2000

BC

SHOOTING CHANT

SHOOTING CHANT

— ✕ ✕ ✕ ✕ —

AIMÉE & DAVID THURLO

A Tom Doherty Associates Book
New York

SHOOTING CHANT

Copyright © 2000 by Aimée and David Thurlo

A Forge Book
Published by Tom Doherty Associates, LLC
175 Fifth Avenue
New York, NY 10010

ISBN 0-312-87061-2

Printed in the United States of America

To Page One in Albuquerque and their wonderful staff,
especially Kay Marcotte, Patricia Montoya,
Ilene Hartfield, and Vicki Reisenbach,
who have always made Ella feel so welcome.

SHOOTING CHANT

PROLOGUE
———— ✖ ✖ ✖ ————

It was shortly after four when Ella Clah left the small, wood frame and stucco public health service clinic near the river in Shiprock. As she walked, she brushed away a strand of long black hair that stirred with the warm New Mexico breeze and drifted down in front of her eyes. Gloria Washburn, a Navajo nurse in her mid-thirties and a friend of Ella's, remained beside her as they crossed the narrow parking lot.

A bit nervous, Ella absently reached up to touch the stone badger fetish pendant she always wore. "And you're sure the blood test is conclusive?" Ella asked her friend, who was almost a head shorter and thirty pounds heavier than Ella's five-foot-ten slender frame.

Gloria nodded. "It's pretty much one hundred percent."

"By the way, it's really important to me that no one else find out about this yet. Don't tell a soul, okay?"

"Sure, but this isn't the type of thing that'll just go away if you ignore it. It's going to affect your entire lifestyle."

"I know," Ella said. "But first I have to get my own thoughts in order."

"Order and then harmony," Gloria acknowledged.

"There are times the old ways make a lot of sense," Ella said.

Gloria stopped by her own vehicle, an inexpensive white sedan with the PHS logo on the door panel. "Well, I'm off to make my patient visits. Some of the traditionalists over by Rattlesnake still won't come in to the clinic. To tell you the truth, they don't even want to see me when I come to them, but I'm pushy," she said with a grin. "That helps."

"Good luck." Ella waved at Gloria then continued to where her own unmarked police vehicle was parked. Gloria was right. Her entire life was about to be turned upside down, but there was no turning back the clock now.

Ella was pulling out onto the highway when the dispatcher's call came in over the radio. "PD to SI Unit One."

"SI Unit One, go ahead," Ella answered. As Special Investigator of the Navajo Tribal Police, she had four officers she could call upon, though only one, Officer Justine Goodluck, was permanently assigned to the SI team at the moment.

"Big Ed wants you over at LabKote, on the west side. One of the Anglo supervisors just reported a dead body in the parking lot."

"Got anything more on that?" Big Ed Atcitty was the police chief in Shiprock, and Ella answered only to him.

"The Anglo who called it in, a Doctor Landreth, reported it was a suicide, but Big Ed wants you to check it out. He also expects a full report from you as soon as possible."

Ella was familiar with the relatively new Anglo-run company whose building she saw from the highway as she drove by every day. The company packaged and sold sterilized laboratory and hospital supplies. LabKote had landed a sweet deal with the tribe, leasing the building and land for five years at very low rates, providing they would hire a certain percentage of Navajo workers for their operation.

"I'm on my way now. ETA in five minutes."

"The county sheriff has also been called in to consult because the victim is a resident of Waterflow, off the Rez, and is not Navajo."

"Who'll be running the show—him or me?"

"Anything pertaining to investigations on the Rez is your responsibility. Unless the FBI wants to take jurisdiction, you're in charge. Big Ed made that clear."

"10–4."

Ella switched on her flashers, then raced down the highway toward the center of the small reservation town. It was time to get to work and that meant setting aside the concerns that had been foremost in her mind until now. But it wasn't easy. The news and all its implications had rocked her world to the core.

ONE

—✖ ✖ ✖—

Ella slowed to forty miles per hour, watching for cars pulling out of businesses and for pedestrians as she passed through the heart of Shiprock. She accelerated across the old steel westbound bridge, then took the curve in the road back toward the south. Traffic, mostly pickups, gave way slowly, but she didn't have far to go.

It was late summer, and the weather had been cool. There was a sense of purpose on the Rez now as everyone got busy harvesting and preparing for the long winter months ahead.

Reaching the turn-off, she drove quickly up the long, straight, graveled lane, surprised by how well it had been maintained. The seasonal rains usually came down in sheets for a half hour each day and roads quickly eroded, etched with deep ruts that scarred the overgrazed region called the Colorado Plateau.

That wasn't the case on this road that led to LabKote, however, despite the fact that this same road also carried fairgrounds traffic and was constantly in use. Ella figured that the company must have hired a private construction company to come out here and maintain the road in order to make it easier for their own employees to get through.

LabKote was housed in what had once been the old cultural center. The employee parking lot was located outside the newly erected chain-link fence and, as she drove up, she could see an Anglo man waiting for her beside a sporty looking sedan.

Ella parked her unit several spaces away in the closest slot she could find, then walked over to meet him. He was well-tanned, slightly overweight, and could have passed for a Navajo at a distance. As she got a closer look at him, Ella decided the man was probably Italian or maybe Middle Eastern. He certainly wasn't from around here, and didn't look Hispanic.

"I'm Doctor Landreth—Ph.D., not medical," he said. "I'm the general manager here. That's Kyle Hansen, one of our engineers," he said pointing to the body inside the car. "He usually came out here this time of day for a cigarette break but, when he didn't come back today, we had Jimmie Herder, one of our security guards, go check on him. He found the body less than fifteen minutes ago and we called the police right away."

As Ella approached the car, she put on her latex gloves automatically, her eyes on the scene. Like most Navajos she had an ingrained aversion to death, but she'd never let traditions interfere with her work. However, as was becoming customary, she put on a second pair over the first. Many Navajo officers did this so they wouldn't even have to touch gloves that had touched the body, or the dead person's possessions.

Ella studied everything as she approached. Both car doors were closed, but the driver's side window was open and the body was slumped behind the steering wheel. The victim's bloody head had rolled to the right, glazed eyes staring sightlessly ahead. A nine-millimeter handgun lay on the asphalt below the victim's left arm, which dangled outside the car. Ella stood by the door and looked inside. An open pack of cigarettes was on the dashboard and, from where she stood, she could see the tip of one blood soaked, unlit cigarette peeking out from beneath the sole of one of his shoes.

She looked at the victim's right hand and noticed, among the gore, what appeared to be nicotine stains on two fingertips.

Ella discovered two shell casings on the ground on the driver's side, and circled each with a piece of white chalk. She then stood up and stepped back, looking at the overall area.

"Is there a problem?" Landreth asked, seeing her searching the area around the car.

"Please step back," she asked, not answering. "You might accidentally disturb a crucial piece of evidence."

Another man came out of the gate, a tall Anglo wearing khaki pants and a light blue print sports shirt. At his waist was a nine-millimeter Beretta in a black leather holster, and on his belt a leather case like those tradesmen used for large folding knives. If he'd had a badge, he could have been mistaken for an undercover cop.

She looked up, a question in her eyes.

"I'm Walter Morgan, director of security here at LabKote. Need any help, Officer . . . ?

"Special Investigator Clah. And, yes, I'd appreciate it if you keep everyone well back from the scene. I'm conducting an investigation here."

"Certainly, Officer Clah. Happy to be of assistance." Morgan turned and gestured to Landreth, who took a few more steps back. The security chief seemed comfortable and confident, almost the opposite of Landreth, and Ella assumed he was probably ex-military.

Moments later, she still hadn't found any matches or a lighter, despite a careful search. It was a small detail, but things that didn't fit always put her on the alert. Unfortunately, until the medical examiner finished her work, Ella knew she wouldn't be able to check the victim's pockets and beneath the car seat.

"Did anyone disturb the crime scene at all after the body was found?" Ella asked, realizing it was time to get out the yellow tape and block off the crime scene.

Morgan looked at Landreth and shrugged. The general manager answered. "I don't believe so, but why does that matter anyway? He committed suicide. That's clear to anyone with eyes. The gun's in his hand, or was, before it fell to the ground. This isn't a crime scene." Landreth took a step forward, pointing at the pistol.

"Suicide is a crime. Now please move back," she said again, then focused on the body. Dealing with Anglos in the public sector could be frustrating. The ones accustomed to being in charge seldom relinquished authority easily.

Morgan shook his head at Landreth, and pointed toward the gate.

"I'll block off the area with yellow tape," she heard a man's voice suddenly boom out from somewhere behind her. "They'll understand perimeters better that way."

Ella turned her head and saw Sheriff Paul Taylor approaching from his white cruiser. She'd met Taylor once at a law enforcement fund-raiser, but they'd only spoken a few words. Taylor was in his late fifties and had thick but graying hair under his felt cowboy hat. Despite his laid-back rural lawman demeanor, the sheriff's pale blue eyes were eagle sharp and she'd gotten the impression he seldom missed anything.

"You certainly got here fast. I just arrived myself."

"I was just leaving Kirtland after refereeing a post–fender bender shoving match," he said. "I'll be back in a minute. Let me get the yellow tape and isolate the scene from non-Navajos."

Ella looked around for the LabKote people, and saw Landreth walking back toward the building. Morgan followed, a few steps behind. She focused her attention back on the sheriff.

Taylor had obviously learned from experience that it was unnecessary to keep Navajos away from dead people. They stayed away on their own. By the time Taylor began to cordon off the area, Ella had put in a call for Ralph Tache, the crime scene photographer, and the two others on her crime team, Sergeant Harry Ute and Officer Justine Goodluck, Ella's cousin. Any shooting had to be investigated, and this one, if her hunch was right, would need to be carefully evaluated before the reports were filed.

Taylor studied the body. "Who is he?" Taylor asked, reaching for his gloves. "This is an expensive little car he messed up."

"The victim has been identified as Kyle Hansen, an employee

here," she said, her tone crisp and businesslike. It was easier to cope with the harsh realities of her job when she distanced herself from them. Remaining analytical and professional was the only way to survive. "From what I can determine the victim took two gunshots to the head. The first one was apparently a near miss; it just grazed his skull, and was not fatal. The easy explanation is that he probably flinched at the wrong time, or was shaking quite a bit and almost blew the job. It's not unheard of for the victim to screw up the first shot. He obviously made up for it with the second shot, which entered right though his ear canal."

"That's what made all the mess inside the car." Taylor shook his head. "But that first shot puzzles me. A round that close to his face . . ."

"I know. You'd think that it would have knocked him out cold, or at least stunned him for a while. Forget flinching. But I'm not the ME. It's up to her to make that determination. I wonder if she can tell how much time went by between shots?"

"Somebody must have seen or heard something. What do you say we go inside as soon as we can and ask the folks a few questions?"

"Good idea. We'll work as a team," she said, watching Taylor's reaction to her assumption.

"Deal." Taylor nodded, and she relaxed, glad there would be no jurisdictional issues here.

As soon as the other officers arrived, Ella went with Taylor to the small guardhouse beside the only gate, but no guard was there, and the gate was open. They were halfway to the main door of the building when Landreth suddenly stepped out onto the sidewalk and blocked their way. "We're in the middle of a sterilization procedure. I can't let either of you go inside without an escort."

"We have to talk to your employees as well as to you. We need to know more about the man who died," Ella said. "We'll also want to take a look at his work station, and his employee file."

Landreth opened the main door and led the way to a small office. "We can talk here."

It only took a few questions to establish that Hansen was used to going out alone during his afternoon break. He was the only smoker on the shift, and no smoking was allowed inside the building. Hansen couldn't leave his work station without being relieved, so the routine was well established.

"So your first indication that something was wrong was when you heard the shots?" Ella asked. She felt sorry for him, he was clearly disturbed by what had happened, but she had a job to do.

"No one heard the shots, not from in here, I don't think. These walls are thick and it's impossible to hear anything that goes on outside."

"What about the guard?" Taylor asked.

"He'd locked the gate and come inside for a can of soda, which doesn't violate procedures by the way. When Hansen didn't come in at the end of his break time, I found out the guard was still inside. I sent him back out to let Hansen in. I figured he was stuck outside."

"What else can you tell us about the victim?" Ella asked.

"He was a genius at his work, but he was messed up personally. His wife divorced him about a year ago and he never got over it. I hate to say this, but I'm not at all surprised that he committed suicide. He was unstable, and everyone who knew him will verify that."

"Was his job on the line?" Taylor asked.

"He wasn't going to be fired. He would have been too difficult to replace, but he certainly pushed it enough times. We had another big argument just a few days ago and, as usual, he was insubordinate."

"What was the latest argument about?" Ella asked.

"He wanted to redesign the software operating the sterilizing machinery. He was always trying to tweak the programs to get a little more out of the assembly line."

"We'll need to see his employee file," Ella said.

Landreth's expression grew stony. "I don't have the authority to show it to you. There's a matter of confidentiality to consider. Our employees could sue us—unless you've got a warrant, that is."

"We could get one fairly quickly," Ella bluffed. "Things move at a different pace on the Rez where everyone knows everyone else. Of course if I have to go to all that trouble, I'll have to make my time count. I'm sure I'll want to go through the entire facility— no matter what it does to your sterilization procedures. And I'd want to look at all the employee records, not just Kyle Hansen's."

"A search warrant doesn't give you unlimited access," Landreth protested.

"True. The Fourth Amendment requires us to specify both the place to be searched and the items we're searching for, but 'items' can mean any papers, books, and records that may help establish the identity of a killer, and the 'place' can be this entire facility."

"Killer? I thought you said it was suicide."

"You said it was suicide, I didn't," Ella said.

"What makes you think it's murder?"

"I won't know for sure until the ME's report is in, but the evidence is not as open and shut as you think. If you insist on standing in our way, there's also a little matter of obstruction of justice you might want to think about."

"Look, let's not get all worked up. I'll get you Kyle Hansen's file, if you'll just sign for it."

"No problem."

As he left the room, Taylor looked at her, his eyebrows raised. "You learn all that bad cop stuff in the FBI?"

Ella smiled. "That guy just annoys me," she replied. "I dislike anyone who tries to tell me how to do my job."

Landreth returned a few minutes later. "Off the record, Hansen was slowly going over the edge. His personal problems kept interfering with business. I would have fired him a long time ago if he hadn't been so important to our production line."

Ella glanced at the employee file Landreth had handed her. "It says here that he was always arguing with his supervisor."

"That's true. I am—was—his supervisor. I hired him to program the machines that sterilize our products. That's precise, methodical work and he was an excellent systems designer. But he had mood swings that really interfered with his performance. One call from his ex-wife or her lawyer, and he'd go into a depression that would last for days. Then he'd just sit there like a stone and no one would be able to communicate with him."

"We'll have to talk to his coworkers. Also, we'll need to question Jimmie Herder since he found the body," Ella said.

"I can't help you with that at the moment. Jimmie took off shortly after he notified us. We've had to call in another one of our security people to man the gate. I've tried calling Jimmie's home several times already just to make sure he's okay, but no one's there."

Ella knew Jimmie. He was a traditionalist and so was his wife. Ghost sickness was a real fear among many of the *Dineh*, The People, but it was particularly so with the traditionalists. It was said that the *chindi*, the evil in a man, remained earthbound after his death and could contaminate the living. Jimmie would have wanted to have an evil-chasing chant done for him and would not have hung around. In all fairness, even a progressive wouldn't have tempted fate by hanging around a corpse unless it was absolutely necessary.

"What about that list of his coworkers?" Ella pressed.

"No, you've gotten all you're going to get from me for now. If your coroner finds that it's murder, then come back and we'll see. But until then, I'm finished." Landreth gave her a hard look. "I'd be risking a lawsuit by giving you anything more and I'm just not willing to do that."

"Okay. Just don't be surprised to see us out in the parking lot tomorrow, stopping people as they come in. I hope that doesn't make them late for work," Ella said with a shrug.

By the time Ella and Taylor left the building, the crime scene team was working the parking lot area, and the medical examiner had arrived.

Taylor's handheld radio at his belt crackled and his call sign came over the air. He spoke quickly, then turned back to Ella. "I'm going to have to return to my office. Let me know what else you find out?"

"You've got it."

As he drove off, Ella met with Dr. Carolyn Roanhorse, the tribe's ME, and one of the few medical examiners in New Mexico not assigned to the Office of the Medical Investigators in Albuquerque. Carolyn was a large woman by any standards, but few had the nerve to point it out to her.

Seeing Ella, Carolyn held up one hand and finished speaking into her tape recorder. After switching it off, she looked up. "You want me to tell you if this is suicide, but I won't be able to give you any definitive answers yet."

"But you've got a gut feeling, right?" Ella pressed.

She nodded. "I could be wrong, but I'd recommend you continue to investigate the possibility of a homicide on this one."

"That was my feeling, too," Ella said. Carolyn's guesses were seldom off the mark, and it was good to have her corroborate her own observations.

Two hours later, after her team had processed the area and the body and the car had been taken away, Ella went to talk to Justine.

"We need to find Jimmie Herder. He's the security guard who found the body."

"Tonight?"

"Or first thing tomorrow. I figure he's probably out trying to hire a Singer. I'll stop by my brother's house tonight and see if Herder's contacted him."

"I'll check with his family," Justine said. "If I find him, I'll let you know right away."

Ella made sure that Landreth knew her team would be back in the morning for one last look around and that a cop would remain to guard the scene until then. Once that was done, she got back into her vehicle and sped down the highway.

She'd agreed to meet her old friend Wilson Joe tonight and speak to the kids in the outreach program, but she was hopelessly late. Wilson was a full-time professor at the college, but he still managed to find time to work with the younger kids on the Rez after hours. It was his way of getting them involved in something other than trouble—the kind of trouble that recently had led to the appearance of gangs on the Navajo Nation.

Right now, the kids were learning about animals and plant life on the Rez. Wilson had asked her to come and tell the kids a little about the Plant Watchers since Ella and her mother were members of that society.

As she drove to the meeting, the monotony of the landscape helped her relax. Ella's mind drifted back easily to the crime scene. That Anglo's death still puzzled her. Instinct told her that there was a lot more to it than what appeared on the surface. The evidence presented a picture filled with too many little inconsistencies. The victim supposedly had shot himself with his left hand, yet the nicotine stains on his fingers suggested he was right-handed. The location and time of the shooting also bothered her. Why would he pick an afternoon break to do the job, and the parking lot at work?

The Navajo Way said that everything had a pattern and only by seeing and understanding that pattern could one find harmony. Inconsistencies marred the order of things and revealed the pattern of evil, and recognizing that pattern was the first step toward reversing it. She wasn't a traditionalist, but some things just made sense.

Five minutes later, Ella parked her vehicle and walked inside the elementary school where Wilson's group met. About ten children were in a room partially used for storage, showing off their pets and some of the plants they'd grown as part of a special project.

Ella smiled at Wilson talking to Alice Washburn, Gloria's eleven-year-old daughter, but she didn't interrupt.

"I've named my rabbit Winnie," Alice said. "She was a gift, though Mom wasn't too happy about her. Winnie just had babies, but only one is still alive. He's really a cool little rabbit already."

As the other children started asking Alice if they could have the baby rabbit when it was old enough, Wilson took Ella aside.

"I was worried that you wouldn't make it."

"I got held up. It couldn't be helped. But I'm glad you're all still here."

"We may have a small group, but they couldn't be better kids. They're interested in just about everything."

"They look like a great bunch."

"I'm really lucky to be teaching them, to be honest. They've helped me more than you can imagine. It's been really tough for me these past few months."

Ella knew he was referring to the death of his fiancée and all the discoveries that had come in the aftermath of that incident. He'd gone through his own version of Hell, facing betrayal, heartache, and almost the loss of his own life.

"What do you think, Professor Wilson?" one of the girls asked.

Wilson glanced down at the pair by his elbow. "I'm sorry, girls. What were you saying?"

"So many people are angry over the show that the Agricultural Society held," Marcie, a little girl of about eight, said. "A lot of the winners were people who had used special Anglo feeds for their animals instead of having them eat what our animals always have eaten—what the land gives us freely."

"It's still fair," Alice argued. "That feed is available to everyone."

"But the animals were even bred in funny ways," Marcie said. "Artificially, or something."

Alice crossed her arms. "So what?" She looked up at Ella. "You have traditionalists in your family, Investigator Clah, but you also went to school off the reservation. Do you believe that if we do stuff like that the gods will be angry?"

"The Plant People will think they're not needed and move away," Marcie said.

"What are Plant People?" Alice asked. "I never understand stuff like that!"

"Because your family's forgotten what it's like to be Navajo," Marcie said.

Ella knew that their were echoing their parents and the old arguments between the traditionalists and the progressives. "Our tribe calls all plants the Plant People because, like people, they can be our friends, or not," Ella answered. "Some plants are good, but others have to be guarded against. That's a fact that stays the same whether you're a progressive or a traditionalist."

"My mother said that the Plant People move away when things aren't right because, like us, they like to live among friends," Marcie said. "That's why we used to have a lot of Indian rice grass and goosefoot which people and livestock could eat, but now all we have are snakeweed and tumbleweed."

Ella considered her answer carefully. The last thing she needed to do was start trouble for Wilson. "I'm not sure why things have changed, but that's why we need our Plant Watchers more than ever. They know where to find the plants we need," Ella said, starting the short lecture she'd prepared on plants and the group of herbalists known as the Plant Watchers.

After completing her talk and answering all of the kids' questions, Ella turned the meeting over to Wilson. He was a natural with the kids and they looked up to him.

Time passed quickly. It was a pleasure to work with younger children. Their outlooks were filled with a freshness and vitality she seldom saw in her line of work, where cynicism often ruled.

As the last traces of the sun began to disappear, the meeting was closed. She stood at the door with Wilson and watched the kids as their rides came to pick them up or they left to walk home. Once everyone was gone, Ella helped Wilson put away the folding chairs. She worked in silence, worries crowding her mind.

"It's not like you to be so quiet," Wilson said at last.

"I just wish there was a way to integrate the old ways with the new. They each have value. Unless we can do that, I'm afraid that the kids will grow up being neither Navajo nor Anglo, and having no idea where they fit into things."

Wilson nodded. "Our culture is slipping away and, with it, our special way of life. I was at a Chapter House meeting a few days ago. One of the elders reminded us that we seldom place pollen in the waters these days, yet we complain when the river becomes polluted and hurts the tribe instead of helping us. He said it'll be that way with everything unless we learn to work with our gods again."

"We're trapped, you know. The new ways seem to destroy the old in so many ways, and yet we need both."

"What happened tonight that made you late? You looked really preoccupied when you came in."

"We had a problem at LabKote," she said without giving him any details. "I have a feeling that we're in for another cycle of trouble."

"The traditionalists hate that place and everything it stands for."

"There was a death there tonight. After that gets out, it'll be worse."

Wilson expelled his breath in a hiss. "Let's not think about business right now. What do you say we go out and have some dinner at the Totah Cafe?"

"I have a better idea. Come by the house with me. Mom would love a chance to cook for both of us."

"I'm not sure that's a good idea. I hurt her, you know. Rose doesn't say much about it, but I know she always wanted us to get married. When I got engaged . . ."

"She was disappointed," Ella finished for him. "But we all have a right to live our own lives. Mom has to accept the fact that settling down and getting married is not for everyone."

"Don't you want a husband and kids someday?"

She smiled. "It's not that simple."

"There was a time when I thought you and I would share a future and start a family."

She sighed softly. "The problem between us has never changed. We're two great friends, but it's never been more than that."

He nodded but didn't answer, gathering another folding chair. The metal rack for storing chairs was against the wall and he walked in that direction.

Ella was bringing him the last two chairs when she heard her call sign come over the radio. As Wilson took the chairs away from her, she nodded a silent thanks.

Ella pulled out her handheld radio and identified herself.

"There's a 27–5 in progress," the dispatcher said, "and we have no other available patrol units in Shiprock. A van's parked outside the public health clinic, which is supposed to be closed now, and the caller reported seeing a prowler forcing open the front entrance."

"I've got it," Ella said. Switching off the radio, she looked over at Wilson. "Duty calls."

"You should have picked a job that's more eight to five. You'd have a life then," he muttered as he walked with her outside to her vehicle.

"Maybe, but being a cop is a big part of everything I like about myself," she said, climbing into the SUV. "I can't see myself ever giving it up."

As Wilson stepped away, Ella switched on the flashers and sped back to the highway. She'd go Code One, a silent approach. There wasn't likely to be any immediate backup for her, so she'd have to make the most of the element of surprise. In the last few hours everything had changed for her, and she had no intention of taking any unnecessary risks.

TWO

Pushing back any thoughts that were not directly related to the work that lay ahead, Ella stayed focused as she raced back south on Highway 666.

When she pulled into the clinic's parking lot less than eight minutes later, lights and flashers already off, she was ready to confront the intruder. She knew what she had to do, and no one in the entire department was better trained than she was.

Ella parked around the back so no one in the building could see her vehicle. She'd already spotted an old gray or light green van parked just outside the ring of light cast by the one street lamp. She slipped off the strap that held her gun secure in its holster, but didn't draw her weapon. Instead, she reached under the seat for her side-handled nightstick, then crept quietly out of her Jeep.

There didn't appear to be a lookout in the van, so her luck was holding. The dispatcher's call had reported that the witness had seen only one intruder, so she didn't expect much trouble. Remaining cautious, however, Ella approached the building's entrance from along one of the side walls, peered around the corner, and checked out the front. It was quiet, but she could see that the door had been forced open.

Ella stepped inside the clinic and waited. It was dark and hard to see, but using the flashlight would give away her position. Once her eyes adjusted, she continued slowly, listening every step of the way.

As she passed the reception area, she could hear the rustling of papers and the occasional thumps when objects were dropped onto the floor somewhere up ahead. Maybe it was a kid searching for drugs, or a cash box. The gang problem on the Rez had escalated in the last few years and, with it had come a lot of problems no one here had really dealt with before.

Holding her nightstick in a blocking position, she inched forward. She wouldn't draw her weapon and risk shooting a Navajo kid. She knew enough defense moves to neutralize any opponent with the nightstick and, in dealing with a burglar, she was more likely to encounter an opponent with a wrecking bar, bolt cutters, or a screwdriver than a handgun.

Ella advanced cautiously toward the sound. As she reached the entrance of the first office, she heard the crash of a large piece of furniture, probably a file cabinet, being overturned.

Ella edged up to the doorjamb. From her vantage point she could see the pale blue glow of a computer screen. It appeared the intruder had been searching through electronic records in addition to everything else. Her instinct for danger switched on to maximum. That didn't fit the profile of a kid looking for drugs. Something else was going on here.

Spotting a short, stocky figure holding a penlight in his teeth and rummaging through a shelf, Ella crept up behind him, alert every step of the way in case the burglar wasn't alone. Before he could turn around, she slammed her baton behind his knees. As he fell to the floor, she delivered another quick blow to his side. Five seconds later, she had him on his stomach and handcuffed.

"Gotcha kid," she muttered, surprised to see he was wearing gloves. Somehow, she hadn't expected a teenager to plan that far ahead.

He tried to twist away and his strength surprised her, but

teenagers could be incredibly fit. "Let's go, buddy. Stand up. I'll read you your rights on the way to the station."

She'd expected some wise talk, but the kid remained silent. She looked around, still sensing something wasn't right about the situation.

Neither seeing nor hearing anyone else, Ella led her prisoner quickly to the office door, wanting to turn on the lights and get a good look at both the kid and the office. It was too dark to make out much at the moment. She couldn't even tell for sure what color hair the kid had, though around here, black seemed a good bet. Suddenly she heard a crackling sound behind her, like that of someone stepping on a piece of paper.

Ella pushed her prisoner to the floor and whirled around to face her adversary.

"Come out now," Ella ordered, waving her baton back and forth. "Don't make it worse on yourself."

Suddenly muzzle flashes lit up the darkened hallway to her right, accompanied by the deafening bangs of two gunshots. Realizing that there were three of them, Ella dove behind a desk as glass shattered behind her.

This was no ordinary break-in, and these weren't ordinary kids. Before she could draw her weapon, one of the trio came up behind her, yanked her off her feet, and hurled her into a coat closet. As her head slammed against the wall, bright lights flashed behind her eyes.

Stunned, she struggled to stand up, but she smashed her head against the metal coat rack then fell back to her knees. Everything went completely black as the door was closed, trapping her inside.

Fighting a blinding headache, she hit the door with her shoulder and heard something snap in the wood. The door moved an inch or two, but remained closed. They'd propped something against it.

It took three more numbing tries, but using a heavy square cardboard box as a battering ram, she managed to force the door open enough to squeeze through.

Pistol in hand, Ella scrambled over the desk they'd jammed

against the doorknob and ran out of the clinic. By the time she reached the parking lot, the van was nothing more than two tail lights a quarter mile away. Ella called in a report, advising officers to proceed with caution against the armed men.

Determined to find some clues that would lead her to the perps, Ella went back inside. As she rubbed her aching shoulder and felt the pain stab through her, she decided to find an aspirin first.

Ella turned on the room lights and looked around carefully. Chaos surrounded her. The trio had completely ransacked the place. Wearing disposable gloves, she searched for the penlight the perp had dropped when she'd grabbed him. She found it beneath a desk a moment later and placed it in an evidence bag she pulled from her jacket pocket. Saliva from where he'd held it in his mouth might eventually identify him, if it got to that point.

Ella was going through the scattered files and papers looking for a pattern in their search when she heard a vehicle pull up. The red and blue flashing lights that told her it was a police cruiser danced rhythmically across the wall.

A moment later, Officer Justine Goodluck walked into the room. At five foot two, clad in jeans and a black windbreaker, her young assistant and cousin looked more like someone's kid sister coming back from a movie than a fully trained officer of the law. It wasn't until one noticed the nine millimeter pistol on her hip and the hawklike sharpness in her eyes that she was taken seriously.

"Are you okay?" Justine asked, looking around. "Your hair and clothes look like you've just come out of a whirlwind."

"Thanks, I know. And, yeah, I'm fine, but my ego's a little bruised," she admitted. "I got too cocky and almost paid the ultimate price. I came in expecting to find one scared teen and walked into a buzz saw."

"I know. I heard your call." Justine put on a pair of rubber gloves, then began to study the evidence.

"I've bagged a penlight he was holding with his teeth. Maybe he drooled enough to pick up a blood type or more, though I doubt we can justify the expense of testing to follow up on a break-in."

"We may be able to lift some prints."

"Don't count on it. The guy I handcuffed was wearing brown leather gloves. Of course, he's also still wearing my cuffs, which should make his life interesting."

"And it'll make him easier for our guys to spot," Justine said with a grin.

"His companions will find a way to get the cuffs off, believe me. They were cool customers, and probably had gloves on, too. I wish I'd listened to my instincts, because if I had, I might not have been ambushed like that. I also should have checked out the van before I ever went inside."

Ella had always had a good track record playing her hunches. Police business was a part of her and she'd developed an intuitiveness about her work that seldom failed her. It was all a matter of training and reading people, though some firmly believed it was part of her family's legacy, a story rooted in legend. But superstitions were no part of her job.

"I knew something was wrong when the guy didn't say anything, even after I cuffed him. A kid caught breaking in would have had some smart-mouthed comment to make."

"Did you get a chance to return fire?" Justine asked, studying the holes in the glass where the bullets had passed through.

"I didn't draw my weapon," Ella admitted. "I came in expecting to use my nightstick against a youngster. I'm pretty good with it, so I wasn't worried." She shook her head, disgusted. "I won't make that mistake again."

Justine gave her a quizzical look. "You've been hesitant to use your weapon lately, Ella, even when the situation calls for it. What gives?"

"I'm capable of using lethal force, Justine, and I will if I have to, but I really don't want that to become an automatic response. If we're ever going to stop the cycle of violence around here, we've got to lead the way by example. That's why I've been practicing with my baton, working on hand-to-hand, and learning martial arts moves."

Justine smiled slowly. "I heard about that little argument you had with Sergeant Manuelito on the effectiveness of the night-stick. Rumor says you flattened him in zero flat at the gym."

"I didn't exactly flatten him," Ella said, unable to suppress a smile. "He was giving me a hard time about wasting my time with the baton when, in his opinion, I should have been out on the pistol range. I decided to show him how effective our night-stick is when combined with proper training."

"He outweighs you by at least a hundred pounds, so he must have made quite a thud when he hit the mat."

"I swear the floor shook. Actually, I tripped him," Ella laughed. "He was waiting for me to come at him directly, so I did a little acting and backed away as if unsure what to do. He advanced then, thinking I was an easy mark, and that's when I swept his legs out from under him."

"You cheated!" Justine said, laughing.

"I proved a point. A nonviolent encounter has definite advantages, such as providing a still breathing suspect to interrogate."

Justine regarded her thoughtfully. "You're changing, Ella. I've noticed there's something different about you lately."

"How so?"

Justine considered it. "Off the record?"

"Absolutely."

"You're nicer to people . . . showing less of an edge some-how." Justine stopped speaking, her eyes suddenly growing wide. "I didn't mean that you're becoming a wimp, or anything like that."

Ella laughed. "The thought never occurred to me."

Justine relaxed. "Good, because I think this change is for the better." Justine shook her head. "I better shut up before I find myself behind a records desk in Window Rock."

"No chance of that. I'll always need you for the forensic work, and to help with my caseload."

"Ah, good old job security. I'll take it any way I can get it."

Hearing other vehicles pulling up, Ella went to the window. "I guess PD called the clinic administrator."

Justine made a face. "Myrna Manus? She's the reason I never get sick. There's a disease with her name on it, I've heard."

Ella shook her head. "Relax. She acts the same way with everyone. Nobody can remember the last time she cracked a smile—though a lot of rude bets float around."

"I've heard them," Justine said with a grin.

A second later Myrna came into the room, cursing under her breath in Navajo. It was obvious she'd been hauled out of bed by the news and had dressed in a hurry. Her blouse was one button off all the way down, and her hair was matted down in the back. She glowered at Ella. "This better be a result of the break-in, not the investigation," she said, waving her hand at the mess surrounding them. "And bullet holes?"

"Not mine. The place was pretty much in chaos when I came in," Ella answered.

Myrna went through the clinic, checking each room, and stepping around errant papers. "What were they after? It couldn't have been drugs. We've made it clear to everyone that we don't keep much of those kind of meds here."

"I saw one of the perpetrators looking through the records," Ella said, then added, "They must have searched the computer files, too."

Myrna stopped by a locked cabinet that had been forced open with a screwdriver or pry bar. "I can see they took our insulin, some antibiotics, and a few asthma meds we keep on hand. But that's not much of a haul." She walked to her desk and looked at the empty bottom drawer, now broken and lying on the floor. "The money is gone, too. We keep about fifty dollars and change in the drawer. The rest is deposited daily."

Ella gestured to the file cabinet, now on its side. "What kind of records are stored there?"

"Mostly patient files that have been pulled for lab workups," Myrna said. "But to figure out if something's missing, I'll need to sort everything out and that's not going to be easy. They did a good job scattering records all over the floor, so it's going to take some time to put things back together. I can start now if you want, but I was told outside not to touch anything."

"Our people will give you full access soon, but first the scene needs to be processed. We're hoping to recover some fingerprints."

"Do you have any idea how many people touch those cabinets? We have our staff, the doctors who come from the hospital, the interns, the cleaning staff, and so on."

"We'll fingerprint them and begin the process of ruling them out, then see what's left." She didn't want to tell Myrna that one of the perps had worn gloves, and if the others had, too, it was going to be a waste of time.

"I'm going to stay right here while your people work. I'm responsible for everything that happens at this clinic, and I intend to see to it that you all do your jobs."

Ella didn't argue. It would be futile anyway. Instead, she looked around for Justine. Finding her dusting the overturned file cabinet for prints, she went over to join her.

An hour later, no longer needed at the scene, Ella finally left the clinic and climbed into her vehicle. She was tired tonight, more so than usual. Too much had happened today. She tried to remember when she'd eaten last, but all she could recall was having a couple of tortillas with cheese nuked in the microwave back at the station before noon. No wonder she was starving. She'd always had a healthy appetite, but it was worse than ever these days, even if it was still only in her mind that she was eating for two.

Ella smiled to herself. She was going to have a baby! She still couldn't quite believe it. No matter how it ended up changing her life, she couldn't have been happier. After all these years of hearing her biological clock ticking away, she was going to be a mom!

The crazy part was that even before she'd taken the tests, she'd known. Of course, missing her period had been a real giveaway. But, in truth, she'd known long before that. Maybe it was a part of the intuition that came with being a woman, or maybe it was simply a matter of being in tune with her own body. Yet how she'd known didn't seem nearly as important now as the fact that she was going to be a parent.

Realistically, she knew that being a cop and a mom would be difficult, but she also knew that like many before her, she'd manage. She would divide her time between her child and her job and make it work. Women were used to reorganizing priorities to accommodate changing circumstances.

As she pulled up in front of her home, Two, her mother's dog, came up to greet her. His entire rear end wiggled along with the tail. She patted the scraggly looking mutt on the head and went inside. "Lonely tonight, Two? You've got me for company now, and it won't be long before Mom's back from the Plant Watchers meeting."

Ella had wanted to go to the meeting tonight with her mom, but it hadn't been possible. She'd try to make it next time for sure. She loved learning about herbs—how to heal with them and how to work with them. It made her feel much more connected to the tribe. Best of all, sharing a common interest with her mother had helped her bridge the gap that had existed between them for so many years. They were closer now than they'd ever been.

The dog laid down in the kitchen beside his kibble dish and let out a sigh.

"Are you trying to tell me you're starving, too?" Ella fed the dog, then started fixing her own dinner.

Thirty minutes later, Ella sat down at the table with two massive hamburgers, some leftover mutton stew, and half a loaf of bread. A quart of milk and a tall glass were at her left hand to wash down the meal. She'd just taken her first bite when she heard a vehicle pull up and then her mother saying good-night to a friend.

Rose came in moments later, leaning on her cane for support. "Hello, Daughter." She looked at Ella's full plate and laughed. "Just a little bedtime snack?"

"Way beyond that. I'm famished after skipping lunch and dinner. Can I get you something?"

Rose shook her head. "No, thanks. I snacked on cookies for half the evening."

Ella looked at Rose. She'd made remarkable progress in the past year recuperating from a devastating accident. She'd almost lost the use of her legs after a drunk driver had smashed into her car. Her mom credited the Plant Watchers and the support of her friends for some of her headway. But at the root of her progress was Rose's own inner strength. She was a formidable woman.

"I'm going to bed early tonight," Rose said. "I want to do some redecorating tomorrow. It's time we turned your father's old office into something more useful to us. Your father has been dead for several years now, and it's not right to waste all that space. That's one of the largest rooms in the house."

"What are you planning to do with it?"

"I know you use the desk and the bookshelves, so I'm keeping that side of the room as it is, but I'm turning the rest of it into my new sewing room. I've been using your brother's old room for that, but since it's right next to your bedroom, I always feel guilty using the sewing machine at night when you're sleeping."

It all sounded logical, but Ella couldn't help but wonder if her mother had guessed that she was pregnant. Relocating her sewing room might have been Rose's way of making it possible for Ella to have a nursery.

Ella looked at her mother, studying her expression, and doing her best to read her, but it was useless. It was impossible for any-one to tell what her mom was thinking unless she chose to reveal it. It had been that way as long as Ella could remember.

Ella remained silent. She wasn't ready to talk to anyone about her pregnancy yet. The baby's father deserved to be the first per-son she told, though she knew it was entirely possible that he wouldn't welcome the news.

After Rose went to bed, a hushed stillness fell over the house. Enjoying the peace and quiet, Ella finished her meal, washed the dishes, then went outside for a walk. It was almost midnight and time for her to go to bed, but she was too restless.

Ella let the night breeze envelope her. It was said that Wind carried messages, but all she could hear tonight was the rustle of the leaves. Suddenly an owl's cry pierced the quiet that surrounded her. She looked up at the pine tree a few yards from the house. An owl was perched in one of the lower branches. It looked at her for a moment, then flew away.

Ella felt a cold chill envelope her. The traditionalists believed that an owl was a sign that terrible things were on the way, and death was at the door. She placed one hand protectively over her stomach. But that was just superstition. The owl meant death only if you were a rodent. Pushing the queasiness aside, she walked back into the house.

SEPTEMBER 10TH

Ella arrived at her office the next morning just as the intercom buzzer sounded. She went to her desk quickly, knowing who was calling even before she pushed down the button. Only one officer beat her into work every morning—Big Ed Atcitty, the chief of police.

"Hey, Shorty, get in here. We've got to talk."

"I'll be right there," she said. He still persisted in calling her Shorty, though at five foot ten she was taller than most Navajos, including the stocky police chief himself.

As she walked in, he gestured silently to a seat while he finished writing something down. Moments later, he looked up. "What happened at LabKote yesterday?"

"Outwardly, it looked like a suicide, but I don't think that's what we're dealing with."

"Does the evidence back you up on that?"

"There are some inconsistencies but, at this point, it's just a hunch. I'll know more when I get Carolyn's report."

"Taylor's a good man. Work with him. I know the victim was an Anglo who lives outside our borders, and I don't want this to turn into a jurisdictional war."

"Understood."

"Now tell me. What's your impression of what happened at the clinic last night?"

Ella took a deep breath then let it out slowly. Though she'd forgotten about the bump on her head, it now began aching again. "At first I thought I was up against a big kid, but it turned out to be men. There were three of them, in fact, and they kept their cool—like pros."

"Were they Navajo?"

"I can't say. I never got a clear look at the guy I handcuffed, and I only saw the outlines of the others. I was navigating by the glow of one computer monitor."

"I heard from Myrna Manus that some files appear to be missing, but she hasn't found a pattern to what was taken. Any indication what they were after?"

"My initial reaction was that they were probably after drugs and cash, but the evidence doesn't entirely support that. I need to dig up a lead or two before I can come up with a theory."

"I've got something else I want you to look into personally." He hesitated. "There's something weird going on," he said slowly.

Although a long silence ensued, Ella didn't interrupt Big Ed. She knew that the rhythms and patterns of speech on the reservation were much different from the way they were on the outside. A long silence here simply meant the person was still thinking, and interrupting them was considered extremely rude.

"My wife, Claire, had a prized ewe she was very proud of," Big Ed said at last. "Our daughter showed the animal at the Agricultural Society's show over at the fairgrounds recently, and she won all kinds of ribbons. The ewe was going to be auctioned, but we found the animal dead this morning. Her throat had been slashed."

"Was she butchered and the meat taken? You see that once in a while around here."

"No, the meat was left for my wife. The animal was the result of artificial insemination and that made some of the traditionalists who were also exhibiting their animals very angry. Claire is sure that Angela Charlie is responsible. She came in second and complained a lot."

"Angela Charlie is a traditionalist, I know that."

"I think her husband, Gene Charlie, is also a member of the Fierce Ones."

The secret vigilante group known as the Fierce Ones espoused traditionalist values and, philosophically, they had some good ideas. Their problem was that they often used underhanded means and strong-arm tactics to achieve a goal. "Is there any evidence linking the killing to Angela or the traditionalists, other than the typical method of slaughter?"

Big Ed nodded. "A couple of things. The large intestine was thrown toward our home. According to the old ways, it then becomes another sheep. Also, we found the head of the animal sprinkled with pollen and laid beneath a juniper. That's said to tell Talking God and Black God to bring another animal."

"Were there any tracks?"

"Whoever did this wore moccasins, or only socks. I checked that part out myself. By now, my wife and her sister will have butchered the ewe and taken the meat. Tracks won't do you any good, but the impressions were so light, they were barely visible." He paused then added. "There is something else. Claire saw a figure in the distance walking toward the Charlie home just before our daughter discovered the ewe. The person had a red skirt on like the one Angela usually wears."

"I'll talk to the woman this morning, then."

"Thanks, Shorty. Let me know how it goes."

Ella watched him. "There's something else that's bothering you about this, isn't there?"

Big Ed nodded. "My wife's ewe wasn't the only animal that was a product of artificial insemination. I suggest you stop by Rex Jim's house. He ran the Agricultural Society show and he knows all the exhibitors. Get a list and follow it up."

"I spent some time at that show myself, at the community policing booth, and I've known Rex for years. I'll take care of it."

Ella returned to her small office and read the preliminary

report Justine had left on her desk. She then wrote down quick notes on what had happened last night to Claire Atcitty, adding pertinent information from her conversation with Big Ed. She'd need to make out a full report later.

Hearing a knock at her door, she looked up. Kevin Tolino, one of the most respected defense attorneys working for the tribe, walked in. Kevin was over six feet tall, lean, fit, and good-looking. He was said to be one of the tribe's most eligible bachelors though, like Ella, he walked the dangerous line between the progressives and the traditionalists, as well as between the Anglo and Navajo worlds.

Ella had known Kevin for two years now, and had been dating him off and on for the last few months. Both of them were considered outsiders by many because they'd lived off the Rez in the past and had adopted many Anglo ways. That common ground had drawn them together initially, along with a natural physical attraction, but in the end it hadn't been enough to sustain their relationship. Although they'd remained friends, they'd both decided a month ago not to date again.

Now she was pregnant with his child and this seemed destined to test the friendship they'd forged. The fact was, she had no intention of marrying Kevin. They'd already proven that would be a mistake. She would raise the baby on her own. Kevin's only choice would be to admit paternity and play a part in the baby's life, or walk away forever.

Ella started to give him the news, but then changed her mind. This wasn't the right time or place. Until she got her own thoughts more organized and there was time to tell him without rushing everything out, she'd wait.

"I thought I'd drop by and make sure you were okay," he said. "I heard you confronted a burglar last night, got jumped by two more, then had to fight your way out of a jam."

"Well, it was something like that. How did you hear about it so soon?"

"I overheard two cops talking at the Totah Cafe this morning."

And that was exactly how news traveled. She wondered how long it would be before everyone also knew she was pregnant.

"So, what really happened? I heard shots were fired, but you didn't even draw your weapon. Is that true?"

"Yeah," she admitted grudgingly. "The call indicated I was dealing with only one perp. I figured it was a teenager, so I'd planned to use my nightstick."

Kevin said nothing for a long time. "When cops underestimate a situation or become complacent, they get killed. Be careful," he said at last.

She nodded once. "Count on it."

THREE

✖ ✖ ✖

Ella left a note for Justine, then decided to go speak to Angela Charlie, Big Ed's neighbor. There had always been conflicts between the traditionalists and the progressives on the Rez but, lately, things were taking on an edge that worried her. What was needed was unity, not the division she kept seeing everywhere.

The term "neighbor," on the Rez sometimes meant the closest dwelling to another but not necessarily within sight, and certainly not across any street. This was true for the Atcitty and Charlie homes. Ella drove down the gravel road past Big Ed's residence, a comfortable looking pueblo-style three-bedroom set down a dusty lane. There was a small unpainted shed out back, and several corrals. A metal loafing shed covered the latest cutting of hay, and there were two apple trees, side by side several yards away. As was typical, there were no lawn or landscaping plants, but a small vegetable garden was on the south side of the house, surrounded by a low wire rabbit-proof fence.

In contrast to the Atcitty's progressive lifestyle, Angela and Gene Charlie lived much as their grandparents did. Two hogans, one of traditional mud and log construction, and the other of unfinished gray stucco, lay at one end of a deeply rutted track that must have been difficult to negotiate even after a light rain.

The stucco hogan was undoubtedly the chief residence, while the old-style was for ceremonial purposes. A cottonwood bough–covered framework provided shelter from the sun for a dozen or so chickens, and a larger pen a short distance away held two sturdy looking horses.

No smoke was visible from the wood and coal stovepipe sticking out of the center of the home, so Ella stopped the Jeep and looked around the brush-covered countryside. The clank of a bell signaled the location of several sheep and goats along an arroyo, where the runoff had enhanced the grazing value of the grass and brush.

Ella shut off the engine, climbed out of her vehicle, and stood by the door, waiting to be discovered. A woman sitting on a large slab of sandstone looked her way, stared for a minute or two, then waved for her to come over.

She recognized Angela Charlie, who was dressed in a simple cotton dress, no belt at the waist, and a wool cardigan sweater. Her hair was in a tight bun, a style more often seen in women twice her age. Angela was probably forty years old.

As Ella approached, she saw Angela wore three silver bracelets and a turquoise ring, but no watch. Who needed a watch around here, where the sun's position told a shepherd all she needed to know?

"Hello, Officer," Angela called as Ella drew near. "I can imagine what brought you here. Have you come to arrest me for sheep murder?"

"I'm here because I want to hear your side of the story with my own ears. Nothing more." As Ella looked down, she spotted a common contradiction between the traditionalists of twenty years ago and those of today. Instead of leather boots or moccasins, Angela Charlie wore canvas and vinyl jogging shoes.

"Then I should tell you that I didn't do it, no matter what that woman down the road says." Angela crossed her arms, and looked defiantly at Ella.

"I haven't heard all the story, so can you tell me why she might say you were responsible for killing her ewe?" Ella pressed carefully knowing that she needed Angela's cooperation to get to the truth.

"The police chief's wife told me herself. She came up a few hours after it happened because she first had to take care of the carcass before the meat went bad. She said she saw a woman in a red skirt walking away from her pen and coming in this direction right before her daughter found the sheep. She knows I have a red skirt—well, at least I did have."

Ella's eyebrows rose. "What happened to it?"

"I don't know. It was gone from my clothesline yesterday. Not that she would believe me. That woman has made up her mind, like I told my other neighbor, across the highway."

Ella knew Angela was referring to Maria Benally, another traditionalist, who was a weaver and sometimes went to the Plant People meetings. According to Ella's mother, who was in a position to know, Maria was a gossip who seldom got her facts right.

"Maybe I should talk to the weaver, too," Ella said. "I'll investigate, and maybe come back later if I find out anything that'll help settle this matter."

"Say hello to your mother for me, won't you?" Angela ended the conversation with those words, and walked back to her rock, shooing away a goat who tried to take a nibble at her shoelaces.

Twenty minutes later, Ella arrived at a more modern residential area in Shiprock, north of the valley elementary school, just below the mesa. She'd stopped by the weaver's home on her way, but had been unsuccessful.

Maria Benally had not been at her loom, which had been covered by a large plastic tarp. Though Ella had waited a good five minutes, the woman either hadn't been in the mood to talk, or wasn't inside her tiny cinder-block and tar-paper home. The absence of a pickup, however, though tracks were visible, suggested Maria had gone on an errand.

Ella drove down the side street in Shiprock, watching preschoolers play in the yards, their moms hanging up laundry and taking care of vegetable and herb gardens. It seemed peaceful and quiet, definitely a low crime area.

As she approached Rex Jim's house, she saw him standing in the front yard talking to a neighbor. He waved at her, and she parked at the curb. Ella had known Rex since her high school days. He'd been a teacher in Shiprock for years until his recent retirement.

He walked slowly, a bad hip obviously giving him trouble again. "Hey, Ella! It's good to see you. What brings you here?"

She left her unit. "I need to talk to you. Can we go inside?"

"Sure thing." He led her across the well-tended lawn and into his living room, then gestured for her to take a seat. "Forgive the mess. I had a party for my granddaughter last night. It was her third birthday and we had close to one hundred people stop by."

It wasn't unusual for that many people to come to a party hosted by someone as well known in the community as Rex Jim. The surprising thing was that there wasn't more chaos inside. "Your house looks fine," she assured him, noting two stuffed plastic garbage bags in the kitchen and an errant length of crepe paper beneath the sofa.

"What's this all about?" he asked. "Is it official?"

She nodded. "I need the list of exhibitors from the last Agricultural Society show," she said, and saw his expression change instantly.

"Have there been *more* problems?"

"Tell me what you mean," Ella asked without answering.

"I heard that late last night Dolores Begay found her blue-ribbon billy goat dead. She spent a year feeding him special bagged feed, consulting with the county agricultural agent, and following all the latest management techniques. I've got to tell you, that animal looked great. They were going to use him to artificially inseminate some goats on a project at Tuba City, but that plan is now as dead as the goat."

Ella looked at him in surprise. "I hadn't heard about this."

"I just found out about it earlier this morning. Dolores thinks that Nancy Bitsillie killed the animal. Nancy was mad because her goat lost out to Dolores's. Nancy raised her animal tradition-ally, and spent lots of time finding the best places for it to graze and making sure it stayed healthy."

"I don't know Nancy. Is she a traditionalist?"

Rex nodded. "Very much so, and that's one of the reasons why the animals's death pointed to her. The head was sprinkled with pollen and left beneath a juniper. Also, it was butchered in a way that allowed Dolores and her family to still use the meat. Tradi-tionalists don't believe in waste."

"So then," Rex continued, "somebody got back at Nancy. They scattered some of the store-bought feed around the corral where Nancy keeps her goats at night, mixing it with the hay in the feeders. Now Nancy's goats have eaten the same feed that she spoke out against."

"So, now Nancy blames Dolores, right?"

"No, that's just it. Dolores was helping at a Chapter House meeting and lots of people saw her there this morning. Nancy thinks it was Norma Sells who scattered the feed in her pens. Norma is a good friend of Dolores, and uses the same bagged feed on her goats. Norma runs the feed store."

Ella felt her skin prickle. "This reminds me of the petty things that went on in junior high school. Maybe it'll stop now."

"I doubt it. Somebody has already gotten back at Norma. She had her entire storage barn trashed about half an hour ago, with feed and fertilizer and manure mixed in together all over the ground. That's what Ethel Yazzie was telling me when you came up. Things are getting worse, not better. The traditionalists and progressives are lining up against each other."

"Do you have the list of those who went to the ag show? I need to contact some of those people and try putting a stop to this before more animals get hurt and property gets damaged."

He shook his head. "I wish I could help you, but I can't. I had the list as a file in my computer, but the machine crashed. I shipped it back to the manufacturer to get as many of the files recovered as pos-sible. But I wouldn't count on getting anything from that hard drive. A virus scrambled everything in it, and it could be gone forever."

Ella had him make out a partial list from memory, then thanked him. "If you get a chance, try to calm people down, okay? Things will only get worse unless everyone starts backing off."

"Too late. It's gone too far already. My guess is that it'll just have to play out on its own."

Ella knew he was right. But anything that set the traditionalists against the progressives was bound to grow increasingly dangerous, and not just for the unfortunate animals.

Ella was back in her police unit, heading to the station, when Justine reached her on the cell phone. "I've located Jimmie Herder, the security guard who found Hansen's body," she said.

Ella had meant to ask her brother about Herder, but by the time things had wound down it had been too late in the evening to call. "Where is he?"

"He's with John Tso. I'm outside his hogan now."

Ella knew the ninety-year-old *hataalii*. Although many people saw Clifford these days, Gray Eyes, as John was known, was still a favorite in the area. "I can't remember how to get to his hogan. Give me directions."

Justine complied. "Shall I wait for you, or start questioning him now?"

"What's happening?"

"I think Jimmie's having a Sing done over him."

"Then don't interrupt the *hataalii*. I'll be there in thirty." Ella placed a call to the sheriff's office, but was forced to leave a message since Taylor was in court.

Hungry, Ella reached into her purse for a grain and fruit bar. She'd barely had a moment's peace since daybreak, and now she was starving again. She made a mental note to stick more nutritious snack food in her vehicle.

When Ella finally arrived at Gray Eyes's medicine hogan, she saw Justine leaning against the side of the car, enjoying the early fall weather, and relaxing in the sun.

Joining her, they waited and, as they did, Ella filled her assistant in on what she'd learned. "We've got the beginnings of a problem that could explode all over the Rez. We have to find a way to defuse this before the entire community gets involved and takes sides."

"But how? From what you've told me things are already taking a life of their own, at least here in the Shiprock area."

"We have to nip this now, even if it means bringing people in to the station. If we can remind them that what they're doing is illegal, maybe we can shake them up enough to have them stop."

"But no one's actually seen anyone else doing these things, right?"

"Just the red skirt in the distance, in that first instance. The rest is mostly gossip rooted in old rivalries, as far as I've been able to learn."

"How can we build a case against anyone, then?" Justine asked.

"We can't, unless we get solid evidence. But we can still question those involved and, if we get them rattled enough, maybe someone will 'fess up' to their part in this. It's the only tool we have."

"And just when are we supposed to do this? We have the Anglo's death to look into, the break-in at the clinic, and now this?"

"We'll do what we usually do when things all come at us at once—juggle."

A few minutes later Gray Eyes came to the hogan entrance and waved at them to approach. As Ella and Justine came closer, Jimmie Herder came out of the hogan to join them.

"You can talk in here, if you want," Gray Eyes said, indicating the hogan with a wave of his hand. "I have to leave to attend to another patient." Without further explanation, he walked to a hitching post where a horse was tethered, took the reins in his left hand, jumped on, and trotted away.

"I hope when I'm his age, I can still be as limber as he is. He's amazing," Jimmie said, then focused back on Ella and Justine, who had followed him into the hogan. "I know why you're here, and you probably know why I'm here, but there's nothing I can tell you that will help. I went outside to tell the man he was past break time and to let him back inside the gate. When I got to his car I saw an arm dangling out of the driver's side. I thought he'd gone to sleep, so I took a closer look. That's when I saw the hand-gun on the asphalt and the body. I ran back inside the main build-ing, reported what I found, then split when Doctor Landreth went out to take a look. I knew I'd have to find Gray Eyes. I was already getting sick. I've never seen anything like that in my entire life, and I hope I never do again!"

"Try to remember. Did you see anything else around the car besides the handgun, maybe matches, a lighter, or a burning ciga-rette. Anything at all?" Ella knew her team hadn't found any of those things in the car, on the victim, or around the car.

Jimmie thought about it a moment. "All I remember seeing beside the car was a pistol, a semiauto."

"Did you ever see him smoke? How did he light his ciga-rettes?" Justine asked, obviously following her boss's line of thought.

"Yes, I've seen him smoke. He usually lit up as soon as he reached his car, and sometimes it was parked where I could see him from the gate. But not the day he died, I'm not sorry to say." He shuddered. "But let me answer your question. He had this fancy silver lighter his wife gave him when they first got married. He showed it to me once. It had his initials on it."

"Okay," Ella nodded. "Now tell me about the man. What did you know about him?" she asked, avoiding the name of the dead out of respect since they were at a traditionalist's medicine hogan.

"I knew very little about him. He'd had another beef with Doctor Landreth recently, I know that. They were always arguing about how to do things, and Morgan had to intercede at times."

"Morgan, the security chief?"

"Yes. Landreth is supposed to be his boss, but, from what I can tell, Morgan is the one who has the final word on just about everything."

Ella made a mental note to get backgrounds on Morgan and Landreth as soon as possible, and see what happened to that lighter. Maybe it was important, maybe not.

As Jimmie left in his truck to go back to work, Justine watched his vehicle disappear from view. "That lighter wasn't at the scene or on the victim. Do you suppose somebody took it?"

"It wouldn't have been Jimmie, or any other Navajo for that matter. If it was missing from the scene, some Anglo took it. But before we assume that, get Sheriff Taylor's permission and go take a look in Hansen's house. He might have left it at home that day."

"I'll also find out what his ex-wife has to say. Maybe he left it over at her place," Justine said. After a brief silence, she added, "I wonder if the people at LabKote realize that no Navajo will ever use that parking lot again. They'll park half a mile away if they have to, but they're not going anyplace that's been contaminated by the dead. Let's face it. Even our progressives usually aren't that progressive," she added with a smile.

"You're right," Ella admitted grudgingly. That aversion was still there even for people like Justine, Carolyn, and her. The only difference was that duty forced them to deal with it.

FOUR

✖ ✖ ✖

Ella sat at her desk accessing credit reports and other background information on the LabKote supervisors, especially Landreth and Morgan. Landreth had been very nervous at the scene, which was understandable under the circumstances, but he'd also seemed particularly anxious to establish Hansen's death as a suicide. It was possible he'd only had the company's best interest at heart, but it still set off a warning bell.

Morgan, on the other hand, was almost too cool and confident. He'd either seen violence and death before, or was playing the role expected of someone who carried a weapon as part of their job. She'd seen the false bravado of many rent-a-cops and rookie officers.

Ella picked up her cell phone, and managed to get Landreth on the line after only two transfers. "I have a few more questions I'd like to ask you," she said.

"I have nothing more to say to you." he replied.

"I'm conducting an investigation, Doctor Landreth. I can haul you to the station if you prefer."

"Look, I'm in the middle of something here. The guy you

should talk to is Morgan. I know the science end of things, but he knows this operation down to the last detail."

"Will you connect me to him now?"

"I can't. He's at home. I'll get in touch with him, then have him call you."

Ella refused to accept his answer and continued to press him until finally Landreth got Morgan on another line, and connected them.

"Come to my apartment," Morgan told her. "We can talk here."

It took almost a half hour to get to Morgan's residence, actually one unit of a duplex located just northeast of Glade Park in the city of Farmington.

Ella pulled up into the steep sloped concrete driveway, parking beside Morgan's vehicle, a nondescript brown pickup with New Mexico tags. She noted the empty gun rack behind the seat, which, in this part of the country, often held an emergency fishing pole, in case the urge to angle became overwhelming.

Ella noted the address on the mailbox but the absence of Morgan's name. Perhaps he'd never gotten around to it, or the place was new to him.

Ella was about to use the brass knocker on the front door when Morgan opened the door.

"Special Investigator Clah, please come in. I had one of my men bring over the personnel files the company keeps on Doctor Landreth and myself, and you're welcome to look them over. How about a cold one?" As he gestured toward a bottle of beer on the coffee table, she noticed the prominent scar on his left arm, just below his wrist.

"No thanks. Still on the job." Ella said, looking around. There were no decorations or paintings on the wall above the cloth sofa, just an American flag flanked by photos of Morgan in a marine dress uniform and desert combat gear, and a framed set of service ribbons and insignia.

"So, you were a marine. Serve in Desert Storm?" Ella wasn't surprised, already suspecting he had a military background.

"That's affirmative. I spent weeks training in the sand, then cruised around on an assault ship while we threatened to invade. The whole thing was a feint, of course. Later we made our advance, but by the time our unit got to Kuwait City, most of the Iraqis had taken off across the desert. Except for a sniper here and there, we didn't see much real action."

"How'd you pick up that scar?" Ella looked at his arm again.

His eyes darkened for a moment as he touched the scar, then he smiled. "From a marine, no less. We had a difference of opinion, and settled it behind our LAV. That's one of our assault vehicles. I got the best of him, but it never got into our records."

"How did you end up in New Mexico?" Ella looked at the file folders Morgan had placed on the coffee table, but didn't pick them up. She preferred to hear it from Morgan first, then compare the spoken and written versions.

"I'm here as a result of the job."

As she walked and passed an open doorway, Ella saw an assault rifle on the table and a shotgun was propped up against the wall. She stopped in mid-stride.

"They're both legal," he said, following her gaze.

"Are all your guards at LabKote this well armed?" Ella asked. "It seems a bit much unless you're expecting Indian attacks."

"My men carry what's needed for their duties, but we always keep a little extra firepower in reserve in case somebody goes postal. Nothing for the public or police to worry about though, I run a tight security staff."

"Where did you work before you came to LabKote?" Ella asked, keeping her tone casual.

"When I left the marines, I did some security work in Europe for several years, then I came back to the States. When I met Landreth and heard about LabKote, I signed on. The rest is history."

Morgan sat down his empty Coors bottle, and gestured toward the files. "It's all in there, one place or the other."

"I'll look over the papers in a minute," Ella said, sitting on the sofa. What do you personally know about Dr. Landreth?"

"He grew up in California, middle-class, and went to UCLA and got degrees in biochemistry and physics. He had his own company for a while, but it didn't work out, so he decided to do something different. He and I clicked from the start, and it wasn't long before we were working together."

Morgan stood and crossed his arms. "That's pretty much it. You can read the files about the rest." He walked into the kitchen area, and took another Coors from the refrigerator.

"What about your family?" Ella picked up Morgan's folder, and noticed he'd listed the names of his parents, but no addresses or phone numbers. No other relatives were mentioned either.

Morgan seemed to think about it for a while before answering. When he did, his voice was without expression. "I lost contact with my parents and my only sister several years ago. We never got along much anyway. I don't even know where they live now."

She couldn't even imagine being without family. "Were you ever married?" Ella probed a little further.

"That's where it becomes none of your or LabKote's business. I don't discuss that part of my past." Morgan's tone suddenly became confrontational. "I don't suppose you want to tell me about *your* personal life?" he added, deliberately looking her up and down with cold appraisal.

It was a creepy feeling. "I think I've heard enough. Let me take a pass through these files, then I'll be leaving."

Ella began to write down phone numbers and Landreth's address. She'd confirm these records from other sources, then leave it at that unless something pointed back at the two supervisors as suspects.

Five minutes later, she thanked Morgan for his time, and left. There was more to learn about Morgan, that was for sure. She sensed that behind the loner stood a man struggling to deal with his own demons. But Ella knew that unless Morgan became more connected to the case, looking further into what made the man tick would become an unpleasant experience, as well as a waste of time.

Hours later, after plowing through a stack of paperwork on her desk, Ella finally took a break. She was standing by the window when Justine came into her office and sat down, a worried look on her face.

"I spoke with Hansen's ex-wife briefly on the phone. She works in Aztec, and her number was in Hansen's file. She said that she rarely saw her ex-husband and that was the way she wanted it. She also told me that the lighter's a silver-plated Zippo with the initials "K. H." on it, and wasn't really worth very much."

"Now some bad news," Justine continued. "Myrna Manus is on the war path. She's got a list of fifteen missing patient files, and some of those belong to influential people, like Senator Yellowhair's wife, Abigail." She stopped and, looking decidedly uncomfortable, added, "Your medical file is one of those missing."

Ella felt a tightening in her chest, knowing what was in the file now. This wasn't the way she wanted news of her pregnancy to get out. She wanted a chance to let Kevin and her family know first, then she'd tell others.

"Did Myrna give us a complete list of everything that's missing?"

Justine nodded. "Big Ed has a copy."

As Justine finished speaking, Ella's buzzer sounded.

Ella was in Big Ed's office a few moments later. Seated in front of his desk, she regarded him silently.

"Your medical records file is missing. Can you think of a reason someone might be interested in it?"

"No, not at all," she replied. "But I doubt they were after information on me. I may have just been part of a handful they picked up. They took fifteen. Maybe that was all they could carry." That was the only explanation that made sense to her. She really didn't see any reason to have to tell Big Ed right now that she was pregnant. There'd be time enough for that later.

"So, why the break-in, and the theft of records? Any theories yet?" Big Ed clipped.

"Maybe blackmail, or a legal advantage? I was thinking of injury or paternity suits and that sort of thing. Getting privileged information could be handy for someone hoping to make a few dollars or stir up trouble."

Big Ed nodded thoughtfully. "You may be right. Get in touch with Kevin Tolino and appraise him of what's happening. I want the police department's role in this to be clear, because Myrna's convinced the clinic could be sued by the patients whose records have been compromised. Those files are supposed to be confidential."

"I'll let Kevin know."

"Keep pushing for answers on this burglary, Shorty. Senator Yellowhair will be calling me the second he learns his wife's records were taken. I can already feel him breathing down my neck."

Ella left the office and went directly to her vehicle. She first tried to reach Kevin on her cell phone, but his secretary told her he was in court. Determined to have something new to report to Big Ed later, she drove over to her brother's home, which was within a few miles of her mother's, but farther back from the highway. Clifford, one of the tribe's best-known medicine men, was always in contact with The People and often knew things long before the police.

She drove across the juniper- and piñon-littered desert slowly and maneuvered down the last section of the meandering dirt track leading to his home. Clifford was outside the medicine hogan by the time she arrived. He'd undoubtedly heard the vehicle a mile or more away on the rough road and had stepped outside to see who was approaching. He waited for her now in front of the wool blanket covering the entrance.

Ella parked, then went to join him as he waved for her to come inside.

"I've been expecting you," he said, motioning for her to sit down on one of the sheepskin hides used as both cushion and blanket.

"You heard about the break-in at the clinic?"

"Yes, but there are more important things happening on the Rez than that burglary. The traditionalists are saying that Anglo ways are undermining our tribe and they have started a movement to close the reservation to Anglos, except for tourists. They want companies like the ones that own the mines, and LabKote, ousted."

"The *Dineh* need the jobs those companies bring, brother. Without work, many would have to take charity from the tribe or move off the Navajo Nation in search of employment. The land can't support everyone as farmers and herdsmen. Why can't our traditionalists face up to that fact?"

He shook his head slowly. "What they see is our people losing track of who they are and becoming just like the Anglos, and that frightens them."

"Change can be frightening," she admitted.

"More so for the old ones. They feel as if their ways and everything they value is becoming obsolete." Clifford gave her a long, thoughtful look. "But this isn't why you came here today, is it?"

"No, it's not," she admitted. "I need a favor. I'd like you to keep your eyes and ears open for me. I may need help to solve that break-in at the clinic. The privacy of many Navajos has been threatened."

"I haven't heard anything about that yet, but maybe I will."

"I'd also like for you to help me defuse another situation, brother. This business with the animals, which began with the agricultural society competition, is getting out of hand. Most of the victims have been progressives, and the circumstances strongly suggest traditionalists are behind these acts. You might as well know that I'm going to start rousting the people that are suspected of being involved in the livestock killings. Maybe I can impress on them that what they're doing is illegal, and that it's helping no one."

"I'll do whatever I can to help you. I don't like what's happened anymore than you do," Clifford said. "But I'd like you to do something for me."

"Name it."

"Mom wants us all to go to our family shrine tonight before supper. I know she'll forgive you if you can't go, but I'd really like you to try and be there. This is her first long hike outdoors. She'll be taking her cane, of course, but she's worked really hard to get herself to this point. It's her first sign of independence after almost an entire year of physical therapy. It would mean a great deal to her to have her two children beside her this evening."

"I know and I'll do my best to be there." Ella stared at the charcoal in the fire pit, trying to organize her thoughts. His mention of children had brought her thoughts back to her own pregnancy. "There's something else I've been meaning to talk to you about," she said slowly. With her own baby on the way, there were other matters she needed to pay closer attention to as well. "Do you remember the details of the legacy said to be part of our family's history?"

He nodded slowly. "How could I ever forget? Loretta and I are getting a lot of pressure from her family to have another child because of it. Many traditionalists feel it's foolish and dangerous not to obey the requirement our ancestors set down for us to always have two children. They believe it could endanger our neighbors and maybe even the tribe."

"But you did have two kids," Ella said softly, remembering Loretta's first child, who was stillborn.

"The traditionalists who have spoken to me recently, and one is the grandmother of your lawyer friend, feel the legacy calls for two living children." Clifford stared at the sand before him. "Be honest. Does it ever bother you knowing people are watching us—waiting to see if the legacy will hold true for us?"

"I've never given it much thought. I'm not even sure what that legacy entails. Mom told me everything once, but it was a long time ago, and I don't remember most of it. But since it's something many of the traditionalists believe about us, and since I'm dealing with a lot of them now, I figured it was a good time to refresh my memory."

It wasn't the whole truth, but Clifford didn't need to know the rest yet. The real reason she wanted to know was because she remembered enough to know that the legacy centered on the children, and she needed to know about anything that might have an impact on her child. "Can you tell me what you know?" she pressed.

"Of course." He started to say more when her cell phone rang.

Ella answered it and heard Justine's voice. "I need to meet with you. I've been processing the little evidence we managed to get at the burglary scene, and I've turned up something interesting."

"Hold that thought," she said, always uneasy about discussing sensitive business over any radio network. "We can meet at the Totah Cafe in half an hour. Can it wait until then?"

"Yeah, that's fine."

Ella looked back at her brother and saw the annoyance on his face. "I'm sorry, but I can't just turn off my phone." She placed it back in her pocket. "Now tell me about the legacy."

"It's what's at the root of the demand made on our family to always have two kids. You see, according to the legacy, there's a very good chance one of us will be good and the other evil. Our family has been known for having special gifts, so the one who turns to evil can only be defeated by the child that remains true to the tribe. One is needed to balance the other. Do you understand?"

"I understand, but I don't believe it. For one, you're not evil and neither am I," she said flatly. "So much for that."

"What *we* believe is not important. How some people will react to us and to our children because of it, is."

He had a point and Ella knew it. "Tell me everything about this legacy. I want all the details, particularly how it began. Maybe there's a way to debunk it."

Clifford stood and looked out the door. A figure, moving slowly, was about a hundred yards away, walking in their direction. "I've got a patient, sister. Our conversation will have to wait."

Disappointed and frustrated by the unexpected interruption, Ella left and drove back to the highway. She was on her way north toward the cafe when she saw Philip Cloud's patrol unit ahead on the highway, going the same direction as she. The young officer had been her friend and a trusted ally for years. She knew that, as a source of information, he was completely reliable. She closed the distance between them, and used her spotlight to signal him. Seeing it, he pulled over to the side of the road.

Ella parked on the shoulder behind his vehicle and got out as

Philip walked back to meet her. "I wanted a chance to talk to you privately," Ella said. "I need your help."

"You've got it," Philip answered. "Just tell me what I can do."

"Things have been very quiet these past few months. We haven't had any burglaries for a while, except for a residential break-in now and then, which is normal. Half of our people still don't bother to lock their doors when they go out. But after the break-in at the clinic, and the livestock killings, I think we're all going to need to stay sharp. Have you heard anything from the gangs, or are there any rumors going around that we should be paying attention to?"

"The gangs have been really quiet for the last nine or ten months. The few hardcore kids left are staying in their own neighborhoods, and vandalism is way down. The Fierce Ones have been keeping an eye on them, I think, and have managed to intimidate the gang leaders. New kids aren't being ranked in either, now that the Fierce Ones are also pressuring parents to control their kids."

The secret vigilante group still made her nervous, but, so far, they'd been more of a help than a hindrance. "Anything else? Anything at all?"

Philip shook his head. "The rains came in time this year, and people are busy with their harvest."

"Have you heard anything that might give me a lead on that burglary at the clinic?"

"A friend of mine is a nurse there, and she says everyone is talking about it. The most interesting theories speculate that someone was either looking for information to establish a paternity suit, or maybe catch a straying husband."

For a moment she considered the possibility someone would try to blackmail her, but then discarded it. Her pregnancy would be common knowledge soon enough, and she intended to ask nothing of the baby's father. He could remain completely anonymous if he chose. There would be speculation about his identity, of course, but children were the property of the mother, from whom they would inherit someday.

"If you hear anything more let me know."

"You've got it. I'll put my brother on the alert, too. His patrol area covers the outlying districts where more of the traditionalists live and, as far as possible suspects go, they have my vote."

"You're thinking that the traditionalists might have targeted the clinic?" Ella really hadn't considered the possibility.

"They're probably innocent, but, let's face it, the clinic does represent the Anglo way of doing things. Our older people have always regarded modern medicine with suspicion."

"Okay, let's see if your brother Michael can get something more for me. And tell him to also report anything he hears about the problem over the animals that were part of the agricultural society's show."

Ella climbed back inside her Jeep. She loved the excitement of searching for the leads that would solve a crime. It was like putting a vital puzzle together. Nothing could compare to fieldwork.

Of course, it wouldn't be easy to remain a cop and raise a child, but other women cops had done it. She wouldn't leave her job. The tribe needed her, and if she didn't honor her duty, she wouldn't be much of a mom. If there was one thing she wanted to teach her daughter, it was the value of responsibility and of being true to herself.

Once it became obvious she was pregnant, she'd have to fight not to be relegated to a desk. Fortunately, she didn't also have to worry that any stigma would be attached to an unwed mother on the Rez. Here, sex wasn't linked to morals. It was just a part of nature. Nature moved in harmony with its surroundings and what was part of nature was not to be condemned.

Still, the news was bound to have an effect on the baby's father. Kevin Tolino was an extraordinary man, one who would do great things for the tribe if things went right for him. The problem was that his career ambitions included politics, and for that very reason she doubted that he'd meet the news that she was pregnant with much enthusiasm. His aspirations had been a large part of the reason why they'd broken up. She couldn't see herself as a politician's wife. Now, if he acknowledged that he was the father, people would wonder why they hadn't married. It was precisely the type of thing that could become an issue all by itself and cost him votes.

With effort, she pushed aside those worries as she approached the Totah Cafe. Justine's tribal unit was already parked outside. Ella went in and joined her at their favorite table on the south side, facing the mesa just above the river.

"What's up?" Ella looked the menu over, hungry again. She was beginning to give new meaning to the phrase "eating for two."

Ella ordered *huevos rancheros,* a mix of eggs and chile, and extra sopaipillas, a delicious fried bread often eaten with honey, then found herself having a craving for milk again. She'd drunk more milk in the past few days than in the last two years.

Justine looked at her in surprise. "Wow, I guess you're starving. Skip breakfast again?"

"I ate breakfast," Ella clipped, in no mood to explain. "So, tell me what's going on? What did you find out that excited you so much?"

"I talked with Myrna for a long time this morning. It turned out that one of the staff here at the cafe found the clinic's missing files in the Dumpster outside. They were in a plastic trash bag, and the only reason they were discovered is because the bag had been ripped open and the files were spilling out. Myrna thinks that they're all there, but it may take a while to sort them out."

"So if the thieves weren't after the files, then why did they haul them away, then just throw them out? Something's hinky about this whole thing. Did they break in to steal some minor prescription drugs and loot the cash drawer, then, on a whim, take the paperwork just to be malicious? I don't buy that."

"Myrna said that they also accessed the hard drive in the computer, you saw that yourself, but the clinic's programmer found no evidence of any computer virus or tampering with files."

"Could they have copied files off the hard drive?" Ella asked, watching the waitress bringing their food.

"There's no way to tell. The only hard fact we have to work with so far is that all the stolen files had just had recent lab work results inserted, and hadn't been placed back with the other patient records."

"So what we have to do now is figure out who would be interested in those lab tests."

"I've got another tidbit to add to the weirdness quotient of this case. I pulled out the slugs I found on the wall and ran a ballistics check. The perp was using an atypical weapon for these parts. They were .380s—you know, 9-millimeter shorts."

"Those are used in PPKs and other small, easily concealed pistols," Ella said, thinking out loud as she reached down for a warm sopaipilla.

"Those guns are a step up from the cheap .32s a lot of gangbangers use, and have a lot more punch," Justine said. "Most people around here would be far more likely to own a hunting rifle or shotgun, or a .38 or .22 if it's a pistol. Of course, most burglars don't carry firearms anyway."

"A lot of the .380s are expensive foreign weapons, too," Ella said. "They're well-designed semiautos and make good backup or off-duty pistols for the cops who can afford them," she added, sampling her food. "What this means is that we're facing well-financed criminals, or very successful ones." Ella ate in silence for a while. "Okay—so we've got an unlikely weapon of choice," she said at last, "and a break-in with no clear motive that involved a three-man team. Taking into account the amount of money and drugs lost, simple burglary seems more and more like a smoke screen. From what we know so far, the entire thing sounds more like an espionage operation than the work of a gang."

After they'd finished eating, Ella placed a few bills on the table and headed to the door, Justine at her side. "Anything else I need to know?" Ella asked.

"Oh, I almost forgot. Abigail Yellowhair's file was one of the ones found in the Dumpster, and so was yours." Justine's eyes stayed on her, her gaze alive with curiosity.

"I'm not sick," Ella said. "It was just a routine test so stop speculating."

"Whatever you say, boss," Justine said with a tiny grin.

Ella met Justine's gaze. Was she getting paranoid, or had her cousin guessed? Pushing the thought aside, Ella started to say good-bye when her cell phone and Justine's rang almost simultaneously.

Justine moved some distance away to avoid interference as she answered the call and Ella flipped open her own receiver. "We've got a situation, Shorty," Big Ed's voice came through loud and clear. "Seems that the Fierce Ones are picketing the tribal offices up on the mesa. The media and press from Farmington are there, and tribal officials are getting nervous."

"That group has always kept their identities a secret. What made them change their minds and come out into the open like that?"

"They're out, but not in the open. I was told they're all wearing homemade masks to hide their faces."

"Any altercations or vandalism yet?"

"No, but people there think it's only a matter of time. They all remember the last time we had a major protest. One of the tribal leaders was accused of taking payoff money and when the council tried to fire him, his supporters staged a protest and one man was killed."

"I'll head up there right now."

"I'm sending as many officers as I can spare, but it'll be limited. I've called in a request to the county and the state police for backup, but for now, we're on our own. The few officers we can muster will just have to handle the situation."

It was always that way. As she closed up her phone, she saw Justine coming toward her. "I got a call from the station," she said. "Some kind of demonstration is going on at the tribal offices on the mesa."

"I know. That was Big Ed on my phone."

"Sergeant Manuelito is in charge up there," Justine said.

"He's a hard-liner. I'll bet he's hoping to kick a few butts," Ella said.

"He wants us in full gear, just in case."

"Hard hats and vests?" Ella shook her head. "That's just going to provoke them."

Justine shrugged. "He's in charge at the scene."

Ella glanced in the back of her Jeep, verifying she had everything, then climbed behind the steering wheel. "Let's get going."

As they raced to the tribal offices, sirens on, Ella felt the tension inside her mounting. The first chance she got, she'd have to order a larger vest to cover more of her torso. For now she'd be okay, but in a few months, it would be a different story—in every imaginable way.

FIVE

—— ✖ ✖ ✖ ——

Ella studied the scene before her, suppressing the chill that ran up her spine. The fifteen or more men in the picket line wore black hoods with slits that allowed them to see and breathe, but they remained silent. On their black arm bands was the symbol of the Fierce Ones, the four sacred mountains painted in white. Only the spokesperson for the Fierce Ones made no effort to hide his identity. Jesse Woody was a Navajo supervisor at the oldest coal mine.

In gear, Ella stood with six other officers in the thin human barrier Sergeant Manuelito had formed between those picketing and the entrance to the tribal offices.

The building itself was a one-story brown brick structure with a lot of glass trimmed with aluminum. In a city it could have passed for a sixties bank, or even a post office, especially with the flag pole outside on the manicured lawn.

Turning back to the current threat, she watched the eyes and stances of the demonstrators, trying to guess their next move.

"What we are protesting," Jesse Woody told the press, "is that our leaders are giving the *Diné Tah* to non Navajos, a railroad car, a truck load, or a pipeline full at a time. Our land was once con-

sidered worthless, good only for sheep or Navajos. But then outsiders came, and started to dig deep holes. They discovered
Mother Earth was rich with minerals and fuels like coal and natural gas. Now, in many places our land's been gutted like an animal carcass and is barren—more like the floors inside these
buildings than a place to grow crops and nourish our animals.
And the Anglos and others still come with their fees, percentages,
and promises, take most of the wealth from our land, and leave us
with dead earth and pennies on the dollar.

"And, instead of feeling the *ch'ééná,* the sadness for something
that will never come back, our elected officials turn around and
give the Anglos new opportunities to destroy what they touch.
This is *our* land, yet we lose a little more of it each day, and with it,
we lose our young people who become more like them and less
like us."

Ella caught the wary look in Justine's eyes. They'd both heard
this type of rhetoric before. People with good intentions pointed
fingers and assigned blame without offering any real solutions to
the problems. She braced herself for trouble in the form of group
action, but the picketers remained orderly, at least for the
moment. They appeared to be more interested in making their
position known to the television crew and reporters gathered
there than in anything else.

The Fierce One's spokesman continued. "What we want is to
allow the Navajo People to meet, discuss it, then vote each time
an outsider wants to set up a business within our borders. We also
want better terms on the leases we give to outsiders, and make
them subject to change or cancellation at any time by a majority
vote. We want what's best for the *Dineh,* yet our so-called leaders
refuse to come out here and listen to us, or even invite us inside.
But no one will leave this building until we are heard."

It was that last sentence that made Ella's body tense up. She
saw the officers on both sides of her brace themselves as well, and
shift to a defensive stance.

Then, unexpectedly, the door to the tribal building opened
and two men stepped out. She recognized Ernest Ben, the head of

economic development. The man next to him was Wilbert Benally, a member of the tribal council.

Ernest Ben came down the sidewalk and stopped before the cameras. "What we need to keep our young people here on our land are jobs. Alliances with Anglo businesses help bring those to us, as well as generate important revenue for our tribe. Without those alliances, our young people will take their education and their dreams for the future and leave the reservation. We all need to work together, now more than ever. If we don't find a way to do that, we'll become our own worst enemy."

"Words like those put our destiny in the hands of outsiders. History has shown us what happens when we place our trust in others. We need to reclaim our land," Woody argued. "Then our gods will provide for the *Dineh* as they did before. The Plant People will flourish and so will our livestock." Jesse turned and faced the cameras. "Our leaders speak to us, but don't listen to the voices of The People."

Suddenly three of the Fierce Ones broke ranks and ran across the parking lot where someone had just left the building via a side door. She heard angry shouts as the protestors tried to block the car the person had just climbed into.

"Take an officer and see what you can do to break that up," Manuelito growled at her.

Ella and Justine jogged toward the disturbance, and soon saw what was going on. State Senator Yellowhair was the person who'd managed to make it as far as his car, but the three protestors were blocking his vehicle. Seeing Ella and Justine, Yellowhair waved frantically.

She had no desire to help him. The fact was she was no fan of the senator's, nor he of her, but it was her job, in this case, to intervene. She slowed to a walk, and continued on toward his car.

"Get these jerks out of my way," the senator yelled out to her. "Do your job."

Ella slowed down even more. Yellowhair was in no apparent danger, and if he was late going somewhere, she certainly wasn't going to worry about his poor sense of timing.

Hearing her name being called by someone at a window, Ella turned her head and saw Lulu Todea, a reporter for the tribal paper. Somehow, Lulu had managed to get inside the building.

"He really *does* need to leave now. His wife is on special medication," she yelled out. "She needs him to pick up a prescription because she can't find her old asthma inhaler."

With a nod, Ella moved forward with her nightstick and ordered the dissenters to step back from the senator's car. Justine backed her up, and the demonstrators gave ground and ran back to join the others.

The senator pulled out into the street with not so much as a backward glance.

"I don't know how he ever got elected with that arrogant attitude of his," Justine muttered.

As Ella and Justine jogged back around to join the others, one of the dissenters threw a soda can at Yellowhair's car when it passed by. The effort was halfhearted, and the truth was she felt like throwing something herself. But it was obviously a signal.

Suddenly, the Fierce Ones made a unified rush toward the tribal building catching the cops off guard. Ella blocked a charging man, using her baton like a staff, but Justine fell when two of the Fierce ones collided with her at the same time.

As Ella moved to protect the downed officer, the men who'd knocked Justine down turned and started swinging at her. Things got out of hand quickly. Glancing around for backup, she realized that the other hooded figures had turned on the remaining officers, swinging fists, pushing, and kicking.

In the midst of the chaos that ensued, one hooded figure came to stand beside her and helped Ella deflect the assault. The man never went on the offensive, he simply blocked and neutralized any moves made against her. Even when two of the hooded figures turned on him, he refused to do anything more than stand his ground and parry their attacks. Then, as the half dozen officers managed to form a small defensive ring preparing for what looked like a renewed assault, sirens filled the air. Four patrol cars with county sheriff and state police markings came screeching up.

All of their hooded attackers scattered, making a run for it, except for the man who'd helped Ella defend herself and protect Justine. Ella knew that without his help, she would have gone down under all the blows.

Still dazed, Justine got up to her feet and, seeing the hooded man standing near Ella, quickly handcuffed his hands behind his back. The man didn't resist.

"No, don't do that," Ella said.

"We have to take him in," Justine said dully.

Ella gave Justine a sharp look. She'd wanted to handle this differently.

"Give me your key," Ella said.

As Justine fumbled in her pockets, Ella focused on the man who had helped her. "We do have to take you in, but I'll sign a statement on your behalf," Ella told the Fierce One. "There'll be no charges against you." Ella removed his hood gently, wanting to see the face of the man who had risked his own life to help them. As she pulled the hood clear, and she saw who it was, she gasped. "Clifford!"

"Are you all right, sister?" he asked quietly. "And you, Cousin?" he looked at Justine with concern.

Ella stood there in shocked silence, unable to think of what to say to him.

Justine quickly uncuffed Clifford. "Go on. Get out of here. You can work this out later with Ella."

Sergeant Manuelito came running up then, trying to catch his breath between words. "Hold on, Goodluck. What the hell do you think you're doing? We don't look the other way for relatives in this department."

Ella, enraged with his attitude, found her voice. "It's thanks to him that I'm still standing and Justine is in one piece."

"But he took part in an assault on a police officer."

"Wrong. He took part in a lawful protest, and when it got out of hand he stood up for what was right," Ella snapped.

"That's for a judge to decide, not you or me. I'm taking him in—unless you plan to try and stop me."

Ella considered it. Manuelito was a tough old guy—built like a wall safe, but she was sorely tempted to make the effort. Yet, knowing it wouldn't help matters, she held back.

Ella looked at her brother. "You'll be out in no time. Any charges against you will be dropped once the judge sees our reports. I'll also get Kevin to take care of the details. He's the best."

Manuelito brought out his handcuffs, but Ella blocked his way. "That won't be necessary. I'll take him in."

Justine stepped in front of Clifford, backing Ella up though Manuelito outweighed her by a hundred pounds or more.

"You're overruling me?"

"I outrank you, and the emergency here has ended. I'm taking him in myself." Ella kept her voice matter-of-fact.

"Without cuffs," Manuelito sneered. "And I suppose you'll manage to lose the prisoner before you ever reach the station?"

"I'm not that kind of cop." Ella's gaze was ice and stone as she stood her ground.

Several heartbeats later, Manuelito moved back. "Okay, have it your way, but I intend to put this in my report."

"Knock yourself out."

As Manuelito walked away, grumbling, Justine gave Ella an apologetic smile. "I'm really sorry. I had no idea it was Clifford who was helping us, and now I've made things worse for everyone."

"This isn't your fault, so don't worry about it. Neither of us knew it was my brother." She motioned for Clifford to follow her to her vehicle. Once they were underway, she finally broke the silence between them. "What on earth were you doing out there? That's very nearly the last group I expected you to be associated with."

Clifford said nothing.

"You're my brother and I love you, but sometimes you've got the brains of a stump."

"Right now you're not acting as my sister. You're a cop. Am I right?"

She nodded. "Yeah, I guess so. I'll read you your rights." She recited them automatically, then glanced back at the rearview mirror. "Are you angry because I'm taking you in?"

"I'm sure you're acting in accordance with your highest sense of right," he said stiffly.

"Which means you're really ticked off at me. But don't worry, this will never make it to court. You'll be out in a few hours." She glanced at her watch. "But not in time to go to the shrine today. Do you want me to tell Mom what happened?"

"Since this is new to me, I'm not sure how soon I'll be able to get to a phone. You better tell her. And tell my wife not to worry."

"I'll ask Mom to reschedule the visit."

"No. Take her up there yourself. She'll need the comfort that'll give her now. We'll all go up again later as a family. It'll signal a healing after this unpleasantness is over."

"All right. I'll handle things, then once you're out, we can make new plans."

Ella called Kevin on the way to the station, then stayed with her brother throughout the booking process. As she'd expected, Kevin arrived a short time later. After filling him in on what had happened, Ella left so he could speak to Clifford alone under client/attorney privilege.

Ella drove home slowly, her mind a whirlwind of thoughts and emotions. Sometime soon, she'd have to find a time when Kevin and she could talk alone. He had a right to know about the baby.

When Ella pulled up in front of her home, she saw Loretta's truck parked outside. Her sister-in-law's presence would not make telling her mother the news about Clifford any easier. With a sigh, she went inside.

Ella looked around for Julian, Clifford's four-year-old son. "Where's my favorite nephew?" she asked as she entered the kitchen.

"He's at my mother's home. We've been waiting for you and my husband so we could go to the shrine. It's been a long time since we went together as a family," Loretta said, standing by the window. "But I expected my husband would get here first. You're the one who's always late."

"Sit down, Mom, you, too, Sister-in-law," Ella said, avoiding the use of names out of respect for their traditionalist views. Names were said to have power and were not to be used lightly. "My brother is going to be a little late getting home today."

Ella related the afternoon's events in a few sentences, wanting to leave the details to Clifford when he was released.

"I had a feeling something wasn't right when you came in the door. Now I know why. I just can't believe my son would have taken part in something like that. All that fighting and disrespect for others . . ." Rose said, shaking her head.

"He wasn't involved in anything criminal at all, Mom. In fact, he helped me out," she said, reluctantly giving them the highlights of what had happened. "His attorney knows all the facts. My brother will be out in a very short time, probably in a matter of hours. Believe me, there's nothing for either of you to worry about."

Loretta glared at Ella. "You said he helped you. Why didn't you help him and keep him out of jail?"

"I couldn't," she said, and tried to explain the circumstances.

"*You* arrested him?" Loretta stood up quickly. "Now I've heard it all."

Ella looked at her mother and saw the disapproval on her face, too. "I didn't have a choice. My brother would be the first to admit it. But maybe one of you can explain something to me. My brother is a man of peace. Why on earth has he allied himself with a group known to use whatever means are necessary to achieve its goals? He must have known the risks that would entail. Even if he never took part in any acts of violence, he'd be caught in the middle, risking his reputation and even his life whenever there was trouble."

"He knew all that," Loretta said. "We talked about it several times. But he thought it was a risk worth taking. The Fierce Ones have done a lot of good things for this tribe in spite of some of their methods. He was hoping that by joining them, he'd become a positive influence, and keep their efforts channeled in the right direction."

"Your brother stands for the traditions of our tribe, and so do the Fierce Ones," Rose said, her voice calm. "They got started to counter the confusion and the values the Anglo culture was bringing into our world. They've done this tribe a lot of good. Your brother must have joined them because he believed that, together, they could do great things for the *Dineh*. Of course, I don't speak for him."

"I value our traditions, too, Mother, but the Fierce Ones are like loaded weapons that can go off without warning."

"This is exactly why my husband never said anything to you," Loretta said, then crouched by Rose's chair and looked up at her. "I promised I'd go with you to the shrine, but my place is with my husband now."

"There's nothing you can do at the station," Ella said.

"Yes, I know. You've taken care of everything," Loretta snapped.

"That's enough," Rose said, her voice stern.

"I have to go, Mother-in-law," Loretta said. "I hope you'll understand."

Rose nodded, then remained quiet until after the rumble of Loretta's truck faded in the distance. Unwilling to interrupt her silence, Ella sat down across from her mother and waited.

"Now, more than ever, I want to visit our shrine," Rose said at last. "Can you drive me there?"

"Of course." It meant at least thirty minutes of rough driving each way, and she still needed to meet with Kevin, but she couldn't say no to her mother now.

At first they rode in silence, then Rose spoke. "In his own way, your brother is doing his best to serve the tribe, just like you are. It would mean a lot to me if you would respect what he's trying to do."

"I do respect what he's trying to do, Mother. I just don't agree with the way he's doing it. Instead of putting himself in the line of fire and facing the possibility of being labeled a criminal, he'd be better off teaching kids after school, like Wilson does. Knowledge like his needs to be passed on. What a better way to work toward the future than by helping young Navajos and providing a role model that helps keep them out of gangs?"

Rose nodded slowly. "But he needs to do more than work with kids. He understands, like I do, that the *Dineh* also need to focus on the present." She paused, then in a firm voice, added, "But please, I never want your brother arrested again. Do whatever it takes to convince him that he can help no one from inside a jail cell."

"What do you want me to do? Most of the time he sees me as a well-intentioned but misguided modernist. He won't listen to my advice unless he already agrees with it."

"In many ways, you're caught between two worlds. I understand that, but our family legacy makes you a part of the old ways, no matter how hard you fight it."

"You told me once about that legacy, and why our family is supposed to have special gifts—"

"Not 'supposed to,' Daughter," she interrupted sharply. "We have them. Yours, like mine, is intuition, and it's far more than what most people call 'woman's intuition.'"

"Mom, I believe you're gifted. I've seen what you can do. When any of us is really in physical danger, you usually know about it first. You're also able to discern what people are thinking with incredible accuracy and, at times, you've been able to see things in your mind before they happen. I can't do any of that. All I have are good instincts when it comes to police work."

"You underestimate yourself. Someday, your abilities will be even stronger than mine. Just so you know, my gifts weren't very developed until I got pregnant. Afterwards, it was a different story. I expect it'll be the same from you."

Ella maneuvered the Jeep onto a dirt road that wasn't much more than two tire ruts. "Tell me something. Did you choose to have two children because of the demands of our family legacy?"

Rose nodded. "Though we'd rather forget about the entire thing, others will never let us do that. It'll follow us for the rest of our days."

"Beliefs connected to the metaphysical and spiritual are hard to argue away, I know," Ella said in agreement.

Rose exhaled slowly. "It's been particularly hard on your brother. People believe that he must have another child—that is, if he really cares about the *Dineh*. What they don't know is that your brother's wife can't have any more children."

Ella gave her mother a surprised look. "That certainly explains why she's so protective of their son. I wonder why my brother never mentioned that to me."

"It's very painful for him. He wanted more children."

"It's got to be really hard on him when people continually pressure him to have more kids."

Rose nodded.

"Remind me how the family's legacy began," Ella said.

"It was generations ago, after the *Dineh* made their first homes in New Mexico, but before the Spaniards came to North America. Mist Eagle, who was from our clan, fell in love with a warrior named Fire Hawk. Though they didn't know it at the first, they were both from the same clan. Later, unwilling to break the taboo against marrying within the clan, Fire Hawk chose another woman to be his wife. But Mist Eagle never stopped loving him.

"One night when Fire Hawk's wife was away, Mist Eagle came to his hogan, pretended to be his wife, and in the dark, seduced him. When the months passed and Mist Eagle discovered she was pregnant, she went to Fire Hawk and told him the truth. Unable to live with the shame he'd brought his family, Fire Hawk took his own life."

"What happened to Mist Eagle?"

"She gave birth to a girl, but she and the child were shunned and they weren't allowed to live near the hogans of other Navajos. Another clan even threatened to kill them if they didn't move away. Mist Eagle faced a hard life alone in the desert with her baby. Eventually, she learned about herbs and how to heal all kinds of sickness. She offered her services to the tribe, but no one wanted anything to do with her—except for the skinwalkers, the

Navajo witches. They were no strangers to incest, since it was one of the ways they gained their dark powers. Mist Eagle learned from these skinwalkers, but she never became one of them."

Ella's heart ached as she remembered her own days of loneliness when she'd first returned to the Rez from California after learning her father had been murdered. Many of The People had called her L.A. Woman back then, and had done whatever they could to avoid her. Yet, in comparison to Mist Eagle's ordeal, hers had been a walk in the park.

Rose took a deep breath, then continued. "One day Mist Eagle came across an old man who'd gone out to the desert to die. She treated him with her special herbs, and the Songs she had learned, and he regained his health. Soon word of what she'd done spread to others, and those who were ill began to seek her out, though they were still afraid of her.

"Mist Eagle helped everyone. Their hatred never really touched her. But anger and resentment over what had been done to them filled her daughter's heart from the beginning. Eventually, the darkness that had been part of her from the day she was conceived became too much for her to resist. She became a powerful force of evil among our people."

"So our tribe sees us as descendants of evil," Ella said.

"We *are* Mist Eagle's descendants. But there's more. Throughout the generations our children all have had special gifts. These were as varied and as individual as the children themselves, but one thing remained constant: the darkness that came with these powers, and the possibility that they could corrupt the bearer."

"Have some in our family actually used their gifts to harm the tribe?"

"Not many, but there have been a notable few. That's why our family decided generations ago to always have two children. That way if the darkness seduced one, the other would be there to balance things and restore harmony."

"Can anyone even remember the last time one of us harmed someone else?"

"My great-grandfather killed his sister after they had shared the same blanket. He hung himself when people found out." Rose paused, then added, "The gifts you and your brother have been given are, by far, the strongest any of us have ever had. Your brother is a healer, and your intuition will never fail you. But the others who watch you and him see only an even bigger threat of darkness and it frightens them."

"Why did you want me to learn about herbs?" Ella asked, suddenly aware of the connection she shared with Mist Eagle.

"I was hoping you and your brother would work together someday. Your knowledge and intuition, along with his gift for healing, would make both of you a formidable force for good. That would put an end to the part of the legacy that feeds on their fears and makes them watch you."

"Clifford and I don't see eye to eye on many things, Mom, but we're allies in a crunch. Remember how we worked together to clear his name and catch our father's murderer? And look what happened today."

"People will only remember that he had to hide from you when your father was killed years ago, and that, today, you arrested your brother. They'll begin looking closer at both of you, trying to judge who will turn to evil."

"Neither of us will. That's ridiculous," Ella said, then, seeing the hurt look on her mother's face, wished she could take back the words. "Mom, I know you believe in this legacy, but trust me. There are a lot of discrepancies in this. I have no special gifts. I'm just a cop with very good training and excellent survival instincts."

"You still believe that in spite of all that's happened to you in the past?"

"I love you, Mom, but you better accept the fact that my intuitions are generally right because they're based on knowledge, observation, and training. Being a cop means listening to everything around you and being alert. It's not a gift, its my job. I'm no different from any other experienced cop."

"No, you're wrong about that, and in the next few months it'll become obvious even to you."

Ella looked at her mother and saw her knowing smile. Her mom knew about the baby. Ella was certain of it. The secret she'd hoped to keep, at least until she spoke to Kevin, was no longer completely her own. And, somehow, that didn't surprise her.

SIX

✖ ✖ ✖

Ella parked at the mouth of the canyon where their family shrine was located. They were in the foothills of the mountains along the northwestern border of New Mexico. The track ended here, so they'd have to walk the rest of the way. As she switched off the ignition, Ella gave her mother a long look. "Okay, Mom. How did you find out?"

"That you're pregnant? Did you really think you could keep a secret like that from me?" Rose said. "I'm your mother."

And that was all the explanation needed. For once she understood her mom perfectly. They knew each other far too well for secrets.

Ella let her mother lead the way, setting her own pace. Rose was still using the cane, but today she employed it more for leverage than support as they climbed. Her limp had all but vanished.

After a difficult fifteen-minute hike, they arrived at a cairn of rocks nestled in a crevice within the canyon wall. "My brother has his son and I'll have my child," Ella said. "That will make a total of two. Maybe people will cut us some slack and relax now."

"I doubt it," Rose said, stopping in front of the shrine.

For a long moment, Rose stood there with her eyes closed in

prayer. Then she placed an offering of pollen and a small piece of turquoise on the rocks. "I've asked the gods to bring you health and good fortune. I chose my offerings carefully, too, so they'll accept them and do as I've asked."

Ella nodded. Unlike the way it was in other belief systems, a Navajo invoked the aid of his gods by compelling them to obey. The *Dineh* never humbled themselves, believing their gods wouldn't respect a request made from weakness.

"Have you told your child's father yet?" Rose asked on her way back.

"No."

"Will he want to marry you?"

"I don't know, but I don't want to marry him."

Rose nodded once. "That's just as well. He wouldn't have been a good husband to you," she said. "He's well respected, but he'll always value his place within our tribe more than he will you or the baby. Most of his clan seems to be like that."

"You know who he is?"

"Of course. The lawyer who lives just south of here. As I said, he's not the husband for you."

Irritated, Ella didn't look at her mother. Rose was right of course, but she hated hearing it put so bluntly.

Later, as they rode back to the highway, Ella's thoughts continued to circle endlessly in her mind, raising more questions than answers.

"There's something I should warn you about," Rose said, interrupting her thoughts. "The lawyer is aware of our family's history. His grandmother is a traditionalist and, of course, there's the matter of his clan . . ."

"What do you mean? What's wrong with his clan?"

"His clan and ours haven't mixed in many years. They were responsible for running Mist Eagle out, and when your great-grandfather killed his sister and himself, it was their clan who stood against our family, making our lives even more difficult. Whether your baby's father has told you or not, I know he's heard stories about us. I really doubt he'll be happy to hear the news that you're pregnant."

The knowledge stung. She wasn't sure what she expected from Kevin, but the truth was she couldn't imagine anyone turning away from their own child. "He still deserves to know."

"Yes, he does," Rose conceded. She paused for a long time, then continued. "Just remember, no matter what happens between you two, your child is a blessing. Your baby will enrich your life in ways you never even dreamed possible. You'll become a new person, even to yourself."

"This child is already precious to me," Ella said quietly. "I intend to be a good mother to her."

"I know," Rose said. "You and I will raise her together. We'll deal with things one day at a time."

Ella noted that neither of them disputed the fact that the baby would be a girl. She smiled. This was one time when not being able to explain something logically made absolutely no difference. She knew what she knew, and that was enough.

By the time they returned home, it was late and the tensions of the day had taken a toll on Ella. She sat in the kitchen, snacking on some cold cereal.

"Will you call the station and make sure your brother is okay?"

"I was going to do that before I went to bed. I would have preferred going by, but I'm just too tired to drive right now unless it's an emergency. But don't worry. Kevin's taking care of things."

"After what I've told you about that clan, you still trust him?"

"Yes, Mom, I do. Kevin's not like that." She could see disbelief in her mother's face, but she held her ground. "He's an honest man, and that's saying a lot about a lawyer. And, like me, he's driven to succeed at whatever he's doing. You can trust him if for no other reason than the fact he's extremely competitive and doesn't allow obstacles to remain in his way for long. He'll see to it that my brother is released."

Rose nodded. "Not the best reason to believe in someone,

maybe, but a good one. Now I'm going to bed. That walk today really tired me out."

As Rose ambled down the hall, Ella picked up the phone. Clifford was probably home by now, but she had to check. There were no sure things in the legal system, even with Kevin at the helm. She'd sounded certain for her mother's benefit, but the more she thought about it, the less sure she felt.

Ella spoke to the desk sergeant and identified herself.

"Your brother is still here. There's some paperwork we need to complete, but it's a matter of finding the forms, and getting the right signatures. That's all."

"That's it? There are no other problems?"

"It's a bureaucratic hold up, nothing more. I wish you would talk to Mr. Tolino before he tries to sue the department."

Ella smiled. "No, I think I'll let him handle things on his own. Good-night, Sergeant."

SEPTEMBER 11TH

Ella left for work early the next morning. She'd called Clifford late last night, and was surprised this morning when she checked back at the station and found he was still in jail. They'd only spoken a few minutes. Apparently Kevin had threatened to sue everyone if he wasn't released by eight A.M. Paperwork was the bane of everyone's existence in the department, but it was worse than usual now, because several of the office staff were transferring their equipment and supplies to the new substation.

Ella tried to stop by Clifford's cell, but the officer on duty turned her away. Kevin had left word that no cops were to get near his client until he was released.

Ella returned to her desk and, as she looked down at her in-basket, noticed that Carolyn's autopsy report had been delivered. She skimmed it quickly, searching for the highlights. It didn't take long to find what she was looking for. Hansen had probably been murdered. The first bullet had struck him hard enough to have knocked him unconscious, in Dr. Roanhorse's opinion. There was also a portion of his left hand without blood or tissue splatter marks.

Carolyn had said that the absence of spray indicated that part of his hand had been covered when the fatal shot was fired, almost as if someone had forced his hand over the weapon and then held it in place. The trigger finger had been covered as well, leading Carolyn to speculate that perhaps someone had helped Hansen commit suicide. That, however, still made it murder, particularly because, in Carolyn's opinion, Hansen had been unconscious at the time someone placed his hand on the pistol and pushed his finger down on the trigger.

She had started to read more when the phone rang. It was Sheriff Taylor.

"I need to meet with you," he said. "Your office or mine? We can discuss the case first, then I'd like to go over to LabKote."

"Why don't we meet halfway then? It'll give us a jump start on things. But first, let me fax you a copy of the ME's report so you can get up to speed."

"Fine by me. As soon as it comes in, I'm off."

Ella wrote instructions for Justine to roust some of the women involved in the livestock killings, and bring one or two in for questioning. After leaving the note on Justine's desk, she set out.

Twenty minutes later, Ella reached a wide spot beside the road just east of Hogback. Sheriff Paul Taylor was leaning against his squad car, reading from a pocket-sized notebook. As she got out to meet him, she noted the edge of wariness on his face.

"I got your message about Herder and I've been following up on it by speaking to some of the Anglos who live off the reservation. When he came in to report the body, witnesses who saw him said he was almost sick. Nobody noticed any trace of blood on him or his hands either, and he would have picked up some splatter if he'd been close to the victim when the second shot was fired. It was a contact wound, with the pistol placed against the victim, according to your ME. That puts Herder in the clear. Everything else I've got so far is hearsay. Hansen was friends with a Jerry

Warren, who also works at LabKote. He lives in Waterflow and I tracked him down and spoke to him. Turns out that Hansen was having some crazy things happen to him lately."

"Crazy how?"

"A pile of broken sticks was left on his doorstep."

Ella gave him a surprised look. "It's a Navajo custom that's supposed to bring bad luck."

"Another time someone broke into his house, but they didn't take anything. What they did do was move his bedroom furniture around."

"What?"

"As I said, just crazy."

"What direction was the bed facing when he found it?"

"The direction it's in now. It's against the north wall. I understand he didn't bother to move things back. He figured it was kids playing around."

"Maybe so, but that's got a Navajo signature. It's said that if you sleep with your head pointing north, you're risking death. It's linked to our custom of burying our dead with their heads facing north."

"I have no idea what we're really dealing with here," Taylor said finally, "but the one connection that remains constant is LabKote and the reservation. I tried contacting Landreth this morning, but he's ducking me."

"What did you need from him?" Ella asked.

"I was hoping to come up with a motive that would explain Hansen's death. I figured we might find a lead if we looked through any personal files Hansen had in his computer. Jerry Warren told me Hansen often E-mailed his wife and friends from his terminal at work."

"Let's go over to LabKote together," she said. "An impromptu visit from an officer of the tribe they lease land and property from might persuade them to cooperate."

Ella led the way to LabKote with the sheriff following in his unit. When they reached the parking area beside the gate, Ella got out of her vehicle. An armed security guard came out of the small booth as they approached. Ella flashed her badge, but he didn't seem overly impressed by her or the uniformed sheriff.

"I'll have to call the plant supervisor before I can let you or the sheriff in, ma'am," he told her. "You'll also need to be provided with an escort. We don't allow any unrestricted access to this facility."

Ella nodded. "Get to it then. We don't have all day."

The guard called in the request on a handheld radio, then turned back to her and the sheriff. "You both will be met by Doctor Landreth shortly."

While they waited, Ella took the opportunity to tell Taylor about her visit with Walter Morgan at his apartment, including what she'd learned about his and Landreth's backgrounds.

"I'm not surprised Morgan is ex-military. A lot of ex-soldiers end up doing security work or joining law enforcement."

After five minutes passed, Ella found herself growing impatient, and spoke to the guard. "Will you contact Dr. Landreth again? We all have schedules around here."

The man got back on the radio, and a minute later Landreth appeared. He shook Taylor's hand first, then hers, disregarding Navajo customs.

As Ella took his hand, she wondered when she'd acquired the Navajo distaste for touching strangers.

"I hope you've come to give me the news that the case has been closed and we can finally start putting this whole thing behind us."

"I'm afraid not. The investigation is just beginning," Ella said.

"That's really disappointing. Hansen's death has created no end of problems for us here, I've got to say. The latest is that none of the Navajo employees will use the parking lot. They insist on parking on the east side, on the fairgrounds lot, and then walking in. It's making the guards—and us—crazy."

"Then it looks like you'll have to adjust," Ella said as they walked through the building's entrance and to Landreth's office. "The reason they're doing that is all part of our beliefs, so don't expect it to change."

As they sat down, Ella's and Landreth's gazes locked. "Let's cut to the chase. We want to access any private files Hansen had on his computer."

"I can't allow that. I have no way of knowing how much personal stuff he's got in there and how much is proprietary."

"We're not interested in your business's secrets. We need to find everything we can about Kyle Hansen, and what's stored in his computer might help," Taylor said.

"His computer should have only things pertaining to his job. I doubt it'll be much help."

"Then let us verify that, and we'll be on our way."

"What makes you think there's anything you can use in there?"

"I spoke to another LabKote employee," Taylor said, "and that worker assured me that Hansen often E-mailed personal friends from his terminal here."

"If that's the case, he probably has those files encrypted, or keyed to a special password."

"We'll have the police department's specialists take a look at that. If they can't crack it, we'll get somebody from the private sector."

Dr. Landreth looked back and forth between the two officers. "I really can't give you access to that computer until I'm certain that what's in it won't jeopardize our technology. Some of our procedures are strictly our own, and to have that information leave the facility could risk losing our edge in business."

"I'm talking about a murder." Ella saw the look of surprise on his face. "Yes, we now know that your employee was murdered."

Landreth cursed, then sat back and took a deep breath, letting it out again. "That's just what we need. Okay, here's what I can do. I'm going to go out on a limb here, so I hope that you appreciate this," he added quickly. "I'm going to go into his computer and give you a copy of all the files that clearly don't have something to do with our sterilization procedures or with our plant operations. You can come with me and verify that, if you want."

"Okay."

Ella and Taylor followed him to a windowless office next to the warehouse section.

Taylor glanced at Ella and gave her a quick half smile acknowledging her victory.

As Landreth switched from one computer program to another, they waited. Soon he accessed a special directory and found what they were looking for. "These appear to be his personal files, based upon the directory name he's placed them in. They're encrypted and he's managed to block our override passwords that are designed to give access to supervisors. In other words, I can copy them, but you'll have to figure out a way to open them up and read them."

"Fair enough," Ella said.

Moments later, he handed them a disk. "There you go. I hope you appreciate the fact that we are cooperating with your agencies. I was under no obligation to give you this without a court order," he said.

Ella nodded. "We know." Somehow, she couldn't quite muster up a thank-you. She had a strong feeling that this was one of the things they'd had been prepared to give her all along as a gesture of good faith.

"I'll have our security chief, Walter Morgan, see if he can find a way to decode those files for you. It may expedite your investigation."

"That would be fine," Ella said.

After they had the disk, Ella and Taylor walked out together. The second they passed through the barbwire-topped metal gate, the doors slammed shut behind them. The sudden hum, and smell of ozone told her that electrical fencing was now in operation. It hadn't been on before.

Taylor scowled as he looked back at the massive structure. "Why do I get the feeling that we've been handed a bone to keep quiet?"

"Yeah, I got that, too," Ella nodded. "They're playing games. But I think it's corporate games in line with damage control. Having one of their own employees murdered at work, and facing the possibility that another employee could be the killer, won't result in good publicity and they know it. They're going to need all the goodwill they can get from the tribe to weather the storm."

"You're probably right," Taylor agreed. "By the way, many of LabKote's employees live on the Rez and I don't have any jurisdiction here, but I'd still like to go with you when you question them. Is that okay with you?"

"Sure." Ella thought of her brother, then of Kevin. She had to make sure that situation had been handled first. "I've got some business to take care of this morning before I can follow through on that," she said. "But if you can, meet me at the Totah Cafe in about two hours—we'll get started."

"I'll be there, or call you if I can't make it."

As Ella drove back to the station, she felt guilty at having put Sheriff Taylor and the interviews off for what was clearly personal business. She couldn't help but wonder if this would be only the first of many times the baby would interfere with her work. She pushed the thought aside. This was a special situation. Even cops had family business to attend to from time to time.

Her thoughts shifted to Clifford and Kevin. Once she verified that Clifford had been released, she'd speak to Kevin. It was time he knew about the baby. To continue putting it off wasn't her style, though after what her mother had told her, she was a little apprehensive about giving him the news. Admittedly, Kevin's reaction didn't worry her nearly as much as that of his clan's. They were a wild card she'd never figured she'd have to deal with.

Ella walked inside the station a short time later, and practically ran into Justine who was coming out of her lab. "You might want to hurry over to the south side of the building. Your brother's just been released, and he's leaving with his wife."

"Here, take this. I'll need it decoded," she said explaining briefly.

"I'll take care of it," Justine said.

Ella jogged to the back of the station and arrived in time to catch Loretta and Clifford halfway down the hall. Clifford gave her a nod, but Loretta wouldn't even look at Ella.

"You should have been released hours ago. Are you okay?" Ella asked, keeping step as they continued down the hall together.

"It wasn't a pleasant experience," Clifford said, weariness evident on his face. "I can't believe I have you to thank for it."

His voice was hard, and it carried. Ella felt the stares of those around her. "I did what I had to do. If it hadn't been me, it would have been Sergeant Manuelito. You know that."

"Maybe. But somehow I expected more from my sister. You could have at least stopped by to see me this morning."

"I checked, but your lawyer didn't want you talking to any more cops. Have you forgotten?"

He stopped as they reached the exit and turned to face her. "Since when have you listened so carefully to other people's rules?"

"We're going home," Loretta said bruskly, walking out the door. "We've had enough of this station to last a lifetime."

Ella was watching Clifford and Loretta walking to the visitor's parking area when she heard footsteps behind her. She turned her head and saw Kevin approach.

"Did you catch Clifford?" he asked, then seeing her nod, added, "I hope he takes my advice and distances himself from the Fierce Ones. They certainly won't do him any good, and it may end up costing him his credibility with The People."

"I'll try to reason with him once he has had a chance to rest." Ella paused. They had to talk, and if she kept putting it off, the baby would be in the third grade by the time she got around to it. "Are you going anywhere right now? I need to talk to you—in private."

"Do you want to go get some coffee?" Kevin's eyebrows rose slightly as he tried to guess what was on her mind. He adjusted his tie, probably a habit when he was trying to puzzle out a mystery.

She shook her head. "Let's just drive down to the river and

take a little walk. It's quiet under the cottonwood trees and it'll help us both think some things through."

"Sounds serious." His expression softened into a smile, but his eyes gave away his concern.

"It is," she said. "It's going to mark the beginning of a whole new life for all of us."

SEVEN

✖ ✖ ✖

Ella stood beneath the shade of an old cottonwood, staring down at the river, which was narrow and shallow this time of year. It was time to tell Kevin, but she also had to make it clear that she expected nothing from him in return.

"It's not like you to hesitate, Ella," Kevin said softly. "What's bothering you? You can tell me anything, you know. We may not be lovers anymore, but I'd like to think we're more than just friends."

"That's a good way to put it." She took a deep breath then let it out slowly. "I guess there's only one way to tell you this, and that's straight out. I'm pregnant."

He stared at her in stunned silence for several moments, then slowly a smile spread over his face. He tried to draw her into his arms, and she didn't resist. They held each other for a moment, but when he moved to kiss her, she pulled away.

"This changes nothing, Kevin, do you realize that?"

"What are you talking about? This changes everything."

She sighed. "Yes, I guess in a way it does."

He laughed. "So, now we get married?"

"No, that's just it. We don't. Kevin, we've got a pretty special relationship, but a baby isn't enough to make a marriage work. You know as well as I do that we've got two totally different outlooks on life. You're on your way up, but I'm happy just where I am."

"So, what are you saying, Ella? Remember that the child you're carrying is mine as well as yours."

She nodded. "I'll never deny you time with the baby, I want you to know that, but I don't think marriage is the right answer for us."

He stared off toward Ute Mountain for a long time. "I wouldn't have picked this time in my life to have a child, I won't lie to you about that. But nature took it's own course. The question is, what do you want to do about it now? Marriage is the only answer I can see."

"It might be for you, but not for me. I know you're trying to do what's best for the baby, and you're also worried what this is going to do to your career. A lot of converted Christian Navajos won't vote for you if you're known to have a child out of wedlock."

"We can't keep the fact that I'm the father a secret, you know. Things don't work that way on the Rez. And this is bound to create trouble on another front, too. Your pregnancy is going to bring all the problems our clans have had with each other right to the surface, and we're going to have to find a way to deal with that. In my opinion it'll be easier on everyone if we present a united front."

Ella wasn't surprised that Kevin knew about the past, but the realization that he'd chosen to begin a relationship with her in spite of that spoke well of his character. The notion that he thought so highly of her was pleasing. But it still didn't change the way she felt.

"I can't marry you, Kevin. And you don't really want me as your wife. We just don't love each other that way."

He pursed his lips. "It's no longer a matter of what either of us wants. There's our baby and our families to consider."

"Your family will never accept my child."

"They'll have to, unless they want to sever their relationship with me."

"It doesn't have to come to that. The baby will be taken care of, you know that. My mom will help me, and I make enough to support myself and the baby."

"I'll help you financially, and not just because it's my responsibility. I want to do this. It's my kid, too." He gazed into her eyes for a long moment. "Are you really sure you don't want to get married?"

"We wouldn't be doing the baby a favor by getting married when we both know, deep down, that it would be a mistake. The only real question is how do you want me to handle this? I can try to keep your name out of it. If I do that, there's a chance many will assume Wilson is the baby's father."

He lapsed into a long silence, then finally spoke. "I don't like that at all, but I need time to think things through. I want to make sure we're doing the right thing for everyone involved."

"There's no rush, Kevin. I'm only on my second month. People won't know for a while yet." Ella paused, then added. "Of course that doesn't include my mother. I had hoped to tell you first, but she guessed."

Kevin laughed. "It would be very hard to keep anything from her," he conceded. "I've heard all about her gifts."

Ella said nothing. Kevin's casual way of bringing the subject up hadn't fooled her.

"You know that's something else people will be speculating about once they know you're pregnant," he added slowly. "Your family's legacy is practically legendary."

"I expect any child of mine will have to go through the same thing I have," Ella said. "People aren't really sure how much of the legacy is real and how much isn't and that makes them nervous around me and my family."

"I wonder how people will react to the knowledge that the father of your child is also a member of the same clan that historically created so many problems for yours," he said, thoughtfully. "I have a feeling it's going to give some in my clan a sleepless night or two."

"As I said, I know there are many things you have to consider. You may find that the best thing will be for you not to claim the baby as your child."

"I just don't like the idea of hiding the fact that I'm the baby's father. It goes against my own sense of right and wrong."

"I know, but remember that no matter what you do, this baby will be surrounded by love, and that I can handle whatever comes."

"I don't doubt that for a minute. The real question is, can I?"

"It may take you some time to figure out all the angles, but you'll come up with the right answer, Kevin. You always do."

As they drove back to the station in Kevin's truck, an uncomfortable silence settled between them. The news had been harder on Kevin than she'd thought. She knew he was torn between the need to acknowledge the baby as his own, and the fear that, in the long run, it would do more harm than good. Kevin couldn't predict how his clan would react any more than she could.

"When do you plan to tell everyone that you're pregnant?"

"Not for a while. I won't quite wait until I'm showing, but I don't want to rush into it either. I need to stay out in the field for now and, once Big Ed knows, I have a feeling he'll want to put me behind a desk."

"You shouldn't stay in the field, Ella, at least not while you're pregnant."

"A lot of people depend on me, Kevin. Right now there's no one qualified to take over my cases. I've got to see some things through before I take leave or accept restricted duty. It's my job to make this reservation a safe place for all The People's children, not just mine. In the meantime, I'll take all the precautions I can, and I'll cover myself every step of the way, but I can't put the entire world on hold just because I'm expecting."

Silence stretched out between them once again. Ella could feel his frustration. There would be no simple answers for either of them—not anymore.

Kevin looked in the rearview mirror, then increased his speed. Noting it, Ella glanced back. "That van's coming up too fast," she said. "Give him more room if he wants it. The entire road, in fact."

Kevin glanced behind him again. "He's going eighty, at least, and closing fast."

As Kevin slowed and started to pull to the side, Ella's instincts for danger came to life. Something was wrong. That van wasn't just speeding, it was going to try to hit them.

"No, don't slow down, speed up. Get out of here!" Ella yelled, reaching for her cell phone. In a breath, the van was alongside them, and Ella felt the bone-jarring thump as the van smashed against them, then heard the screech of tires as Kevin tried to keep them on the highway.

Ella's hand was shaking as she tried to punch up 911 on her phone. She'd almost managed it when the van suddenly slammed into them again.

"I can't hold it," Kevin yelled. His truck veered to the right and careened off the highway. Bouncing heavily, they flew off the shoulder and into an alfalfa field.

"Hold on!" Kevin yelled, keeping a death grip on the steering wheel as he pumped the brakes.

Ella reached over to help him steady the wheel, but they hit a patch of sand just then and it was like hitting a wall. The rear end of the pickup rose off the ground, then the air bags popped and they were slammed back into their seats, blinded by the fabric and deafened by the noise.

In almost slow motion the truck tipped over nose first, and Ella blacked out for a moment.

When she opened her eyes again, she felt an odd sensation, then realized she was hanging upside down in her seat belt. Pushing away the collapsed air bag, she looked to her left. "Kevin? Are you okay?" She undid the safety belt, held out her arms to stop her fall, and landed on her knees atop the ceiling of the cab.

Kevin tried the same, except his knees collided with the steering wheel. "That hurts," he grumbled.

"You still okay?"

"Yeah, I'm in one piece, more or less," he said, operating the door latch, then kicking it open. "Can you get out on your side?"

"Yeah, my door's banged in, but it's not jammed against the ground. Your roll bar saved us."

A moment later they stood by the side of the totaled vehicle, the smell of gasoline, dust, and hot oil intermingling. Kevin looked at her, worried. "Are you sure you're okay . . . and the baby?"

"The baby at this stage is so small, it's well protected. Besides, my stomach wasn't hit, just both my shoulders."

As she spoke, she looked over at Kevin and saw blood streaming down his arm. "But you're hurt," Ella said quickly. "Let me find my cell phone. If it still works, I can get the paramedics."

Kevin sat down on a large boulder at the edge of the field. "I'll be okay. It's just a cut . . . and my arm feels like it may be broken. You know, all in all this is turning out to be one helluva day."

She gave him a thin smile. "For me, too."

Ella retrieved her phone, called for a rescue team, then contacted the police department. Next, she rejoined Kevin, carrying the first aid kit he kept behind the seat. The blood flowing from the cut on his upper arm had slowed down considerably, so she decided against trying to bandage it because of the possible break.

"What was it with that van? Do you have an enemy who works in a repair shop? I really didn't get a good look at the driver, but I saw the logo on the side of the door. Near as I can remember, I haven't got any unpaid repair bills," he joked halfheartedly.

Ella had seen the logo on the side of the van as well. It was from a well-known appliance repair shop. "I don't know what's going on. The driver didn't handle that van like he was drunk. I got a partial on the plates and I've already called it in. Let's see if our guys can catch him."

Hearing sirens wailing in the distance, Ella started to walk back to the road. "It's a good thing we weren't far from town. I'm going to lead them over here. Don't move too much until they check you out."

Kevin didn't argue. As she made her way to the road, questions filled her mind. If it had been a deliberate attempt, had it been aimed at her, or at Kevin? It was his vehicle, after all. An attorney in his position made almost as many enemies as a cop. Every time he won a case, there was a new disgruntled loser to contend with.

Ella tried to recall if the van had been in the area of the police station earlier, but couldn't remember. Although she had plenty of old enemies that would have been very happy to see her crash, she didn't think she'd ticked off anyone lately.

Ella greeted the paramedics, then led them over to Kevin. One stayed with him, but the other one came to where she was standing. "I'm okay," she said, but the paramedic refused to accept her answer. Not in the mood for an argument, she submitted to the usual field tests for unseen trauma, and had some small cuts on her hands and knees tended. By then, Sergeant Joseph Neskahi had arrived on the scene.

Ella spoke to him while the paramedic bandaged her cuts. "Go to Ben E's Repair Shop. Talk to everyone there until you can narrow down who the driver was. We want to lock up whoever was behind the wheel. Impound that van when you find it, too."

"I'll take care of it," Neskahi said as they loaded her into the ambulance. "Do you want me to break the news to your mother before she hears it from someone at the hospital?"

"If you could, I'd sure appreciate it, Sergeant. Just make sure she understands that I'm fine. Tell her I said so personally."

Ten minutes later, Ella allowed the doctor at the Shiprock hospital to check her over. Although she kept telling everyone that she was fine, no one seemed to believe her, especially after she advised the doctor that she was pregnant.

By the time she emerged from the ER with a clean bill of health, except for her cuts and bruises, Rose and Wilson Joe were waiting for her. Wilson seemed a bit cool, but she put it down as his way of dealing with the news the car accident had happened while Kevin had been at the wheel. He'd never been a big fan of Kevin's.

"Are you all right, Daughter?" Rose asked as they walked down the hall.

"I'm fine, just banged up a bit. Kevin got the worst of it."

"We overhead one of the nurses say that his arm was broken," Wilson said stiffly. "What happened?"

"Other than being forced off the road, I'm not sure." Ella gave them the few details she was certain about.

As they reached the lobby, Ella saw Kevin Tolino's mom and dad waiting. She was about to go over and reassure them when Kevin came out with a cast on his arm. They began talking immediately, and not wanting to interrupt, she waited.

After a few moments, Kevin came over to join her. He greeted Rose warmly, then took Ella aside. "I'm going to head home," he said. "We can talk more tomorrow. Okay with you?"

"Sure. I'm going to go home with Mom, then I'll catch a ride or use Mom's truck to go back to work. I may need to talk to you later."

He nodded. "Officer Jimmy Frank was questioning me while they were setting my arm. I've got to tell you, although I've got enemies, I can't think of a single one violent enough to pull a stunt like this. You better take a long look at the criminals you've been chasing. There's no doubt in my mind that you were the intended target today."

"That could very well be, but we've got to consider all the possibilities."

"I better get going. I don't want to keep my parents waiting. I hope you'll cut yourself some slack and take the rest of the day off, too. You've been through enough."

Ella shook her head. "I'll be diving into this case right away. Every minute that passes works against my investigation."

"Is that dedication or obsession?"

His tone was critical, and that surprised her. She was sure his intentions were good, but if Kevin thought that the baby now gave him the right to dictate what she could or couldn't do, he was sadly mistaken. "I'll handle things. Just go home, feel better, and let me take care of my business."

Ella saw the flash of anger on his face just before he turned away. He wasn't used to having anyone completely disregard his advice.

Rose smiled as Ella joined her. "Be it far from me to criticize you, Daughter, but taking the rest of the day off couldn't hurt."

"You heard us?"

"Yes. If he hadn't wanted me to, he should have whispered softer."

Ella laughed. Kevin's voice had been quiet, but he hadn't counted on Rose's sharp hearing. Though her mother's face had taken on wrinkles with age, her hearing was excellent.

Ella noticed Wilson's near silence as he drove her and Rose home. Something was on his mind, but right now she just didn't have the energy to try and find out what was bugging him.

"I know the lawyer believes that this accident was caused by an enemy of yours," Rose said. "Do you have any idea who it might have been?"

"No, but I think my friend was too quick to jump to conclusions. The only thing I'm certain about is that it was deliberate, not an accident."

"Should the rest of your family be told about this?" Wilson asked, "Or is the threat one you feel sure won't spill over to them?"

She knew what he was thinking. Skinwalkers were known to have multiple targets—the primary one, and others that could also be used to accomplish their goal. Wilson's experience with them certainly entitled him to some paranoia. But she had made other enemies who were just plain old criminals. The threat from one of them seemed more likely.

"I really don't know anything at this point," Ella said. "But maybe a little caution won't be a bad thing." She looked at her mother. "Would you consider staying with Loretta during the day?"

"Absolutely not," Rose said flatly. "I can take care of myself. I may have to use a cane, but my senses are sharp. If anyone comes by, I can call you or your brother for help."

"You know that it takes time for our police to respond, even if we drop everything and race over. And my brother is often away with a patient. Just for a few days, won't you stay with a friend while I'm not home?"

"No. I won't be run out of my home. It didn't work on me in the past, and it won't work now."

Ella sighed. She hadn't expected any other response, but it was still worrisome. "I'll see if I can increase the patrols around home. And, if you see anyone or anything that doesn't seem right, don't wait. Call in, okay?"

Wilson glanced over at Ella. "I can stay for the rest of today, if you'd like," he offered.

"That's not necessary. I'm not so old that I need a baby-sitter," Rose said sharply.

Wilson glanced at Ella, cringing slightly.

Ella made a helpless gesture. "You heard her."

A half hour later, Ella sat in the kitchen with her mother. She'd showered and changed, and although she now felt the bruises even more than she had before, she was ready to tackle the rest of the day.

"Well, things certainly have to get better from this point on," she said sipping a glass of cold milk.

"Your life will get even more complicated as time goes on," Rose mused, "not less."

Ella sighed. "By the way, did Wilson seem a little edgy to you on the way back from the hospital?"

Rose nodded. "But it was to be expected. He overheard the doctor mention to the nurse that you were pregnant."

Ella closed her eyes, then opened them again. Trying to keep a secret on the reservation was hopeless. She wondered why she'd ever thought she'd be able to pull it off. "I'll have to talk to him later."

"This is just the beginning of how it'll be, Daughter. Your love for your work and the love you feel for your baby will always tear you in two different directions. One day you'll find yourself coming apart, and it won't be at a seam."

"My baby will have all the love I can give her, but I can't stop being who and what I am."

"Discovering that you're going to have a child must have taken you by surprise. Are you sure you're prepared for what's to come?"

"No, I'm not prepared. I didn't expect this. But now that it's here, there's no turning back. And, you know what? I wouldn't want to. I want to be a mom."

Rose smiled. "It's not all sunshine and clover. Some daughters are difficult," she said.

Ella laughed. "Gee, I wonder who you mean?" She finished the last of the milk, then stood. "I'm going back to work. Is there anything you need from me before I go?"

"Not a thing. Just be careful."

Ella drove off in her mother's truck and, on her way to the station, called Justine. "Anything new turn up on any of our pending cases?"

"We tracked down the van that ran you off the road. Sergeant Neskahi learned that it had been stolen earlier today. Then one of our cruisers found it abandoned about three miles from the site of your accident, partially stripped. We have it in impound now."

Ella muttered a soft curse. "Fingerprints?"

"We're going to focus on that next. The sergeant is there now, and I'm on the way."

"When you're done, check into the criminal cases Tolino's involved with and see if there's anyone who might be out gunning for him," Ella said. "Then ask for his cooperation on his civil cases."

"I'll take care of it.

"Did you get a chance to bring in any of the people involved with the livestock killings?"

"Joseph Neskahi worked on Nancy, and I took Mary Lou and Norma Sells. I think we rattled them a bit, but not enough to make a difference. We didn't get anything useful out of any of them, and nobody changed their stories."

"Keep on it."

"10–4."

Ella was nearly to the station when she saw thick black smoke billowing from the Sells Feed Store storage barn. Ella called it in as she pulled off the road to see if she could help. Norma Sells was fighting the blaze in the sheet-metal building with a handful of Navajos who'd come to help, but it didn't take a professional to see that it was already too late. Even if the fire department arrived right now, the supplies inside were doomed. What they had to do now was keep the flames from spreading to the wood-framed store not twenty feet away.

As Ella jumped out of her vehicle, Norma handed the garden hose she was using to another woman, then jogged over to her. "I hope the police will finally do something now."

"What do you mean?"

"I gave Officer Goodluck a written statement. I *told* her to go arrest Nancy Bitsillie, that she was the one who killed Mary Lou's goat, but she said they couldn't without a witness or proof. Then my barn was trashed, and I had to throw out half my feed. Later on, after someone spread *our* premium goat feed all over Nancy's corrals so that her goats ate it instead of the traditional forage and hay, she came here and accused me of a lot of things. She's crazy, I'm telling you. Just plain crazy."

"So, you think Nancy was the one who made the mess in here before, with the manure and all, then came back and set this fire?"

"Who else? I'm telling you, she lost it when Mary Lou's goat won. She's one of those traditionalists who thinks anything modern is evil and should be destroyed. That doesn't seem to keep her from driving a pickup, though."

"I'll check out everyone's story, but first, what can I do to help here and now?"

Norma shook her head. "Nothing. I'll just have to let the fire burn out. We'll just keep wetting down my store so the fire won't spread. But you can throw Nancy's butt in jail. At least I'll know she can't get at me again."

Ella called in her report, then drove directly to Nancy Bitsillie's home, which was down near the bosque east of the river. The trailer house with a roofed over porch wasn't quite the hogan the usual traditionalist might have, but as was typical, they'd constructed a six-sided log and mud ceremonial hogan in the back. Ella saw Nancy and her two brothers standing on the porch as she parked and walked up.

Nancy stepped off the porch as Ella came up. "That crazy woman is blaming me for the mess in her feed store, isn't she?"

"Someone set a fire there a short while ago. I think you'll agree that things are getting out of hand. I'd like to ask you a few questions and maybe together we can figure out what's going on," Ella said, keeping her tone nonconfrontational. She wanted Nancy's cooperation, not another battle.

Nancy glared at her. "I *knew* you'd side with her though. You come from a family of traditionalists and you should know better. Your problem is that you spent too much time on the outside and it corrupted you."

"My sister was here all day yesterday," Wilbur called from the porch. "She's not guilty of anything. If anything new has happened, it still couldn't be her. All three of us were stacking hay until just an hour ago."

Ella saw the anger in the pair's eyes as they came closer. There was more going on than anger over a goat being killed. Things had escalated way beyond that, and she wasn't sure how to stop it now. "Who do you think ruined all the grain and hay at the Sells Feed Store?" Ella pressed.

"You'd like to blame the traditionalists for everything, wouldn't you?" Nancy said.

"I just want everybody to stop losing their tempers. Nobody needs this kind of tension here. We have to stand together, not split ourselves apart."

"As it always is with those who've abandoned our ways, you talk out of both sides of your mouth. Maybe you should listen more to your brother instead of turning against him and arresting him. He *knows* who he is."

"I have *not* turned against my brother," Ella said, her anger spilling to the surface. Realizing what was happening, she stopped and took a deep breath. "I'm not getting into this with you." She met Nancy's gaze. "Where were you during the past hour?"

"I told you—" Wilbur began.

Ella gave him a sharp look. "I want her answer, not yours. When I want to hear from you, I'll ask you the question."

He glowered at her but remained silent.

"I was here, making some mutton stew after putting away the hay, just like my brother said," she answered, her voice taut. "Now unless you plan to arrest me, please leave."

Nancy stepped back into the trailer house, leaving Ella standing there with the two brothers.

Ella gave them a curt nod, then went back to her vehicle. As she passed by their pickup, she reached out and felt the hood. It was cool and no noise ticked from a cooling engine. If they had set the fire, they hadn't used this truck as transportation.

Ella climbed into her SUV, thinking about what had just transpired. Nancy's words had cut deep. She and Clifford were being seen as each other's enemies, though it couldn't have been further from the truth. Yet, because of the legacy, she knew that everyone would be watching them carefully now to see what would happen between the two of them next. The prospect made her uneasy.

She arrived at the station fifteen minutes later and Sheriff Taylor came out the side door.

"I was here looking for you, and heard about the truck accident." he said, coming up to her. "I didn't think you'd be back to work so quickly."

"There's a lot to be done," she said simply, and saw the look of recognition on his face. A kindred soul—she was sure he knew exactly how she felt about her work because he was the same way. "What brings you here?"

"I think I've spoken to all the LabKote employees that live off the reservation except for Walter Morgan, and you've done that. I've also interviewed the two Anglo supervisors who live in my jurisdiction. Their stories are almost identical—word-for-word identical."

"So it looks like they've had time to rehearse."

"Yeah, which doesn't exactly make me trust them. But I've got nothing really new, either. I also spoke to the two Navajo workers who live off the Rez, but their stories are vague. About the only thing they seem to have noted about Hansen was that he was very depressed when his ex-wife refused to reconcile with him. One of the women thought he was really sweet and very much in love, though the other one called him 'pathetic.' She said that he was always whining about his wife."

"That makes a case for suicide," Ella said. "But why do it in the parking lot at LabKote? And if someone helped him off himself, they're guilty of murder themselves."

"I don't buy the whole suicide angle. I got the impression he still hadn't given up on the idea that he'd eventually win her back."

"Let's continue to look into it and see what other people have to say. Who's next on the list?" Ella asked.

"There's Leonard Bidtah and his wife Bertha. Also Wilma Francisco. They worked the same shift as Hansen. The rest of the employees, according to one of the supervisors, wouldn't have seen much of Hansen except coming or going, since his work kept him isolated."

"I know the Bidtah's. They don't live too far from here. We can go there now. Wilma may be more of a problem. She lives with her parents and they're traditionalists. But let's take it a step at a time."

Ella drove the sheriff in her tribal vehicle, leaving her mother's truck at the station. As they reached a residential section of the Rez and she saw Taylor looking around, she tried to see things through his eyes. The beige, cookie-cutter modular homes weren't stacked next to each other as she'd seen in other housing projects, but there was a lot of clutter in several of the front yards.

Old vehicle carcasses left to die where they'd stopped were now children's playhouses and targets for stones. Dogs and kids played in the midst of poverty, oblivious to their status as they ran up and down the streets. To her, it was home, and to the ones living there, it was just life. To an outsider, places like this probably spoke more of hardship and stagnation, and strangers living on the edge of disaster.

"You were in the FBI, Investigator Clah?"

Ella nodded.

"Why didn't you stay with the bureau?"

In other words why had she chosen to live here, of all places? She could read the question on his face as clearly as she could see his pale blue eyes and weathered features. "You see a never-ending cycle of poverty here, don't you? I see that, too, but there's another side of the Navajo Nation someone who wasn't raised here probably won't ever see. That's why I'm here."

EIGHT

—— ✖ ✖ ✖ ——

As they entered another area of mobile homes, Taylor mulled over her words. "You mean intangibles, like your culture? Is that why you returned?"

"It's more than that. It's what we call the *hózhq*. It means all that's good, orderly, and harmonious. It's a feeling I find only here, and what makes us one with the land and gives us an identity that's more than the name Navajo. To be honest, I didn't always see that myself. It's one of those things that you don't miss until you're no longer around it."

"It sounds a bit like a cowboy and his boots," Taylor said, nodding. "I was offered a job back East years back. I packed up all my things and left, intending to start a new life, but it didn't work out for me. It was pretty enough with the green and all, but I like it out here, with the sagebrush, bare mesas, and dry river beds. My boots, my hat, my horse, and even my pickup truck are a part of me. I couldn't see trading them in for taxi cab rides and air so thick you can see what you're breathing in."

Ella parked in front of a new-looking double-wide mobile home. Trash had accumulated in a pile by the side of the house, ready to be burned, if it didn't blow away first. A tricycle lay on its side beside a chicken-wire fence that held several hens. An old dog looked up, but didn't bother to growl or bark as they climbed up the three wooden steps leading to the front door.

"Here it doesn't matter but, at the Francisco's, we'll have to wait in the tribal unit until we're invited in," Ella whispered.

As Ella brought her hand back to knock, a middle-aged woman opened the door.

"Ella, I haven't seen you since last year's tribal fair in Window Rock. How have you been?"

"Fine, Bertha. Working hard."

Bertha nodded sympathetically. "Yeah, don't we all. At least there's a new place to work here in Shiprock. Leonard and I both have good paying jobs for the first time in years." She gestured for them to sit. "But tell me, what brings you here?" She looked at Sheriff Taylor. "We don't get that many *bilagáana*—white—lawmen on the Rez except for the FBI. What's going on?"

"Sheriff Taylor and I need to ask you and Leonard a few questions about an employee from LabKote," Ella said.

"Oh, you mean the one who killed himself?" She didn't wait, but continued. "I heard that you were looking into that."

Ella didn't bother to ask for more of an explanation. "Can we speak to Leonard, too?"

"I can help you now, but you'll have to wait to talk to my husband. He went to the store."

"Okay. That's not a problem," Ella said, taking out a notepad from her jacket pocket. "I already know you worked the same shift, but how well did you know the deceased?"

"Better than Leonard did, I'd bet, but we weren't really friends or anything. I was his secretary. I compiled and bound his reports, placed orders for shipping supplies, kept expense accounts, and stuff like that. He wasn't easy to get along with, but he liked talking to a woman, I think, because we tend to be more sympathetic."

"What did you two talk about?" Ella asked, "aside from business matters, that is."

"We spoke about his wife a lot. He loved her very much. I

didn't mention Leonard too often to him, though, because it just reminded him that his own marriage had broken up. He also wasn't too happy with his work, and sometimes he'd let off some steam."

"What was wrong with his job?" Taylor asked. "I understood he had a pretty important position."

"He did, and he was well paid. But he was always finding things wrong."

"Like what?" Taylor pressed.

"Oh, the processing machines that sterilized the labware didn't operate at the level he wanted, or shipping was taking too long for something, or not long enough. With him, it was always something. That was just his nature, you know."

Ella nodded. "How was his overall job performance?"

She considered it for a long time before answering. "Good, I'd say, but I know that Doctor Landreth and him had some problems getting along, mostly because Doctor Landreth wouldn't let Mister Hansen breathe without looking over his shoulder."

"Why do you think he was doing that?" Taylor asked.

Just then the door opened and Leonard came in. "I thought I recognized your Jeep, Ella. Are you investigating Hansen's death? I'd heard that the police didn't believe it was suicide."

Taylor glanced at Ella, then back at Leonard. "Does everyone know about that?"

"Pretty much everyone at work, anyway," Leonard said, sitting next to his wife. "Poor Hansen was a nice enough guy. And he drove a great little sports car, too."

"Do you think Doctor Landreth had a reason to be looking over Hansen's shoulder all the time?" Taylor asked.

"Nah, that's just Doctor Landreth's management style," Leonard answered. "He's always a bit nervous, or insecure. He tells you to do something, then watches like a hawk to make sure you do it just the way he said. And he's almost as paranoid about security as Morgan is."

"He's not that bad," Bertha said, then stopped. "Come to think of it, he is."

"So would you two say that Landreth was victimizing Hansen?" Taylor asked.

Leonard shook his head. "No man, I'm telling you, he was like that to everyone. Well, except for Mister Morgan."

"But the thing is that it bothered Kyle more than it did other people," Bertha said. "He was very precise about everything he did, and it really annoyed him to have Doctor Landreth constantly second-guessing him on everything. Kyle—Mister Hansen, liked having the final word and Landreth never let him have it."

Taylor looked at Leonard. "You work on the assembly line?"

"Yeah, mostly boxing up the sterilized packs when they reach the end of the line. I'm a shipping clerk, and I fill and box up orders from customers. The critical stuff's all automated."

"Have you ever had any kind of run-in with Landreth?"

Leonard laughed. "Me? I doubt he even knows my name. Heck, the only reason Hansen ever spoke to me was because my wife was his secretary."

Leonard looked at the cuckoo clock up on the wall. "I've got to get going. I'm on the evening shift."

Ella stood and walked with Taylor to the door. "Thanks for your help. Both of you."

"Don't discuss what we spoke about here today with anyone else, will you?" Taylor asked. "It could slow down our investigation."

"People will know you were here. They saw you drive up," Leonard said. "But we'll say that you asked us a couple of questions, and then Ella wanted to visit. They won't believe it, but they won't make a big deal out of it either."

They were underway a few minutes later. "They sure gave us a new perspective on these people," Ella said.

"Yeah, but I still don't have a clear grasp on what we're dealing with here. Office politics can generate rivalries, but I just can't see Landreth plotting to kill one of his subordinates," Taylor said. "He'd rather lord over them."

"What kind of background did you get on the victim?" Ella asked. "Anything interesting on his life away from work?"

"Near as I can figure, he didn't have one. I've spoken to his neighbors, checked church and social organizations, but it all came down to the same thing. After his marriage broke up, Hansen became a loner."

"He must have had some friends," Ella said, unable to imagine what it would be like to be that alone. On the Rez, between family and friends, people always had someone to count on.

"I think he was a very lonely man because he cut off most of the ties he had with his past after his divorce. He apparently would go to the small park near his home to watch the kids play baseball on a regular basis, but no one spoke to him and he didn't speak to anyone."

She shuddered. She couldn't imagine living that way.

"Tell me about this Wilma Francisco we're going to next," Taylor said. "What do you know about her?"

"She's young, in her early twenties I guess. Her parents are traditionalists and she lives with them in one of our outlying areas."

"You mean in a hogan and that type of thing?"

She shook her head. "No, that's usually a path only the real old ones prefer. This is a house the tribe probably helped fund, but they have a ceremonial hogan in the back. If they're like other families in that area, they probably live off their garden patches and alfalfa field, a few fruit trees, and a small herd of sheep they graze up in the hills. Some work with arts and crafts as well, too."

"It's probably different for a young woman from a family like that to work for an ultra tech company like LabKote."

"That depends," Ella said hesitantly. "Our traditionalists are usually very poor people, money wise. When things like the need for a new wood stove comes up, they do what they have to in order to survive."

"Don't we all."

It took twenty minutes of hard driving. Unfortunately, by the time they got there, the small, cinder-block house seemed deserted.

"You think we wasted our time?" Taylor asked.

"No, they're here. See the trace of smoke coming from the wood stove? They're just trying to make up their minds about us." She gestured past the sheep corral. A loom was set up in the shade of a cottonwood branch arbor. "They've been weaving."

Minutes passed by slowly, but eventually an elderly woman came to the door and waved for them to approach.

Ella could sense Taylor's uneasiness as they approached. This had to be a jolt from everything he was used to, and she sympathized. Fitting in, even for her, wasn't always easy.

Emily Francisco stood in the porch, her eyes filled with distrust, as Ella greeted her. "What has brought you here, Policewoman?" she asked.

Direct and to the point. There'd be no chitchat here today. Ella explained that they needed to talk to Wilma, and felt the temperature drop ten degrees.

"Why do you want to talk to my daughter? Is it about that place where she works?"

"In a way. It's about one of the employees. Can we talk to her?"

She pursed her lips and gestured Navajo style at a young woman walking back toward the house in the twilight with a scraggly looking dog. "There she is." She regarded Ella with open suspicion. "You're keeping secrets from me, Policewoman, but it's not necessary. We all know about that company. It brings money, but it's not a good thing for the tribe. It's the start of the end, you know."

She'd heard it all before but, although she disagreed, this was not the time to argue about such matters. "Thanks for your time," she said, then walked over to meet Wilma, Taylor at her side.

Wilma's smile faded the second she recognized Ella. Taylor noticed and muttered, "I think she'll be trouble."

"No, give her some slack. She knows that we were at the plant, and is probably worried about what we'll ask her."

Wilma came up to them rather than continuing toward the house. She stopped when she reached a large, crumbling sandstone boulder, and sat down. "What brings you here, Officers. Is it about the dead man?"

Ella nodded, nothing that Wilma had refrained from using the name of the dead. It was a custom among the traditionalists not to mention the recently deceased by their names. Otherwise, their *chindi* might come. The *chindi* was worse than a ghost. It was pure evil. The good in a man went on to merge with Universal Harmony, but it's counter was said to remain forever earthbound.

"What can you tell us about him?"

Wilma shrugged, not looking directly at either of them. "What do you want to know?"

"Whatever comes to your mind," Ella replied.

"I barely knew him. Most of the men flirt with me or ask me out, even some of the married ones, but he never did."

Taylor checked down at his list. "You're the quality control manager?"

She smiled. "It's a fancy title, but all I do is randomly select sterilized packs of labware coming off the line and send them on to quality control. There, the lab techs conduct tests to make sure the petri dishes and such meet LabKote specs. That's it."

"And when they don't?" Ella asked.

"They're cleaned up, and those that can be reprocessed go back through the system. Nobody gets into trouble, if that's what you're thinking."

Ella watched her. Wilma was uneasy about something, but it wasn't the lack of eye contact that gave out signals. In contrast of the way things were off the Rez, here, a younger person from a traditional background never made eye contact with an older one. It was a sign of disrespect. But the feeling that Wilma was holding something back still niggled at the back of her mind.

"Was Hansen difficult to work with?" Taylor asked.

She saw Wilma stiffen as if she'd been slapped, then with effort she relaxed. "No. At least he tried to remember our customs," she said pointedly.

Ella saw Taylor's eyes narrow slightly and knew he had no idea what he'd just done. She would make it a point to explain it to him later. He'd gotten off lucky that Wilma was a young woman working in a nontraditional profession. The older ones would have terminated the interview immediately.

"Try to remember," Ella persisted. "Was he considered a good employee, or did he get into trouble often?"

"He was hard to work with. He did get into trouble a lot, but it was only because he demanded so much of others—including the big bosses. He was the most precise person I've ever known. I can tell you that he was always making me do things over. If the quality control report had even one misspelled word, I'd have to do it again. He seemed to know and notice absolutely everything."

"How did he get along with his supervisor?" Taylor asked. "Did they argue a lot?"

Ella smiled, realizing that this time he'd avoided mentioning names. The sheriff was a fast study.

"The dead man had his own way of doing things and his Anglo supervisor was the same way. They clashed a lot because of that."

"Do you like working at the plant?" Ella asked, still sensing that something wasn't being said. When Wilma gave her a startled look and hesitated, she knew she'd hit the target.

"I like the pay," Wilma said cautiously. "But I get nervous when I can't figure people out and that place . . ." She shook her head. "I guess I've just been listening too much to my mother. Don't mind me."

"No, stay on that. Tell us why you're uneasy."

She took a deep breath then let it out again. "I've been thinking a lot about this. Maybe it's the competition thing, you know?"

Ella nodded, but Taylor gave her a puzzled look. "I don't get it."

Wilma looked at the ground, gathering her thoughts, then finally spoke. "Outside the Rez everyone works and works and works and they never have enough. Here, we work only until we have enough to pay for what we need. Then we go back to our sheep, or our land. When I look at the Anglo workers, I see that they're always busy trying to get ahead, but even when they get a promotion, they're still not happy for long. Whatever it is that they're looking for, is never where they look. Do you understand?"

Taylor nodded, but didn't comment. "Was the dead man," he asked, using her own term, "ambitious like that?"

She nodded. "He liked being upper level and feeling important. He often bragged to others that the plant would shut down
without him. But it hasn't."

"Did he have any enemies?" Taylor asked.

"Not that I know about. But it's hard to say because, sometimes, competition crosses the line and gets into some really nasty
stuff."

As they reached the small-frame house, Ella said good-bye to
Wilma then walked back to the vehicle. "She opened an avenue of
investigation for us, but I'm not sure you caught it."

Taylor smiled. "You mean when she said that Hansen believed
the plant would shut down without him?" He saw Ella nod and
smiled. "Yeah, I was thinking the same thing you were. I wonder
if someone actually believed that."

"I know traditionalists don't want the plant here. Most of them
aren't militant, but there's the Fierce Ones, and they make up their
own rules." Ella considered the matter carefully. "You better let
me tackle that group alone. I'll have better luck than you."

"Amen to that."

Ella dropped Taylor back off at the station. "I'll keep you
updated, particularly if I learn anything new."

"Your brother is one of the Fierce Ones, isn't he?" Taylor
asked.

"Yes, but he's strictly nonviolent. He's a *hataalii*, one of our
healers." Seeing the expression on his face, she knew what he was
thinking. "I won't cut the group any slack just because my
brother chooses to align himself with them," she said answering
his unspoken question. "Don't worry about that."

"At least you have a connection who may be able to give you
some reliable information," he said, still unconvinced.

"Give me some time to see what I can turn up."

Ella watched him walk back to his unit, parked across the lot.
She couldn't blame him for suspecting her objectivity. There was
something to guilt by association, and that was one of the many
reasons she wanted Clifford to stay away from the Fierce Ones.

Yet, instinct told her that he never would. He had chosen his path and, because he believed it, would follow it through with loyalty and courage.

SEPTEMBER 12TH

The following morning, as usual, Ella arrived at work early. As she walked into her office, Justine came in right behind her. Ella sat down at her desk, silently noted a message to call Sheriff Taylor after noon, then looked up at her assistant. "What's happening on the cases?"

"Nothing on the break-in. I'm still tracking down people and talking to employees at the clinic, but so far I've got nothing. I haven't been able to crack Hansen's files yet, either."

"What about the van that ran Kevin and me off the road?"

"I've been looking into that myself. I processed the van for prints but someone sprayed the interior with oil and that makes lifting prints almost impossible."

"Who would have known enough about police work to do that? Do you have a theory yet?" Ella asked.

"Sorta," Justine said slowly. "We know the van was stolen, and that it wasn't joyriding teens or a drunk. I've been wondering if perhaps it might have been the Fierce Ones settling a score with you. They weren't happy when you stood against them at the protest, or when you arrested Clifford."

Ella leaned back in her chair and silently weighed Justine's theory. When she'd reasoned that she hadn't made any enemies recently, she hadn't considered them.

At long last, Ella shook her head. "No, I doubt it could have been the Fierce Ones. Clifford would have known and, if anyone tried to come after me, he would have had their heads. He's really something to see when anyone attacks his family."

"What if they kept it from Clifford?"

She smiled. "Trying to keep anything from my brother is nearly impossible. Believe me."

"Okay. It was just something for you to think about."

Ella nodded once. "I'm going to drive out to the college. I'm going to see if there's some information I can pick up around campus about the break-in at the clinic."

Ella called Wilson and arranged to meet him, then drove over. The time alone on the road, which followed the river valley to the northwest, gave her a chance to think. Too many leads seemed to be pointing back to the Fierce Ones, and when an answer seemed that clear, it was either the unqualified truth, or the results of someone's conscious effort to mislead her. The problem was that her usually sharp instincts were fuzzy on this. What she needed was more information.

By the time she arrived at the college, Ella couldn't quiet the uneasiness that gnawed at her. She was missing something important, she just knew it.

Ella walked to Wilson's office, which was located along the perimeter of the massive, stylized hogan. It was early September and the semester had just started. Students clustered below trees, reading quietly, doing homework, or talking about their schedules. Everyone walked with purpose here, as if they had too many things on their mind which, of course, they did.

Ella reached Wilson's office and saw him sitting at his desk, grading papers, totally oblivious to her until she rapped sharply on the door.

"Hey, Professor, wake up!" Ella said, and laughed when he jumped.

"Don't you know it's bad manners to give the professor a heart attack?"

She sat down across from Wilson. "You and I have to talk, but between my schedule and yours it's quite a trick to find time alone with you."

He smiled. "Yeah, Ella, but it's always been that way. What brings you here?"

"I'm searching for leads in my cases, as always. Have you heard anything, whether gossip or gospel, about the clinic break-in?"

"I heard some of the students talking, but nothing you can

use. The story is that nobody's privacy is safe anymore, and if you want your medical records kept confidential you better leave the Rez to see a doctor."

"That's not the kind of thinking that we need, you know. We already have a lot of trouble getting the older people to go to the doctor. If the younger ones start balking, too, we may have a serious problem on our hands."

"That's why I try to come down hard on that type of talk, but the fact is that, in the long run, the kids will make up their own minds. Unless the clinic improves their security or does something to assure people things are okay now, they're going to see a drop in the number of patients."

"We'll have to weather this just like we've done all the other bad times." Ella leaned back and regarded Wilson. "Speaking of medical files and confidentiality . . . I have a bit of news for you. But, for now, it's for your ears only."

Wilson's face didn't betray his thoughts. He sat back and waited. Though Ella was certain that he already knew what she was going to say, he did nothing to tip his hand.

"I'm pregnant."

He nodded, not faking any surprise. "Are you happy about it?"

Ella smiled. "Yeah. I haven't worked out everything yet, but I'm definitely happy about this."

"What about your job?"

"I'll still be a cop. There are a lot of cops with kids, you know."

He smiled. "The father? Is it who I think it is?"

"It's Kevin and, before you ask, he knows but I don't intend to marry him."

Wilson met her gaze and held it. "I'm glad."

There were many ways to interpret his statement, but Ella had a feeling that if she asked him to clarify, she'd get an answer she wasn't prepared to deal with. Instead, she continued. "There are things he and I need to work out, of course, but I expect it'll be that way from this point on."

He nodded. "Will he take on any financial responsibility? If not, the Navajos won't consider him the baby's legitimate father—not even if they know he's the biological father. To claim fatherhood around here, you have to earn it."

"He'll do the right thing," she said, but didn't elaborate.

He took a deep breath, then let it out again. "Your baby is going to make some of our old enemies resurface, you know, if not now, then soon enough. They may try to get your child so they can control you. You'll have to stay on your guard."

She understood his concern. Both she and Wilson had lost people they loved because of the skinwalkers. But she didn't really believe they'd be a threat to her or the baby—at least not for a very long time.

"They've been quiet for a while. Let's not look for trouble. The last thing we need is to stir them up. But, if they start something, we'll finish it for them," she added firmly.

"Maybe once others know the news, I can do a little digging from behind the scenes and see what kind of plans they're making."

"No, please don't," Ella said, a little more sharply than she'd meant to sound. "You play an important role in our community," she added, her voice gentler. "The kids and your colleagues look up to you. But if you go after people you suspect may be skin-walkers and start frightening people, you'll focus the wrong kind of attention on yourself. That would serve no one, least of all me or you."

"All right. I'll stay out of this. But there is something I want to say to you. I've heard about Clifford's involvement with the Fierce Ones, and we all know that's a vigilante group. You spoke of my position in the community and how I should guard my reputation, but that's even more so for him. He's one of our most gifted Singers."

"Why don't you try talking to him? Tell him what you just told me. He might listen to you."

"I doubt it, he's not that way. But I'll see what I can do."

"Thanks." She started toward the door, when Wilson called her back.

"Do you have to leave right away? I'm really desperate for

judges right now. I'm sponsoring a pet expo on behalf of the middle school science club. The exhibition is right here on campus. How about volunteering? It would only take another twenty minutes of your time."

"I really should be getting back."

"But it would really mean the world to the kids, and you'd be helping me out, too," he insisted. "Besides, Big Ed's niece is part of it, so if you're a little late, I'm sure he'll understand."

"You're not going to take no for an answer, are you?" she said, laughing.

"Now you're getting the idea."

Wilson led her across campus to the agricultural center, then to a small room that faced an enclosed courtyard. The animals were in pens, each with a small presentation notebook explaining what the animal's use was, and how it served the family that kept it, and ultimately the tribe.

Ella joined those already involved and judged everything from chickens to rats, using a checklist Wilson provided. As she reached a crate in the corner, she recognized Winnie the rabbit, Alice Washburn's pet.

"Whatever happened to the bunny this rabbit had? I remember Alice saying that most of the litter died."

Wilson looked grave. "That's a strange story. The one that survived was born blind. Her parents wanted to have it destroyed, but Alice refused to agree. As it turned out, the bunny compensates pretty well and Alice adores him."

"So, it's a good ending, though not a perfect one." Ella said, and continued judging the exhibits. When they finally finished, she handed the score sheets to Wilson.

"Now you owe me," she teased.

"You're entitled to be treated to dinner," he said. "Let me know when you have some free time."

"I will," she said.

"About your baby . . ." Wilson started to say something, then just stopped. He looked away, embarrassed.

"Go on. You don't have to measure your words with me."

"If Kevin decides to bow out, and you find yourself needing anything, let me know. I'd like to help you in any way you'll let me."

Ella took his hand and gave it a squeeze. "You're a good friend. You've always been a big part of my life, and I expect you'll be a big part of my baby's life as well."

As Ella drove back to the station, she couldn't shake the feeling that trouble was shadowing her every move. Even her conversation with Wilson had seemed odd. She'd expected more active disapproval from him. Things had gone too easily and smoothly to trust.

She sighed. Cynicism and pessimism were an occupational hazard for cops. She'd have to stay focused on the things she knew, as opposed to speculation. Her top priority had to be gathering more evidence.

As she walked inside her office, Justine came to meet her. "We got an updated list from Myrna Manus. Not as many things as she thought are missing from the clinic. There are the drugs we knew about and some cash, but all of the medical files have been found. Now the bad news. When she sorted through the papers, she discovered that a few of the records were missing. The really odd thing is what was taken. Myrna said that every missing record pertained to a pregnancy test."

Ella suppressed a shudder. "Could it be that the test results for pregnancy in those cases just hadn't been placed in the files yet?"

"That makes a lot more sense. They probably run quite a few. It's likely that they'd occasionally make filing mistakes with all the paperwork handled there," Justine said. "I'll have Myrna check with her people on that."

"Good," Ella answered. "But if they were really after those pregnancy test results, and took them all, this still gives us some important evidence. We know that three violent, highly motivated burglars broke into the clinic. They didn't count on us finding out about the missing pregnancy test results so soon, however. These new findings suggest the crime was planned and not as random as they wanted us to think. What we're missing is the motive."

Big Ed suddenly appeared at her doorway, and walked inside her office, his face too expressionless to pass as natural. When he shut the door behind him, Ella knew there was trouble ahead.

NINE

———✗ ✗ ✗———

Justine started heading for the
door, ready to give them privacy, when Big Ed suddenly gestured
for her to sit down. "Both of you need to hear this," he said. "Senator James Yellowhair was just kidnapped, apparently on the way
to work. I want you two on this case as of right now. Everything
else takes second place. Is that clear?"

It took a moment for Ella to process what he said. She couldn't
remember the last time someone of that stature in the tribe had
been kidnapped. In fact, she didn't think it had ever happened
before.

"What do we know about this so far?" she asked, her thoughts
already focused, and her training taking over.

"I'll tell you what I've heard, but I'll be quick because I want
your team at the crime scene, pronto. Twenty minutes ago, Joseph
Neskahi found the senator's car abandoned near the main highway about two miles from the senator's home. He called it in
when he saw the state government plates and, while he waited,
he found the letter the kidnappers left stating their demands. Just
to make sure it wasn't a hoax, Neskahi had another officer go
check at Yellowhair's home, but he wasn't there or at his office."

Big Ed glanced at Justine. "There was some blood on the upholstery, so you may want to type that and get whatever you can. I want frequent verbal reports on this. I'll have to keep the tribal president current on what's happening, and I expect answers fast. Are we all clear on this?"

"We'll get started right now," Ella said.

As soon as Big Ed left, Ella looked at Justine. "I want you to go to the crime scene, get that abandoned car processed, then head for the Yellowhair home. You're friends with his family. You're more likely to get them to talk freely to you than I am."

"I'm on it."

As Justine left, Ella, working on a hunch, used her cell phone to call Lulu Todea at the tribal newspaper office. Ella didn't really like the woman, but if anyone would know the senator's current enemies, it would be she.

Ella asked to speak to Lulu, then started down the hall, toward the station exit. Through the connection, she could hear excited voices at the newspaper office.

"Hey, Ella. I was just about to call you. What do you hear about Senator Yellowhair?"

"In regard to what?" Ella asked, suddenly wondering how much Lulu knew already. The kidnapping had been discovered by the police a half hour ago at most. Ella reached the exit, and stepped outside into the parking lot.

"Okay, let's not play cat and mouse," Lulu said. "I've got a deadline. I know the senator's been kidnapped and I know that there's a certain group behind it."

"Which group?" Ella asked, feeling her blood turn to ice. There was only one group she knew about who'd use tactics like those—the Fierce Ones.

"That's the weird part. One of the kidnappers called here not five minutes ago. He referred to himself in the plural—'We have taken the senator,' 'We have made our demands known,' and so on. I tried to ask him some questions, wanting to find out who the group was, but it didn't work. The man just cut me off."

"Do you have it on tape?"

"I didn't get a chance to do that," Lulu said after a moment's hesitation. "The call came out of nowhere."

Ella wondered if Lulu was telling the truth. "What else can you tell me?" She climbed into the Jeep, and started the engine.

Lulu hesitated. "Well, I've got a theory. I think the reason they didn't give me the name of the group is that we all know which group would do that around here. The Fierce Ones."

"Yeah, but doesn't it strike you as odd that they wouldn't claim responsibility outright?" Ella pressed.

"At one time when they were anonymous, I think they would have been willing to do that, but things are different now that the identity of so many of their members is public knowledge. Actually, you should breathe a sigh of relief. Considering that your brother is a member of the Fierce Ones, you're probably better off that they're keeping the group's involvement a secret for now."

Ella knew that Clifford wouldn't take part in anything violent. Yet, even though it was technically kidnapping, holding someone against their will for a while wouldn't be something out of the question for him—providing the motives behind it were good and the person wasn't hurt. "What are the demands, did they tell you?"

"All I know is that it's all spelled out in the note they left in Yellowhair's car. Your officers must have it already and I expect you'll get it from them shortly. Now how about giving me something in return? I'd like to know what's in the note."

Ella had just pulled out onto the highway, and was headed in the direction of Yellowhair's home. "I'm on my way to where the senator's abandoned car is right now. I'll let you know as soon as I see the note."

"The Anglo press is going to get into this, all the way to Albuquerque and beyond. Will you give it to me first?"

"I'll do my best. But if the kidnappers call you back, Lulu, be ready to record everything."

"I'm working on that already."

"And could you make me a list of Yellowhair's enemies?"

"There are a lot of them, you know." Lulu reminded.

"Pick your top ten, those you'd do a story on," Ella sighed, then hung up.

Next Ella called Blalock, the FBI resident agent. She didn't particularly like the man, but she needed the bureau's resources and possibly manpower, particularly if the evidence indicated that Yellowhair was being held off the Rez.

"I can meet you at the kidnapping site. I'm just twenty or so minutes away," FB-Eyes, as Blalock was known, confirmed after hearing her account of the situation.

"Good enough."

Ella had known Blalock for years, and they'd found their own way of getting along. The Anglo FBI agent had learned the hard way to make allowances for cultural differences and, now, was always sure to be seen in the company of a Navajo officer whenever he investigated a case on the reservation. Ella had noticed that his approach to the *Dineh* had mellowed considerably, too, from the first time she'd met him. Then again, she'd mellowed, too. She wasn't nearly as cocky.

As Ella sped down the highway, she forced her body to relax. She couldn't allow the tension to get to her. She could and would do that for the baby, at least. Shifting her thoughts away from work momentarily, she looked at the passing scenery while heading northwest. The desert looked relatively lush this season, especially in the lowlands and fields along the San Juan River. Instead of the dry, dusty air and the smell of baked earth, the ground was covered with flowers, clumps of wild grass, and big thickets of brush. Sheep and goats fed freely and, outwardly, it looked like a good year. But there was an undercurrent that lay just beneath the tranquility that extended to the horizon. It whispered of other influences that threatened to corrupt the land and start a cycle of sorrow.

Ella focused her thoughts back to the job at hand as she arrived at the scene. Neskahi's patrol car lights were flashing, and Justine was already there. Also present were round-faced Sergeant Tache, the department's crime scene photographer, and Detective Harry Ute, whose job was to collect evidence. While

Justine, their only fully qualified forensics expert, went over every inch of the car, the other two worked the surroundings.

Ella walked up to Neskahi and saw the worried expression on his face. "What have you got for me, Sergeant?"

Neskahi had placed the note in an evidence pouch, labeled with the time and location, and his signature. "You'll find this interesting," he said, handing it to her.

Working carefully, and wearing latex gloves, she read it.

"This is the Fierce One's platform, all right, that the tribe should replace all non-Navajos on the tribe's payroll. But this next demand of theirs is crazy. We can't give any group a list of all non-Navajos working on the Rez, let alone arrange to have it appear in our newspaper along with their job titles. That sounds like they're going to target these people." Ella shook her head, then continued. "Our job is to serve and protect, not bird-dog Anglos taking tribal money."

"Did you notice that the insignia of the Fierce Ones doesn't appear on the note, nor do they identify themselves clearly," Neskahi pointed out. "Their demands are also extremely unreasonable. They want the tribe to replace every single non-Navajo worker, or pair the person up with a Navajo to be trained for that job, no later than one month from now. And if the tribe doesn't comply—for whatever the reason—they'll kill their hostage, and take another one."

Ella finished reading it, then shook her head. "Something's not right about this. I realize these demands sound as if they're coming from the Fierce Ones, but this isn't their usual style." She lapsed into a troubled silence. Many would think that she was trying to protect her brother if she didn't come down on the Fierce Ones now, but she was sure that there was more going on than met the eye. She couldn't shake the feeling that they were being led on a wild-goose chase. "The Fierce Ones would have never made such impossible demands on the tribe."

As Justine pulled out and headed down the road to Senator Yellowhair's home, Ella went up to Harry Ute. "I want you in on this investigation full time. I'm going to need more manpower in my unit."

"Done," he said, as he carefully continued to study the area for anything—hair, clothing fiber, or footprints that might have been left during the incident. "What would you like me to focus on?"

"Dig as hard as you can and compile a list of Yellowhair's enemies, political and otherwise. Go beneath the surface and get all the details you can."

"I'll take care of it."

Seeing Blalock's sedan pulling up, Ella went to meet him. She filled him in quickly as they walked over to the victim's car.

"It looks like you've got some built-in suspects already," he said after he'd read the ransom note. "But I've got to tell you, in this case, that's just going to mean major-league trouble. If this is the work of the Fierce Ones, that group has a lot of support and sympathy in this corner of the Rez, despite their violent tactics. Investigating individuals within that group is going to be next to impossible. They'll cover for each other."

"Are you saying that you think it's a hopeless cause?"

He shrugged. "The fact is, the bureau has never done well against individuals or groups that have wide-spread support in the community. We still have a few fugitives running around in the wilderness back East because local sympathizers make sure they get whatever supplies they need."

"I'm aware of that, but it's not the same situation here."

"Are you trying to tell me that the Fierce Ones don't have an enormous amount of clout?" Blalock gave her a skeptical look.

"No, I'm not saying that at all. I know better. What I'm saying is that there's a possibility they're being framed. These clues are pointing directly to them. Something about it stinks. None of these guys are stupid."

The federal agent considered what she said for a long time before speaking. "You may be too close to this case, Clah."

His words shouldn't have surprised her. Clifford's association with that group was going to haunt her on this. "I'm just looking at how things have been laid out and following my gut instincts. This has nothing to do with a conflict of interest."

"Okay. How do you want to handle things?"

"First, I'll make a stop by the tribal paper. I'll fill in Lulu—that's in exchange for a bit of cooperation the paper's given us. With luck, now that they've had a chance to think about it, they'll remember something extra about the caller."

"Are you considering complying with the kidnappers' demands and giving the paper that list of Anglos working on the reservation?"

"No way. We couldn't get every name anyway, there are too many legal roadblocks to overcome. But we've got to look as if we're willing to bargain, and we're going to need the paper's continued cooperation to do that convincingly."

"My advice is to make a big show out of considering their demands and trying to meet them. Have Chief Atcitty contact tribal leaders and get them to hold meetings on the issues. Then, in a week or so, have the paper report that they're working on the list the kidnappers wanted, but they have to find a way to avoid legal repercussions before printing it." He paused, then added, "The operative word is *stall*."

Ella led the way back to her vehicle. "You want to ride with me or the other way around? It doesn't really matter at the paper, but it may be a plus at the Yellowhairs' if we arrive together."

"Will your unit be safe here?"

"I can arrange for one of our people to drive the Jeep back to the station."

Blalock considered it for a moment, then nodded. "That's probably the best thing all the way around."

Ella handed the keys to Tache and asked him to drive her Jeep back, then they got underway. They rode in silence, Blalock staring at the passing desert, lost in his own thoughts.

"Are you still looking forward to retirement, Dwayne?"

"Oh, sure," Blalock smiled. "I've got four more years, but when you add up all the time I've already been with the bureau, it doesn't seem so long."

"Won't having all that time on your hands drive you crazy?"

"Funny you should say that. I've been giving that a lot of thought lately myself. Originally, I'd thought of retirement as something that would open new doors for me. I'd intended on starting a new career, maybe private investigation or security consulting. A lot of ex-agents do that."

"Do I hear a 'but' in there someplace?"

"Well, it's dawned on me recently that I'll be in my mid-fifties, and I probably won't want to start a new career at that stage in my life. Opening my own business would take a lot of hard work, and risk my savings."

"You could work for an existing firm." Ella suggested.

"Yeah, but I'm used to working on my own out here. As a resident agent I have a certain amount of autonomy. I haven't punched the clock in a long time."

"I hear you," Ella said. "So, what you're really wondering is if you should stay in, even after you reach the magic number."

"Yeah," he nodded at last. "Pretty stupid, huh? I spent the last ten years looking forward to retirement, and now I don't think I want it nearly as badly as I used to."

"That's the way life is. Just when you think you have everything figured out, something new comes along to change your outlook."

"Leaving the bureau worked out really well for you, didn't it? You ended up with a good job close to your home, where you can call most of your own shots."

"I knew I was needed here, even if no one else was aware of it at the time," she added with a tiny smile. "But I didn't have as many years in the bureau as you do, either. The change was easier for me on a number of counts."

Once again silence stretched out between them. Ella's gaze drifted to the towering line of weathered peaks that stretched out in the western horizon, making it look as if they were moving into a wall of stone. The wind had risen now, and the whistling of the air rushing past the car rose to a crescendo, then settled quickly to a dull hum, only to rise again.

As they pulled in to the office of the tribal paper, clustered among other tribal offices in the red-orange sandstone hills around Window Rock, she felt Blalock tense up.

"What's up? You allergic to the press all of a sudden?" She teased.

"Something like that. For what it's worth, Ella, I wouldn't trust any of them to keep a story under wraps for long, especially if they think a rival reporter is about to scoop them."

"I've learned the hard way, when my mother was hit by the drunk driver, who to trust at this newspaper. I'll talk to the editor-in-chief. She and I go back quite a ways. She won't endanger anyone by printing a list like that but, you're right, news is news, and I can't expect them to sit on the rest of it forever. The way I figure it, I've got one bargaining chip. I can offer them a chance to get the full story first, after the case is wrapped up, and selected bits and pieces in the interim in exchange for their continued cooperation. I think they'll go for it."

As Blalock and Ella walked inside the newspaper office, she could feel the tension in the room. People stopped working for a second as they noticed two law enforcement officers had just entered. They knew a story was brewing and the excitement was akin to that at the police station before a big bust.

Lulu hurried out from her office at the back to meet Ella. "I've been waiting for you. You promised to let me know what was in the note." Lulu nodded in greeting to Blalock, who simply nodded back.

"Can you get Jaime? We need to have a meeting," Ella said.

Lulu hesitated a second, obviously not wanting to take second place, but then agreed and led Ella and Agent Blalock into her editor-in-chief's office. After making sure everyone had chairs, the reporter deferred to Jaime's position.

Jaime was Ella's age, but at least twenty pounds heavier and a foot shorter. She was dressed in what some jokingly referred to as Reservation Chic—a checkered flannel shirt and jeans. Her expression was guarded as she acknowledged Blalock with a nod and then focused her attention on Ella. "I understand you made a deal with Lulu. She gave you information and now it's your turn to reciprocate."

"And that's why I'm here," Ella said, giving them the details of the letter. "You can print everything except for an actual list, which you probably know we can't provide anyway. Are we in agreement on that?"

Jaime toyed with the silver and turquoise ring she wore on her right hand. "When we don't publish a list, how will that affect the welfare of Senator Yellowhair?"

"What you have to ask yourself, is how it will affect the lives of the people whose names you did print," Blalock said. "Also, what about the jobs of those here at the newspaper if the Anglos listed decided to file suit against the tribe?"

Jaime mulled it over. "You realize that they're bound to know some of the names already, like the new preacher at the Christian church, and the university students who are interning at the hospital. They're all pretty much high profile."

"True, but there are many, many others in New Mexico and Arizona. Look at it this way, Jaime. History has shown us what can happen when we start making lists based on race or religion. So work with us, and buy us some time."

After a long, silent pause, Jaime nodded. "All right. The paper has a responsibility, too. We can't ignore that. But I want you to honor your bargain with us." Her gaze shifted to Blalock. "And it'll be binding on you, too. Are we in agreement?"

"Totally," Blalock replied, then turned to Lulu. "By the way, did you recall anything about your caller that may help us out? Have there been any more calls or contacts?"

Lulu shook her head. "Just what you already know."

"Do you have any clues or suspects other than the obvious?" Jaime added.

"Not really, it's just too soon. But we've got an interagency team working on the case. We'll turn up something soon. It's a top-priority case." Ella said.

By the time Ella and Blalock left the newspaper office, the FBI agent was visibly restless. "You know, I'm starting to get a bad feeling about this case," he said. "The more I think about that note, the more convinced I get that we *are* being jerked around. A first grader could figure out who the kidnappers are supposed to be just on the basis of that note and current events. So, that means that there's got to be a reason why the Fierce Ones aren't taking credit for it openly. If they know people will assume it's them, why not go the rest of the way and admit it? And if they weren't prepared to do that, why pursue an action like this that'll point directly to them? They've *got* to know that because of the circumstantial evidence, we're going to be all over them, whether they take credit for the kidnapping or not. It doesn't really add up right."

"I agree," Ella said.

Blalock continued. "Is there anything else going on that could tie into this kidnapping? I read about the protest at the tribal offices and know that Yellowhair got the Fierce Ones ticked off when he crossed their picket line, though apparently he did have a family emergency. By any chance did he make any other enemies that day?"

"Not that I know of, so I guess that leads us back to the Fierce Ones again. I'll be talking to my brother soon, and maybe he can give us a lead we can follow up on."

"Would he tell you if he knew his own group was responsible for this?"

"Probably not directly, but Clifford isn't a good liar, at least around me or my mother. Both of us can tell when he's holding back."

As they headed east toward Highway 666, which would, in turn, lead to the senator's home, she remembered the last few times she'd visited the Yellowhair family. It had been after his daughter's death in an auto accident, and the situation had been tense and grief filled. Now she'd have to face Abigail Yellowhair with more bad news. She would have given anything to avoid this, but she had a job to do.

They'd been traveling for forty minutes when Blalock broke the silence. "Why is everything so far from everything else out here?" he muttered. "It gives a person too much time to mull things over."

"That's a bad thing?"

"Not for law enforcement, but it is when you think of the criminals. Too much time for them to plan, you know?"

Passing the kidnapping site again, they headed down the long, gravel road that would eventually take them to Yellowhair's home. As they left the highway behind them, Ella felt that peculiar tingling feeling that always warned her when something wasn't right. She tried to pinpoint what was wrong, searching around her from left to right, and in the side mirror.

Picking up her nonverbal cues, Blalock loosened his seat belt, and threw back his jacket, insuring he had easy access to his pistol. "Should I speed up or slow down. You're on to something, I can tell. What did you see?"

"Nothing, but something's not right. Can't you feel it?"

"My gut instincts have been out of sync from the first day I came to the Rez." He looked around on his side of the car, alert for trouble.

Ella spotted the remains of a dead sheep near the side of the road. "There should have been a predator or two near that—or birds, if nothing else. But the carcass is just sitting there for the flies and bugs."

"Maybe another car passed by recently and spooked them."

"The road's pretty straight. I don't see anything in either direction, do you?"

"No," he answered his voice taut.

Ella could see dwellings ahead, and several cars parked beside them. Nothing seemed out of the ordinary. The senator's house was off by itself in the distance, on a parcel of land the tribe had provided for his use. When he'd become a state senator he'd hired his brother-in-law to renovate his old house, and now it was an impressively large stucco building with a red tile, pitched roof. It was a display of wealth that always left a bad taste in Ella's mouth.

Ella considered the possibility that her anxiety was just a reflection of her dislike for Yellowhair. He'd always been bad news as far as she was concerned. But it was more than that, and she knew it. The badger fetish she wore at her neck for protection felt warm against her skin. The logical explanation was that it probably was no warmer than usual, but since she was always more aware of it in times of trouble, it seemed that way. Yet, no matter how she rationalized it, the fact remained that the fetish had always been an accurate warning sign. To discount it now would be foolish.

They were less than a mile from the senator's house when she saw movement and a flicker of light from atop a rock on the mesa to her right. "Sniper, two o'clock!" Ella yelled.

Blalock pulled hard on the wheel just as a bullet cut across the sedan, followed an instant later by another. Ella heard one impact on metal, and another shatter the windshield and rear window almost simultaneously. As the brakes grabbed, the car spun around sideways in the road and came to a stop in a cloud of dust, facing in the direction of the sniper.

Ella dove out the passenger's door, hearing Blalock do the same on his side. Suddenly another round passed by her so close that she felt a tug of cloth and the sensation of heat against her skin.

For a moment she thought she'd been shot, but as she hit the ground and rolled into the drainage ditch, she was aware that she wasn't in any pain.

Pistol out, she took a defensive position behind a low ridge of road grader-formed sand. She heard Blalock, now behind the car, making a call for backup on his handheld. As she looked down at her arm, a tremor that started at the base of her spine ran through her. She could see a small hole where a bullet had pierced her jacket and passed through between her arm and her side.

"You hit, Ella?" Blalock said. "Say something, for God's sake!"

"No, but he almost got lucky." She'd had close calls before, but it was different now that she was carrying a child, and she was almost sick to her stomach. She was going to start wearing a vest full time now, no matter how inconsequential or routine her day's work seemed to be at a glance.

Blalock fired off two shots toward the rocks where the sniper had been hiding, but there was no evidence anyone was there now. Silence descended around them. "I would have had to be lucky as hell to hit that guy. He's too far away for anything except a rifle and scope."

"Just in case he's still around, stay out of sight and don't give him another shot. Its possible he may have only changed position. We'll have backup soon, and then we can make our move. Justine is at Yellowhair's, and should be here any minute now."

As she finished her sentence, they heard a siren, and saw a vehicle heading their way from the Yellowhair home.

"Cover me." Ella zig-zagged back to Blalock's sedan and dove inside. Reaching for the radio mike, she instructed Justine to go straight up the mesa, then yelled for Blalock. "Jump in, Dwayne. We'll cover her."

Blalock got back inside the sedan, which was still running, slammed down hard on the accelerator and sped uphill. "The sniper may have missed, but he did deliver his message," he said, glancing over at the hole in her shirt.

"Yeah, but what exactly was his message?" Ella asked. "Was it a warning not to question Yellowhair's family, or a warning against looking into the case at all?"

"You're overanalyzing, Clah. I would have said it was his way of letting us know he wanted us dead."

She smiled. To the point—that was Blalock's style. "The one thing I'm sure about is that there's a connection between the kidnapper and the sniper. Otherwise he wouldn't have known we'd show up here."

Before long, several patrol units were involved, and a countywide manhunt was underway. Roadblocks were established, and the entire force was put on alert.

Ella and Blalock managed to locate the place where the sniper had been from the obvious impressions in the sand where he'd laid, prone. But clues were scarce, except for some distorted footprints.

"He did a really good job picking up after himself," Ella said, looking around for spent brass cartridges and finding none. "Unless we can recover at least one bullet, we won't even be able to identify the caliber of the weapon he used."

"There are vehicle tracks here," Justine said, pointing them out to Ella. "They lead down to that farm road, and then probably to the highway. From the size of the tread pattern, it's a pickup or SUV, and the tires are pretty new. I'll have a make and model, with luck, in a few hours," Justine said. "Can I use your reference material?" She looked over at Blalock.

"I'll fax my tread patterns to the station ASAP," FB-Eyes agreed.

"There's one clear boot-print here among the rest," Ute said, as he crouched by a soft sandy area near the gravel-filled ground at the top of the mesa.

"Size ten," Blalock said, studying it. "Pretty common around here."

"But we can probably get a brand name. Those ridges on the heel look distinctive," Ella said, crouching by it. "Every little piece helps."

"Are you trying to bolster your own spirits, or mine?" Blalock shot back.

Ella resisted the urge to kick dirt onto his expensive wing tips. FB-Eyes had mellowed, but he could still be one colossal pain in the neck when he chose.

"He may not have left us much to work with, but we'll get him," Justine said. "Maybe one of the roadblocks will get lucky. He probably didn't throw away that rifle, and it's hard to hide one in a vehicle."

"I don't want to rely on luck. I need you to scour this entire area. Find something else we can use," Ella growled.

"If it's here to find, we'll find it," Justine said. "But this was done by someone who knew what he was doing."

"You know we'll do our best," Ute added.

"You guys always do," Ella said more gently, realizing she was starting to push the others a little too hard. She had confidence in those working with her, but things had taken more of an edge for her now. She was locked in a battle with an unseen enemy and it was a battle she had to win—for her sake and that her of her child's.

TEN

——— ✖ ✖ ✖ ———

Ella led the way back to Blalock's car, determined not to let anyone sense her frustration. "Let's see what kind of damage your sedan took."

"Hopefully it won't have to go into the shop for more than a day. The bureau can take forever to supply me with a loaner."

Blalock approached the sedan, concern in his eyes. He crouched by the passenger side and studied the bullet hole, which had penetrated behind Ella's door and out the driver's side. "This one must have hit us just before we swerved to the right. The other went through the front and back windshields. The third, you know about personally."

"We have to find a way to get Abigail Yellowhair to talk candidly to us," Ella said.

"Will that be a problem?" Blalock's eyebrows rose.

"My problem has always been with the senator, not his wife, so let's see how things go. Justine, I'm sure, already picked up some useful information for us, though it was probably all hearsay or off the record."

"If you trusted Officer Goodluck to go question the family, why are we going up there, too?" Blalock asked.

"The reason Justine can get information for us so successfully is because the Yellowhairs see her as a friend more than a police officer. If I don't interview Mrs. Yellowhair, they'll start to distrust Justine and I'll lose the advantage she gives us by soliciting unguarded comments."

They arrived at the stucco, Spanish-style house a few minutes later. Ella signalled for Blalock to wait with her in the car.

"Don't tell me that someone living in a pretentious place like this one is trying to pass themselves off as a traditionalist," Blalock scoffed. "I thought any display of riches was frowned upon."

"Yeah, I thought the house was a bit much myself the first time I saw it, but the tribe supported him when he said he needed it to be this way. He argued that he would have to entertain many influential state politicians here, and his home had to be the kind an outsider would automatically respect."

"So, if he's really just a pragmatist who tries to fit into every crowd, why are we waiting?"

"Courtesy. It can sometimes gain trust. I've always thought that Abigail leaned toward the traditionalists, despite her husband's work."

A moment later a tall, slender Navajo woman came to the door and waved at them to approach. She was dressed in a long, dark blue skirt and a simple tunic blouse woven loosely in gentle yellows for summer. It was fastened at the waist with a concha belt. It was a relaxed style, but it gave her an air of elegance and an undeniable sense of presence.

Ella met her by the door, and then followed her inside, Blalock a few steps behind them.

"I've been expecting you to come by," Mrs. Yellowhair said to Ella, then included Blalock in that statement with a glance.

"I'm sorry that every time I come it has to be under such difficult circumstances," Ella said, remembering the last time.

Abigail nodded, her face serene. "When do you think the kidnappers will free my husband?"

"I don't know," Ella answered, determined to be as honest with her as possible. Abigail deserved that much from her.

"You want to know who I think might have done this to him, I suppose?"

Ella nodded. "I need to know everything you can tell me about the people who consider the senator an enemy, and might be out to hurt him and you."

"My husband makes enemies with the same ease that some people make friends," Abigail said. "He's a difficult man for people to understand. He can be completely charming when the situation calls for it, but he can also be a hard-liner when he feels things should be done in a certain way."

"Has anyone made any threats against him, or the family within the past few weeks or months?" Ella asked.

"There's Avery Blueeyes, the tribal councilman. He opposes every bill and every measure that my husband supports. Another man, Atsidi Benally, who teaches our language to the college students, also resents our family because he sees my husband as too Anglo in his thinking, and the wrong leader for our people."

Ella had heard of both men. Avery Blueeyes was a politician through and through, and served on many tribal committees. What he wanted was Yellowhair's job representing their district in the state legislature.

Atsidi was an old man with a lot of connections, and a strong following in the Four Corners region. He was so conservative and traditional, he made Clifford look like a left-wing liberal. Atsidi wasn't a member of the Fierce Ones because he claimed that they fought like the whites—hiding their identities and trying to manipulate the laws the whites had instituted on their land. Now that the Fierce Ones were no longer hiding their identities and had modified some of their tactics, maybe he'd become more sympathetic to them. He might have even suggested the kidnapping to them. Or maybe he was acting with yet another group that was still unidentified.

"But the worst one of all is that half Navajo who lives off the Rez."

It took Ella a moment to register who Abigail was referring to. "You mean the Navajo talk show host?" Ella paused, trying to think of his name. "Something Branch?" she said at last.

"George Branch. A political conservative who's just to the right of Attila the Hun," Blalock commented. "He's about as obnoxious as they come. But that seems to be a trend these days for these talk show jocks. Creating issues to build ratings is their stock and trade."

Abigail nodded. "All that is true but, with Branch, there seems to be pure hatred behind his show business animosity toward my husband. He almost cost my husband the last election because of the comments he continually made on his radio show. Branch made a lot of thinly veiled accusations and repeated irresponsible gossip that branded my husband as corrupt. My husband was livid."

"Wasn't there some ruckus about the senator demanding equal airtime, even though the law doesn't require it?" Blalock asked.

Abigail sighed, then nodded. "My husband wanted a chance to rebut the statements made against him, but Branch said my husband should get his own show if he had something to say. Tempers flared, and it ended up in a shoving match at the station between him and Branch. After that, Branch intensified his attacks on my husband. He capitalized on that incident to make my husband look even worse."

Ella noted that Abigail hadn't used her husband's name, but hadn't hesitated to use anyone else's. The small discrepancy said a lot about her. Names were said to have power, and knowing an enemy's name and using it weakened that person and made him vulnerable. Abigail was loyal to her husband, even in something like this.

"Do you realize that Mr. Branch even got a restraining order to make my husband look dangerous and unstable? What was worse, he ranted on about the incident every day until the election."

"I remember," Blalock said. "I listen to Branch once in a while to keep tabs on him. People in his position can sway a lot of opinions and trouble usually follows them."

"And those are the people you think would pose a danger to your husband?" Ella asked.

"They're the only ones who come to mind right now."

Ella reached into her jacket pocket and brought out a card. "You can reach me at that number day or night. If you remember anything you feel might be important, or if you need to talk, don't hesitate to call me. We'll also have an officer here with you at all times, of course."

"Thank you." Abigail met her eyes. "My husband never could understand you, but I always have. I know how difficult it is to be in a family that doesn't share your views. It sets you apart and, though you'd give anything for it to be different, it's not something you can change."

Ella understood then that although Abigail longed for a simpler life, it was one she knew she'd never have. "It *is*, hard, but everyone has the right to be themselves," she said. For a moment Ella felt a kinship with Abigail. If not being able to follow her heart was the price of being a politician's wife, she was glad she'd refused to be part of that world.

After consulting with the Navajo cop assigned to monitor the telephone and protect Mrs. Yellowhair, Ella walked with Blalock to his sedan. "She hasn't had an easy life. I never realized that until now."

Blalock nodded. "It takes more than a fancy house to make a home."

When they returned to the ambush site, they found Justine standing by her vehicle, clipboard in hand.

Ella and Blalock approached her. "Any progress?" Ella asked.

"We've been looking for the missing rounds but, so far, we haven't had any luck. I was hoping that if I followed the trajectory, I'd get lucky, but no such luck."

"Where's Harry?"

"He's still walking around out there with a metal detector. He refuses to give up. If the bullet didn't ricochet, it had to impact on or beside the road, and he wants to find it."

"Good for him. We need a lead, and we need it badly," Ella said. "And please tell him to contact Lulu Todea at the newspa-

per. She's supposed to be making us a list of Yellowhair's enemies. He can add those names to the ones he's compiled already."

"Okay, I'll do that. And I'll be out here for a while longer,
unless you need me," Justine said.

Ella shook her head. "We're going to pay George Branch a
visit."

Recognition flashed over her features. "Ugh. I can't stand that
blowhard. I don't know how he manages to stay on the air."

"He feeds on people's fears and prejudices, telling them what
they want to hear," Blalock said. "If his listeners would look past
all his simplistic answers, they'd see that he really offers no solutions to anything—just more confusion."

"Good luck with him," Justine said.

As they got underway, Blalock glanced over at Ella. "Think
Branch could be our sniper?"

"I don't know, but I'll be sounding him out carefully, that's for
sure. I really don't like being used for target practice."

Blalock studied her expression for a moment, then looked
back at the road. "There's something you're not telling me.
What's bugging you?"

"As a Navajo and as a cop, I've been taught to look for the pattern and identify what's not part of it, or out of place. A kidnapping, and then a sniper incident here on the reservation so close
together doesn't add up and make a picture I can understand.
And, coupled with everything else that's happening . . ."

"I know you're trying to tie everything together, but maybe
what we're dealing with is a series of unrelated events."

"I think you're wrong. They're connected. I just don't know
how yet."

"Look at it logically. We can't link the clinic robbery to the Yellowhair kidnapping. There's no common thread. And, although I
admit that the attempt to kill you appears, on the surface, to share
a link to the abduction, there's no way to be sure. You've made a
lot of enemies in your time. You're going to drive yourself crazy if
you keep trying to group everything into a tight little package."

Blalock ran a hand through his hair. "Let's focus on one thing at a time. Branch is half Navajo, and that has given him some credibility when he talks about tribal matters, but he's still a troublemaker. In my opinion, he'd fit in real nicely with the Fierce Ones."

"I don't know. I think the Fierce Ones wouldn't want a wild card like Branch in their group. Sooner or later, they'd try to muzzle him and all hell would break loose."

By the time they reached the radio station outside the Rez, it was early evening. Ella walked inside the building, stopped by the candy machine, and bought two chocolate bars.

"Since when did you become a junk food junkie?" Blalock asked.

"What can I tell you? I'm into chocolate."

Twenty minutes later she'd finished the candy bars and they were still waiting for Branch to see them. Her patience wearing thin, Ella waited by the corridor, pacing.

Finally, Branch came out. He stood close to six feet tall and was built like a fifty-five gallon drum. He swung from side to side as he walked, and she couldn't tell if that was his version of a macho swagger, or whether it was an attempt to accommodate his enormous bulk. His size alone made her doubt that he would have been able to move fast enough to shoot at her and Blalock, then get away before they reached him.

"I hear you folks need to talk to me," he said, his rich baritone voice reverberating in the small reception area.

"We'd like to speak to you in private," Ella clipped.

"Let's go to my office then," he said, then led the way around the corridor until they reached a large, cluttered office.

He waved in the direction of the two chairs by the desk. "You'll have to forgive the chaos in here, but I like it this way. I can't stand an orderly place that looks as if no one works there." He gave her a long, hard look as he seated himself behind the desk. "Aren't you a little bit out of your jurisdiction?"

"That's why Agent Blalock is here. There's no place around here that's not in his jurisdiction."

"So, you're working a case together? What's going on?"

Blalock cleared his throat. "State Senator James Yellowhair has been kidnapped."

Branch muttered an oath and grabbed the phone. Ella reached out and covered the keypad with her hand so he couldn't enter a number. "You're not working for the news channel, you run a talk show. There's no need for you to spread the story just yet."

Branch let go of the receiver and regarded her mockingly. "Whatever you say—and for someone who's out of her jurisdiction, Officer Ella, you do and say quite a bit, don't you?"

"Okay, let's cut the crap," Blalock snapped. "You and the senator weren't exactly pals. Where were you earlier today, probably before dawn?"

Branch's eyes widened. "I have no intention of answering that question. You can't pin this on me, though I'm sure wherever Yellowhair is, he would absolutely love that."

"You don't deny that there's a lot of bad blood between you and the senator, do you?" Ella asked.

"Of course not. But he and I need each other. There's no such thing as bad publicity, you know. I keep his name out in front of people, and that's exactly what he wants."

"You almost cost him the election," Ella said.

"Are you kidding? I handed it to him. Without me, he would have lost. He's made plenty of enemies on his own, without any help from me."

"So, you're saying that you two have been engaged in a self-serving mock combat for the purposes of gaining publicity?" Blalock pressed. "Was this all prearranged and mapped out, like pro wrestling?"

"Absolutely not!" He leaned forward, resting his elbows on the desk. "Listen here, Agent Blalock, allegations like that can really create problems for me. Be careful what you say, particularly in public, or I'll sue you for libel so fast you won't know what hit you."

"Save it," Blalock snapped. "Theatrics don't impress me. You're a public figure, so as long as you have a radio show, you and the contents of your programs are fair game. So, let's get down to it. What was the deal between you and Yellowhair?"

"There was no deal. We hate each other's guts, but our inter-action gave my ratings an enormous boost, and gained him instant name recognition, so we both came out ahead. I still think he's corrupt, mind you, but I just don't actually come out and say that on the air."

"But you do insinuate it," Ella countered.

He smiled. "Sure, but I'm careful how I word things. Trust me, if Yellowhair had anything on me, he would have taken me to court months ago." Branch paused, then glanced at Blalock. "But the bottom line is that he's been kidnapped, and you want to get him back. Okay, that, I get. But what part do you want me to play in this?"

"You know Yellowhair, and have done extensive research on him, I'd be willing to bet. Tell me, who hates him enough to kid-nap him?" Blalock asked.

"If, instead of that, you'd asked me who hated him enough to want him dead, I could have given you several names. But this is trickier. If you kidnap a guy like him, you tend to make him more sympathetic to people, not less."

"Okay, so who would have wanted him dead?" Ella said.

"Avery Blueeyes for one."

"Because he opposed the bills Yellowhair sponsors?" Blalock asked.

Branch gave them an incredulous look. "Oh, please!" He then glanced at Ella, and with a surprised look, added, "You two really don't know, do you?"

Ella didn't move. She hated this man's superior attitude, and it was taking all her willpower not to reach out and wipe the smug look off his face. If only mild pistol-whipping were legal in New Mexico. "Enlighten us."

"Avery owned hundreds of acres of land adjacent to the Rez outside Farmington. He spent close to a year trying to get one of the high-tech computer companies to set up shop there. He very nearly succeeded, too, but then Yellowhair sponsored a bill in the state legislature that offered tax breaks to Anglo companies on the Rez. When Avery opposed the bill, Yellowhair accused him of a conflict of interest and made him look really bad. In capsule form, Avery had to back off and let his deal fall through. He lost a bundle of money on that, too, but if he'd closed the deal, he would have lost the faith of those he worked with on the tribal council and, eventually, The People themselves. After that fiasco, Avery hated Yellowhair with a passion."

"So, he's the person you think is behind the kidnapping?" Ella asked.

"You're putting words in my mouth, little lady."

Ella gripped the sides of the chair so tight her knuckles turned pearly white, but she forced herself not to move.

"What I *said* is that Avery would have cheerfully killed him. But kidnapping? No. That just doesn't sound like that old boy. He'd be more inclined to shoot Yellowhair in cold blood. Like me, he collects guns," he said, a challenge in his voice. "But don't get excited. We both have federal firearms permits and follow all the current regulations. We both believe in the right of every free man to own and bear weapons in defense of himself and his possessions."

Blalock rolled his eyes. "Please. Let's not get into the issue of gun control. We don't have time for one of your rants."

"Rant?" He shook his head. "It's the truth. The feds are being controlled by the liberals who want to take guns away from our law-abiding citizens. The constitution has become a joke. It's time to stand up for ourselves."

"Let's go," Ella said, not even looking at Branch.

By the time they left the station a short time later, Ella had lapsed into a tense silence.

"Hey, Clah, chill out. He was just being annoying. It's what he does best."

"Yeah, I know," she muttered. Ella took a deep breath, then let it out again. "We're going to have to find out where Branch was at the time of the kidnapping."

"I'll handle that while you take on Avery Blueeyes. He's on your turf, and from what I've heard, is a tough customer."

Ella nodded. "He is, particularly to non-Indians. But I've got to tell you, I can't see him in the role of a kidnapper."

"How well do you know him?"

"His wife is a good friend of my mother's and they used to come over a lot when I was still in high school. But that was years ago before he got elected to the tribal council."

As they got underway in Blalock's bureau sedan, Ella glanced back at the radio station. "Did you get the feeling that Branch was going to do his best to turn the kidnapping into another promotional opportunity for his radio show?"

"Oh, yeah. There's no way he's passing that one up. But who knows, if he stirs the water enough, something may come to the surface."

Blalock drove Ella back to the station and dropped her off. As she walked toward the entrance, Justine came out of the station to meet her.

"I've gone over every inch of the van that ran you and Kevin off the road. As you know, most of the interior was sprayed with oil, so that made lifting prints almost impossible. But under the seats we found cola cans and snack food wrappers, along with a student notebook. We lifted a few prints, but none of them match those on file in our police databases."

"Let me take a look at what you've got," Ella said.

She followed Justine to the lab. The PD had expanded Justine's facility by knocking out a wall and giving her more room for equipment, and responsibilities, as she'd proven herself. "You know, I remember when you first came to me," Ella said. "Your credentials both as a cop and a fully qualified lab tech sounded impressive, but no one really knew how things would work out." She waved her arm around the lab. "The fact that the tribe has expanded your facilities here really shows you how much you're valued."

"I keep working at it. You know how many times I've been back to Quantico to the FBI Academy for additional forensics courses. The lab work associated with police work keeps getting more complicated and technical, but also more accurate."

Putting on latex gloves, and handing Ella a pair, Justine set out the various items she'd taken from the van.

Ella studied them, then focused on the doodling on the cover of the notebook. "There can't be that many students interested in entering the Air Force Academy, and that's where that logo's from. See the labeled ribbon around the bottom of the shield, and the eagle on top? I remember it from high school when the science club took a trip there and to the zoo at Colorado Springs. Have you heard of any high school seniors trying to get into the academy?"

Harry Ute came in just then. "The Air Force Academy? My nephew was talking about that place the other day. Ernest Ben's boy, Charlie has applied. He needs a letter of recommendation from a congressman or U.S. senator, and Ernest and James Yellowhair had a huge disagreement over that. Yellowhair's only a state senator, but he could have helped by using his political contacts to help Charlie. The problem was he refused to do it. Yellowhair told Ben that he didn't appreciate his opposition to some of the land issues he'd brought up at the state level, and saw no reason to help Ben or his son now."

"Yellowhair seems to be more popular every time we turn around, doesn't he?" Ella mumbled.

"Don't underestimate James Yellowhair," Harry warned. "He has political enemies because he's known for playing hardball. But he's also very good at reaching out to the everyday voter. He presents himself as the underdog, and people come flocking to him."

"Well, considering he barely made it in the last election, I wouldn't say 'flocking,'" Ella said.

"That was a close call but, as usual, he took his lumps and still managed to land on his feet. If he comes out of this kidnapping alive and healthy, he's a shoo-in at the next election. You'll see."

She didn't like the approval she heard in Harry's voice, but decided to keep quiet about it. Ute's politics were his own business. "We'll need to talk to Charlie, and maybe his father, too, depending on what we get from the boy."

"You'll get less static from the kid," Harry said. "Ernest is really protective of his son. Charlie's a bit on the spoiled side, but he's a good kid, and pretty smart."

"Why don't you come with me, Harry, and we'll track him down?" Ella suggested.

"That'll work. Charlie knows me, and won't hold anything back."

Ella placed the notebook back in the clear, tagged evidence pouch, then signed it out in her name. "I'll take this with me, but I'll keep it inside the pouch so it's not compromised," she told Justine. "In the meantime, see if you can track down and question Avery Blueeyes and Atsidi Benally for me. Then, I want you to concentrate on the clinic B and E. We need some definitive answers."

"I've talked to just about everyone about that break-in, but I'm still batting zero."

"Keep at it. We don't have any other choice."

Ella drove across Shiprock to the high school on the southwest side of town. The old high school, where Ella had graduated, was on the north side of the river. The new facility, built near the site of the old helium plant, was bigger and better, and maintained in tip-top condition, if Ella remembered from her last visit there when they'd had all the gang problems.

Harry was quiet, not even gazing out the windows as they crossed the river, but being glum was so much a part of his personality that it was something she expected.

He cleared his throat.

The unexpected sound coming from Harry startled her, and she flinched. "Something on your mind?"

He nodded. "I wanted you to be the first to know, Ella. I'm thinking of quitting the force."

Ella stared at him for a second, then focused back on the road. Nothing could have surprised her more. Harry was almost an institution in the Navajo Tribal Police. His skill at collecting evidence was second to none, and badly needed.

"Why, Harry? This is as much a part of your life as it is mine."

He said nothing for several long seconds, then when he spoke, his voice was even lower than usual. "It's not an easy decision, because the Rez has been my home since I was a kid. Almost everyone I know lives here. But it's time for me to leave. I've been offered a chance to join the U.S. Marshals service and that's a job I think I'd really be good at. I'm a good tracker and I'm low profile. People don't notice me in a crowded room, you know. I blend."

"Congratulations, then. It's an opportunity few officers ever receive. I think you'd be a great addition to their team, but you're needed here, Harry. You're the best at what you do. I wouldn't know how to replace you."

"If the department absolutely can't replace me, I won't leave, but I think they can. Someone else will come along. You'll see. That's the way things always are."

"We'll try, Harry. It's just hard losing one of our best cops."

Harry's possible resignation had come as a shock to Ella. Sooner or later she'd planned on taking maternity leave, but if Harry was also gone and there was trouble . . . The department was shorthanded anyway when it came to good, experienced officers.

They drove into the asphalt parking lot on the north side of the high school campus a short time later. Ella noticed that the kids walking through the lot toward the athletic fields seemed totally relaxed. Laughter flowed easily from a group seated on the outside steps eating bags of chips and drinking sodas.

"They're not immune to trouble. It touches them here, too," Harry said, as if reading her mind, "but what kids have that the adults don't, is a deep-seated conviction that nothing can really harm them."

They entered the main lobby and walked down the hall toward the principal's office. Moments later, they were ushered inside by one of the school secretaries. Ella introduced herself to the new principal, Wallace Curtis. The teacher turned school administrator was well respected in the community.

"What brings the police here?" he asked, his expression guarded. "Has something happened to one of our kids?"

"We just need to talk to Charlie Ben. Can you find him for us?"

He gave them a surprised look. "What could he have done? Charlie's one of our top students. I have a problem thinking of him as involved in anything that concerns the police."

"We just need to ask him a few questions," Ella said.

"I'll have to be present. He's a minor, and as a representative of the school, I have to witness your interviews."

"That's not a problem," Ella said and Harry nodded his assent.

Principal Curtis checked student schedules on his computer, then left. Ella walked to the window and stared outside at the mesa rising above the river valley to the north. "Why don't you handle the questioning, Harry? Charlie may be more at ease if you do it, and we may get answers."

"I don't think he'll have any to give us. He's a straight shooter," Harry said. "But I'll do it. Let's see what we get."

Several minutes later Principal Curtis entered with a tall, broad-shouldered Navajo boy who moved like a bundle of compressed energy. His hair was combed but looked damp, as if he'd just stepped out of the shower.

Charlie sat down and regarded them nervously. "What's going on? I haven't done anything wrong," he said before Harry could even say a word.

Harry smiled at him. "Nothing to worry about, Charlie. I'm Artie's uncle. Remember me?"

"Yeah. But why are you here?"

"We found one of your spiral notebooks inside a van that was used to commit a crime," Harry said. "What we want to know is how it got there."

Ella placed it on the principal's desk in front of Charlie and watched as surprise, then confusion crossed his features.

"Wait. How did you get that? I threw it away yesterday or the day before. That's one of my *old* notebooks. Check it out if you don't believe me," he said, pulling a new looking spiral out of his book bag. "I use these to keep track of homework assignments and football schedules for teams in our district. Look through that one and you'll see that all the pages are full."

Ella sensed the kid was being completely honest with them. He could see his hopes of getting into the Air Force Academy going up in smoke if he got into any trouble, and having the cops looking into his life was scaring the blazes out of him.

"I cleaned out my locker after school and dumped the old stuff in the trash can outside by the gym. Someone must have picked it out of there." He looked at it even closer. "That looks like nacho sauce or something on the cover. I keep my notebooks clean." He pulled several different color notebooks out of his bag. "See?"

"His word is good enough for me, Investigator Clah," Principal Curtis said. "I can't say this about all of our kids, but you can believe whatever Charlie tells you."

"Don't worry, Charlie. We believe you," Ella said. "You just confirmed what we already thought. Somebody put that in there to mislead us. Tell me, have you seen anyone, probably an adult who didn't seem to belong here, hanging around the trash, or the school?"

He thought about it, then shook his head. "I'll keep a lookout though, if you think that'll help you guys."

"It would." Ella handed him her card. "Give me or Harry a call anytime if you think of something. And let your principal or teachers know if you see any strangers hanging around campus."

As her cell phone rang, she stepped away to one corner of the room, leaving Harry to wrap things up with Charlie and the principal.

"Clah here," she said, expecting the call to be from Sheriff Taylor. She suddenly remembered his earlier message to call him after noon.

It was Big Ed, however. "Shorty, we got a problem with the Fierce Ones. Now they're picketing over at LabKote. The security guards have warned them and informed us that they have instructions to mace or shoot anyone who tries to enter illegally. Things could get ugly fast. You're already in the area, so get over there with Harry. You'll be in charge on the scene."

"Chief, that's really not—"

"You have your orders, Shorty. So far nothing but threats have been made, but the guards there seem mighty squirrelly, at least that's what our dispatcher reported. I'll send you backup, but the most I'll be able to spare will be two patrol officers in addition to Justine, Harry, and you. Evaluate the situation when you get there, and if you think things could escalate, call me. I'll call the county and Farmington PD if I have to. You copy?"

"I copy, Chief."

"One more thing. I heard from an officer on the scene that Clifford is there, too."

"He didn't use a mask?"

"None of them have, and that's why I don't think they mean to create a problem. It's the guards who are making me tense."

"Is there anything that identifies the protestors as members of the Fierce Ones, or could it be an independent action?"

"They have those black arm bands with the four sacred mountains in white, just like before."

"I'm on my way," she said, then gestured to Harry. Thanking the principal and Charlie Ben, she rushed back to the car with Harry.

"We're needed over at LabKote. The Fierce Ones are protesting there. So far there has been no violence, just threats, but from the sounds of it, the situation's like a powder keg—it won't take much to make it blow."

ELEVEN

—— ✖ ✖ ✖ ——

Ella filled Harry in on what she knew as they sped south toward LabKote, sirens and lights on.

"I expect that they've zeroed in on that company now because they heard about the death of Kyle Hansen and want to make sure a Navajo takes over that position," Harry said. "And that brings up another possibility we're going to have to deal with. Sooner or later someone will accuse the Fierce Ones of having murdered Hansen so he could be replaced with a Navajo."

"That's not really the MO of the Fierce ones," Ella said. "It's more along the lines of what the Anglo Brotherhood might have done, except in reverse. That group would have been perfectly capable of killing a Navajo to insure an Anglo would get a particular job. They gave us some serious problems in the past, but they've all but disappeared. We don't have anyone on the Rez now who would use those tactics."

"Tactics are subject to change depending on the situation, particularly with an unpredictable group like the Fierce Ones," Harry said.

By the time they reached LabKote, she'd used the radio network to brief the two patrolmen and Justine, who were already there, standing by.

As she got out of her Jeep, Ella spotted Clifford. Her brother gave her a nod, and continued walking in the picket line, which moved back and forth, blocking the gate. Everything seemed calm and orderly.

Then Ella glanced over at the three grim-faced guards standing inside Labkote's fence, and her short-lived optimism faded. They had left the outside guardhouse unmanned. All three were armed with riot guns, pistols, and Mace. She could also hear the hum that signalled that the electric fence was on.

For a company that only sold sterilized laboratory supplies and glassware, this seemed a bit much. Then again, she had no idea how much money it would cost to replace the equipment or decontaminate the clean areas if anything was compromised.

As she started toward the fence, intending to talk to the security guards, Clifford and Glen Lee came up to her. Ella had known Glen almost all her life. He had a small farm, livestock, and a large family. He wasn't what anyone could term a rabble-rouser.

"Join us on the line," Glen said. "As a cop, your support would mean a lot to the community."

"I can't do that, and you know it. I'm here as a cop, not a private citizen."

"There won't be any trouble today," Clifford said. "If someone tries to leave the plant, we'll step aside. We'll do the same with anyone who needs to go in. This won't play out the way it did at the tribal offices."

"I'm glad to hear that," Ella said, seeing the reporters from a Farmington TV station pulling up in a van. "Stay away from the fence, too. It's more than just a hot wire."

Glen nodded. "Talk about paranoid," he muttered. "These LabKote guards are packing a lot of firepower, don't you think?"

"They just look afraid to me," Clifford said. "I think they've seen too many old cowboy and Indians movies where the Indians attack the fort, you know?"

Glen laughed. "Maybe so."

"I'm going to go talk to them," Ella said.

"Jesse Woody has been trying to do that since we first arrived, but the guards won't let him in, and the supervisors won't come out," Glen said.

"The security guards are probably undertrained and nervous. Let me see if I can get them to relax a bit."

As Glen moved away, Ella took Clifford aside. "This isn't the place I would have chosen to talk to you, but I need to ask you something directly. Would the Fierce Ones get involved in a kidnapping?"

"You're talking about Senator Yellowhair?" Clifford asked. "I heard about that," he added, then shook his head. "No, that's not something our group would do."

The kidnapping wasn't general knowledge yet, but on the Rez news seldom needed to make the papers before everyone knew about it. "You really should give your involvement with this group some hard thought, Brother. You're in with a crowd that's known for acting first and thinking later."

"No, not anymore. They want me to remain part of their group, and I've threatened to quit—and, work against them—if any physical confrontations or destruction of property takes place. I'm going to lead them in a new direction, you'll see. Our tribe needs the Fierce Ones, but they have to be a strong, positive force."

"It sounds as if you'll be taking over Jesse Woody's position as spokesman," she said with a tiny smile.

Clifford shook his head somberly. "I'm a Singer, first and foremost. It's my duty to be available to anyone who needs healing. I won't turn away from that."

Ella looked over at LabKote's covered loading dock and caught a glimpse of a tall Anglo man wearing jeans, a baseball cap, and a fatigue jacket, holding a Colt .223 semiautomatic rifle. A cold chill ran up her spine as she recognized Morgan. There was something about the look on his face. She'd seen it before in police officers who had been in too many confrontations to see the prospect of another with either fear or anticipation. It was a settled look, one that, in many ways, was a lot more dangerous than either of the two more common responses.

She hadn't confirmed Morgan's background yet, but it would be something she'd want to do soon. She was still searching for the person who killed Kyle Hansen, and as she looked at Morgan now, she had no doubt that he would be perfectly capable of committing the act.

Ella had her officers stand between the protestors and the electric fence, not to safeguard LabKote's people, but on behalf of the protestors. The press was also being kept way back because of the danger posed by the electric fence, but they still were able to use their cameras to film everyone.

The protestors remained orderly, but Ella couldn't quite push aside the feeling that things could go downhill fast if one of the protestors made the wrong move.

Justine came up then, interrupting her thoughts. "If the protestors pull something like they did at the tribal offices, we're going to have some people maced, shot, or electrocuted. What should we do if one of the guards starts shooting? Stop them, even if we have to shoot back?"

"You bet. But I don't think it'll go that far. Look at the security guards." Ella's eyes darted back to the LabKote security team, and to Morgan. "The oldest one is what, twenty? They're inexperienced and torn between wanting to mix it up and afraid of what'll happen if they do. But it's clear that Morgan, the man wearing the baseball cap and fatigue jacket, is in charge. Look at his posture and the way he holds that assault rifle. I've got a hunch that if anyone can keep those guards from making a crucial mistake, it's Morgan. He's maintaining control over his men."

"I wish I could be as sure as you are," Justine said.

"I'm not certain enough to lower my guard, if that tells you something," Ella admitted. "But something about LabKote's people is bugging me." She paused, trying to figure it out. "No, to be more precise, it's Morgan who's worrying me. I know he has a military background, the marines, but he really looks out of place here."

"How so?"

She considered it. "He looks too calm," she said at last.

Justine nodded. "Yeah, you're right. He's like a shark in a goldfish pond. But where would someone like that fit in?"

"In some war-torn country no one can either spell or pronounce, because he likes the excitement," Ella said. "I wonder why he left the marines?" Seeing Ted Landreth come out of the main building and move toward the protestors, her attention became riveted on him. "Get ready. Something's up."

Landreth stood just inside the fence and waited for Jesse Woody to approach.

"I'm here to see if we can work out the grievances you seem to have against our company. We can talk in my office, but you'll have to come in unarmed, and alone."

Jesse held out his arms, palms upward. "I'm not armed. None of us are."

"Good, then you won't mind if you're frisked before we let you inside the building?" Landreth said.

"Not at all," Woody answered.

Landreth waved to Morgan, who signalled one of the security guards on a handheld radio. The guard activated a portable transmitter, and the gate opened.

Morgan spoke into the radio again, and the other guards stood in the gap as Woody passed through. Once Woody was clear, the guard closed the gate again, and Morgan came up to quickly and efficiently frisk Woody for weapons.

Now that Morgan was standing close to the fence, she watched him carefully, noting he still wore a handgun, and had the black leather case she assumed held a folding knife instead of Mace. Morgan was certainly a man who believed in being prepared.

Morgan looked up and his eyes held hers. She didn't look away and, for what seemed like an endless moment, she saw the open challenge in his gaze. Then someone called him and he nodded to her, then went back to the building.

Jesse stayed inside for nearly forty minutes, but when he came back out, there was a smile on his face and the protestors visibly relaxed.

Jesse exited the fenced-in area with less ceremony than when he'd entered, and met with the others and the press that had come to cover the event. "LabKote supervisors have agreed to meet with us again and discuss our demands. They don't know of any Navajo who is qualified to take over the job that's now open, but at least they're willing to let us look, and then give them a recommendation. It's a start—a good one."

As the group dispersed, and the press returned to their vehicles, Ella breathed a sigh of relief. Justine came up to her then. "If it's okay, we're going to go back to our regular duties now."

Ella nodded. "That's fine. The crisis is over but, before I leave, I'm going to talk to Morgan again."

"You're going to put pressure on him?"

"No, he doesn't strike me as the type who reacts well to that technique. I just want to ask him a few pointed questions—like why he and his men were so heavily armed. The situation certainly didn't call for it."

"You want me to go in with you?" Justine asked.

"No, that's not necessary. I've met with him before, and I don't think he's going to give me any trouble. It's not to his advantage, especially now that this incident has ended. If I read LabKote correctly, they're hoping all the publicity they've been getting will fade away as quickly as possible."

"Is there anything in particular you need me to do next?" Justine asked.

"You can do background checks on Walter Morgan and Ted Landreth, just to confirm what they've given me already. Find out if those pregnancy tests were filed or not, and get me a list of whose files were taken besides mine and Mrs. Yellowhair's. I also want you to try and find Avery Blueeyes and Atsidi Benally as soon as possible."

"I'll do that. I also spoke to the Blueeyes' family earlier and they claim Avery is fishing somewhere, but they don't know where. I considered putting out an APB, but we don't have enough legal justification. We have no evidence, circumstantial or otherwise, linking him to the kidnapping," Justine said. "I got a chance to question Atsidi, but he has an iron-clad alibi. He was on a field trip to a historical site with his students when the senator was kidnapped. Of course, that doesn't mean he wasn't an accomplice."

"For now, concentrate on Blueeyes, then. We can't put out an APB, but we can find him and bring him in for questioning."

"I'll keep digging. Even if he's holed up somewhere, I'll find him," Justine said, getting into her unit. She waved good-bye, and drove off.

As soon as all those outside LabKote had gone, Ella went up to the booth at the front of the gate, where a guard had been stationed. "I'd like to talk to your head of security," she said flashing her badge. "Walter Morgan."

"I'll see what I can do," the guard answered. "I don't suppose you have an appointment."

"No, but maybe I can get a warrant, if you insist on forcing the issue. I'm still investigating the death of one of your employees."

The guard picked up the phone and had a quick, soft-spoken conversation with someone on the other end. "Mister Morgan will be out in a moment."

This time there were no games. In just a few minutes, Morgan came out and met her.

"Hello again, Investigator Clah," he said as the gate was opened. "I understand you want to talk to me."

"I do. I have a few questions regarding your security measures."

He smiled, but his expression didn't soften. "I figured you might. I saw you standing out here, watching my people more than your own." He gestured toward the building. "Let's go to my office."

She watched Morgan as he remained just a step or two ahead of her, setting the pace. He was clearly a man who liked remaining in control, especially on his own turf.

A moment later they were inside a small office that was as stark and as spartan as she'd expected from someone like Morgan. Like his home, there were no family photos anywhere. A security camera was attached in a corner near the ceiling, looking down on the entire room. Morgan's assault rifle rested across his desk, which held only a computer and keyboard, and there was a large metal gun cabinet against one wall. Another small table held a tape recorder and telephone console. Most people's work spaces said something about them, but this office was more like an interrogation room.

"I understand that you had your security people make it clear that you'd shoot any trespassers," Ella said. "Were those riot guns and your Colt loaded?"

Morgan picked up the assault rifle, removed the clip, and showed her the full magazine. "Does this answer your question? We have the right to protect this facility from criminals. Trespassers are criminals that may become a threat to our operations and destroy valuable equipment and inventory. I think a show of force usually prevents violence—when people know you can back up what you say, they're less likely to test you. That's also why my guards and I are armed to the hilt," he added.

"What property in this plant is worth the price of a man's life?" Ella insisted.

He suddenly laughed. "Subtle as a brick, aren't you? It's my job to protect this place, and I do it to the best of my ability. And, for the record, we do have the support of law-abiding Navajos. Your tribal council and president have visited our facility, and they all approve of the way we are handling things, including the employment question."

"Then you don't think the Fierce Ones have a valid argument?"

"I'm not from around here, as you know from looking over my personnel file, and I don't know enough about the situation on the reservation to answer that. But I do know that they shouldn't have any beef with LabKote. We hire many Navajos. My next in command, for example, is Navajo. He supported my decision to shoot if anyone tried to get in."

"Who's the guard?"

"Jimmie Herder. You may not have seen him today because he was covering the rear of our facility. We're not the Evil Empire, Investigator Clah."

"I never said you were," Ella clipped.

Ella knew that with every answer she gave him, he was sizing her up just as she was doing with him. The main difference between them was that this was clearly a game he enjoyed playing.

"Look, you're obviously starting to feel uncomfortable about LabKote. Why don't you let me give you a guided tour? Some of the machines we use are worth hundreds of thousands of dollars each. If they get damaged, we'd have to shut down and we can't just go to the local hardware store or Radio Shack for parts. Any downtime means big losses for this company. LabKote is not a large operation, and we've been undercutting our competition to get a customer base. We make only a small profit, so we can't afford any significant losses if we plan to stay in business. That's why we're so protective of our facility."

"Are you trying to tell me that you're operating on a shoe-string budget?"

"Our financial situation is proprietary information," he said, "but come on. If you get a good look at everything here, it'll set your mind at ease. Better the devil you know than the devil you don't know."

Ella followed him down the hall, her gaze taking in every detail of the facility. There was a large warehouse area where the sterilized packets were boxed and prepared for shipping. Large, garage-type doors along one end opened onto a long loading dock. Shrink-wrapped packets of plastic petri dishes and other lab supplies were carried into the packing area by a moving conveyor belt which passed through an opening in the wall. About a dozen Navajo men and women were filling orders as she was shown around.

Morgan then led her out of the warehouse and farther down the hall, stopping by a window that revealed the interior of a large room that was secured with a steel door and an electronic lock. This looked like another warehouse, with large garage-type doors against one wall. The doors were covered with some kind of insulating material, however.

"That's where Hansen worked. You can't see his booth from here, but you can see it if you look up at the security monitor," he said pointing to the far corner. "We keep that in place to make sure everything's as it should be."

She could see shrink-wrapped, sealed packages moving slowly down a conveyor belt, pausing every few seconds by the large machines. "I'm assuming this is where everything is sterilized, and those are the machines responsible. Can you tell me about them?"

"I don't know all the technicalities, I'm no scientist, but this is the place where we kill any microbes that might have survived the earlier cleaning process and still be viable inside the sealed packages. It's done with short bursts of gamma radiation. To insure safety, the machines are shielded and, in addition, the building's added shielding prevents the highly focused, short-duration gamma rays from getting beyond the room. Notice the material on the doors. One of the reasons we have such tight security is because we could have a nasty accident if some intruder walked through the processing area and into a beam of gamma rays."

"And I suppose that the person running the machines has to have a high security clearance?"

"With our organization, yes, but this is not a top secret process or government operation. Our machine operators are critical to the operation and everyone's paycheck depends on them, so we make sure that they can work without interruption during a processing cycle."

"What kind of security is there to keep a worker from wandering in there at the wrong time?"

"You've already seen our cameras and, since the operation beyond this door is completely automated, only the operator or his supervisors have key cards to open these particular electronic locks."

He took her to another window. "This is our quality control area," he said, gesturing to the room inside. "The reason for the heavy rubber seals around the door is that we have an air lock system in place here. There are also special micropore filters. In this room our quality control people search for contaminants among random samples taken off the production line. Like the processing room, this is a restricted area. Only lab personnel with special suits have electronic keys that allow them access."

Ella glanced through the window. Beyond the closet-sized air lock, and through another window in an interior door, she could see people in white moon suits working. The large, stainless steel machines had openings equipped with heavy gloves that the techs would use to reach into the chambers. It looked like a scene from a science fiction movie, not something anyone was likely to see on the Rez.

"The next room contains our incinerator," he said, going to the end of the hall. "All waste material from quality control is turned into harmless ash with the help of a high-temperature furnace."

"You mean the bacteria or other microbes that turned up on containers that failed the tests?" Ella asked.

He nodded. "Finding any that actually got past the gamma rays is a rare event. Most of what's burned is growth medium, like agar, and the containers we opened up and tested. That's our operation in a nutshell," he said with a smile. "You can see now that we don't have anything to hide. It's for the public's sake that we keep such a tight lid on our work. We can't have people just wandering in or trespassing."

Ella was about to thank Morgan when a high-pitched alarm sounded. She jumped, startled by the shrill sound, and braced herself for an emergency, but seeing Morgan take it in stride, she forced herself to relax.

"Look fast, and you'll see the gamma ray equipment power down," he said moving to the corresponding window. "The equipment's beam is automatically shielded when the large outside doors open, and of course the machines shut down." He gestured to a team of men in yellow fireman turnout gear. They were moving into the room via one of the garage-style doors, now opening. "That's our emergency response team. Had there been a fire, they would have put it out. A spill of one of our cleaning solutions, or an electrical short would also be handled and corrected as well. Of course, as I'm sure you realize by now, this is only a drill. We have several a week between processing runs, just to keep our people sharp."

It had all looked very practiced and routine, but she had a sneaking suspicion that it had been staged for her benefit. What she couldn't decide was why Morgan had felt compelled to arrange a drill for her. Was it pride, or just a way to get her to go away and not come back?

They were going back down the hallway toward the front entrance when Ted Landreth came out of his office. "Do you mind stopping by my office when you're finished?" he asked Ella.

"I think Mr. Morgan and I are done with the tour," Ella said, curious to see what Landreth wanted. She looked at Morgan, who nodded.

"I'll go log in my report," Morgan said, leaving.

Landreth offered her a chair, then sat down behind his desk. "I'm hoping you can help me. I need a way to show the Fierce Ones, and any other concerned group that our company is really very beneficial to the tribe. For example, in exchange for a very favorable lease agreement, we've made substantial donations of valuable lab supplies to the high school and college laboratories. The tribal council knows all that, but obviously The People don't. I think we're due for another press release. I'll have our public relations people come up with something."

Ella nodded absently, then stood and walked to the opposite wall where several photos had been hung. Several tribal officials were pictured with LabKote supervisors. The photos were filled with men smiling and shaking hands, despite the fact that even casual physical contact with a stranger was something most Navajos preferred to avoid. Morgan wasn't in any of the photos, but silently she noted that one of the photos showed Senator Yellowhair and Ernest Ben with Landreth.

"I don't think the Fierce Ones dispute the good you do for the tribe," she said, returning to her chair. "They'd just like to see more of our people benefit from the higher paying jobs—like the one Hansen had before his death."

"Yeah, I know that, but Hansen had advanced engineering degrees in computer software design and programming. His job requires some highly technical expertise as well as a formal education. Remember that certain additions to our machinery, the safeguards that protect everyone, for instance, were Hansen's own design. He was an undeniable asset to us. That was the reason we didn't fire him for insubordination months ago."

"Are you saying he's practically irreplaceable?"

"Just about, but I'm sure that if we look hard enough, we'll eventually find someone who can take his place."

"Who's doing his job now?"

"Carl Fine. He's one of the supervisors. But all he's doing is running the production line according to Hansen's established procedures, which are installed as custom software and written up in a manual. It's only a temporary arrangement. Carl just doesn't have the training or expertise that Hansen had."

"So, how do you intend to comply with the Fierce Ones' demand that the position be filled with a Navajo?"

"I'll ask tribal employment services for help, and at the same time conduct a regional job search through the universities in Arizona and New Mexico. Maybe we can hire someone qualified who *is* Navajo. We'll certainty try. If that doesn't pan out, perhaps we can get someone to train as a tech and work alongside whoever ends up taking Hansen's job."

She nodded and stood. "If that's all you had for me . . ."

"No, actually, I have a favor to ask you."

She stood by the door. "I'm listening."

"I understand from Morgan that your brother was out there today with the Fierce Ones."

Ella wished she had more background on Morgan. He was good.

"Can you explain to him that we'll do our best, but Hansen's job can't be filled at the drop of a hat? He might be more inclined to believe you and then spread the word to the others."

"You told all this to Jesse Woody already, right?" Seeing him nod, she added, "then it's been said. It won't become more true if you tell it more often."

He didn't crack a smile, and neither did she. Ella stood and walked down the hall. She was surprised when Landreth didn't follow her, since she'd been told that no one was allowed inside unescorted, but before she got ten feet, Morgan came to meet her.

"Can you come back into my office for a moment before you leave, Investigator Clah? There's something I'd like to show you."

She followed him wordlessly, knowing instinctively that he already knew she'd agree. Curiosity was the founding trait of an investigator.

Ella entered Morgan's office and saw him take a sheet of paper from the top of his desk. "Sheriff Taylor had asked us to call him if we found anything that would be of interest to him regarding Hansen's case, so I did." He offered her the page. "This is what I faxed him this morning. It's a printout of a letter we found on a computer disk Hansen hid in the middle of some papers in his bottom drawer. It took us a while to work out his password so we could gain access to the file, but we finally did."

"What was the password?" she asked.

Morgan smiled. "We tried his wife's name, his name, listed birth dates, and all the regular stuff, but Hansen's brain didn't run on regular channels. That's when I decided to try something more his speed. His password, as it turned out, was 'gamma.'"

It was another sign of what kind of person Morgan was. Like her, he would keep working a puzzle until he had answers. Pure and simple, he liked to win. "Good work."

She read the letter. It was addressed to his ex-wife. In it, he was pleading for a reconciliation. To Ella, the letter had the sound of a work still in progress, not something he was ready to send.

"The guy sure was a whiner. No wonder his ex jettisoned him," Morgan said contemptuously.

His assessment was so blunt and so much in line with his macho style that she had to smile.

"What? You think I'm an insensitive clod?"

"The thought occurred to me," she said. "But, in all fairness, I don't much care for anyone who uses this tactic. It's equal parts guilt and begging."

Morgan grinned at her. "Yeah. That's the way I see it, too." He handed her the disk. "Here's where we found the letter. It contains nothing else besides the printout, but I figured you'd want to have it."

"Thanks."

He returned with her to the gate. "We're two wolves, aren't we?" he observed. "We wouldn't beg, even if they kneecapped us."

"Begging doesn't do any good. If you have to, you've already lost," she said as she got back into her vehicle.

As she drove away, Ella checked in with Justine, giving her the code word that would decode the files.

"I'll try that right away," Justine said.

"Any other news?"

"Not yet."

A peculiar restlessness gnawed at Ella. She wanted answers, but none seemed forthcoming. As usual, their investigation was becoming an exercise in patience. A phone call to Sheriff Taylor only confirmed what she already knew. After agreeing to keep in touch, Ella disconnected the call.

She was halfway to the station when she caught a glimpse of an old truck behind her. There were no other vehicles on this stretch of road at the moment, so it was easy to spot.

She passed two more turnoffs, but the driver stayed with her. If this was a tail, it was such an obvious one that it couldn't have been a pro in the truck behind her.

Deciding to check it out, Ella slowed her vehicle down, then drove up a dirt track. There was a canyon ahead that she could use to turn the tables on him.

The thought that perhaps Big Ed had assigned someone to follow and back her up occurred to her. He'd done it in the past. Ella considered the possibility then discarded it. No cop would have been that sloppy, and they would have signalled her by now.

The other driver followed her up the dirt track, then slowed down as she disappeared into the canyon. He passed her position cautiously, still searching for her. Ella bided her time, then pulled out behind him. Unfortunately, he was still too far away to ID.

Spotting her, the driver suddenly tried to turn around, found he couldn't, then floored the accelerator pedal, heading straight into the desert. The only thing out in the direction he was going was the local landfill.

Ella stayed in pursuit and called it in on her radio. She didn't think she'd need backup, and that was just as well since no one would be available for several minutes anyway.

The beat-up truck in front of her stayed on course, though it was a rough trip, even for a four-wheel drive. They were going forty, but with all the bumps and uneven terrain, it felt as if they were on a wild, uncontrollable, roller-coaster ride.

As they drew closer to the landfill, the terrain cleared to low, scattered brush. Ella saw the massive bulldozer ahead in a scooped out basin, burying refuse, and pressed down harder on the accelerator. The last thing she wanted was an innocent caught up in this.

Suddenly, the driver pulled to a stop, leaped out, and disappeared behind a pile of rubble.

Ella was only seconds away from where his truck was parked, when one shot rang out. Every instinct she'd perfected as a cop told her the story. The bulldozer operator had come face-to-face with his destiny. There was a killer on the loose now and, like predatory animals, they made cunning adversaries when trapped.

TWELVE

———— ✖ ✖ ✖ ————

Ella reached for her shotgun, called in a situation report, and requested an EMT unit. As she left the Jeep, she was careful to stay behind the protection of the engine block. Experience and training took over now, and she knew what she had to do.

The foul-smelling landfill resembled a large crater, with the bulldozer and several mounds of refuse lining the high earthen rim. Ella waited for an eternity, but everything was still. Even the crows, ever-present residents of the landfill, began to land and resume searching for scraps.

She crouched, moving forward low to the ground, shifting her vantage point from trash mound to trash mound, then searching for the shooter before moving again. A few birds took flight, but most remained, not seeing her as a threat.

Directly ahead, about halfway to the bulldozer, she saw a small mountain of discarded furniture. It would do for cover. Ella sprinted toward an upended sofa, expecting to be shot at for the few seconds she was exposed, but nothing happened.

The cry of the crows, their feeding interrupted, distracted her, but she fought to concentrate on the man who'd brought her here.

As Ella moved around to one end of the sofa, she saw a body lying on the ground, bleeding from the chest.

She drew near cautiously and recognized Rudy Joe, the dozer operator. He'd told her once that he worked out here at the landfill because he liked the outdoors all year round. Who'd have thought that statement would turn out to be his epitaph.

Ella crawled over to Rudy and felt for a pulse. He was still alive, having been shot in the chest, but well to the side and below the heart, catching a rib. The blood loss, however, was heavy. Maybe it was kinder that he'd passed out. To be aware of what was going on, under these circumstances, would have been torture.

She remained quiet, but still the shooter remained hidden either behind the dozer or another heap of trash. The rim of the crater was too steep to climb easily at this, the low end of the landfill. Did the man expect to get away if he just didn't reveal his position? Surely he must have surmised that if he left, he'd have to try it on foot, because to reach his vehicle he'd have to get past her, and that would never happen. The man was connected to one or more of her investigative trails, and she had no intention of letting him escape.

Ella moved forward again, looking all around her. As she maneuvered closer, the bulldozer's engine suddenly came to life. With a powerful roar, the machine lurched forward, crushing everything in its way.

She had to make a quick choice. If she tried to run to either side to flank him, she'd put herself in the open and he'd shoot at her. But if she stayed where she was, she'd be buried under tons of garbage or crushed by the machine's massive steel blade or steel treads.

Ella fired off three shotgun blasts in rapid succession, but the buckshot either ricocheted off the blade, or passed over the head of the operator, who was using the blade like armor plate. The bulldozer kept coming at her, and she was forced to give ground. If she couldn't get to one side soon, he'd trap her with her back to the wall of earth that bordered the pit.

To survive, she'd have to disable the machine or hit the driver. As she tried to get into a better firing position, she suddenly realized that this had all been a setup. She'd been manipulated into coming out here where she'd be all alone.

Angry that she'd made such a tactical mistake, Ella grew even more determined to turn the tables on her enemy. She would *not* die out here. She had a future, and this man would not rob her or her baby of that.

Hearing the wail of a siren over the sound of the bulldozer, she smiled. She was no longer by herself. A heartbeat later, she saw Officer Philip Cloud up above at the rim of the pit. As the bulldozer bore down on her, Ella gestured for Philip to move to his left. She'd run to the right, and if one of them was quick enough, they'd outflank the driver and get close enough to shoot.

The driver had seen the police car arrive and slowed the bulldozer, suddenly aware of Philip. When the officer slid down into the crater, the bulldozer quickly turned in its tracks and roared toward him. Philip tried to move laterally to the machine, but the dozer was agile and continued to keep him in its path.

Ella had wanted to capture the man alive, but now the life of a fellow officer took precedent. With only seconds before the bulldozer trapped Philip, she raced out and took a position behind cover in line with the side of the machine.

Ella dropped the shotgun and pulled out her pistol. It was more precise and she was better with it. Bracing her hands combat style, she aligned her sights, held her breath, and squeezed off one shot. The man dropped to his right, falling out of the bulldozer onto a pile of rusted out car parts.

The dozer slowed immediately, ran into the wall of earth that surrounded the landfill, and climbed almost to a forty-five-degree angle before the engine died. It slid back three feet, then stopped.

Ella swallowed the bitter taste at the back of her throat. Another corpse, another face that would either keep her awake, or haunt her dreams for months.

While Philip checked on Rudy Joe, she picked up her shotgun, checked the bore for debris, then moved forward slowly and cautiously, though she knew the man was dead. Few ever survived a bullet behind the ear.

The first thing she did as she drew near was kick the gun well away from him. Then she crouched down and turned the body face up. She'd expected a Navajo, this was their land after all, but the light-skinned man before her was no one she recognized.

Philip jogged up and glanced down at the man. "Do you have any idea who he is, and why he did this?"

"Not a clue." She reached into his pocket and pulled out his wallet. "There's a Colorado driver's license with the name, Thomas LaPoint, but no LabKote ID," she said, surprised. "I assumed . . ."

"There are other Anglos working on the Rez, and other Anglo run businesses," Philip said. "The highways bring many people through our land."

"Yeah, I know, but LabKote was fresh in my mind. I just came from there."

"Things are never what they seem to be around here. Have you ever noticed that?" Philip said in a hushed tone, then walked back with Ella to tend to the wounded bulldozer operator.

Rudy Joe was stabilized about ten minutes later and transported to the hospital. While her team processed the scene, Ella stayed with Dr. Roanhorse while she continued her preliminary examination of the body.

"I'll do an autopsy and find out if he had any drugs in his system that affected his judgment, or if there was any medical reason for his violent behavior. Suicide by cop seems to be a modern favorite, but, from what I've seen here, I doubt that was what he was trying to do. Judging by what you and Officer Cloud told me, he wanted you dead, not himself."

"What I can't figure out is why he set up this one-on-one confrontation. If he wanted me dead, he should have stacked the deck."

"Be thankful for his bad judgment."

"I wish I could figure out what this was all about," Ella said.

"When I can't, it usually means I'm missing something, Carolyn, and whenever that has happened in the past, it ends up costing me."

"Do you have any idea who this guy is?" Carolyn asked, gesturing to the corpse, "other than the name on his toe tag?"

"No, do you?"

Carolyn shook her head. "If I were you, I'd go talk to people at the mine, at LabKote, and over at the hospital. All those places hire quite a few Anglos. Of course, he could just be someone from off the Rez who was here visiting or just looking around. We have a lot of curious people who come and do the tourist thing, then leave."

"All I have to go on for now is a name and address on the driver's license and this motel room key we found in his pocket." Ella walked over to the perp's vehicle. The old truck looked as if it were being held together with superglue and rust. The doors didn't match the paint job, the fenders were dented, and the entire body seemed misaligned on the frame, undoubtedly the result of a hasty repair after the vehicle had been involved in an accident.

Justine joined Ella and, together, they processed the interior. While Justine dusted for prints, Ella checked out the contents of the glove compartment. Except for some melted candy bars, there was nothing there.

Ella continued to look around for a LabKote ID. She'd been heading back from the plant when she'd spotted the tail, and it seemed a logical tie-in. She checked the floorboards, and between the seat cushions, but there was nothing to be found.

"I ran the plate through DMV, and the tag is stolen," Justine said. "There is no registration either. Are you looking for something specific?" Justine asked.

Ella explained why she suspected a possible link to LabKote.

"I'll keep looking," Justine said.

After going through the interior completely, and verifying again that there was no LabKote sticker in the truck, Ella took a deep breath.

"We should go check out his motel room," Justine said. "We may find something there."

"Take the team over and get started on that as soon as you can," Ella said, "but leave the motel staff to me. I'll interview them."

Justine took the key, which was labeled Sagebrush Motel. "Okay, boss. First I'll make arrangements to have this vehicle impounded, then make sure it gets to the garage where I can process it completely later."

Seeing Tache taking photos, and Ute working the perimeter, Ella knew her team had things covered. She could do more from the office now than by staying here. "I'm going back to the station," she told Justine. "I'll file my report, then go interview whatever staff I can find at the motel."

"I'll meet with you later then," Justine said.

Ella glanced back and saw what was irreverently called the 'croaker sack' being loaded into the back of Carolyn's van. A shudder ran up her spine. The aftermath of killing another human being, even in a righteous shooting, was never easy. The dead always exacted their revenge, carving a place for themselves in the nightmares that would haunt her for as long as she lived.

The first thing she did once she got back to the station was check with the armament officer and sign out an extra long kevlar vest. No questions were asked, especially after the latest incident.

Ella spent the next thirty minutes running the dead man's ID through law enforcement and other databases. At first, there was nothing unusual, except that Tom LaPoint, a Colorado resident according to his records, hadn't had any priors and what he'd done today seemed completely out of character. But then things began getting really strange. According to the records, Tom LaPoint had died in a car accident four years ago in Denver.

After accessing his photo through the Colorado Division of Motor Vehicles she finally found an answer she understood. The man she'd shot was not Tom LaPoint, and the listed address was a phony. The photo on the computer screen showed a completely different person than the individual who'd tried to kill her. Her attacker had assumed the dead man's identity.

She leaned back in her chair, trying to mentally review everything she knew and come up with more answers, but a rational explanation eluded her. It now seemed unlikely that the gunman had come from LabKote, so maybe he'd been parked somewhere nearby, waiting for her.

Hearing the buzzer on the intercom sound abruptly, she jumped. It was starting—the jumbled nerves, the tension that would stay with her for weeks, making her peer into every shadow. That was why many cops outside the Rez were forced to take time off after an incident where a shooting death had occurred. But there'd be no respite for her here. It was the drawback of a police department plagued by shortages of every imaginable kind. If she couldn't cut it she'd have to go on unpaid leave, or be replaced permanently.

"Shorty, I just heard about what happened over at the landfill. Get in here. We have to talk," Big Ed's voice boomed over the intercom.

Ella stood up slowly. She wasn't in the mood for the battery of questions she'd have to answer, and what was worse, she knew Big Ed expected answers and she didn't have any to give him.

When Ella walked into his office, she saw the concerned look in his eyes. "I heard about the incident. What can you tell me about it?"

Ella briefed him. "The only thing I know for sure is the person who attacked me and Officer Cloud is *not* Tom LaPoint. That's a stolen identity. Maybe Justine and the others will learn something from his motel room."

"But you say he doesn't seem to be connected to LabKote," Big Ed said thoughtfully. "So, let's try looking in a different direction. The Fierce Ones are very active now. In the past, they've used some sophisticated games to achieve their goals. Could they have hired someone, or a group of Anglos, to support their contention that the Anglos are a threat to the Rez?"

Ella said nothing for several moments. Her brother would

have never gone along with something like that and he would have had the clout to stop them. If she said that, however, it would be perceived as loyalty, not a cop's instinct. "That doesn't sound right to me," she said.

"Maybe that's because you're thinking of the Fierce Ones as one unit, not as individuals who have banned together. Individuals could form another group within the larger one. Think of Jesse Woody, and Billy Pete, Shorty," Big Ed reminded her. "Those men have a tendency to fight by their own rules."

Ella knew Billy Pete; they'd gone to school together. Billy was part of the Fierce Ones, though he'd yet to openly admit it. Yet, as she thought back to the tribal office demonstration, she remembered that he hadn't been one of those arrested. He'd also been absent at the LabKote demonstration.

"I don't even know if Billy is still in the Fierce Ones. He wasn't at either of the demonstrations, near as I recall," Ella said.

"You mean he wasn't arrested," Big Ed said.

Billy was a smart man. She had no doubt that if he was up to something like what Big Ed had suggested, he would have laid low during any public demonstration. "Okay, I'll look into it."

Big Ed gave her a long, hard look. "Do you need some time off?"

The short answer was yes, but Ella knew he couldn't really spare her now. "I'll be okay," she said.

Ella returned to her office, lost in thought. Big Ed's theory of a group within a group bothered her. It was logical enough, considering the personalities of the men involved. *She* should have thought of it.

Forcing herself to look at things dispassionately, she wondered if perhaps her brother's involvement *was* clouding her judgment. Maybe she was prejudicing the case she was trying to make. Unsure of herself, she made up her mind to be twice as hard on everyone—including Clifford—from this point on. People's lives were at stake, including her own and her baby's.

Ella sat at her desk, writing the report on the shooting at the landfill. Policy required it be done ASAP, while memories were still fresh and untainted. Reliving all the details exhausted her, but she continued working. When the intercom buzzed sometime later, she welcomed the interruption. Ella depressed the button and identified herself.

"This is Tache," the voice at the other end said. "I returned from the motel ahead of the others because there was nothing for me to photograph there. I spent my time developing some photos of the crime scene instead and they're ready for you now."

"I hope you got me a close-up of his face."

"You shot him through the head. There's some distortion."

"Is there enough of it to make an ID?"

"Yeah, you weren't using a rifle, and it was a clean shot, but it's going to rattle any civilian who looks at it. I can use a scanner and computer software to edit out the wound somewhat. I'm assuming you want it to try and ID him, right?"

"Right."

"Okay. I'll bring the best shot I can doctor up for that. It'll take about a half hour."

"You can do that later. Bring me what you've got now, and we'll go through it."

Although the man's face and the death mask he'd take to his grave were indelibly etched in her mind, she'd have to study Tache's photos carefully for a clue. Her primary responsibility now was to find out who the man was, and learn what he was doing on the Rez besides trying to kill cops.

A moment later Tache came in. His round face, normally cheery, looked as glum as Harry Ute's normal expression. Then again, he'd spent time the last few hours photographing a corpse.

"You okay?" she asked.

"I was about to ask you the same thing," he answered quietly.

"Yeah." She spread out the photos he handed her. It sure wasn't pretty. Her stomach did a somersault, but she swallowed and forced her expression to remain neutral. "I'll take this one with me now," she said at last, choosing a close-up that showed the man's face but less of the wound that had caused his death.

"I took that one at the morgue. Doctor Roanhorse had cleaned up the body by then. When I saw Justine and you searching the car, and heard that no one, including me, had ever seen him, I had a feeling you'd want a shot to show around right away."

"Thanks. I appreciate this."

"Don't mention it. I'll get a duplicate ready for distribution among the other officers."

Ella began gathering her things. She didn't want to finish her report right now. She needed some fresh air. Grabbing the photo and sticking it inside an envelope, she stood to leave just as Justine came in.

Ella filled her in on what she'd learned about Tom LaPoint.

"I'll keep checking and see if I can find out who he is," Justine said. "The motel was a waste of time. It was as if he'd never checked in. There wasn't even a comb in there."

"Work on his identity. I want LaPoint's name—his real name," Ella said. "And we need to find out where he lived. I suspect the motel room was just a place for him to crash in case he needed one after getting rid of me. Too bad we only found that key and the key to the pickup."

"I'll get you answers," Justine said, handing Ella the motel key. "One way or another."

THIRTEEN

✖ ✖ ✖

Ella left the station in her Jeep, and immediately rolled down her window. She felt sick. Allowing the fresh air to hit her face helped, but the feeling persisted as the Anglo man's face stayed before her mind's eye. Suddenly Ella began to tremble uncontrollably. No matter how hard she tried, she couldn't make it stop. Taking short, shuddering breaths, she pulled to the side of the road and took the vehicle out of gear.

With effort, Ella finally managed to bring herself under control without emptying the contents of her stomach. Navajos saw death as failure to grow, the end of all possibilities, and that's what she'd taken from the Anglo stranger. Sorrow gnawed at her, though the Anglo had given her no other choice.

She remained parked for several more minutes before finally continuing to the motel on the main highway near Kirtland. It was just a few miles north of the reservation border, and business was brisk. The motel had a bar and lounge for people who liked to stop for a drink, and was handy, because no businesses had liquor permits inside the reservation.

Ella went inside, and walked over to the front desk of the small lobby.

The woman looked at the photo Ella handed her then cringed. "I've never seen that guy. I just started working here yesterday afternoon, and I didn't check him in. But you might try the lounge. The employees there might recognize a guest or regular customer."

Ella asked for the name of the motel guest in room 110, and the clerk identified him as Tom LaPoint, which was no surprise. Undeterred, Ella went into the lounge and flashed the bartender her ID. The name tag on the woman's uniform identified her as Barbara Sanchez.

"You're out of your jurisdiction, so you must want to buy a drink, right?" the woman behind the bar challenged.

"I want some answers." Ella showed her the photo. "Have you ever seen this man?"

The woman made a choking sound and, for a moment, Ella was sure she was going to burst into tears. "So, you *do* know him," Ella said gently.

"His name was Tom, but I don't know his last name," Barbara Sanchez said in a shaky voice. "He came in several times these past few days and would usually have a rum and cola, or a draft and some nuts."

"Did you go out with him?"

"No. I'm not supposed to date the guests and customers."

"Okay, so I won't tell anyone. Did you date him anyway?" Ella pressed.

"I would have, had he asked me, but he never did. I think he might have . . . eventually. He was a little shy." She stared at the bar, purposely looking away from the photo.

Ella slid the photo back in the envelope. "Did anyone ever meet him here?"

She shrugged. "He met friends briefly a few times, but mostly he came in alone and left alone."

"Who did he meet here? Can you give me any names?"

"I don't know who they were. One was a Navajo man who wore a Kansas City Chiefs' cap. The other was an Anglo, a real mystery man. I only saw him the one time. He wore sunglasses in here, can you believe it? It's dark enough, don't you think?"

"What color was his hair?"

"Can't tell you, he had a cowboy hat on, and he only stayed for a few seconds. Tom didn't finish his drink that day. He met the guy near the doorway, then left."

Ella nodded, then slipped her card across the bar. "If you remember anything else, give me a call."

Ella spoke to the waitress and a room service clerk, but no one else was able to give her any leads. She checked on room 110 but it was just as Tache and Justine had described it, untouched.

Ella drove back to the Quick Stop just inside the reservation. Everyone came by here for gas or groceries sooner or later. The prices were high, but it was a good place to get a gallon of milk or a loaf of bread without going into Shiprock.

Assured from her jeans and T-shirt that she wasn't a traditionalist, Ella showed the manager the photo. The young Navajo woman turned as white as the day old popcorn inside the machine. "I've never seen him," she said in a shaky voice.

"Are you sure?"

"Yes. Now please leave and take that horrible photo away from here. That may be a part of your line of work, but it sure isn't part of mine!"

As she turned away, Ella felt her chest tighten. The remark had struck home. Had she hardened herself too much in order to survive the demands of her work? She looked at the photo and tried to see it as someone outside law enforcement would, but it was no use. The picture was nothing in comparison to the actual, vivid details recorded forever in her mind.

As she climbed back into her unit, she began to shake again. A pregnant woman, according to tradition, should have avoided the face of death but, in her job, there was no escaping it. Ella took a long, deep, steadying breath, then switched on the ignition.

She had to concentrate on the case now. It was the only way to put what happened into perspective. Calling in, Ella gave Justine the details of what she'd learned about LaPoint's possible contact. "I'm going to need Billy Pete's address. He's always wearing that KC baseball cap, and I'm betting it's him the bartender saw. Check around the office. I'm sure we've got a file on him that lists his address."

"I don't need to. I know where he lives. I've known him for a long time. He's been a friend of my brother's for as far back as I can remember."

Ella got the address and started back to Shiprock. She knew the eastern residential area that Justine had mentioned. It was a section of small, closely spaced cube-shaped houses. Mostly young people lived there, since the inexpensive tribal-built houses weren't really large enough for big families. The biggest advantage they had was that they were only a ten- or fifteen-minute drive to the power plants, the major employer around besides the tribe itself.

Ella knew Billy worked at the mine, but it was almost six now, and unless he was on the night shift, there was a good chance she'd find him home.

As Ella approached Billy's home, she saw him pulling up in his truck. Ella parked behind him, blocking him in case he decided to try and duck her, then walked up the open carport. "Hey, Billy."

He gave her a guarded look. "Hey." He adjusted his Chiefs' cap, then leaned back against his truck. "What brings you here?"

"There's been a shooting." Without giving him any more warning than that, she brought the photo out from her jacket pocket and handed it to him. "I've been told you know this man."

Billy looked at the photo, then paled slightly. "I don't know why you'd think that. He's a stranger to me."

"Look again," she said.

He complied, but then shook his head. "Never seen him before, sorry."

"There's an eyewitness that will swear differently."

Billy glared at her. "You don't honestly believe I had some-

thing to do with this man's death, do you?" he asked her, his
voice taut. "You've known me since I was a kid, Ella."

"I know you didn't shoot him—I did that when he tried to kill
me and another officer. But I need to know everything *you* know
about him."

He hesitated.

"Don't even think of lying to me," she said, her voice firm.

"All I can tell you is that his name is Tom something. I can't
remember his last name. I met him one time at the mine. He was
talking to Jesse about a truck or something like that. Ask Jesse.
Then I ran into him a few times in the Palomino Lounge, you
know, the one at the Sagebrush Motel. It's the closest place a guy
can get a cold beer around here without going into Farmington."

"And?"

"He's a stranger to me, for all intents and purposes. We barely
talked. He noticed my Chiefs' cap and bought me a beer once."

"Were he and Jesse good friends?" she pressed.

"Ask Jesse. You know better than to ask me that. One Navajo
doesn't speak for another," he said.

She looked at his cap, then gave him a wry smile. "That's a
convenient excuse. Since when did you become a traditionalist?"

"I'm not, but I *do* believe in our ways, and I think the old customs should be treated with respect." He gave her a long, hard
look. "Sometimes you still sound like L.A. Woman."

She forced herself not to cringe. That had been the nickname
many had used for her when she'd first returned to the Rez from
southern California. After being back home for several years, and
after everything that had happened to her since, she'd thought
everyone had forgotten about it. Hearing it mentioned so easily
now stung, but she was determined not to show it.

"What was this guy like?" she pressed. "I'd like your impression of him."

Billy considered it. "He seemed lonely, like a fish out of water
here, and trying too hard to make friends. I asked him what he
was doing on the Rez, and all he said was 'research.' I thought he

was some kind of college graduate studying Indians, since we get so many of those who come by."

"I'll check it out. But you said Jesse knows him?"

"I saw them together once at the mine. That's all I can really tell you."

Ella gave him a long, thoughtful look. "You and I used to be friends once, Billy. Why can't we trust each other anymore?"

Billy shook his head sadly. "We both changed. There's a lot happening on the Rez right now, but I believe we can't restore harmony using the Anglo system of law. To defeat our enemies, we have to hold fast to our own traditions."

"It's how we define 'enemies' that really separates us," Ella said. "As I see it, anyone who undermines the stability and order of our tribe—a lawbreaker—is an enemy, whether or not he sees it that way."

Billy began walking toward the front door of his house. "It's time to say good-night. I've told you all I know."

"Or just all you're going to tell me?"

He shrugged, unlocked his door, then turned. "Do what you have to, Ella. I'll do the same."

As she got back into her police unit, Ella felt a vague sense of disquiet. It really bothered her to think that some of her own people saw cops as enemies of the tribe. All the cops she knew were highly dedicated men and women who put their lives on the line to serve The People. This was their home, too—a place where they lived, loved, and raised their children. Without them, there would be no harmony or beauty, only chaos, despite all the arguments that attempted to twist the truth.

Ella put her unit in gear and drove away from Billy Pete's home. It was time to get back to work. She had a job to do.

Ella reached for the mike to request Jesse Woody's address, when she heard her call sign over the radio. She answered, identifying herself, and waited for the dispatcher to tell her the nature of the call.

"We've got an Officer Needs Help call near you. He's asking for you specifically. I'm going to patch you through to him now."

The dispatcher had her switch frequencies, and in moments Sergeant Neskahi's voice came over the air.

"If you can respond, I can use the assist," Neskahi said. "John Brownhat's wife is dead, and it looks like she fell off her mare. Her husband found the body when he came home from work, and he insists her death was no accident."

"What does the scene tell you?" Ella probed.

"It's inconclusive. The horse seems gentle enough, but you know how they can spook one minute and be okay the next. John is understandably very upset, and wants someone to come and investigate. He's certain that the horse would never have thrown his wife and that there's no way she just fell off."

"What do you think?" Ella asked.

"Admittedly, she's a good horsewoman, but accidents do happen. She might have had a heart attack or something. There's no way I can tell," Neskahi said. "But John wants answers, not guesses. He's on the phone with the chief now. He's not going to let this go."

"I'm on my way," she said.

Moments later, as she neared the fork in the highway at the center of Shiprock, she was called on the radio again. This time, Big Ed came on.

"Shorty, I need you to assess the scene over at John Brownhat's and then report back to me. If there's a chance it's homicide, I want you on the case."

"I'm already on the way, Big Ed," Ella affirmed. "Sergeant Neskahi called me for assistance."

"I've also sent Carolyn Roanhorse out to take a look," he added. "She may even get there before you. John Brownhat is a close friend of the tribal president and I've got enough pressure on me right now."

"10–4."

Ella picked what she thought would be a shortcut to the Brownhats, but, as it turned out, the gravel road had been partially washed out in the last rain, and it wasn't much of a timesaver. By the time she arrived at the solitary home that stood a few miles north of Ship Rock, the geological formation for which the town was named, she saw Carolyn had already arrived.

Ella parked her unit, then walked toward the others. It was twilight now, and the ground was obscured by the grayness of the hour. A saddled pinto mare stood by, grazing on a patch of tall grass, oblivious to everything but her appetite.

Sergeant Neskahi left the ME and came up to Ella as she approached the scene. In a low voice, he filled her in. "The victim died of a broken neck, according to Dr. Roanhorse's preliminary examination, but that's what you might expect from a fall from a horse."

Ella studied the mare, which no longer had its bridle on, though it remained saddled. "That's the horse?"

"Yeah. I took the bridle off so she could feed freely, and maybe not wander away in the dark. That mare looks as if a three-year-old could ride her, but you know as well as I do that horses are unpredictable. Just when you take your mind off what you're doing and relax, something goes wrong. A hamburger wrapper drifting in the breeze could turn a nice ride into rodeo time. But then again, Elisa Brownhat raised and trained horses, so she would have known how to handle almost anything. She was one of the best horse people around."

"Yeah, I know," she said. "It does seem as if there's a piece of the puzzle missing."

"That's exactly the way I feel," John Brownhat said, approaching Ella from behind.

Ella turned her head, startled by the silence of his approach. She'd never even had an inkling that he was there. She knew his reputation as a hunter and a tracker. Even when game had been scarce, the Brownhats had never gone hungry. But she'd never seen Brownhat's skill until just now. He had walked from his house across an area filled with grass, brush, and rocks without making a single sound.

"My wife did not fall off that mare. You should know that in the seven years we've been married, I never once saw or heard of her falling off a horse, even when she was training them. She sometimes bailed—got off fast—if the horse was giving her too much trouble. But she never took a fall."

Ella met his eyes. In the twilight, they burned with anger and sorrow. "I'm very sorry about what happened, Sir. I'm looking into this myself, and if there's something not right about this, I'll find it."

Brownhat nodded. "You have certain talents, I know," he said.

There it was. The legacy followed her as if it were solid, incontrovertible fact instead of a legend. "Right now what I need you to do is go inside and let us work. I'll come and talk to you again before we leave."

"Some of the tracks have been brushed away," John told her. "Look carefully. Some other person was here when my wife died."

"You've checked the area?"

"I know what you're thinking, but I haven't disturbed anything. You can easily recognize my tracks, and they haven't confused any of the other signs." Having said that, Brownhat turned and went to the house.

Neskahi expelled his breath in a hiss. "He's really a skilled hunter. He found the tracks by the road. I probably wouldn't have looked that far from the body."

"We owe it to him and to the victim to check everything out. If there's something more to what's happened here than a riding accident, we need to find evidence to support it."

Ella unhooked her handheld radio from her belt, and requested her crime scene team. A moment later, the dispatcher told her that Big Ed had already done that for her. Tache, Ute, and Justine were in transit.

Seeing Carolyn kneeling by the body, talking into her tape recorder, Ella approached quietly, not wanting to interrupt her.

After a minute, Carolyn glanced up at her. "I can't tell you much from the body, not until I've had a closer look," she said, preempting Ella's questions.

"Any signs of violence?"

"It appears that she has a broken neck, and there are bruises on her jaw, and probably elsewhere, but you'd expect to see some of that after a fall from a horse."

"But on her jaw?"

"I know," Carolyn answered. "That one can go either way. It could be evidence of a homicide or not." Carolyn struggled to get off her knees. "I should go on a diet, but I just like eating dessert too much."

Ella smiled and gave her a hand. Carolyn was a large woman by anyone's standards, but in the past few months she'd added another ten pounds at least. "You just need to do more exercise," Ella suggested quietly.

"I dislike any activity that makes me sweat," Carolyn said curtly. "Besides, life is unpredictable and I'd hate for anything to happen to me, like a heart attack, while I was doing something highly unpleasant. If I have to die, I'm going to do it licking cookie crumbs off my lips." She signalled Neskahi to help her put the body into the sack.

Ella saw Neskahi cringe, then quickly cover his reaction up. "You very seldom ask me to help you with the bodies," Ella said. "Why's that?"

Carolyn grinned. "I like to force the macho cops to do something that makes them weak at the knees. It's my version of fun, so back off."

Ella bit her lip to keep from smiling. It would have been too cruel to poor Sergeant Neskahi, who was approaching so slowly it was as if his feet had suddenly turned to lead.

Hearing vehicles approaching, Ella saw her crime scene team driving up. "I better go fill my people in."

"Good luck. I'll see you tomorrow?"

"Count on it," Ella answered.

Ella watched Justine leave her unit and come toward her. Her assistant never complained about the long hours. Like Ella herself, Justine seemed to thrive on police work. It was free time that they had difficulty handling.

Ella filled her team in, and then watched as they brought out floodlights and began working the area. Neskahi assisted, as he often had in the past. Ella examined the blanket and the saddle, looking for cockleburs or something that might have upset the animal earlier. Finding nothing, she led the horse away, staying on the harder ground and traveling in a straight line, making sure that she didn't obliterate any clues or tracks in the process.

After putting the animal in a corral adjacent to the house, she returned to join her team. Harry moved with his usual unerring intuition finding clues where no one else would have thought to look. She saw him sketching the pattern of hoof marks on the ground, then measuring the strides and entering them onto his drawing. He knew, as she did, that a spooked horse would change its stride, and maybe even rear and come down hard, making deeper impressions on the ground. They might also duck their heads to unseat a rider, and that would leave a distinctive pattern as well.

Ella stood beside him. "What do the tracks tell you?"

"There's no sign here that the horse did much except walk at an even rate. There are also no drag marks from a rider with a foot caught in the stirrup. If we are to believe she fell, then the way it happened was that the horse was walking, stopped, and the woman flew off, landing about five feet away face down. Considering Elisa's skill as a horsewoman, that just doesn't seem likely."

"Make sure you say all that in your report. And keep up the good work," Ella added. The tribe would be hard-pressed to find someone with Harry's eye for detail and his love of the job. She felt a twinge of frustration, knowing that only he could decide whether to stay or go, and there was nothing she could do to sway him one way or another.

Justine walked the cordoned-off perimeter alongside Officer Tache. Together, in a spiraling pattern, they searched the ground methodically.

Ella approached them, staying in their tracks. "Anything?"

"I'm sure that the area around where the victim was laying was swept clean of tracks—though it was skillfully done. Someone used a branch to eradicate the trail then dusted the ground with sand. We used to do that as kids when we were playing. I recognize the technique," Tache said. "Someone's playing us and the evidence here."

"I made plaster casts of some boot-prints we found up by the road," Justine said. "I'm working from memory, so I may be wrong, but they look like a match in size and type to the ones we found where the sniper ambushed you. They don't match the ones the victim's husband is wearing either. I checked. Brown-hat's feet are smaller."

"So, what the evidence is telling us is that someone was here with the victim, and that whoever it was wanted to hide that fact," Ella said. "Also, this person knows how to obscure his trail."

"Unless she was murdered, it isn't likely anyone would go through all that trouble," Justine said.

"Let's not jump to conclusions," Ella said. "It's also possible that there was an accident, and whoever was with her didn't want to get blamed or didn't want it known that he was here with her. It could have been someone with something entirely different to hide."

"Like what?"

"An affair, maybe, or any of a dozen other possibilities."

"So, you don't think it was murder?" Justine pressed.

"It probably was, but I think we have to keep our minds open," Ella said. "Don't overlook any possibility until we know something for sure."

"There's something else you should know right now that could figure into this. I got a fax from the clinic, and Myrna Manus gave me a list of all the patients whose files had been stolen. She also said that the pregnancy tests results had already been placed in the file folders, though not every patient with a stolen file had a pregnancy test run. So, whoever took the files in the break-in kept just the pregnancy test results." Justine kept her voice low.

"Let me guess. Mrs. Brownhat's file was one of those that was taken." Ella wondered if Myrna had mentioned her own test as well. "Did Mrs. Brownhat have a pregnancy test run?" She asked.

"Myrna wouldn't say. She told me that any other information

would remain confidential unless you got a court order or every patient's permission." Justine shrugged. "I just thought it was too coincidental not to mention."

"You did the right thing. Let's wait and see what information I can get from the husband first."

Ella went inside the house, leaving her team to finish processing the area. They'd be returning tomorrow in the light of day to make sure they hadn't overlooked something.

The problem right now was what to tell John Brownhat. He would demand answers, but she couldn't give him much without compromising the investigation. She also didn't know if she should mention the pregnancy tests, especially when she didn't know if his wife had even had one done.

As she approached the house, John came out to the porch and waved at her to come inside.

Ella followed him into the living room, then sat down on an old, wood-framed couch.

John's expression was unguarded and sorrow was naked on his face. "Someone murdered her while I was at work," he said, still in shock.

"I think you may be right," Ella said, "but we need to get more evidence together before I can tell you anything for sure."

He nodded "I want to know who did this," he said in a whisper. "Find him."

Ella nodded. "Can you think of anyone who may have wanted to do her harm?"

John took a deep breath. "My wife had her own way of doing things, and she wasn't good at holding her tongue, even when the situation begged for it."

Ella said nothing as he lapsed into silence. Eventually, he continued.

"Last week we were at a Chapter House meeting. She spoke against what she called the 'stranglehold' our traditionalists had on The People. As you can imagine, since those meetings are filled mostly with traditionalists, her views got some people really angry."

"Anyone in particular?"

"Billy Pete was there, and they got into a shouting match after the meeting. My wife called him a brainless sheep, following the one with the bell, and he wasn't too happy with that."

"Do you think Billy could have killed her, or made her fall somehow?"

He shrugged. "I don't know. But, if he did, I want him to go to jail until he's too old to walk."

"He will—if he's guilty," Ella assured him.

"Is there anyone else she may have met—planned to go horse-back riding with, for example?"

· Brownhat considered it for a long time, then shook his head. "I don't think so, but I don't know. You see, my wife and I were satisfied with our marriage, but we seldom spoke about what we did when we weren't together. She trained and broke horses during the day to make extra money, and I work at the new coal mine. By nightfall we were both too tired to do much of anything except have dinner, watch a little TV, then go to bed."

"I'll let you know if we uncover anything important," Ella told him, standing up. "And you know where to reach me if you think of something that may help us out." She left her card on the coffee table and started toward the door.

"My wife wasn't the most popular woman around here," John said as he joined her at the door, "but I loved her, and she didn't deserve this. Not now, especially," he added.

"What do you mean, 'not now'?" Ella asked, suspecting she already knew the answer.

"We were finally going to have our first child. For years and years she tried to get pregnant, but luck wasn't with us. Then after we'd given up all hope, it happened. We had so many plans, but now . . ."

"I'm so sorry," she said. His sorrow and regret cut right through her and she fought not to shed a tear.

"Find whoever did this," he said. "Give me that, at least."

Ella had to clear her throat first before speaking. "I will. You can count on it."

FOURTEEN

———— ✖ ✖ ✖ ————

As she stepped out of the
house, she saw Harry Ute conferring with Justine and Tache. Ella
wondered if she looked as exhausted as they all did.

Forcing herself to focus solely on the case, she approached her
team. "You'll all be back at dawn? This man has animals to tend
and graze, and he probably starts early, working at the mine and
all. We know he'll avoid the taped perimeter, but his animals
may not."

Tache nodded. "I'll be here at daybreak. I've done the best I
can with the bad lighting conditions, but there's no telling what
kind of quality or detail the photos I took will have."

Harry Ute and Justine both agreed to be on hand at daybreak
as well.

"We'll meet in my office at nine tomorrow, and review everything we have. Let's see if we can come up with some leads to follow." Ella looked at their weary expressions. "You're all doing a
terrific job. I'm very proud to be working with you."

Their faces perked up considerably as they all joined in to
stow away their equipment, and Ella knew they'd needed to hear
that. Sometimes she forgot to tell them how valuable they were to

the tribe. Maybe it would have made a difference with Harry if she'd remembered to do that more often.

After everything was put away, Justine walked with Ella to their units. "I knew Elisa," Justine said. "She was magic with the horses, but she also had an uncanny ability for getting people really pissed off."

"So I've heard. There was a ruckus at the Chapter House meeting last week. Get me something on that. Apparently she had a run-in with Billy Pete."

Justine raised her eyebrows. "Billy's many things, Cousin, but he's no killer."

"Check it out anyway. There are some really weird things happening on the Rez right now and people are changing."

"Billy couldn't hurt anyone, not like that."

Her words were so firm and resolute, Ella felt a prickle at the base of her spine. "Is there something I should know about?"

Justine hesitated. "It's personal."

"If your personal life touches any of our cases, I want to know. It ceases to be only your concern when it's linked with your professional duties," she said a little more harshly than she'd meant.

Justine eyes grew wide and she looked instantly contrite. "Of course. Maybe I should have told you before, but it didn't seem to matter then."

"*Told me what?*" she demanded, out of patience.

"I've been dating Billy Pete."

Had Justine told her that she'd planned to run away on an alien spacecraft, it couldn't have surprised her more.

"When the heck did all this happen?"

"We've been dating for a few weeks. Remember when things were really slow, and we were all trying to find ways to stay busy?"

Ella nodded.

"Billy came over to see my brother Leonard, but he was gone and we sat up almost all night talking. It turns out we have a lot in common. It was nice," she said, averting her gaze, embarrassed. "And it got nicer."

"You're not pregnant, are you?" Ella could have kicked herself for asking that particular question. It was really none of her business, and she'd only thought of it because the subject was on her own mind constantly now.

Justine gave her a startled look. "Good grief, no!" she blurted, then laughed. "I'm not ready for kids, not by a long shot."

At least that was one thing she didn't have to worry about. Ella breathed a sigh of relief, promising to herself to avoid that topic around those who didn't know about her yet.

"But I do know Billy and, believe me, he's no killer."

"Have you ever discussed any of our cases with him?" Ella asked pointedly.

"I *never* name names or get specific, but, yeah, sometimes we talk about things—in general terms," Justine said.

"Stop doing that from this point on," Ella said, hoping that the feeling she was getting was way off the mark.

"He won't discuss our private conversations with anyone else," Justine assured her.

"Our business *is* confidential, and since Billy's name has come up on several occasions during the investigation, you have to treat him accordingly. He's a suspect, Justine, or at least a potentially important witness. Don't kid yourself."

Hurt and anger flashed in Justine's eyes. "I'll do my duty, Special Investigator Clah, but you're sorely mistaken if you think he's capable of doing something like this. Billy Pete is a man of principle."

"I don't doubt that you believe that, but you now have a professional responsibility to follow my orders on this matter."

As Justine strode back to her own vehicle, Ella felt a cold chill envelop her. Although her cousin and assistant was a good cop, she was still young and in a lot of ways, naive. If Billy Pete was involved with the Fierce Ones as they all suspected, it wasn't exactly a leap to think he was using Justine to find out what the police were doing and how their investigations were progressing.

It was too late tonight to go track him down, but she intended to talk to Billy the second she had a chance. She wanted to make a few things crystal clear to him about her cousin.

Angry that she had missed something as important as this, though she spent more time with Justine than she did with her own mother, Ella drove across town to the hospital. She needed to talk to Carolyn, both as the tribe's ME and as a friend. Carolyn was the only person Ella knew who would never, under any circumstances, become associated with any of the factions at war in the tribe. Carolyn was a law onto herself.

Ella stepped out of the elevator at the hospital. Everything had been renovated here lately. The faint smell of paint still lingered in the cold corridors that led to the morgue, and she felt a slight wave of nausea. She wondered if it was the beginning of morning sickness, or just a manifestation of the heightened senses she'd been experiencing lately.

And, as she drew near to Carolyn's office another, unmistakable scent filled the air. It always reminded her of the inside of a refrigerator when something stored there had gone bad. It wasn't overwhelming, just inescapable. And, curiously enough, it didn't really stay on her clothing after she left the place, though she would continue to smell it for a while, like a bad memory that lingered.

For any Navajo working here day after day, the job could be punishing, but for Carolyn it was simply a debt she paid daily to the tribe that had financed her medical education.

As Ella walked inside the cluttered office next to the morgue, she found Carolyn at her desk.

"I haven't even begun the autopsy, and I'm having dinner now, so don't start with me. It's past dinner time, I'm hungry and crabby, and in no mood."

"Yes, ma'am." She eyed Carolyn's egg salad sandwich with envy. "That looks good."

Carolyn gave her a surprised look. "You haven't been able to even chew gum in here in the past. You must be starving if this sandwich is tempting you."

"I am," Ella said with a sigh. "Can we go upstairs to the cafeteria? I really need to put something in my stomach. I've been feeling queasy lately."

"Sure," Carolyn said, putting her sandwich in her in-and-out file, and walking out into the hall with Ella. "But don't tell me you came over here at this hour just so you can share hospital food," she added as they entered the elevator.

"I wanted to talk to you."

"Business or personal?"

"Both."

Carolyn nodded. "Yeah, it's hard to separate things like that, isn't it?"

Ella sighed. "What's worse is that I just got all over my assistant's case for that same reason."

"Your cousin Justine?"

"Seems she's been dating a person who's become a suspect. And, I've got to tell you Carolyn, it makes my skin crawl. I have a strong feeling she's being used. The worst part is that she thinks she's in love."

Carolyn grimaced. "And you're feeling protective of her, I gather. It's hard to mind your own business, or keep it strictly business, when you suspect someone you care about is being used."

"I like her, and not just because we're related. If I'm right about what's going on, I'm going to wring the guy's scrawny neck. I don't care how noble his intent is—the end does not justify the means, not in my book anyway."

Carolyn nodded slowly. "Do you realize that just a few weeks ago, we were all trying to fill our time because things were so slow. Now we're all working to capacity and then some?"

Ella nodded as they walked down the hall. "Yeah, but you know, I prefer it this way. I feel ... useful. You know what I mean?"

"Sure. We're not in our respective lines of work because we like free time. If we'd been looking for that, we'd have chosen different careers. But there's something ugly going on right now. Even I can feel it and let's face it, I usually stick solely to facts I can measure and weigh."

"I know exactly what you're talking about, Carolyn. Too many weird things are happening—people who are normally peaceful acting out of character, problems with the livestock, and murders with evidence that only adds to the confusion instead of solving the crime. I haven't been able to get any of it out of my mind. But I have to admit that it hit me hard when I learned that Elisa Brownhat thought she was pregnant. Her file was taken in the clinic break-in, and apparently the record of that test was stolen. As a matter of fact, all the pregnancy test results were stolen. It was only by accident that we were able to retrieve the files and discover that little detail."

Carolyn gave her a surprised look. "Just the pregnancy tests? That's odd. I'll verify if she was pregnant, and let you know. But does that tie into her murder, or provide some kind of motive?"

"I don't know. But that infant never had a chance and that makes me sick."

Carolyn said nothing, but her eagle-sharp eyes remained on Ella.

As they joined the cafeteria line, Ella took the beef enchilada plate, the salad, and milk. She still couldn't quite get over the fact that she was actually drinking cow's milk. It certainly wasn't a drink most Navajos normally sought out, and it had never been something she particularly liked. It was supposed to be too early in her pregnancy to have cravings, so she wrote it off as an instinctive urge to eat a better balanced diet for the baby.

By the time she reached the cashier at the end of the line, her tray included sliced peaches and a banana.

"Boy, you really are hungry," Carolyn said.

"Yeah. I've been running around like crazy, and I never get a chance to eat a decent meal, particularly a balanced one. Today was even worse than usual."

"Have you heard about the other livestock problems? I mean besides what people have been doing to each other's animals."

"No, what's going on?"

"Apparently a rash of deformities has shown up in newborn chickens, ducks, and rabbits. The county extension agent paid us a visit. He's looking into it because the incidence rate is way up, and he wanted to know if we'd also seen an unusual upswing of birth defects here at the hospital."

"Have you?"

"Nope. Our numbers on that are no higher than usual. Of course, the gestation periods of the farm animals we're talking about is roughly a month, give or take a few days."

"What do you think is causing this problem?" Ella asked. Unlike the traditionalists who undoubtedly had their own theories by now, Carolyn would never blame anything on the esoteric, and right now she was interested in cold, hard facts.

"It could be anything from a statistical fluke, to bad breeding habits or poor stock selection among locals."

Ella said nothing. A sense of disquiet ate at her, but she pushed it aside, attributing it to a flux in her hormones.

"I've known you for a very long time, and I can tell when you're holding back on me. What is it that you're not saying?"

"You're right. There's something I haven't told you, but I'd like you to keep this under wraps for now."

"You've got it."

"I'm pregnant."

Carolyn's eyes grew wide, and she opened her mouth to speak, but then closed it again. "I'm speechless."

"That's a first."

"How did this happen?"

"The usual way, Doctor," Ella teased.

Carolyn laughed. "Wow. I can't believe this. It would explain your queasiness lately, though. Are you happy about it, or pulling your hair out by the roots?"

"Both," she said. "I admit I was careless, and it certainly wasn't planned. But, you know, I'm really glad things turned out this way."

"Is Kevin the dad? He's the only guy you've ever been even remotely serious about since you came back to the Rez."

"Yes, it's Kevin. The poor man is still trying to figure out how to take the news. He wanted to get married when I told him, but there's no way that's going to happen. When we first started to date, all I could see were the things we had in common, but, as time went by, what we *didn't* have in common overshadowed everything else. He can play as big a part in the baby's life as he wants, but marriage between us wouldn't work in the long run."

Carolyn nodded, and then leaned forward, resting her elbows on the table. "I want the baby to know me as Aunt Carolyn. I assume you won't have any objections to that."

Realizing it hadn't been a question, Ella laughed. "Why do I get the feeling that if I said no, you'd start reciting a list of the favors I owe you?" She raised a hand, stemming Carolyn's reply. "Of course you'll be Aunt Carolyn. You're a dear friend of mine. What's part of my life is also part of yours." Ella paused. "Of course when I ask you to baby-sit for the umpteenth time, you may change your mind."

"Never."

Ella sighed, finishing the last bit of her meal. "But now you know why all these deaths are weighing me down. I want my child born during a time of harmony, not during a time of trouble. I hope I can close those cases out before then."

"Not to mention that it would be really handy if you could take off work the last trimester and make things easier on yourself."

Ella smiled. Carolyn always had a gift for getting to the heart of the matter. "Taking time off until the last possible moment is out of the question. I'm always juggling too many cases, and there's no one who can take over. On top of everything else, Harry Ute is thinking of quitting and going to work for the feds."

"That man has been on the Rez all his life," she said. "That's probably why he wants to do something different for a change."

"I guess, but it's going to make things really tough for me."

"Does he know you're pregnant and will need maternity leave?"

"Not many people know I'm pregnant. Just Kevin, Mom, and you. And Wilson, who found out by accident."

"Big Ed's going to be delighted, no doubt," she said wryly.

"Yeah. I have a feeling I'm going to need a spatula to scrape him off the ceiling," Ella said.

Carolyn checked her watch, then stood up. "I better get back to work. If you want autopsy reports anytime soon, I'm going to have to start tonight. With luck I may have something for you by tomorrow."

"I need some leads—badly," Ella said.

"I'll see what I can do for you."

Ella watched her friend go, then stood and walked out to her tribal unit. Looking at her watch in the glow of the parking lot light, she realized it was a bit past nine. She considered going to Jesse Woody's before calling it quits tonight since this was such a good time to catch him at home. As one of the few Navajo supervisors at the mines, and also the current leader of the Fierce Ones, he was usually busy during the day and evenings. Tired but not in the least bit sleepy, Ella decided to head out to his house, and see if she could catch up to him there.

Ella verified his address with the PD then sped down the darkened highway. Pushing her worries back into the far corners of her mind, she concentrated on the empty road, which was illuminated only by the vehicle's headlights and the full moon.

Ella arrived at Jesse Woody's home an hour later and was surprised to see so many vehicles parked there. She glanced at the cars and pickups, checking to see if any looked familiar. In the dark, it was hard to see them all. The lights were on inside the low wood-framed house and she could hear loud voices. Wondering if she had inadvertently come at a time when the Fierce Ones were meeting, she left her unit to see for herself.

As she started up the stone outlined path to the front door, Jesse Woody came out and met her.

"What brings you here tonight, Investigator? Surely no one complained about the noise. Our home is at least five miles from our closest neighbor."

Ella noticed that the sound level inside had suddenly dropped. "Am I interrupting something?" Ella asked.

"Just a small gathering of friends dropping by."

"A weekday party, is that it?"

"You bet. Now what can I do for you?"

Ella opened the envelope in her hand, brought out a pocket flashlight, and showed him a photo of the man she'd been forced to shoot and kill at the landfill. "I understand that you know this man."

Jesse looked at the photo, pushed her flashlight aside, and took a step back. "You know better than to bring something like that here."

"Keep in mind that I could have asked you to view the body instead of just the photo. Now talk to me. Do you know him?"

"No."

"Think again, very carefully this time. Obstructing justice is a serious offense, and could result in some jail time for you."

Jesse met her gaze with a steely one of his own. "If you already know the answer, then why bother asking me?"

"I want his name—not the name he went by, his *real* name."

Jesse gave her a startled look. "I'm not sure what you mean. He told me his name was Tom LaPoint."

"Where did he work?"

Jesse shrugged. "Maybe nowhere. He came by the mine several times during the past few weeks, and tried to get me to hire him. I didn't formally interview him or consider him for a job because he never filed an employee application."

"Do you usually fraternize with people who are asking you for a job?" she asked, playing a bluff.

Jesse's eyes narrowed. "Be more specific."

"I have a better idea. You start being more specific, and I won't haul you to the station in Shiprock."

His expression hardened. "Don't threaten me."

"It wasn't a threat. It's a guarantee. Ask anyone inside if I ever bluff."

Jesse said nothing for several long moments. "I saw him at the mine on a few occasions, as I said. The only other time I met him was once when I took my horse for a ride out into the desert. The guy was out there in an old pickup, driving up and down the dry arroyos, passing the time. He followed me home afterwards, which I didn't like. I wanted him away from here, so I accepted his invitation to meet him at the Totah Cafe. We had a cup of coffee, then I left."

"What did you two talk about?"

"He was curious about life on the Rez. He said I was lucky because I would always have a place to call home and that was something a lot of people didn't have these days. I reminded him that the U.S. government restricted us to this place a long time ago, and that it wasn't our choice to live on a reservation. He then talked a bit about freedom for minorities, but, as he spoke, I got the distinct impression that this was the last place on earth he wanted to be. As he said repeatedly, he didn't belong here. I finally asked him why he stuck around and, after a few moments of thinking about it, he told me that, for now, this was where he was supposed to be."

"What the heck does that mean?"

"Beats me. Maybe he was getting metaphysical. I just wanted to go home, and asking him would have meant staying even longer at the Totah Cafe."

"You really have no idea what he was referring to?"

"No, I don't, and I'm being honest with you. The guy was a weird one. He struck me as one of these dispossessed people who wants to be part of something, but has no idea what. So they go from one thing to the next without any kind of plan or direction."

Ella nodded. She'd met people like that before. "Thanks for your help."

Ella was about to call it a night when her brother Clifford came out of the house and walked over to them.

"Sister," he said, then glanced at Jesse. "I think she should come in and hear what's been happening."

Jesse shook his head. "She's your sister, but she's also a cop. Tonight she's here on business, not as a friend."

"The police department is not our enemy," Clifford said calmly, then looked at Ella. "Come inside with us."

Ella looked at Jesse, who nodded curtly, obviously still against the idea, but unwilling to argue with Clifford about it.

When Ella stepped inside the Woody's home, she saw several men she recognized, including Billy Pete. At least four of them were wearing knives at their belts. It wasn't uncommon out here for men to have hunting or folding knives with them, but it made her a bit edgy. Someone who looked like Jimmie Herder was in the kitchen, but she only caught a glimpse before he stepped back out of her view.

"Tonight, we met here as friends who share the same concern," Clifford said. "Nothing more."

Ella understood the warning not to bring up the Fierce Ones, or mention them as a group.

"Lilly Mae Atso came by here several days ago and spoke to Jesse," Clifford said. "She was very worried because she'd taken her goats to the fairgrounds to feed on the hay and grain leftover from the livestock show and, while there, noticed a lot of dead insects and some baby birds that had died in their nest. She was convinced that the fairgrounds have become evil and wanted us to warn others."

"Remember that the Anglo man from the plant got killed in the parking lot not far from there," Jesse said.

"What makes you think these things are related?" Ella asked.

"You know better than to ask that," Clifford clipped.

"She doesn't see the link because she believes, like many others, that *we* had something to do with that Anglo's death," Jesse spat out, disgusted. "But that's just not true. We want Navajos to get the high-paying jobs on the reservation, but we don't kill people in order to make that happen."

"Relax. I haven't accused anyone," Ella said firmly.

"Let me continue and maybe you'll begin to see the connections," Clifford said. "Evil corrupts and that's exactly what's been happening. Our people have started turning against each other and traditionalists are blamed for a lot of things we know they couldn't have done."

"You're talking about the livestock killings, right?" Seeing her brother nod, she added, "Do you have any evidence that proves the traditionalists in question were framed?" she asked.

"Not your type of evidence, but do you realize that every single instance of violence tracks back to the fairgrounds in one way or another?"

"The animals were killed on their owner's property."

"Yes, but all the people involved in the trouble were present at the fairgrounds exhibition at one point or another during the two-day event."

"I know. They were competing against each other and, as I understand it, the main source of contention seems to be the methods used to breed and raise the animals. But trying to link the violence to the fairgrounds itself is reaching."

Clifford shook his head. "The evil that's at work there fosters violence. Each one of those people is gentle by nature. Can't you see that there's more working here than mere differences of opinion?"

"I'm a cop, and I deal only with hard facts, not spiritual beliefs. If you want me to look into something specific . . ."

"I'm telling you what you need to do to find answers, Sister. You can't just focus on one aspect. Look beyond that—"

Ella held up her hand, and nodded. "I'll check out the fairgrounds and look things over. But I think you're refusing to see what's right in front of you. Since the beginning of time, opposing viewpoints have made people do a lot of crazy things." She paused, looking at the hostile faces of those around her. "Will there be a Blessingway done at the fairgrounds?"

Clifford shook his head. "Not yet. We need to know more about what we're facing."

Ella didn't comment. They were all chasing shadows, but that's the way it often was with mysticism of any kind.

"I promise I'll check out the area and see what I can find. Just remember that I'm dealing with people who are *killing* livestock."

"What about the dead insects and birds?" Clifford insisted. "How do you explain that?"

"A soil contaminant?" she suggested. "I don't have an answer for you yet, but when I do, I'll let you know."

She didn't believe in esoteric evil, but whenever wildlife started dying for no discernible reason it merited a closer look.

Maybe there was a link between that and the deformities affecting newborn livestock.

None of this exonerated the Fierce Ones, however. They were still suspects. It was entirely possible that they'd contaminated the soil themselves so they could blame LabKote. If that were the case, she knew they would have selected a contaminant of short duration, then used the ensuing crisis to blame LabKote. Citizens would have rallied behind the Fierce Ones and, as an extra bonus, they would have been asked to deal with whatever "evil" had been unleashed there. By the time they had the right ceremonies performed, the contaminant would have broken down and they'd come out as the good guys. They would have accomplished their goal of shutting down the plant by turning people against it, and then used The People's own fears to force them to embrace the old ways more closely.

If that was their plan, though, what part did they want her to play in it? Were they going to try and use her to implicate LabKote and add legitimacy to their plot?

"Look into this, then let me know what you learn," Clifford said, interrupting her thoughts.

"All right," she said, giving her brother a long, thoughtful look. Did Clifford realize how bad things were beginning to appear for his group? Somehow she doubted it. He had a tendency to see only what he wanted to see. She doubted he was aware of even half the possibilities running through her mind. "I'll have the county lab techs do a workup. Maybe somebody at the fairgrounds just misused some bug spray."

"See it through yourself," Clifford warned. "The Anglos who work for the county don't care—they *can't* care—not like we do. This is *our* land, the *Diné Tah*, and it's up to us to find the answers."

Ella said nothing, but noticed the nods and general agreement on the faces of the others. To try and explain to them that the county people knew their jobs was useless right now. All she'd do was stir up more ill will for the PD. "I'll look into this myself, but they'll have to run the tests. That's out of my field."

"Understood."

There was another possibility she had to consider, too. It was possible that LabKote *had* leaked something into the soil. But if that turned out to be the case, it would be a separate problem altogether. A spill on the fairgrounds still wouldn't exonerate Norma, Nancy, or the others who had gone after each other's livestock or property. It would be just one more problem to face, on top of the kidnapping, the murders, and the rest of the strife between the traditionalists and the modernists.

Leaving the gathering, Ella drove back home. It was past eleven when she entered her house and all was quiet. Trying not to wake her mother, she walked down the hall silently, then almost tripped over Two, who was lying there in the dark.

As she opened the bedroom door, he trotted in and jumped on the bed. Ella undressed and, wearing an old FBI Academy sweatshirt, started to crawl into bed. Realizing, however, that she wasn't at all sleepy, she changed her mind, stood up, and went to her computer.

After answering E-mail from friends, she switched to a computer puzzle game Wilson had given her a few months ago. The software took a photograph scanned into the computer, reduced it to components of varying sizes and shapes, then disassembled them. It then became a computer jigsaw puzzle that Ella had to reconstruct. After several weeks of work, her favorite landscape photo of Shiprock was emerging slowly on her computer screen.

As she worked, Ella wondered how long it would take before she'd be able to piece together all the things happening on the Rez and get a clear picture that would reveal the truth.

FIFTEEN

—— ✖ ✖ ✖ ——

Ella was up and on the road again the next morning after an early breakfast with Rose. The sun was just coming up as she drove north toward Ship Rock and the turn-off to the Brownhat residence. It was crisp outside, but still too early in the year for the first frost of fall.

As she topped a low hill, Ella noticed an old green pickup by the road, the hood up. She slowed, looking for the driver, and noticed an elderly man farther ahead, walking toward town.

Giving someone a ride if they needed it was still common on the Rez, despite the warnings against picking up hitchhikers. As an officer, she usually tried to help out unless she was on a call. Ella drove up beside the old man and saw that it was Atsidi Benally, one of the men Abigail Yellowhair had mentioned as an enemy of her kidnapped husband.

Justine had already spoken to the man and he had an alibi, but Ella decided that this would be a good time to talk to him herself. It was hard to imagine Atsidi kidnapping anyone, or being involved in something like that. He looked thin and frail, though he was probably a lot stronger than many men over the age of sixty-five.

"Need a ride into town, Uncle?" she asked, using the term to denote respect, not kinship. "I see your pickup decided not to go all the way this morning."

"I thought I recognized your Jeep," Atsidi stopped, catching his breath. "How's your mother?"

"Getting stronger every day, Uncle. She's going to be using that cane for firewood this time next year." Ella knew that Atsidi respected Rose for her work with the Plant People, and for maintaining her traditional beliefs as much as she had, though Ella's father had been a Christian preacher.

"If I catch a ride to the first gas station, do I have to wear handcuffs?" Atsidi joked, coming around to the passenger side and getting in. "Your policemen have asked many questions about that weasel senator who got himself kidnapped. If you didn't drive this way everyday yourself, I might have thought your stopping to help was no coincidence."

"I know you and the senator have had your troubles. I don't care too much for the man myself, if the truth be known." Ella nodded, checking for oncoming traffic, then pulling back out onto the highway. She noted the smell of piñon and smoke on the old man's flannel shirt, and thought instantly of the many traditionalists who, like him, still used wood and coal stoves for heating and cooking. It was a pleasant smell, which spoke of history.

"I heard that your brother, the *hataalii*, has gotten himself mixed up with those gangsters who act like cops without badges. No offense, of course." Atsidi observed, shaking his head slowly.

"None taken. We've talked about it, as you may have also heard. The Fierce Ones are no longer keeping their identities a secret. Do you think that will make them more sympathetic to The People?" Ella knew Atsidi was against any secret organizations, but had supported many traditional movements. He was a natural leader, and people listened to what he had to say, especially at Chapter House meetings.

"The People can't be forced to follow the old ways. It has to be a matter of choice. The Fierce Ones work like many Anglo groups who try to use fear to make others follow them, but there are better ways to accomplish the good they're trying to do."

"Like kidnapping?"

"Force is not the answer," Benally repeated more firmly this time.

Ella believed him. His words held the ring of truth.

"You can stop here," Atsidi motioned with his head toward the grocery store and gas station at the intersection just ahead, outside Shiprock. "Maybe I can return the favor if you ever have a problem with your fancy police car."

Ella pulled over, and Atsidi climbed out with a grunt, shutting the door a little too hard, something probably learned from habit in his own weather-beaten truck.

Ella waited until he crossed the road in front of her, then turned around and drove off in the direction she'd come. She'd passed where the Brownhat's lived, but this short visit with Atsidi Benally had at least eliminated him in her mind as an accomplice in the Yellowhair kidnapping. It just wasn't his style. He was too direct. Of course, there was always the possibility that the old man was as good at fooling her as he was at leading the traditionalists.

Later, after another hour at the Brownhat scene, her crime scene team met for their morning meeting. Ella looked at the somber faces around her. Although no hard evidence pointing conclusively to murder had been found at the site, they all agreed that John Brownhat had been right about the nature of his wife's death.

"How long before we have the autopsy report?" Ralph Tache asked.

"Dr. Roanhorse will call as soon as she has something. She knows that time is crucial to us," Ella said.

"Where should we focus the next phase of our investigation?" Harry asked.

"I want you to talk to her friends. Question anyone she was close to, and get everything that led up to the confrontation she had with Billy Pete at the Chapter House meeting." She looked at Tache. "I want you to concentrate on finding a link between the break-in at the clinic and Elisa. I have reason to believe that Elisa was pregnant, though that hasn't been confirmed. Her file was one of those taken during the break-in, and all the pregnancy results from those records are still missing. See what other connections you can dig up. For example, was she seeing a traditionalist who might have resented her going to the clinic?"

"You mean was she having an affair with one?" Justine asked.

"Find out. I want a connection, folks. Dig one out, if it exists. And remember not to let the kidnapping get far from your thoughts. We'll have to give that our time, as well."

Tache and Ute walked out, but Ella called Justine back.

"Wait. Before you get started checking on Elisa, I want you to come and help me with something else." Ella filled her in on what she'd learned at the meeting the night before.

"I don't get it. What exactly do you want to do at the fairgrounds?"

"I'm going to call Wilson, and have him meet us there. I want to look over the area with a fine-tooth comb and take soil and water samples."

"Big Ed would have your butt in a sling if he found out. That's not our jurisdiction. You should have the county environmental or health people do that."

"I know it seems like someone else's job, but it's also part of the unrest on the reservation right now, and something we have to take into account when we're looking for motives for the crimes we're trying to solve, including the kidnapping." She paused then added, "I also want to stay high profile when we go out there so the people at LabKote will see us. Let's see what kind of trouble we can stir up. If they've done something wrong, I want to make them squirm."

"I just hope we can find some answers that'll help us figure out what's been going on," Justine said.

"I hate to even contemplate the thought that the Fierce Ones may have put something in the soil to blame LabKote, but if we find a contaminant, at least people will stop going at each other for a while—and that'll give us some time to prove where it came from," Ella said.

"I can't see how the Fierce Ones would benefit from doing something like that. If people believed that LabKote leaked something from the plant onto the ground, then things would blow up and get even nastier. The traditionalists would blame the progressives and it would become an open war."

"If there's a contaminant there, I really doubt that LabKote's to blame. They'd know something like this would be tracked back to them, and no one there is stupid. They would have cleaned it up pronto. Plus, from my knowledge of what they do, I don't think they use toxic chemicals. It's mostly a sterilizing plant, and they don't even use chemical disinfectants to achieve that goal, they use radiation."

Justine's eyes narrowed and she started to speak, then stopped.

"Go on," Ella prodded.

"I don't think this is the case, mind you, but adding to your train of thought, what if the Fierce Ones have someone on the inside? It's possible they could frame LabKote without the supervisors even knowing about it."

"You mean if they've managed to get one of their own hired by the plant?" Ella expelled her breath in a hiss. "I think I saw Jimmie Herder at the meeting, come to think about it. The amount of harm one of those men could do, if they got in the right position, is considerable. I wonder what Jimmie has access to?"

Justine shuddered. "Jimmie may not end up being the only insider at LabKote. You know the Fierce Ones are pushing to replace Hansen with a Navajo. Do you think they've got someone in mind?"

"I don't know, but start looking into it."

Justine and Ella met forty minutes later at the gravel parking lot west of the fairgrounds exhibit hall. Not too many months earlier, the area had been the site of youth gang violence, and Ella remembered one particular incident just like it was yesterday. Shots had been fired between two rival gangs in cars, the Fierce Ones had tried to put a stop to it by ramming the cars with a dump truck, and one vehicle had overturned, injuring several young men. She's had the place staked out, and had been able to react fast enough to prevent further violence.

"Where's Wilson?" Justine called out as she stepped out of her department vehicle. "Am I early?"

"Right on time, actually," Ella confirmed by looking at her watch.

"Wilson called me on my cell phone. He was just getting into his pickup. Apparently he had some trouble locating the sample bottles he wanted. They had to be sterile, and that meant going through some new inventory in the science storeroom at the college. It was donated by LabKote, by the way."

"I could have brought some from the department lab if I'd known. The only thing I ended up bringing was my camera so we can document the sites from where the samples are taken." Justine looked back toward her unit, and confirmed that the camera was on the seat. "Good thing biology and ecology are Wilson's fields of training, because this isn't something I've been taught to do."

"This is the type of puzzle Wilson enjoys, too, so he was eager to get involved. He insisted on supplying everything we needed since we're going to fund the analysis out of our budget." Ella brushed back her long hair, fastening it into a ponytail with a silver barrette.

"Here he comes now," Justine gestured toward the battered old pickup Wilson still drove to work. "Ever notice how many teachers around here, even college professors, drive old Ford and Chevy trucks. Is that the Rez in them speaking, do you think?"

"Wilson says it helps make him a good role model for his students. It lets them know that if they want to be rich someday, teaching isn't the profession for them," Ella said, laughing as Wilson drove up beside them.

"Not too many Cadillacs in the police parking lot either. Know how a Navajo cop gains social status?" Justine repeated a common department joke.

"They marry a New Mexico teacher." Ella echoed along with Justine as Wilson stepped out of his truck.

"Hi, ladies. What's this about New Mexico teachers? Another poverty joke?" Wilson looked back and forth between the two women cops.

"Enough talk about money," Ella said, then winked at Wilson. "We're police officers and teachers because we're dedicated. Right, Professor? Money doesn't matter to us."

"If you really believe that, there's definitely something alien in the environment and it's affecting your brain function. Shall we find out what it is?" Wilson reached into his truck and brought out a detailed topographic map of the area, unfolding it on the hood of his pickup.

"What's the plan?" Ella moved over beside Wilson, and Justine joined them.

Five minutes later, all three were gathering samples according to Wilson's predetermined strategy. Wilson would place a length of wire with a labeled card attached into the ground, and Justine would take a reference photo with a building or ground feature visible. Ella would then collect soil samples while Justine took a few leaves or blades of grass from the closest plant.

Wilson concentrated on finding small dead animals to bottle. He collected grasshoppers, bugs, and spiders, then located a bird's nest in an eave of the exhibit hall. Inside were two dead hatchlings. Those went in their own labeled container, too.

After taking samples in every quadrant, including several spots around the agricultural building and display hall, they moved closer to LabKote's fence. Drainage patterns showed where the most recent rains had run off, and samples were taken there as well.

Working together, they gathered around a clump of grass growing next to the fence where water had collected after draining off the roof. Wilson inserted a wire "flag," and Justine stepped back to take a photo of the location.

Ella, out of the viewing field of the camera, noticed a LabKote guard walking in their direction and cleared her throat.

Justine took the photo, then lowered the camera.

"Just what the hell are you three up to?" The Anglo officer growled, resting the palm of his hand on the butt of his holstered pistol. "This is a restricted area, and you could get severely injured if you touch the fence. Can't you see the signs?" He pointed to a red warning sign in English, Navajo, and Spanish.

Wilson responded first. "I'm an ecology professor at the local college, and we're collecting soil and organic samples from this public use area for a class project. Do you want to help us?"

"Um, no. I have work of my own to do. What kind of samples did you say you're taking?" The guard looked at Ella. "Aren't you one of those cops who was here the other day?"

"Yes." Ella decided to be noncommittal. She knew it wouldn't be long before Landreth and Morgan found out what they'd done. She hoped it would worry them, especially if they'd dumped some kind of contaminant.

Ella remembered that during the fifties and sixties a uranium mill only a few miles from where they were standing had allowed radioactive "tailings" to get into the ground. Although the out-of-state owners had been forced to stage a massive cleanup, buildings that had stood for decades had been torn down because some of the raw materials in their foundations were too "hot." She hoped history wasn't repeating itself.

"Aren't you pleased that science teachers take such a positive interest in our environment, and pass that appreciation on to their students?" Justine volunteered with a smile.

"I notice all you students seem to carry handguns instead of book bags," the guard commented, seeing Justine's handgun at her belt. "Professor, when do you think you'll be done and away from this fence?" The guard, knowing they were giving him a hard time, tried not to lose his cool.

"Just a few more samples around the perimeter and we'll be gone. You can watch, if you find it educational," Wilson said with a straight face, gathering up the canvas bag containing their samples.

Ten minutes later they were finished and back by their vehicles, a hundred yards away from LabKote.

"I would have liked to have taken a few more samples down by the river where the runoff from this part of the mesa drains, but I can't because I have to get back for a class in half an hour," Wilson said, handing the sample bag and topographic maps to Justine. She'd be sending the samples to the Albuquerque lab for analysis.

"We'll take care of that," Ella said. "You've already done more than enough. Thanks for all the help. Justine will make sure you get a printout of all the lab results." She looked over at Justine, who nodded.

"I'll take care of it," Justine said. "Ella, do you want me to gather the sediment samples, or start packing up what we have for shipment?" Justine waved at Wilson as he drove off, then placed the bag on the seat of her car.

"Just give me four sample vials and the map, and I'll do it myself. I haven't been down to that spot near the river since I was in high school, and I'd like to go down there," Ella said. "Get everything else ready, and I should be back to the station in time to add this to the box and catch the afternoon FedEx pickup."

"Okay, boss. Don't start getting nostalgic and go for a skinny-dip in the river. The water is probably pretty cold this time of year," Justine teased as she placed four of the unopened containers in a plastic bag, and handed them to her. "Make sure to take two samples from each of the two spots already marked on the topo map. That way you won't need the camera."

"I hope we're wrong about this contamination," Ella said.

"If we are, we're going to have to come up with some new theories about what affected the dead insects and birds we found. If we don't, the traditionalists will have their own explanation ready."

"No doubt," Ella said, then watched as Justine climbed into her vehicle. "See you at the station in about an hour."

"Right, Cuz." Justine drove off, and Ella walked over to her Jeep, placing the hard plastic vials on the passenger-side floor. The route she'd have to take was bumpy, and this way she wouldn't bounce them off the seat and break them with her foot. At least with the Jeep, compared to the school bus she'd gone in years before, the ride would be more comfortable and much quieter.

Ella drove south on Highway 666, one of the deadliest highways in a state with one of the worst highway fatality records, and turned east on a dirt road she hadn't been down in months. The first few miles were graveled and relatively well maintained considering the rainy season had recently ended, but the track she took back to the northeast was probably as bad as it had ever been.

As she got within a mile of the bluffs overlooking the San Juan River, the road became a collection of ruts laden with rocks rounded in an ancient riverbed, and it was impossible to travel a foot without a bounce or lurch to the side.

Ten minutes later she reached the edge of the bluff, which overlooked the tamarisks, willows, and cottonwoods that comprised the bosque lining the river on both sides of the valley. The bluffs came up nearly to the bosque, and defined that side of the river valley.

She remembered the last time she'd been here, her senior year in high school. The entire graduating class had collected boulders, arranged the rocks on the hillside to form the year they were graduating, then whitewashed the rocks so the giant numbers were visible all the way from the high school in the valley. Later, they'd gone down to the bosque, cut willow switches, and used them to roast hot dogs and marshmallows over a fire one of the teachers had constructed on a large sandbar.

Billy Pete had been there, too, and kept telling her a hot dog wasn't cooked until it was black all over. She'd preferred her own cooking, but she'd shared a can of cola with Billy, and a bag of chips.

Thoughts of Billy reminded her of Justine, and the age difference between her cousin and her old classmate. He wasn't old enough to be her father, exactly, but he did have quite a few years on her. It bothered her, because she'd always thought of Billy as a friend, and as someone who wouldn't have taken advantage of another person. But things weren't the same on the Rez now as when she was a kid, and that knowledge kept her eyes open to the bad as well as the good. At least the tension between her and Justine had eased a bit.

Ella climbed out of the Jeep, grabbed the bag containing the vials and her handheld radio, then started inching her way down the narrow trail where the road had finally given up. She'd have to walk the remaining quarter mile or so down the cliff side to the narrow strip of sand beside the muddy river.

The hike down the sloping trail took only five minutes, including a brief stop to check her map. As she stepped around clumps of willows growing like red, leaf-covered fishing rods stuck together at the handles, Ella heard a vehicle from somewhere on the bluff. It was probably teenagers coming to neck, or, unfortunately, to drink.

Ella concentrated on the sound of running water, letting it act like a natural tranquilizer. This was one of her favorite spots. She thought about her child, and of the times in the future when she'd walk beside the river with her, sinking their toes into the warm sand and smelling the musty richness of the water that had given the Navajo Nation a chance at life.

Ella took out the vials and began gathering samples, making sure with her map that she had the proper locations: both sides of an arroyo where runoff flowed from the bluffs. As long as she took two samples upstream and two downstream from the spot, they'd have the samples according to Wilson's strategy.

As she was placing the cap on the last vial, instinct told her she was no longer alone. Stepping slowly away from the water's edge, she set the container in the plastic bag with the others, and stuck them in her pocket.

She's been a cop long enough to hear a dozen stories about

complacent officers getting killed. Remembering the tales revital-
ized her instincts for survival now.

Ella flipped the snap off her holster and crouched down low,
looking around carefully among the clumps of willows for signs
of movement. The bubbling flow of the river, the sound that had
helped her relax, now masked the footsteps of whoever was stalking her, adding to the danger.

She remained still and, after a minute, she saw a shadow farther upriver shift to the left almost imperceptibly. Taking out her
pistol, she crept forward silently. Every instinct she possessed
told her it wasn't just a teenaged boy hoping to catch a girl
bathing. As she edged toward the figure hidden in the shadows,
she saw movement along the base of the bluff as well. There was
someone else stalking her, and that second person was closing in
from behind.

Hearing the rustle of brush ahead, Ella tried to get a fix on her
target and bring her pistol to bear.

Suddenly, a large man wearing a mask and a dark sweater
crashed out from the brush and slashed at her with a big bladed
knife. He missed her hand, but caught the barrel of her pistol,
jerking it away from her just as the second man appeared and
rushed at her like a bull.

Ella kicked out, knocking the second one into the man wielding the knife. She reached for the backup derringer in her boot,
but one of the men grabbed her by the foot, and twisted it around
painfully. Ella fell to the ground hard but kicked again with her
other foot, catching him on the wrist, and he grunted, letting go.

Everybody scrambled to their feet at once. Ella was outnumbered, and neither one of her pistols was within easy reach. When
both attackers moved to cut off her escape, each wielding deadly
looking knives, she knew that there was only one option left. As
both of the men lunged at her with their blades, she leaped into
the muddy water.

SIXTEEN

———— ✖ ✖ ✖ ————

The water hit her like a wave of ice, but she fought to stay focused on the real threat—the men after her. The river was barely three feet deep here and she stretched out, trying to keep low in the shallow water as she rode the current.

It wasn't hard to stay on the bottom, her clothes were dragging her down anyway. Ella held her breath as long as she could, then surfaced for air and a quick look.

One of the men was running along the bank, but falling behind steadily because of the brush and the difficult terrain. She'd walked the route only minutes earlier, and knew there was a sharp bend in the river only fifty yards away. Taking a deep breath, she dove down, allowing the current to carry her once again.

Ella knew her attackers would probably assume she'd head for her Jeep to rearm herself with a shotgun or rifle, then come back after them after she'd called for backup.

What the perps had no way of knowing was that she still had her backup pistol. That, along with the element of surprise, were her biggest advantages now. Ella came out on the opposite bank, and took cover until she had her derringer out of her boot. It was wet, but clear of debris, so it would fire safely.

Then, using the dense vegetation and river noise to hide her, she moved back up the river. It took fifteen minutes of hard running, and careful, slow stalking to reach the area where she'd been ambushed. She knew the terrain here, and now the men were in front of her not behind her. Moving double time, she hoped to catch up and surprise them.

Although the demanding pace helped warm her chilled body, she couldn't stop trembling every time the breeze came up. Focusing away from her discomfort, she kept her mind on the trail. She pushed herself to the limit, but it wasn't long before she had to admit defeat. Freshly crumbled marks up on the hillside told her that the men had climbed back onto the mesa. It looked like they'd assumed she'd gone for help and decided to cut and run.

Spirits low, she returned to the ambush site, found her handheld radio, and called in a report of the incident. After locating her handgun in a clump of tall grass, she checked the weapon to make sure that it was still loaded, the bore was clear, and the action functioned properly. Then she placed it back in her holster. At least one thing had gone in her favor. The sample vials inside the plastic bag were still in her pocket, and hadn't come open.

Ella went back to her Jeep, taking a different route in the unlikely event the men were planning a trap for her there. Looking around carefully, she approached the vehicle from behind. The area seemed deserted.

Ella's clothing had nearly dried off, at least on the surface, but her body wouldn't stop shaking and the tips of her fingers were numb with cold. Unwilling to take chances, she forced herself to ignore her need for warmth and methodically checked the Jeep for tampering before climbing inside.

Five minutes later, the heater on full blast, she headed for home, which was not only closer than her office, but also held a change of fresh, warm clothes.

*   *   *

An hour later, Ella sat in her office with Justine, writing her report of the incident. The samples they'd gathered were on their way, and the map was spread out on a table in Justine's lab, drying.

"I'm glad it was you instead of me, Ella. I've never been much of a swimmer—let alone with my clothes on." Justine sat across from Ella's desk, folding and unfolding the receipt for the FedEx package that had just gone out.

"It was more a matter of letting the current take me and holding my breath," Ella admitted.

"You could have been killed, or cut to ribbons by those guys," Justine said somberly. "We have officers on alert, but other than what they were wearing, we have zip to look for."

"They were after me, and wanted to put me away for good without making a lot of noise that would carry toward town. What bugs me is that either the perps knew where I was headed, or they were able to follow me and I never saw them."

"The terrain leading up to the bluffs is wide open. I doubt they could have been too close." Justine pointed out.

"I wonder if the guard at LabKote tipped someone off to what we were doing, and they were afraid of what I'd find near the water. Or does that sound a bit thin?"

"There were others who knew we'd be in the area," Justine said. "Remember the gathering at Jesse Woody's house? That was when you agreed to run the tests."

"I know, and that group included my brother and Billy Pete." Ella noticed how Justine cringed when she'd mentioned Billy. "But the Fierce Ones wouldn't have done this. They would have realized that if anything happened to me down by the river, they would become prime suspects. It's too obvious."

"What other suspects *do* we have? Not the tribal politicians. That isn't their style," Justine said. "But, like you, I seriously doubt that the Fierce Ones had anything to do with this. It's so obvious it smacks more of a frame, or dumb coincidence."

"There's another possibility," Ella said slowly. "Do you think somebody is framing them, instead of the other way around?"

"That could very well be," Justine answered.

"If we could only figure out why somebody is trying to get me out of the way permanently, I have a feeling our investigative trails would converge and narrow." Ella wished her so-called legacy was as powerful as some thought and could show her the truth, but no revelations seemed forthcoming.

"Well," Justine pointed out, "at least the samples we took are on their way for testing, and we've been promised a twenty-four-hour turnaround on the preliminary results. Soon we'll find out if there's anything out there to worry about."

Ella looked at the report she'd been working on, trying to remember where she'd left off. Big Ed had asked for paperwork on everything, and oral reports on the kidnapping, and she was already way behind.

"Shorty, time to talk." Big Ed came into her office. "And you, too, Officer Goodluck. I'd like someone to explain why this department has all of a sudden become the Environmental Protection Agency. I got a strange call from LabKote about your activities and I checked it out. What's with these soil samples and dead birds you're sending off to be tested?"

"I'm responsible for the tests," Ella said. "We're trying to find out if LabKote, or someone else, has contaminated the fairgrounds area. If there's something criminal going on there, we need to know fast. The traditionalists are starting to label the place 'evil.' "

She explained what Clifford had told her about Lilly Mae Atso and her goats, and the effect the fairgrounds seemed to have on those who'd been there at the animal husbandry show. Ella also mentioned Kyle Hansen's death as a possible related event.

"We need to find a motive for the murder of Kyle Hansen," Ella said. "As I've indicated in my reports, we've pretty much concluded that it was no suicide. One possibility, when we look at some of the animal mutations around here and the reports of irrational behavior by those who attended the show, is that an environmental agent is responsible. If Hansen knew about a spill of some kind and threatened to blow the whistle . . . Well, that sort of thing has happened before though, admittedly, not here."

"Clifford's opinions may have validity at some level," Big Ed agreed. "I'll reserve further judgment for a while since gathering those samples almost cost you your life down by the river, but be careful what you're stirring up. What ends up coming to the surface may not be what you expected and surprises can get you killed."

Big Ed lowered his voice. "In line with your brother's comments about the evil in the fairgrounds, what about our old enemies, the skinwalkers? They're dark witches who, by their very nature, thrive on chaos. They've marked you for death. Do you suppose the ones who made it out alive after our raid last year are trying to retaliate? Creating trouble at the fairgrounds may just be a side benefit for them."

"I'd been wondering about that as well, Ella," Justine said. "Two men tracking you, then attacking with knives sounds like a more traditional approach to murder. Could skinwalkers be on your trail? If so, this may have nothing to do with our current investigations."

"The attack on me by the river felt more like a military operation than one I would associate with our people. No illusions, no magic or Navajo-sounding words, were used against me—only stealth. And, let me remind you, we still don't know if the ones after me are Anglo or Navajo."

"I've heard that you and Clifford aren't exactly seeing eye to eye lately," Big Ed said.

The chief's matter-of-fact tone didn't fool her. He was thinking of the legacy. She could sense it as clearly as she could the breeze coming in through the open window.

"What are you saying—that he was one of the two men?" She shook her head. "You know better than that. He'll defend himself and others, but he would *never* attack anyone."

"Some might say that it's possible he sees you as a threat to our tribe and acted in its defense."

Anger twisted through Ella. "My brother would never harm me, and this type of speculation is ridiculous. If you're going by the legacy, then trust the instincts I'm supposed to have. He is *not* involved. Besides, I know the way he moves through the brush. I'd never have heard him coming at all."

Big Ed nodded. "Okay, Shorty. I just wanted to see for myself where you stood on that."

"Whatever mistakes my brother may have made associating with that vigilante group, he's no danger to any of us," Ella said firmly.

"All right. Then let's stay on track. We have to find Senator Yellowhair and we have to find him alive. I suggest you two concentrate on that, and let this bird pollution thing run its course. Kyle Hansen is already dead, I'm sorry to say, but, hopefully, the same isn't true for the senator."

After Big Ed left, Justine gestured to the report she'd left on Ella's desk. "That's something you should read right away," she said, then returned to her office.

Ella studied the report filed by Harry Ute and Justine. After reading about their latest find, she telephoned Blalock immediately.

"My people located a bullet from the sniper attack on us," Ella said. "Harry got hold of a better metal detector, went back on his own, and found a full-metal-jacketed 30–06 bullet, pretty much intact. It even had a paint scrape that matches your car."

"Was your lab tech able to get a manufacturer?" Blalock asked.

"Yes, but it won't be much help. Justine found that the bullet is old U.S. military surplus, and could have come from almost anywhere. She pointed out that rifles have been chambered to that caliber since around 1906, and you know how common they are among hunters around here." Ella knew her brother and father had both hunted with 30–06 rifles, and she'd fired the weapon as well. They were almost as common as 30–30 Winchesters on the Rez.

"So, we're going to have to find the weapon actually used against us before we can match the bullet," Blalock grumbled. "Peachy."

They discussed the frustrating lack of evidence linking Branch or any other suspects to the kidnapping. "The kidnappers have made no new demands," Ella said, "but I bet they're watching the paper to see when the list they want will be printed."

"They'll have a long wait. We'll keep monitoring Mrs. Yellowhair's phone, and hope somebody decides to call her," Blalock said. "I'm still interviewing Yellowhair's contacts and associates but, so far, I've got nothing new. Officer Goodluck passed me a tip that Avery Blueeyes is at Navajo Lake, since that's out of your jurisdiction. But that's a large area to search and, so far, my people haven't found him."

"Something tells me he's staying low profile on purpose," Ella said.

"Maybe, but I've got to tell you, in my book, the Fierce Ones still look like our best prospects."

"But it's just not their style to kidnap someone and stay in the shadows. They prefer a more in-your-face approach." Ella then told Blalock about the soil and water samples they'd taken, and the subsequent attack on her by the river. "I'm beginning to suspect that someone's trying hard to frame the Fierce Ones."

"What other group would have an interest in that? I don't know of any non-Navajos with that kind of agenda, and there are no other activist groups on the Rez with any substantial amount of power."

"I know all that, but the Fierce Ones have never taken on a battle where they couldn't rally local support. Dealing with the youth gangs and graffiti a while back is one example. But kidnapping is something else. It's hard to justify, even to the most traditional Navajo."

"Let's keep digging," Blalock said at last.

Ten minutes later, Ella dropped a quick update in Big Ed's mail slot, then left for the parking lot. It had been a long day and it was time to go home.

As Ella drove down the empty, darkened highway, she wondered about the world her child would inherit. She'd wanted her daughter to grow up in the Rez she'd known, safe anywhere at any hour, but those days were long gone. A new era was beginning, and it was in that new Rez her child would have to find her place.

SEPTEMBER 14TH

Ella woke early before her new clock radio went off, and felt a large lump at the foot of her bed. The lump moved, then groaned slightly, settling in another location atop the covers.

"When did you start becoming a foot warmer, Two?" Ella sat up and scratched the long-haired mutt behind the ears. Two moved his head slightly to lick her wrist, then stretched out full length.

"Mom will make you start sleeping outside full time if she finds you've been getting on the furniture, boy," Ella whispered. "Let's make this our little secret."

Two looked at her solemnly, then slithered off the bed onto the floor. Shaking loose hair all over the place, the mutt trotted out of the room and into the hall, then laid down on the floor just within her sight.

"You'd rather not keep secrets, right?" Ella said, then sighed. "Neither would I." Ella stared across the hall at what had once been her brother's room. She'd have to tell Clifford about her baby soon, but she was worried about how the news would affect him. Would he be pleased, or worried about the legacy? It seemed nothing was simple these days.

Ella went through the morning shower and dressing ritual, noting her breasts seemed tender. It was another sign of her pregnancy, she knew. Five minutes later, she walked into the kitchen. As she did, she saw Rose was already there beside the stove, making scrambled eggs for a breakfast burrito.

"Good morning, Daughter. I placed your boots out on the porch so they could dry out thoroughly today. It's a good thing you keep them well oiled, or the river water would have shrunk them up enough to fit Julian."

"Thanks, Mom. I'm glad I held on to my old pair. I'd forgotten how soft and comfortable they were. Can I help you with breakfast?" Ella moved to the counter, where Rose had placed a plate with two baked potatoes.

"Just chop up those potatoes into cubes, then get the cheese and green chile salsa out of the refrigerator. The tortillas are already on the table."

A half hour later, Ella was finishing her second burrito and sipping a glass of milk when the phone rang. "That's probably for me, Mom. Maybe there's been some news about the kidnapping." Ella reached for the phone on the wall, suspecting from the early morning hour that it was probably Big Ed Atcitty.

"Shorty, we've just got a call from the tribal offices up on the mesa. It looks like we can add Ernest Ben to the list of kidnapped people. Go straight there. I'll have the other people on your team meet you."

"I'll be at the scene in fifteen minutes or so, Chief. Who else knows about this?" Ella asked.

"Just the maintenance man at the tribal office for now. The kidnappers left their calling card there, so to speak. You'll see when you get there. This will all become common knowledge soon when the rest of the staff show up for work, so get going. I've already had someone check the Ben residence, just to make sure this wasn't a hoax and he wasn't there. But, on the plus side, there were no signs of violence either. He's recently divorced so we checked with his ex, but she hasn't seen him either."

"I'll call Blalock and fill him in," Ella said, then hung up.

"Did they find the senator? Your expression suggests bad news. Is he dead?" Rose asked.

"No, at least I don't think so. But we probably have another kidnapping. Keep it to yourself, though, until I can confirm it. We don't want to frighten his family if this turns out to be a false alarm."

"Who's missing?"

"Ernest Ben, head of the tribe's economic development." Ella stood, took another swallow of milk, then checked to verify her handgun was in place. "Gotta go. Thanks for the great breakfast."

"Come by for lunch if you get the chance, Daughter. Oh,

wasn't the man you're going to check on involved in the altercation with the Fierce Ones at the tribal offices?"

"He was there, all right," Ella said, remembering. "That makes two people connected to that incident who are now missing." Ella regretted her words almost instantly knowing that her mother was going to be worrying about Clifford now. "You know that officers are going to be talking to the Fierce Ones again, don't you, Mom?" Ella asked gently.

"I was just thinking of that. Will you be questioning your brother yourself?" Rose asked. "You know how people will talk if you do, especially after everything that's happened already."

"Maybe Justine can take care of that. Everyone knows she works on my team, but it still might take some of the edge off the gossip." Ella put on her jacket, and started out, hoping today would be a better day than yesterday.

"Take care of yourself. Your daughter needs you," Rose said.

The words rang in her ears as she left the house, and got into her Jeep. The sun was rising over the hills far to the east, illuminating the Jeep in a strong light, and forcing her to lower the visor. It would be a few more minutes before the valley below felt the warmth of the morning rays but, by then, she'd be on Highway 666, speeding north toward Shiprock. As she drove down the dirt road, she noticed an old woman herding goats. The woman, her attention on the animals, never even turned her way.

"That's where I found them," Andrew Tallman pointed up at the aluminum flagpole halfway between the curb and the front door of the brick tribal office.

"The pants were hanging by their belt loops from the snaps on the flagpole rope, flapping in the morning breeze. Right?" Ella asked, verifying the facts. Andrew Tallman, in his late sixties, was obviously a man of few words, and it had taken nearly fifteen minutes to determine he really didn't know much about Ernest Ben at all, except for what was in the note.

"And when you took down the pants you noticed the belt with his name on it. Is that right?" Justine pressed. She looked half asleep, but Ella was glad that her assistant's brain had already woken up.

Andrew nodded once. "I found the note in his pocket, read it, and called the police." The custodian/maintenance man cleared his throat. "I didn't think about fingerprints until it was too late. Sorry."

"Don't worry about that anymore, Mr. T.," Ella said. She was glad that Tallman had eventually placed the note between the pages of a novel he'd been reading so that the workers, who'd arrived before the officers, wouldn't touch it as well. Maybe they'd still be able to find some useable fingerprints besides Tallman's.

"May I go? I have a lot of work to do," Tallman said, his English slow, but sure.

"I'm finished with all my questions now, Sir," Ella told him. "Thanks for your help."

He walked off, visibly relieved to finally be able to raise the U.S., New Mexico, and Navajo Nation flags.

Justine got Ella's attention again. "I'll check the note for fingerprints when I get back to the lab and can fume it with ninhydrin. In the meantime, I hand wrote a copy of the note's text so we can work with it."

"Read me what it says again," Ella said.

"Okay, here goes:

> To tribal officials and representatives of the *Dineh: Hosteen* Ben has been selling out to the Anglos. We will keep him and *Hosteen* Yellowhair until the Navajo Nation is 'owned and operated' by The People alone.

There's no signature," Justine said.

Ella shook her head. "It's consistent with the way a traditionalist would talk, using '*hosteen*' instead of mister. The tone and wording is similar to the Yellowhair message, too. Check with the linguists and handwriting experts Blalock has access to and see if they think the notes were composed by the same person."

"I'd bet on it," Justine said. "Speak of the devil, here comes FB-Eyes now." Justine pursed her lips to point toward the approaching light blue government sedan.

"Let him send the note to the Albuquerque bureau lab for prints, if he volunteers."

"We can get a faster turnaround if you let me do the work here," Justine reminded Ella.

"Do you really expect to find any prints?"

She hesitated. "Not if the note came from the same kidnappers," Justine admitted, "and based on what we've seen, that's a pretty good bet."

"Then let Blalock and the bureau be the ones who spend the time and money not finding anything out. We have a kidnapper or two to track down," Ella said.

"And that's why you're in charge around here not me, right boss?"

"Right. Now let's brief Blalock while we have something to eat inside. The lunchroom usually has snacks available, and all this investigating has made me hungry. I wonder if they have any fruit rolls or granola bars?"

SEVENTEEN
—— ✖ ✖ ✖ ——

Blalock insisted on having a quick look around while Ella briefed him, and that effectively squashed Ella's plan to get something to eat. Meanwhile, Justine, Harry Ute, Ralph Tache, and Joseph Neskahi searched the grounds and immediate area for anything the kidnappers might have left behind.

A while later, Justine joined Ella who, along with Agent Blalock, had managed to find a box of doughnuts. Ella gestured to a doughnut and a Styrofoam cup of coffee she'd set aside for Justine.

"What's next, boss? You don't think Ben was kidnapped from this location, do you?" Justine asked.

"Not really. His vehicle still hasn't been found. I'd vote he was taken after he left work last night. That's more in keeping with the kidnappers' MO. We have officers on the lookout for his white Dodge Ram pickup but, unless we get some evidence of a struggle when we find the truck, we'll be back to square one," Ella said.

"Give me a good photo or two of the victims, physical descriptions—height, weight, and the usual. I'll have a thousand flyers made up that we can circulate," Blalock said.

"We can distribute some of those among the Four Corners law enforcement agencies and blanket the entire state using local newspapers and the media," Justine said.

"Somebody, somewhere, must have seen Ben or Yellowhair just before or after they were taken," Blalock said. "And if either of those men is being held in this area, a neighbor or postman could end up giving us the lead we need."

A call came through on Ella's handheld radio, interrupting them. "Dispatch to SI Clah. Officer Cloud has found Ben's missing vehicle on a side street north of the tribal offices. Please see the officer at 1288 South Fifth."

"10–4, dispatch."

Ella looked at the others. "If the MO for the kidnappings has remained the same, Ben was taken from his truck just like Yellowhair. Let's get over there and see what we can find."

Ella returned to her unit and switched on her flashers. At least now they'd have a chance to search for physical evidence that might lead them somewhere.

Some time later, they gathered by Ben's truck. "He made a normal stop," Justine told Ella and Blalock. "There are no dents or scrapes on the vehicle, and the road shows no skid marks."

Tache and Harry Ute were going over the cab itself, which contained an unopened six-pack of beer sitting on a water-soaked seat, and the receipt from a liquor store not far off the Rez. Ben's jacket was over the seat, as if placed there casually.

"I think that Ben left work, drove east toward Farmington far enough to reach the liquor store, bought some cold beer at the time printed on the receipt, then started back toward his home," Blalock said.

"But something made him pull over, and that was when he was kidnapped," Ella added. "I could think of only a few things that would make someone pull over that time of night."

"An ambulance," Justine suggested.

"Or a cop." Blalock added.

"Or a car with someone in it that Ben knew," Ella said.

"When you do the background on Ben, check and see if he has any radical friends or associates, will you?" Blalock asked.

"Such as the Fierce Ones?" Ella felt her muscles tighten from the tension. "The problem with any theory involving them is that we still don't have *any* physical evidence against that group."

"Which means we have to start putting some serious pressure on the Fierce Ones," Blalock said, "but you guys will have to handle that without me. They'd never talk to the FBI about anything. I'd just get the runaround."

"Get started on those flyers, Dwayne," Ella said. "I'll have all the personal data I have on Ben and Yellowhair faxed to your office so it'll be waiting when you get back to Farmington."

"We should all pray that we break this case soon," Blalock said, walking over to his car. "I can feel the heat coming from politicians already, and it isn't ten A.M. yet."

"That's nothing compared to the heat we're gonna get from the tribe," Justine mumbled.

"That's a fact," Ella said.

Leaving Justine and the crime scene team at the site, Ella returned to the station and walked directly to Big Ed's office. He was on the telephone, but waved her to a chair.

When he finally hung up, Big Ed took a minute before speaking. She could tell from what she'd heard of his side of the conversation that the chief had just been leaned on heavily by the tribal president.

"You know who that was, Shorty, and you can guess what's bothering him. The head of our tribe wants action on these kidnappings, and he wants it yesterday. You and I both know kidnappings can take either a few hours to solve, or years. But when the Navajo Nation's president is under pressure, it'll come back on me. And when it comes to me, it goes to you. Now tell me what I need to know." Big Ed picked up a big mug shaped like a pig, and swallowed a mouthful of coffee. Grimacing, he put it back down in disgust.

"It looks like the work of the same kidnapper or kidnappers as before. The MO was pretty much the same: taking the victim at night from their vehicle, and leaving a note for us to find." She handed him the copy Justine had made of the text, and he skimmed it. "That's the newest. The original is going to the FBI lab."

" 'Owned and operated,' huh? That seems to fit with the demands made when Yellowhair was taken. Any theories about the identity of the kidnappers?"

"None except for the obvious, and it bothers me because I know that's precisely what we're supposed to think. We do have some ideas about the actual kidnapping strategy, if you want to hear them." Seeing him nod, she continued. "The victim apparently pulls over for the kidnapper's vehicle, and that sounds like it's either a police or emergency vehicle, or a person the victim recognizes and trusts enough to stop."

"We'll have to check out our own people to see who's sympathetic to the Fierce Ones, or worse, if somebody is a member of those vigilantes. Personally, I don't think that will pan out. I'd like to think our cops are above that, but I'll check that out myself." Big Ed leaned back in his chair, rocking back and forth while he spoke.

"Personally, I lean toward the notion of somebody posing as a cop," Ella said. "That would be easy to carry out. All you'd need is a similar model vehicle to the ones we use here and a red emergency light or, in the dark, and with a spotlight, just the flashers would do."

"So, the victim pulls over, the spotlight blinds them, and when they roll down the window to greet the officer, they get a gun in their face. It would be pretty simple," Big Ed agreed.

"And that would tend to rule out Blueeyes from the list of suspects unless he had someone working with him," Ella said. "I think if he was going to do something illegal, he would act alone. The fewer witnesses the better for a man like that."

"No definite word on his whereabouts?" asked Big Ed.

"Not yet."

"Okay. Then take that new theory of yours to the next level. Go see if anyone in the area where the kidnapping occurred remembers seeing flashing lights around the time the crime went down," Big Ed said.

"Ben's vehicle was found in a residential area, so we may be able to find a witness, providing he was actually taken at the spot where we found his truck. I'll get some officers and go canvass the neighborhood right away."

"Do what you have to do to get the victims back safe and sound," Big Ed said. "I'm counting on you, Ella."

An hour later, Ella knocked on the door of Pauline Salt's home, one of four apartments constructed of brick and metal in a style reminiscent of the late fifties or early sixties. This was an area inhabited by the teachers and staff of various federal and tribal institutions, including the public health hospital. It wasn't necessary for her to follow tradition here and wait to be seen before approaching the door.

Although the other homes she'd visited had constituted a waste of time (the residents were all at work), this time she could hear someone moving inside.

A cranky voice spoke out, telling her to "wait a minute."

Then a middle-aged Navajo woman in a blue robe pushed aside the curtain of the narrow window beside the door and looked out through half closed eyes. "What is it?"

"I'm from the police." Ella held up her badge so the woman could see it and her ID. "I'm sorry to disturb you, but I need to ask you a few questions about something you may have noticed in your neighborhood last night. Can you open the door so we can talk?"

There was a pause as the woman disappeared, then the door opened and Ella was invited inside. "Sorry. I work the night shift and I don't usually get out of bed until the afternoon. I'm a little out of it right now."

"That's okay. I won't stay long. I just needed some information."

"I recognize your face from the papers. You're the police department's special investigator, Ella Clah, right?" The woman finally smiled, pleased with herself.

"Yes, I am. And you're Pauline Salt?"

"How did you know? Oh, right, my name is on the mailbox."

The woman was a nurse, Ella noted from the photos of her on

the wall, including a diploma from the University of New Mexico Nursing School. This explained her nontraditional use of names.

"I assume you're working on Senator Yellowhair's kidnapping?" Pauline sat down on a comfortable-looking sofa, and stifled a yawn. "I've never met the man or voted for him, so I'm not sure how I can help you."

"I am working on a kidnapping," Ella admitted, withholding specifics. "Did you work the night shift last night?"

"Yes, I did."

"What I need to know is if you saw anything unusual on this street late last night, or early this morning."

"I'm afraid I didn't see anyone at all on the street when I got home."

"And that was at . . ."

"Around twelve thirty A.M."

"And the street was totally deserted?" Ella pressed.

"Well, not quite," she said after a brief pause. "When I was drawing the curtains and getting ready to go to bed, I saw a cop down the road pulling someone over." Pauline yawned, then smiled. "Excuse me."

"Did you notice anything about either vehicle?" Ella knew that this was what she was looking for. No officers had pulled anyone over on this street last night, according to their watch reports. She'd checked. "Was one of the two vehicles a new-looking pickup?"

"That's right. A big fancy white one. I could see it clearly because the cop had his spotlight on it."

"What about the cop car?" Ella asked.

"It was one of those Jeep-type vehicles, what they call a sports utility vehicle nowadays."

"Did it have an insignia on the side, like regular Navajo police cars do?" This could be a good lead, if she could get more information.

"It was like yours, with no markings, but it wasn't blue, it was white. It had a red blinking light stuck up on the roof that looked like it was ready to fall off. It was over the driver's side, like someone had stuck it on there really fast. I guess it had a magnet on it."

"Did you notice the driver, or the officer?"

"No, just shapes. I can't say for sure, but I think there were three or four figures in the police car. Maybe the officer had a partner, or the driver had passengers. Were they arrested? Why are you asking me this anyway? It was one of your own officers, wasn't it?"

"No, it wasn't, at least we don't think so. I'd like you to do a favor for me, and maybe help a crime victim at the same time. Tell me everything else you remember about last night, and then I'll tell you a little more about my investigation, but it'll have to be in confidence."

Pauline's eyes grew wide and she nodded. "Of course."

Ella got every detail Pauline Salt could remember, then finally told her about Ernest Ben's kidnapping. "But please don't tell any-one what you know. It could compromise our investigation. "Ella started to walk out the door, but stopped in mid stride. "Don't even talk to another police officer, unless I call you first and tell you it's okay."

"No problem," she said. "I can keep confidences. Don't worry."

Assured Pauline would be discreet, Ella left. The best thing she could do was to keep Pauline anonymous to everyone, except the cops she personally trusted. If anyone thought Pauline could identify the kidnappers, she'd be in danger.

By the time Ella and Justine finished canvassing the neighbor-hood, it was past lunchtime, and they grabbed a sandwich at the Totah Cafe. By then, news of Ernest Ben's kidnapping had reached the radio and television stations. As she watched the broadcast, Ella was pleased to see that Blalock had come through for her.

The television newscaster showed the flyer Blalock had pro-vided for them, and read off the description of both missing Navajo officials.

"We've got every agency in the area looking for that phoney cop car. Something's bound to turn up," Justine said, referring to the information they'd deliberately kept from the reporters in order to protect Pauline.

"That vehicle's probably hidden away by now, but every dealer in New Mexico and southern Colorado is going to have an officer visit them and look over their sales records. Blalock and the FBI can get law enforcement teams moving like no one else can."

Ella finished her chef's salad, and eyed a piece of pie on the counter across the room. She knew she'd have to start eating more nutritiously with a child developing, but fattening foods just tasted better somehow.

"Wait until that George Branch character does his show tonight. He really laid it on thick about tribal corruption when the senator was kidnapped. I wonder what he'll say this time?"

"Blalock is going to record his broadcasts from now on. He's still a suspect, though he couldn't be doing this alone if Ben was taken by more than one man."

Justine looked across the room toward the door, stared hopefully for a moment, then looked back at Ella.

"Who did you see come in?" Ella asked. She hadn't looked, not wanting to be obvious, but was curious about Justine's reaction.

"It was Billy and a couple of his coworkers from the mine," Justine said with a shrug. "But he didn't see us, or he would have said hello."

"I wonder how they're reacting to the latest kidnapping?" Ella watched Justine for a reaction.

"Billy and his friends don't look too happy, judging from their expressions. Whoever is doing this is trying to make the Fierce Ones look bad, and I have a feeling that's going to stir up its own brand of trouble."

"Then we better catch the bad guys quickly. We don't need any more problems. Time to get back to work partner," Ella said, walking out the side door with Justine.

Ella was halfway across the parking lot when she glanced behind her automatically and saw Billy Pete watching Justine from the window. Aware of Ella, Billy shifted his gaze to her, gave her a nod, then turned his attention back to his friends.

EIGHTEEN

——— ✖ ✖ ✖ ———

That night at home Ella decided to tune in to George Branch's show. She'd only heard a few minutes here and there in the past because she'd found the man so one-sided and annoying.

After listening to the first ten-minute segment, she was glad Blalock had elected to start recording the broadcast. Branch had chosen the recent lawlessness on the Rez as his topic. His ranting held few surprises, but Branch suddenly got Ella's attention when he mentioned that she'd been attacked beside the San Juan River. This attack had not been made public. Only officers around the station, her mother, and the attackers themselves knew about that. Branch assured his listening audience that Ella had undoubtedly been yet another target of the kidnappers operating on the Rez. He then pointed out that as a police officer, she would have been an excellent hostage for anyone hoping to force tribal government action.

When the phone rang, she grabbed it immediately. Blalock's voice came over the line. "Are you listening to George Branch tonight?" he asked.

"Unfortunately, yes. Are you recording it?"

"You bet."

"Did you just hear him say something about me being attacked along the river?" Ella asked.

"Yeah, I heard it. Have you considered his theory that you may have been a kidnapping target?"

"No, not really. They came at me with knives, remember? But if it hadn't occurred to the bad guys before, it will now, thanks to that moron."

"That's true. So, what do you want to do about it?"

"First, I want to find out who his source is. He just broadcast information we'd deliberately kept under wraps. Let me call you back when his show is over. Maybe he'll say something that'll help us figure out where he's getting his information."

"I'll be waiting for your call," Blalock said then hung up.

Before the George Branch Show was over, Ella got two more calls, one from Justine, and the other from Big Ed. Both wanted to know the same thing—how did Branch know about the attack as well as the other details he'd mentioned? They knew they could rule out Pauline Salt, the nurse who witnessed Ben's abduction. She knew nothing about Ella's knife attack.

Branch took no listener calls or responses during this evening's broadcast, but Ella wasn't sure if that was his regular format or just for tonight's show. The half-Navajo radio personality blasted law enforcement, capping the tirade by attacking Dwayne Blalock and calling him "the Feeble Brained Idiot," what he claimed FBI should stand for in Blalock's case.

After the show, Ella spoke to Blalock.

"I'm going to look into every detail of that loudmouth's life. His butt is mine."

"Go for it. In the meantime, our PD will have to dig hard to make sure the leak isn't one of our guys."

As Ella placed the receiver down, she smiled for the first time that evening. Branch had wanted to provoke a reaction with his broadcast tonight, but what he'd get would be far worse than he'd ever expected. Blalock wasn't the kind to let anything slide.

SEPTEMBER 15TH

Ella woke up early to the sound of Two barking outside. Half asleep, she put on a robe and an old pair of moccasins and walked to the kitchen.

She opened the back door a foot and saw the mutt standing in the driveway, barking at some shapes on a hillside in the distance. "What is it, boy?" As she called, Two turned his head to see if she approved. His tail wagged one or two hesitant twitches.

Ella stepped outside onto the back porch, and squinted to see what was causing his reaction. Silhouetted in the pre-dawn glow in the east were a herd of goats and a human figure. From the shape, it looked like a woman in a long skirt.

"Come on in, boy, we're not going to be attacked by goats any-time soon," Ella said, and Two barked one more time before trot-ting over toward her, tail wagging continuously.

The door opened behind Ella, and Rose let them both back into the house. "Good dog," she praised. "What is it, Daughter? A skunk?"

"Just a woman and her goats. I think it's the same person I saw the other day farther up the road."

"I think she's doing more than herding goats, Daughter." Rose grumbled. "Do you know who she is?"

Ella's eyes narrowed. "No, I haven't gotten close enough to identify her yet."

"If you do, I think you'll see that she's your lawyer friend's grandmother. And she's here to keep an eye on you, I'll bet, because she knows you're pregnant. She's afraid, like many oth-ers, that either you or your brother will become you-know-whats and turn to evil. In many people's eyes, the tensions between you and your brother support the legend's claim that one of you will choose evil and become the other's mortal enemy."

"I guess they see me as the one who'll become evil since they're watching our house."

"They're watching your brother's, too, according to his wife."

"If they think I have the energy to attend or conduct strange ceremonies at night, they're nuts. And the whole concept of wearing the skin of a coyote, becoming one, and running around at night doing mischief . . ." She shook her head as she considered the belief about the skinwalkers. "I've got news for them. Sometimes at the end of my work day, I barely have the energy to get undressed before crawling into bed."

"You're too modern in your thinking." Rose paused then continued, "There's something else you should know."

Seeing her mother hesitate puzzled Ella. It wasn't like her to do that. "Go on."

"I know you like facts, but I'm not sure about this," she warned, "But it's possible that your lawyer friend's family knew he was seeing you and, while that was going on, they felt no need to keep tabs on you. They knew that he, in his own way, would keep track of you and what you were doing. But now that you're pregnant, things have changed. None of them expected this," Rose exhaled loudly. "I'm not sure if they'll now pressure him to marry you, and in that way keep an eye on your baby as it grows, or go in a different direction entirely."

"What do you mean?"

"The way I see it, if he is able to convince them that the baby is his, then everything will be all right. It'll be their kin as well as ours. But if he doesn't . . ." she let the sentence hang.

"You think they'll believe my teacher friend is the baby's father?" She said, referring to Wilson Joe. "With his connection to the evil ones, I can see how that might create a stir."

"There's that possibility, of course, but there's another that worries me even more. Remember that Mist Eagle's legacy started when two from the same clan shared a blanket. They may already know that your brother can't have more children since his wife is infertile, so their minds may turn to the unthinkable."

"You mean they'll think Clifford and I . . ." She shuddered. "That's disgusting."

"Eventually, they'll figure out it's not true, but until they're certain it could create some very big problems."

"There's DNA testing, Mom."

"That means nothing to them."

"So, you're saying that the key to my keeping my baby safe is convincing them that Kevin is the father?"

"I think so. But you have no intention of meeting with his clan and trying to reason with them, do you?"

"Absolutely not. And if they come after my family I'll throw the lot of them in jail. I don't care if they're the same clan as the tribal president. I'll take them down, Mom. Don't doubt that for a minute."

Anger filled Ella until she began to shake. Superstition was nearly impossible to fight. It was rooted in fear, and nothing good ever came from that emotion. "I'm guilty of nothing and I won't be put on trial by anyone, particularly Kevin's family. If any of them come near this house, I'll arrest them."

"That won't help."

"Maybe, but it'll make me feel a lot better, and I'll guarantee that their night in jail will be as uncomfortable as possible."

Rose looked at her daughter. "New meets old. This is going to be some battle you'll wage."

"I'll win, too. You'll see," Ella said, struggling to keep her temper. "Do you suppose Kevin knows about all this yet?"

"Why don't you ask him, Daughter?" Rose's tone suggested she already knew the answer.

"I'll do that, all right, next time I see him. And, if the old snoop gets any closer, let me know."

Ella walked over to the refrigerator. "Want breakfast now?"

It was still early when Ella arrived at the police station. Despite the hour, there were messages waiting for her. Two were requests for interviews from a local newspaper and an Albuquerque television station, and the third was a "see me as soon as you get here" request from Big Ed.

Ella walked down the hall toward the chief's office. As usual, Big Ed was in. "Good morning," Ella announced at her chief's door.

"I'll be the judge of that, Shorty. That crank on the radio has an agenda against us, and he's spreading his half-truths and redneck politics over parts of four states. Now that you've had a chance to think about it, how do you think he found out about you being assaulted by the river?"

Ella thought about it as she eyed a box of doughnuts on the chief's desk. She'd brought along some granola bars and an apple for snacks, but they were in the Jeep. Besides, doughnuts always looked better than granola.

"You can have one, but not until I get your answer," Big Ed leaned back and started rocking in his chair. "Skip breakfast, did you?"

"Not really," Ella shrugged absently, still wracking her brain about the leak. There were only two possible answers she could think of. "Chief, either one of our officers leaked the news to Branch, maybe inadvertently via a relative or friend, or he's getting information from the other side."

"The perps? Why would they contact him?"

"Publicity. It helps generate fear and lack of confidence in the PD and strengthens their own position."

"Okay. Let's take a closer look at our findings. What do we have so far?"

Before Ella could speak, Justine popped her head around the door jamb. "I got your note, Big Ed, and I'm here."

Big Ed waved the young officer in as he looked to Ella for an answer.

"We've got two murders, a break-in at a clinic, and two kidnappings."

"Don't forget those incidents involving the modernists and traditionalists and their animals. People have lost some prize livestock recently," Justine pointed out.

"Tell me about it. My wife's still upset." Big Ed sat up and offered a doughnut to Ella, then Justine. Neither declined the offer.

"So many things are happening back-to-back, instinct tells me to look for common ground," Ella said, "but I haven't been able to find any."

"What course of action will you follow?" Big Ed started rocking in his chair again, this time with a doughnut in one of his hands.

"I'm going to start by having a serious talk with George Branch. I'm anxious to see how he explains knowing things he shouldn't." Ella glanced at Justine. "While I'm there, I want you to call the lab about those samples and see if they can fax you the results as soon as they're available. We need to start ruling out possibilities as well as suspects."

"Get on that now," Big Ed said. "Time's wasting."

"I'm on it." Justine said, and left the room.

"I'm also going to need additional officers to help us do the legwork on these kidnappings, Chief," Ella said. "Is there anyone you can spare?"

"I figured you'd be asking, so I started checking. To be perfectly honest, I'd rather have our people talking to Navajo cops than ask Blalock to bring in extra agents. Unfortunately, so far, I've only got one man available, but I'm still trying to switch other schedules around, so I may have more soon."

"Who's the officer?" She asked.

"Sergeant Manuelito."

He was the officer who'd pressured her into arresting her brother. One look at the chief's face told her he was aware of it, too.

"It's your call. Do you want him?"

Ella hesitated. She needed the help, but she wasn't sure the sergeant was the right choice. "I know Sergeant Manuelito has a lot of experience, but I wonder if he's the right man to be dealing with the traditionalists. He's new to this part of the Rez, and is really gung ho."

"What do you expect from an ex-marine? But he's a good cop to have on your side when the going gets tough."

Ella nodded at last. "I'll have him follow up on any leads we get on that white SUV, and have him help check with the dealerships. That should keep him from tangling with the Fierce Ones. I know he'd like to bust a few heads, but we don't need that right now." Ella stood. "If that's all, I'll get to work."

"Keep me up to speed, Shorty," Big Ed said.

Ten minutes later, Ella was on the road toward Farmington. She'd checked George Branch's address and found he lived in an old farmhouse near Waterflow.

As she sped down the highway, she watched farmers picking up bales of alfalfa from the fields. With cooler weather coming on, this was probably the last cutting, and they had to get the bales stacked and covered before the next rain.

Arriving a short time later, Ella found that Branch's property included an old, neglected apple orchard, and a large lawn, probably impressive in times past, but now overgrown and full of weeds.

In the gravel driveway was a gas-guzzling bus of an SUV with a custom paint job, heavy bumpers, and fog lamps. She hadn't seen a foggy day here in the San Juan River Valley in years. Branch either was making good money, or had a second job.

Ella walked up the flagstone path and knocked on the screen door loudly. She'd decided not to call ahead, hoping to wake Branch up, suspecting he slept late after working past ten P.M. five nights a week. When no one responded, Ella opened the screen and knocked on the front door even louder than before. She then heard a curse and the sound of footsteps.

Moments later, the door opened and Branch stood there in a T-shirt and sweatpants. He was barefooted on the hardwood floor. "Oh, it's you, Clah. Check out my program last night?"

"I need to ask you a few questions regarding a criminal investigation, Mr. Branch. Can I come in, or would you prefer coming with me to the police station?"

"The Navajo Nation stops on the other side of the river, and so does your jurisdiction. I don't have to go anywhere with you, and I don't have to let you in my home, either." Branch stood up straight, and brushed his unruly reddish brown hair back. His expression was one of arrogance.

"Okay, it was just a request. I'll ask one of the cooperating agencies in this investigation to make it happen. You've met Special Agent Blalock and, as I'm sure you can imagine, he's looking forward to interviewing you again. He'll probably have to detain you for, say, three or four hours while we discuss your connection to a kidnapping. And, don't worry if you're late for work, we'll call and explain to your employers. I'm sure they can find someone to take over your show if our bureaucracy at the station makes you late."

Branch's face grew cold. "Come in."

Ella had placed a tape recorder in her pocket, and now, unobtrusively, she turned it on with her thumb. There was no way Branch was going to distort this interview so he could use her or the interview as material for his show.

Ella took a seat on the couch. "I want to know who is leaking information to you."

"My source is anonymous. I can't give you a name."

"Are you aware that your informant must either be one of the criminals or someone in contact with them?"

"Or a friendly cop," Branch said.

Ella didn't ease up on him. "Or all three. I wonder what your listeners would think of your credibility if I let word get out that we have reason to believe you're in contact with the perps and are withholding evidence in a kidnapping case."

"Chill out, Clah. All I know is that someone called me at the station with the information. The guy never identified himself. I tried later on to get the Navajo PD to confirm what I was told, but the officer on watch hung up on me after I identified myself."

"Does the station have caller ID installed?"

"No. We have a policy of not trying to confirm the identity of our callers. It could damage my show's free speech, no government snooping policy."

When he began to preach about free speech, law and order, and liberals ruining the country, Ella gave up. This was all she was getting out of Branch today. "Call me if your informant contacts either you or the station again."

"I'll think about it."

"Do you understand the words 'obstruction of justice'?"

He took her business card. "Always happy to cooperate with the police."

Ella was driving past Hogback ten minutes later when her cell phone rang. It was Justine.

"I just starting getting faxes from the lab in Albuquerque on those samples we took," she said. "It looks like good news for the town, but bad news for the investigation."

"You mean there are no contaminants present?" Ella asked, surprised.

"Nothing except normal background radiation, which is a little high because of our geology and the old uranium mill. There are no unusual levels of toxic metals, organic poisons, or even sewage," Justine said, sounding disappointed.

Ella understood how she felt but, admittedly, Justine always took things like this harder than anyone else. Her young cousin had been put on the special investigator's team primarily to serve as a lab tech and conduct basic forensic work. Whenever lab work failed to provide leads, even if she hadn't done the tests herself, Justine always took it personally.

"Are there any other tests pending, or is that it?" Ella asked.

"They're doing microbial cultures, too, which can take several days, but I really doubt a bacterial agent or virus could be responsible for killing the insects and birds we saw at the site. I believe most pathogens are more species specific, but I'll check with Dr. Roanhorse, just to be sure."

"Do that. And find out how many more days it'll take for the autopsy and toxicology reports to come back on Elisa Brownhat. In the meantime, we'll just have to keep focused on the kidnappings. Human lives are at stake."

Just as Ella said good-bye to her assistant, she heard an emergency call come in on her unit radio asking for any available units. "This is Sergeant Manuelito at the Bitsillie residence, just west of Hogback at the windmill. I need backup. I have a suspect resisting arrest."

"10–4 Sergeant," Ella said, answering the call. "I'm less than five minutes from your location." Ella called the dispatcher, informing her she would respond.

Activating her emergency equipment, Ella accelerated and reached the dirt road turnoff quickly. As she entered the private road with a controlled skid, Ella looked ahead at the small gray stucco Bitsillie residence.

The Bitsillie's were traditionalists, and had a log hogan behind their more modern winter house. A rough-cut log corral held several goats, and a white pickup was parked beside the corral. Manuelito's police unit was at the end of the road, fifty feet from the hogan. Beneath a cottonwood branch arbor she could see a uniformed officer pushing a man with his baton. An old woman and man stood nearby, waving their arms.

Then something about the white pickup suddenly became familiar. In a heartbeat, Ella knew why. The truck belonged to her brother, Clifford.

Ella jumped out and ran over to the arbor, where Clifford and Sergeant Manuelito were circling each other. "What's going on Sergeant? Why do you want to arrest my brother? And what are you doing here anyway? You're supposed to be tracking down a white SUV."

Ella caught Clifford's eye. He was watching Manuelito with a look she recognized from their teenage years as his "do you believe this idiot?" glare.

"Are you going to back me up or not, Investigator Clah? Your brother is resisting arrest." Manuelito's face was red, and he was obviously angry and frustrated.

"Resisting getting pushed around is more like it," Mrs. Bitsillie shouted angrily. "The *hataalii* was here treating my husband for a sore shoulder when this wild Navajo came speeding up in his car, getting dust in everyone's eyes. He was rude to me and my husband, and especially to the medicine man."

Mrs. Bitsillie continued, shaking her finger at Sergeant Manuelito, "I don't get angry very often, but if you'd have tried to grab me like you grabbed the *hataalii*, I would have socked you right in the nose, even if I am an old woman."

"What happened, Brother?" Ella approached Clifford, who looked more relaxed than anyone else there. Old Man Bitsillie was shaking, and his fists were clenched in anger as he glared at Manuelito. He'd lost the ability to speak a few years ago; he was even older than his wife.

"This officer came up like a whirlwind and demanded that I tell him where I was last night and where I'd driven my pickup. He wanted me to leave my patient and come to the police station. When he tried to grab my arm, I avoided him and wouldn't let him get close. The woman almost got struck when Sergeant Manuelito tried to use some sort of nightstick hold on me."

"Destea here wouldn't answer my questions, and he resisted arrest when I tried to take him to my vehicle. The old woman wasn't in any danger," Manuelito said. "Are you going to take his side again because he's your brother? What kind of cop are you?"

"Step over here with me a moment, Sergeant. Consider that an order." Ella was going to remain calm, though she wanted to grab Manuelito's baton and feed it to him. It was obvious the man had lost his cool.

Manuelito glared at Clifford, then walked over to Ella's vehicle. "These are your people, too, Sergeant, and you're really acting like a jerk. Is this the kind of role model you think a cop should present to those we're supposed to be protecting? You're on my team now, and while you're on it, you're going to calm down and behave like a professional."

"I was just doing my job. We're supposed to be looking for a white vehicle, and the Fierce Ones are possible suspects in these kidnappings. Clifford Destea has a white pickup. It's not an SUV, exactly, but the witness who saw it might have made a mistake. It was night, after all."

"What you say makes sense, but did you find out if my brother has an alibi?"

"We didn't get that far. He refused to answer, and I didn't have any choice but to ask him to come in to the station. He's under arrest now. Are you going to take him in, Special Investigator?" Sergeant Manuelito demanded.

"Wait here, Sergeant. I'll see what I can do to clear up this situation." Ella walked back to Clifford, who was talking to Mr. Bitsillie about his back. Mrs. Bitsillie held some herbs Clifford had given her.

"I'm done here, Sister. Now what do you want me to do? I'll drive myself to the police station if necessary, or ride with you. But don't ask me to go with that man. He has too much anger inside him to think rationally at the moment. Perhaps he should find another profession before he hurts an innocent person."

"Did he hit you with the nightstick?" Ella looked her brother over for signs of a injury.

"He tried a few times, but no. I think his lack of success was what made him angry. I was wondering what I should do if he tried his pistol next."

Clifford was speaking as calmly as if he were addressing a child, but Ella could see a glint of anger in the back of his eyes. Perhaps knowing him so well allowed her to spot things about her brother no one else could, except, of course, for their mother.

"He's going to place you under arrest but, with the Bitsillie's as witnesses on your behalf, he's going to end up looking like a fool," Ella said, "which is understandable in his case. There's nothing I can do at the moment, but I can come down hard on him later. The police chief will probably do the same."

"Here we go again," he said, expelling his breath in a hiss. "If you don't mind, I'll drive my own truck. I'd rather have it closer to home. You and the sergeant can be in front and back of me. How do you think he's going to react to that?" Clifford pursed his lips toward Manuelito, who was leaning against his vehicle, trying to look bored.

"Who cares? I'll lead the way, and you follow me. He can do what he wants. When we get to the station, I'll make sure he isn't left alone with you. If he tries something, and you're forced to defend yourself, it'll just make your case worse unless there are other witnesses. But I'll tell you this—I'm getting him reassigned. That's within my authority." Ella walked with Clifford toward his truck.

"You know, and I know you know, that I haven't done anything illegal. When's all this going to end?" Clifford took out his keys and climbed into the cab. His voice was cool and calm, and from her experience too relaxed to be normal for her brother. But with Clifford, the more collected he seemed, the angrier he was inside.

"I don't know, but my taking you in again is going to make both of our lives interesting. The rumor that there's some sort of rift between us is going to grow even stronger. But let's not defend our actions here today with anyone outside the PD. It'll only spark more talk. What do you say?" Ella asked.

"Okay, but this is getting out of hand, and I intend to put a stop to it. Don't be surprised if I do something you don't like, Sister," Clifford said.

"Like what?" Her brother was so matter-of-fact she knew there was going to be trouble.

"You'll see, Special Investigator, you'll see."

Ella scowled, then turned to the sergeant. "Let's go, hotshot," she said quietly. "I'm leading the way, and the medicine man will follow in his own vehicle. You follow him, then do the paperwork at the station."

As Ella climbed into her Jeep, she thought about Clifford's last words. "Just what the hell did you mean by that, Brother?" she whispered, alone in the vehicle. Her only answer was the sound of the road beneath her tires.

NINETEEN

———— ✖ ✖ ✖ ————

Ella decided there was one thing she could do to make things easier for Clifford. Plan in mind, she proceeded to alter their route. When they reached Shiprock, she continued on past the turnoff to the main station. Clifford stayed right behind her, following in his pickup as they approached the old westbound bridge across the river.

"Unit SI five to SI one," Manuelito came on the radio immediately. "You missed the turn, Investigator Clah. Where are we going?"

Ella deliberately waited a full thirty seconds before responding. "SI Five, I'm heading to the westside substation. Do you copy?" Clifford would be a few miles closer to home at the new, modern facility, and avoid some of the publicity, hopefully.

"10–4," Manuelito responded.

A few minutes later, after Clifford and Ella were inside the small, new facility, Manuelito joined them and formally placed Clifford under arrest. Ella wasn't surprised. Manuelito was one of the most stubborn cops she'd ever encountered.

"I'll call Kevin Tolino for you," Ella volunteered as Clifford was led to the booking desk, which was, literally, a small desk manned by one clerk.

"Please do that, Sister, but don't tell him to come down here to bail me out. I'm going to stay. I'm not going to let him try and talk the sergeant here into dropping the charges either. Tell him instead to go get a statement from the witnesses. This time I'm going to court. I think there's one cop who needs to learn a lesson, and the tribe's best lawyer is going to help me teach him."

Sergeant Manuelito had looked up the second Clifford had mentioned going to court and, now, he was a shade paler. "What do you think you're doing? Trying to give the police department a bad image?"

"That seems to be your goal, not mine. I'm just going to see that justice is done." Clifford held out his hands, wrists up. "Aren't you going to handcuff me, Sergeant?"

"Are you sure you want to do this, Brother?" Ella just shook her head slowly. "I'll provide bail money."

"Your lawyer and I can work something out," Manuelito insisted, his voice fading. He turned to Ella. "Do something. He's your brother. You really want him in jail?"

Now Ella smiled. "I can't tell him anything. My brother never listens to me. I've got a feeling that you'd better find a lawyer of your own. You've really gotten yourself into a hole this time, Sergeant. If I were you, I'd stop digging and look for a way out."

Ella watched as Clifford was booked and escorted by another officer to one of the two holding cells in the back. Sergeant Manuelito paced back and forth for a while, then cursed to himself and left the station.

As soon as things had settled, Ella called Kevin. "We have another problem here with my brother," Ella said, and explained.

Kevin started to laugh. "Good for Clifford! The sergeant deserves it. Tell your brother I'll get on it right away. But first, how are you doing? I heard about the knife attack on Branch's radio program. I started to call you at home but since I wasn't sure how much Rose knew, I decided against it."

"I'm fine. Branch sensationalized it as usual," she said. For a

moment, Ella was tempted to ask Kevin to speak to his grandmother and get her to stop watching her and the house, but this
wasn't the time. That was more of a face-to-face issue that would
have to wait.

Just as Kevin said good-bye, Justine came into the station. "I
overheard your radio traffic. What's going on?"

Ella explained about Clifford and Sergeant Manuelito.

"You believe Clifford's side of the story, don't you, Ella?" Justine asked as they walked outside to their vehicles.

"Of course I do and, unless Manuelito gets real lucky, he's
going to end up before a review board. I doubt Clifford will sue
him, he's not that kind of person, but he seems intent on scaring
the hell out of the sergeant." Ella was beginning to appreciate her
brother's strategy. "The sergeant was assigned to our team, but
now I'm not sure I want him. If he asks you for information concerning the investigation, refer him to me."

Ella stopped by her Jeep. Administrative matters like these
had to be dealt with according to established protocols, but she
had the authority to get Manuelito transferred back off her team
and she intended to do just that. He was putting roadblocks in
her way, not helping.

"By the way, I got the background information on Walter Morgan and Ted Landreth," Justine said. "There's nothing we didn't
already know there. The only thing I'm curious about is why
Morgan never went back home after he got out of the marines,"
Justine said.

"What do you mean, never went home?"

"According to the information we have, he was raised in the
St. Louis area, joined the marines a few years out of high school,
and served until the end of the Persian Gulf conflict. When he
came back to the States, after spending several years in Europe,
he stayed in California. Wouldn't he have ever gone back home? I
know I would have."

"Morgan didn't seem to get along with his family, at least
that's the impression I got. Maybe he left home under a cloud.
Was there a wife listed in his background?" Ella remembered

Morgan saying it was none of her business, which had only aroused her curiosity even more.

"Nope. And if he was living with someone, no mention of that is in his records either," Justine recalled.

"Did you get his parents address? There wasn't one in his file. Morgan said he'd lost touch with them." Ella said.

"From what I found, they're living in the same town he grew up in. I guess Morgan just didn't want anyone to contact them about him. He may want to cut those ties for his own reasons," Justine said.

"Let's call the National Records Center and the Veterans Administration and get all we can on the man's military service record. He's coming across as the kind of person that sends up all kinds of warning flags to people in our profession—a bit strange, a loner, and dangerous."

"The kind of person who's associated with crime and violence," Justine agreed. "I'll put things in motion when I get back."

"Anything else?"

"I used the word 'gamma' to finally break the code on Hansen's computer files. There's a whole subdirectory full of memos he wrote, all business and boring, about production schedules and stuff. The only personal files were a letter to his parents and a Christmas letter. You know, the kind people send out to everyone on their list. If there was anything else, it has already been deleted in such a way it can't be retrieved."

Ella nodded. She hadn't really expected it to be any different. "Okay."

"What's next on our investigations, boss? Blalock and all our other officers are either tracking down and interviewing people connected to the victims, or looking for that white SUV. Mrs. Salt is still the only witness to the Ben kidnapping, right?" Justine looked over at the highway as a white vehicle passed by. It was a van.

"So far. You know, it just occurred to me that there *is* a thread connecting LabKote to the kidnappings." Ella looked back into her notebook for what she'd jotted down after her last visit to the lab.

"What?" Justine asked as she tried to sneak a look at Ella's notebook.

"I remember seeing some photos of LabKote employees and tribal officials on one of the walls there. You know the kind, the 'tribal cooperation with private enterprise' publicity shots. Well, guess which two politicians were in those photos, all chummy with LabKote?"

"Don't tell me. James Yellowhair and Ernest Ben."

"The very ones. And who would you want to pay under-the-table money if you were looking to move in on this part of the Rez? The same two Navajos," Ella said. "Ben essentially runs the tribal section responsible for approving outside business ventures, and Yellowhair is our most influential politician, outside of the tribal president. Big Ed had said that the tribe had checked out the operation, but maybe LabKote got the fast-track courtesy of a little inside deal."

"But if those two are LabKote's biggest friends on the Rez, why would people from LabKote kidnap them?" Justine shook her head. "The Fierce Ones would have more motive."

"Maybe—unless one or both of them got greedy and started asking for more money. Or it's possible I'm way off track here, Justine. But let's go out on a limb. I'll ask Blalock to use his FBI sources to check the bank and investment records of both politicians. In the meantime, I want you to see if either politician made any big purchases, either a few months before LabKote got permission to operate on the Rez, or within six months after that time."

"You think LabKote decided to kidnap them instead of paying them more hush money?"

"It's possible. Or maybe Yellowhair and Ben found out something that threatened to shut down LabKote. We could speculate endlessly, like we've already done with Morgan, but before we go any further looking for a fire, let's see if we find any smoke. And play it real cool around Morgan."

"Gotcha, but people are going to think you're just avoiding going after the Fierce Ones."

"My job is to find the truth and that's all I'm worried about. Let's go to LabKote."

Within seconds, they were headed south down Highway 666, Ella leading in her blue unmarked vehicle.

When Ella finally pulled into LabKote's parking lot, she saw that the section where Kyle Hansen had died was completely deserted, though it was actually closer to the gate. Clifford's words warning her that an evil presence had taken over these grounds echoed in her mind. She could certainly understand why he felt that way. Trouble seemed to gravitate here. Ella reached under her seat and grabbed her police baton, slipping it into the empty loop of her belt.

"That fence is almost glowing. Smell something burning?" Justine said as they walked toward the main gate entrance and the adjacent guardhouse.

"I think that's from the scorching leaves that have blown onto the live wires. The idea of such high voltage scares me. What would happen if some teenager tried to climb it?" Ella said.

"Maybe they're trying to keep dinosaurs in there. Remember the movie, *Jurassic Park*?" Justine said, laughing.

They walked up to the gate and were met by the guard, who poked his head out of the door just as they arrived. "Hello Officer Clah. Do you and the other officer have an appointment? I don't see you on my visitor's list."

The man held a clipboard, but Ella noticed he also had two canisters of Mace and an extra clip for his handgun on his belt. The security here was quietly up-gunning from last time. Just inside the small gatehouse, she could also see a shotgun resting against the wall.

"No, we don't have an appointment, but we need to see Mr. Morgan, your security chief, and ask him a few questions relevant to our investigation." Ella didn't mention which one, assuming the guard, and Morgan, would think she meant Hansen's murder. "We'd like to go in right now. Can you escort us?"

"No, I'm not allowed to leave my post except in an emergency situation. You'll have to wait." The guard stepped back into the guardhouse and picked up his portable radio transmitter.

"Just open the gate," Ella demanded. "You can watch us all the way to the door."

"I don't think that would be a good idea," the guard said. "But don't worry. It'll just be five minutes or so before someone comes out."

"Don't waste my time. Open the gate. We promise not to get lost along the sidewalk," Ella snapped, walking over to the entrance.

"If you really insist," the guard relented. "Here we go." He punched in a code number on a handheld keypad, like a garage door opener. The gate opened to a width of six feet, then stopped.

Ella went in and Justine followed. The gate shut behind them a few seconds later, and the guard stepped back into his small structure, picking up his handheld radio again.

"Nice going, boss," Justine said as they walked down the sidewalk toward the same door Ella had been through before.

"Sometimes being assertive is all it takes," Ella said.

"Somebody must have a dog," Justine remarked, pointing to some tracks. "That's an interesting addition to their security."

As Ella looked down, she spotted a set of boot-prints left in the dirt. "Now these look familiar. Those ridges on the heel are distinctive."

Ella's assistant bent down and studied the tracks. "It seems to be the same size and pattern as the boot-prints found at the sniper's location and near the Brownhat body, but I can't say for sure. I wish I had my camera, or could make a plaster cast."

"Uh oh." As Ella looked up, she saw a long black dog with big white teeth emerge from around the corner of the building and head in their direction. "Don't run, but get ready for a Doberman."

Justine reached down into her pocket, then felt around her belt. "I must have left my Mace in the unit."

"I've got my baton, at least. Something told me I'd be needing it." Ella stepped around so that she was between Justine and the dog, which was approaching quickly, but not at a run. It wasn't growling, but she didn't know if that was good or bad.

"Hey, guard. Call your dog!" Justine yelled toward the gate. The man was out of view, but Ella knew it was intentional. He'd let them walk right into this.

"Here it comes." Ella stood still, holding the stick at both ends and out so it would be the first thing the animal would encounter.

The long, sleek animal, standing much taller than Ella expected a Doberman to be, came up within ten feet, stopped, and bared his teeth in a low snarl. His stubby, wagging tail gave him away, though.

"Good boy, aren't you a pretty boy?" Justine called in the sweetest voice she could muster. "How about a cookie?"

"You've got cookies?" Ella glanced out of the corner of her eye.

"Actually they're peanut butter and crackers from the station vending machine, but dogs don't care. Please watch him while I unwrap these."

"Good boy, that's a nice puppy," Ella lowered the baton, and held out her hand a few inches, palm up. The big male beast took a step closer and sniffed, his stubby tail wagging a bit faster.

"Here boy, have a cookie," Justine tossed a cracker under-handed so it landed in front of the dog. He grabbed it immediately and gobbled it down, then sat.

"Good boy, sit. That's it." Justine called. "Now come!" The vicious-looking dog trotted up and sat down right in front of Justine, licking his chops. She held out another cracker, and he scooped it right out of the palm of her hand.

"Okay, we can go now," Ella announced. "Bring your new friend with us."

Ella walked to the door, with Justine following and the Dober-man at heel beside her. Ella knocked, and when the door began to open, Justine sent the dog to fetch a cracker she threw. "I don't want to get him in trouble with his boss," Justine whispered.

As Dr. Landreth greeted them, the Navajo security guard, Jim-

mie Herder, appeared at the far end of the compound and whistled. The dog ran immediately toward him, cracker in mouth.

"It's too bad Morgan wasn't there, and Landreth wasn't more
help," Justine complained twenty minutes later at the Totah Cafe.
"Was Landreth that boring when you talked to him before? If I
heard another word about mutual cooperation and shared prof-
its, I'd have cut my wrists with those slick brochures he kept
handing me." She took a sip of coffee, and ate another french fry
from the big plate she and Ella were sharing.

"But did you notice that the photos I'd told you about were
gone? In their place was a flowchart for production, and a map of
the U.S. showing the location of LabKote's many customers. They
must sell to hospitals and labs all over the country." Ella picked
up a french fry, dipped it in her ice cream, then popped it into her
mouth.

"That's gross, Ella. How can you do that with strawberry ice
cream?" Justine moved a handful of french fries to one side, and
salted them.

"So you prefer chocolate french fries, huh?"

Justine made a face. "So, what do we do next?" she asked, taking a sip of cola.

"I'm going to talk to Clifford. Did you see that security guard
at LabKote, Jimmie Herder? The Navajo who called the dog?"
Ella finished off her share of the fries, and started eying Justine's.
"He was wearing boots, I think. I wonder what size and pattern
they are?"

"He's also the one who discovered Kyle Hansen's body, right?
I think he's related to Billy."

"I'm sure he's also one of the Fierce Ones. If memory serves,
he was at Jesse Woody's house that night, trying to stay out of
sight. What I'd like you to do is check and see if he really is
related to Billy. Then call me as soon as you know."

"I'll get on it right now," Justine said.

"I'm going to go talk to Clifford. I'm betting that Jimmie

Herder is their man on the inside and that the Fierce Ones know more about LabKote than we do right now."

Ella drove to the west side substation where Clifford was being held. As she entered the small gravel parking lot, she noticed a pickup with a rental sticker on it.

"I thought it might be you, Kevin," Ella said as she walked into the small lobby of the facility and saw the attorney standing by the booking desk.

"Hi, Ella. I hope you're not here to interview your brother. I've told Clifford not to talk to *any* police officers on case related issues unless I'm present, and I have to go now to speak with your boss." He gave her a long, hard look. "Of course if you're here as his sister, that's a different story but, if you are, you'll have to wait for visiting hours."

"He's going to stick it to the sergeant, then?" Ella asked. "Not that Manuelito doesn't deserve it."

"He's tired of putting up with that nonsense, and I don't blame him. To make sure the charges of harassment and assault get a fair hearing, I don't want him to talk to anyone else who was there, you included. I'm also going to have to subpoena you to get a statement, unless you're willing to give one on your own."

"I'll tell the truth about what I saw and about what the parties involved told me, if that's what you mean. I'm interested in real justice here, not protecting a cop who appears to have stepped over the line. But Big Ed Atcitty may have something to say about when and where. I'll explain the situation to him, and then get back to you," Ella said.

"By the way, what did you want to talk to him about, Ella?" Kevin asked.

"I'll let you know when I ask him," Ella said, heading out the door. "Spontaneous answers are always the most informative." Just then her cell phone rang. Ella waved good-bye to Kevin, and stepped outside the building.

Ella flipped open her cell phone and heard Justine's voice come through loud and clear.

"Jimmie Herder is in the same clan as Billy. I also called

Blalock, and asked him to pressure the Marine Corps directly into releasing Morgan's service record. We don't have the time to go the conventional route."

"Good work."

"Did Clifford verify Jimmie's involvement?"

"Kevin insists on being present when I question Clifford, so I'll have to wait a few hours, maybe more, before I get any more information."

"Kevin won't let you talk to your brother? Strange, huh?" Justine said.

"Lawyers excel at being irritating," she answered. "What I want you to do now is get me a copy of that letter Kyle Hansen supposedly wrote his wife. I want to ask her about the letter and see if she ever received it or one just like it."

"You don't think Hansen actually wrote it, right?"

"We got that piece of evidence through Morgan and he doesn't strike me as the kind of person who would volunteer any information unless it serves him. If you think back, he and everyone connected to LabKote wanted to establish Hansen's death as a suicide, and they answered all our questions in a way that supported that idea. I'm now wondering if they also came up with that bit of evidence to try and convince us. That's another thread in this web of events I want to either cut or pull in for a closer look. Of course, it may be that all they intended to do was protect their company, not allow a murderer to escape justice," Ella said.

"I got a report from Neskahi. He spoke to Billy about Elisa Brownhat, but Billy was at work the day in question and quite a few people can vouch for him. The sergeant has questioned most of Elisa's friends, too, but so far he has no indication of who might have been with her that day."

"Tell him to stay on it."

"Will do," Justine said.

Ella disconnected the call, and got into her vehicle. On the way to the main station, she called Wilson Joe to tell him about the early sample test results.

He was surprised and relieved at the same time. "At least this means we can rule out something in the water and soil. That's a big plus. I wonder what the organic results will be. Something killed the baby birds and the insects we found in the area."

Ella offered to have Justine fax him a copy of the data they'd received, then disconnected. By then, she was at the main police station.

Justine met her by the vending machines. "I had to give up my crackers to keep from being munched, so I need a new supply." Ella's cousin laughed. "Want a candy bar?"

"Sure, I'm starving. Did you get me a copy of Hansen's letter?" Ella took the chocolate nougat, and immediately popped it out of the wrapper.

"It's on your desk."

Ten minutes later, Ella put down the phone and called Justine into her office. "Guess what? There's no way Kyle Hansen wrote that letter. In it, Kyle addressed his wife as Kathy, and as she just informed me, Kyle always called her Kat. She hated to be called Kathy, and he knew it."

"So Morgan, or whoever wrote the bogus note, guessed wrong and goofed. That's interesting," Justine said.

Just then, Ella's phone rang. After a very brief conversation, she hung up, walked to her office door, and shut it.

"What's up, Ella? Who was the caller?" Justine lowered her voice even though they were alone, recognizing that her cousin wanted to speak confidentially.

"It was George Branch, the radio gadfly. He didn't want me to say his name out loud. He told me that his source had just called and told him that Judge Raymond Chase is going to be the next kidnap victim." Ella looked the address up in the tribal phone book while she spoke.

"Can we trust the tip?" Justine asked.

"The information Branch got from his source was right on target before, so I'm not taking chances. I'm going to have the judge's house staked out and see if we can stop this one. If it turns out to be a hoax, at least we will have made a mistake on the side of caution."

"I guess we really don't have a choice," Justine said.

"I'll get Blalock on the phone and update Big Ed while you find Sergeant Neskahi and Philip Cloud and ask them to meet me here. If this is on the level, we might have a chance to get the kidnapper this time."

"Anything else, boss?" Justine said as she headed for the door.

"Yeah. Make sure you wear a vest. There's always the possibility somebody could be setting us up."

TWENTY

————— ✖ ✖ ✖ —————

That evening Ella sat alone in her vehicle, which was parked directly across from the judge's home, and hidden in the long shadows of night. She was restless, wishing something would happen.

"This could turn out to be a long, boring night," Justine's voice came over the handheld provided by the FBI for this particular operation.

Their group was small, but Ella couldn't have asked for better backup. Agent Blalock was on the case, Sergeant Neskahi was watching the rear of the home, and even Big Ed Atcitty was playing a role.

"Just keep an eye on everyone coming or going, especially any vehicles not on the list or someone on foot." Ella set the handheld down for a moment and shifted in her car seat, trying to get comfortable in the extra long vest as she kept looking from side to side. Her intuition told her danger was near, she just hadn't been able to find it yet, and the tension was getting to her.

Earlier, Big Ed had notified Judge Chase, the most important official in the Navajo court system, about the danger, but Chase had already scheduled a retirement party that evening for another judge, and had insisted on going through with his plans.

The police and FBI, at the judge's insistence, had been instructed to remain inconspicuous and, because of the large number of guests, the request had been easy to fulfill. Big Ed, an invited guest, was inside, monitoring the situation from there.

"Having so many people could either work to our advantage or help the bad guys, I don't know which," Ella said, as she kept her eyes on the new arrivals.

"It's a distinguished crowd," Justine called back on the radio. "I either recognize or know all these people. It's like a Who's Who of VIPs on the Rez."

"Judge Chase is known for being a tough judge. Many Navajos who've gone through his courtroom are convinced that it's because he's half Navajo and always had to prove himself to people. He had to work hard, and expects everyone to pull their own weight, too," Justine said.

"I can see how someone like him would have made enemies," Ella said.

"He's sure a lot different than the other half-Navajo we've been dealing with lately," Justine answered.

"You know what? Something's not right here. Judge Chase's photo wasn't there at the LabKote office," Ella said, thinking out loud. "Near as I can figure he has no connection to LabKote. I just can't see how he fits into anything. Yet I'm getting the feeling something is about to go down."

There was a brief silence, then Blalock came on. "There's movement in the bushes behind you, Clah. I can't tell what's back there."

Ella adjusted her rearview mirror, ducking down slightly to make herself a harder target as she reached for her weapon. She could feel the badger fetish getting warmer against the skin of her neck, a warning she'd never failed to heed. "I'm going to take a look."

She'd just placed her hand on the door handle, when she saw

the bushes stir. A glowing object was suddenly hurled toward her car, shattering the rear windshield.

Ella threw the door open and dove out, hitting the gravel road and rolling away as the interior of her car burst into flames. She scrambled to her feet, vaguely aware of the screams and shouts coming from the house.

Chase appeared at the door to his home, but Big Ed pushed him back inside, looking around, gun in hand. Justine was running after a shadow through the underbrush, with Blalock trailing her, several yards behind.

Ella wavered slightly as she tried to stand. Philip Cloud, dressed in civilian clothes, came to her side. "You okay?" he asked, holding her arm and shoulder.

"Yeah, I'm fine," she muttered, shaken by how close she'd come to being toasted. "Did you get a look at the perp?"

He shook his head. "When I heard FB-Eyes warn you, I came out the back door to get into position. But, before I could get around the side of the house, whoever it was threw that firebomb."

As they were walking away, her vehicle's gasoline tank suddenly exploded, shaking the ground beneath their feet and shattering windows in the house. The powerful rush of air rocked them, and flying pieces of debris whistled by.

Two of the guests grabbed garden hoses and turned the spray on her flaming vehicle. As they worked, Ella's gaze went to the others watching from the lawn and front porch. Chase's home was too isolated and too well guarded for anyone to have sneaked up that easily. The perp may have been one of the guests.

As she studied the familiar faces, she began to rethink her theory. The people here, as far as she knew, had no reason whatsoever to want her dead.

Justine came back several minutes later to join her. "He's gotten away, at least for the moment."

"Did you get a good look at him?" Ella asked her assistant, who was still catching her breath.

"I never saw more than a figure in the dark. I followed him, but he hopped onto a trail bike, then jumped an arroyo and kept going. I couldn't stay in pursuit, but Blalock approached from a different angle so he was already on the other side of the arroyo. He got a better look, I think. Neskahi caught up to Blalock in his car, and they took off after the suspect. I know Big Ed's already called for roadblocks, but if the biker travels cross country, and that's what I'm guessing he'll do, we won't catch him right away."

"Don't underestimate Blalock, or the sergeant. Both are persistent."

"It's not that. I saw the way the perp handled that bike. That was no kid raising hell just for fun. It will really help if Blalock is able to tell us whether the bomber is Navajo or not," Justine added.

"Let's see what he says when he gets back."

Ella and Justine searched the grounds and found a spot in the brush where the attacker had been hiding, possibly for hours. The boot-prints they found were all too familiar.

Ella went inside the house and, with Justine's help, questioned all the guests while Big Ed joined forces with Blalock, out searching for the attacker. At the end of two hours of questioning, Ella knew nothing more than when she'd started. No guests were unaccounted for, and none had seen anyone outside just before the bombing.

As Ella wrote a few notes to herself on the pad she kept in her shirt, Justine approached. "So, it looks like you were right. This was all a setup, and you were the target, not Judge Chase. The guy who firebombed you was extremely patient. He probably got set up here before we did, and just waited. Blalock said he was wearing camouflage fatigues. This fellow in the boots is really starting to get on my nerves," Justine said, annoyed. "Branch is responsible for this, so I think I'll head over to his house and roust him."

Ella bit her lip to keep from smiling. Justine was only a little over five feet tall. It would be hard, if not impossible, for her to give Branch anything to worry about.

"We'll do it together. Let's go now. I want every bit of information that man has and, if we wake him up in the middle of the night, we'll have a temporary advantage."

As Ella climbed into Justine's vehicle, she could feel her body thrumming with tension and fear. She'd been a target before, but it was different now. Her unborn baby deserved a chance to live, and this incident had just been too close.

"Are you okay?" Justine asked.

With a burst of will, Ella forced her body to grow still. The baby needed her, but so did the tribe. She was fighting not only to keep her baby safe, but so that everyone else's babies could grow up safe on the reservation. This was their home, the land prepared for them by the gods who had given them the four mountains and four rivers to protect them. It was The People's right to live here in peace and to have a safe place to raise their children.

"It was a close call," Ella said at last, "and I'm determined to see to it that no one ever takes me by surprise like that again. One way or another, I'm going to catch this boot-wearing jerk and throw his sorry butt in jail. But this guy is crafty. He comes in darkness and disappears like the wind."

"We've had tough enemies before, boss. We'll catch whoever it is."

It was close to midnight when they reached George Branch's home. The old farmhouse was dark, and everything was quiet inside and out except for the crickets in the yard. Branch's SUV was parked in the driveway, and the tiny blinking red light on the dashboard indicated the vehicle had an alarm system.

"Let's go give him something to think about," Ella said.

She knocked loudly on the front door, identifying them as the police, then continued knocking until a half asleep George Branch came to the door, turning on the porch light.

"What the heck are you two doing here? Just because you don't sleep doesn't mean no one else does."

"We need to ask you some questions right now, Mr. Branch," Ella said. "Would you prefer to do this at the station?"

He turned on the light in his living room, and motioned for

them to come inside. "What is it with you? What's so damned important it couldn't wait until morning?"

"You set me up," Ella said, pushing him so he fell back onto the sofa in a sitting position.

"I have no idea what you're talking about and I'm too sleepy right now to try and figure it out. Save us both some time and spill it."

"That was no kidnapping attempt your informant clued you in on. Someone tried to roast me alive, and I'm holding you responsible," Ella snapped, then recapped the events for him.

Branch's eyes finally opened wide, and he leaned forward to listen. "You don't really think *I* had something to do with that, do you? Think about it. You've annoyed me a few times, but that scarcely gives me a motive for murder. A lot of people annoy me, and I don't go out and try to kill them."

"Have you considered the fact that you've been set up, too?" Ella pressed. "They used you like they tried to use me. They wanted you to look responsible when I ended up dead."

His jaw dropped open and, for a moment, he said nothing. Finally gathering himself, he shook his head. "I did what you told me to do. I passed on information. What happens after that has nothing to do with me."

"What happened tonight was attempted murder. Think of the term 'accessory' and you'll get a clearer idea of where you stand," Justine said.

"I had nothing whatsoever to do with what happened," he roared.

"Why should I believe you? You've done nothing except play games," Ella demanded.

"What do you want from me?" Branch groaned.

"You can start by telling me who tipped you off?" Ella asked calmly, sitting down across from the sofa. Justine remained standing, but took out a pen and small notebook.

"I never saw him. He called me at the station."

"And you didn't recognize the voice?"

"No, I really didn't. I was about to go on the air, and there were a dozen other things going on at the time. Believe me, if I knew who it was, I'd take you to his house myself."

"That's not good enough. You're giving me nothing, Branch."

"I can't give you what I haven't got!" he moaned.

"Try harder," Justine insisted.

"I can tell you a bit about what's been happening behind the scenes in Shiprock, if you want," he sighed, and seeing Ella nod, continued. "I heard from Avery Blueeyes yesterday. He got scared to death when he heard about the kidnappings. He's terrified he's being set up as the one responsible."

"Why would he think that?" Justine asked.

"I already told Officer Clah how Yellowhair really ruined Avery's land deal. Well, the other person who stood with Yellowhair against Avery and backed his position was Ernest Ben, the head of economic development. That was one of the rare times those two men stood together on an issue."

"We've been looking for Avery lately, but his family says that he's fishing somewhere, maybe Navajo Lake. But that's a big place. Do you know where we can find him?"

"Not a clue. But I don't think he's out in some boat on the lake. He's around, he called me from a cell phone. I can tell because there was a certain kind of interference—you know, the type where it fades in and out. If I were you, I'd look in Farmington, Aztec, Bloomfield, or thereabouts. Even if he tried, he couldn't stay low profile here on the Rez where everyone knows him."

Ella stood up slowly. "I want you to understand one thing, Branch. If I *ever* find out that you've been holding out on me, I'm going to be all over you. Your life will become one never-ending string of misery. If you so much as breathe wrong, we'll bring you in."

As she walked toward the door, she glanced into the adjoining room. The door had been closed before, and she'd assumed it was a bedroom. Now, seeing inside for the first time, she had to admit it looked more like an armory. An expensive wall-length gun cabinet was filled with a variety of old and new, expensive, high-quality pistols and rifles. Ella remembered the .380 auto used at the clinic break-in, and was about to ask Branch a few more questions, when she saw him following her line of vision.

His eyes glittered, and his expression hardened. "You didn't see those last time, did you? If I'd wanted you dead, Investigator Clah, I wouldn't have fooled around with some knife or messy firebomb." He waved an arm toward his collection. "I'm a gun rights activist, if you didn't catch the message from my program."

"Have any weapons from your collection ever been stolen, or turned up missing?"

"Not ever. The door to that room is lined with steel, and is kept locked except when I'm at home. I also have a sophisticated alarm system set up in there. My entire house is modified to offer certain surprises, too. Suffice it to say that I've never had a gun stolen. I'm almost waiting for someone to try. Take a closer look, if you want. These guns, for the most part, have never even been fired."

"What do you mean 'for the most part,'" Ella said.

"I belong to an association of gun collectors. Every once in a while we hold special functions, and we get to show off some of our classic weapons on the firing range."

"You said you had surprises for a would-be thief all over the house," Justine said. "What kind of surprises do you think would stop a determined thief?"

"There's nothing illegal here, I assure you," he said. His expression turned hard. "But, just so you know, from now on, whenever you want to talk to me, I want my attorney present. I've done my best to help you but, instead of being grateful, all you've done is accuse me of a crime. I've had enough. I'm not going to be railroaded by anyone—you or any other crazy group on the Rez. Being a nice guy never pays off—least of all, for the nice guy."

They left Branch's house, heading down the highway back toward the Rez. Silence stretched out between them until they reached the community of Shiprock. "Where to now?" Justine asked.

"I want to stop by the station, then I'll need you to drive me home."

"And pick you up tomorrow?"

"That, too. I don't know how long it'll be before Big Ed can find me a replacement vehicle."

The station's graveyard shift was now in place, but the office staff was long gone, and the hallways were all but deserted. Their footsteps echoed as they walked toward their offices.

"I hate this place at night," Justine muttered.

"It's just as alive as it is during the day. The main difference is that it moves at an entirely different pace. I don't think I'd mind working graveyard if I was out on patrol."

"I would. That's how I got started. You're awake when the world's asleep, and vice versa. I didn't have any kind of life outside my job."

Ella chuckled. "And you have one now?"

Justine smiled. "Not much of one."

"You still seeing Billy?"

"Sorta," she said with a shrug.

"What's that mean?"

"Our relationship isn't working out," she said, her tone betraying her disappointment. "I like him, Ella, a lot. But he's got some ideas that just aren't compatible with mine. It's not traditionalist as opposed to progressive, either. He wants to be the most important thing in my life, and I guess I'm just not ready for that. I've got a career and other demands that have to take equal billing."

Ella smiled sadly. She recognized the arguments all too well. "There was a time in my life when every man I met had the same problem. They wanted me in a job where I could be with them anytime *they* were off work. But our lives aren't that way."

"And being cops is part of everything we like about ourselves," Justine finished. "Is that why you didn't remarry after you got into law enforcement?"

"There've been men in my life, some who I thought I loved, or could love, but the fact is, that my job always stood between us."

"Do you regret it?" Justine asked, her voice a bare whisper.

Ella shook her head. "Not generally. I mean there are times when I look at certain couples, like Big Ed and his wife, who've been married forever, and I wish I could have found that kind of friend and partner. But I don't regret the choices I've made. I really don't see how I could have made different ones."

Ella reached her desk, and started going through the pile of files and mail that had accumulated there. "This is what I was looking for. The autopsy is in for Elisa Brownhat." She scanned the pages quickly. "She was about eight weeks pregnant. From the report, it's clear that she died of a broken neck, but the other bruises aren't consistent with those of a fall from a horse. There are no bruises on her body except faint ones on her jaw and the back of her neck—as if somebody grabbed her hard and twisted her head, snapping her neck." Ella rubbed her eyes. "So it's now official. What we probably have here is another murder. We still don't have the toxicology results, which haven't come back yet, but I doubt she was high on something that might have made her fall, especially considering the placement of the bruises. Carolyn hasn't been wrong yet when it comes to determining cause of death."

"I spoke with many who knew her, and she wasn't carrying on an affair, apparently. Nobody had any reason to kill her that I could find, and I remember Neskahi saying Billy had an alibi," Justine said slowly. "But Elisa did show her horse at the Agricultural Society's exhibition. Have you noticed that everything seems to be happening to the people who were near the fairgrounds that day? Even Kyle Hansen, who was next door, fits into that category. But what's the motive behind all this? It doesn't make sense."

Ella closed her eyes for a moment. "You know, I'm too beat to think. Lately I've been exhausted almost all the time. Take me home, and we'll get started again tomorrow morning at eight. If we're lucky, we might yet get six hours of sleep tonight."

SEPTEMBER 16TH

Ella woke up shortly after daybreak. Two was standing by the window, growling. Automatically reaching for her weapon, which she kept on the nightstand, she got out of bed and peered outside. The same figure she'd seen before was standing on the dirt road about fifty yards away from the back door. It was the old woman with the goats. Kevin Tolino's grandmother was at it again. She didn't seem to be a threat, but it was still annoying.

"She's still coming around," Rose said, coming up behind Ella.

Ella jumped.

"You won't need that gun," Rose said. "That old woman's not here to harm us, just to watch."

"This is really annoying. I'm going to get Kevin to put a stop to it. And if he can't, then I'll do it for him."

Rose walked out and Ella showered quickly. As she came out of the bathroom, she saw that Two was still by the window. He was no longer growling, and when she checked, the figure was gone.

"You keep watching, Two. And if you ever feel compelled to bite them, even the old lady, I'll back you up."

TWENTY-ONE
——— ✖ ✖ ✖ ———

Justine arrived at Ella's home early. As they got ready to leave, the phone rang. Ella felt her muscles tighten. Lately, whenever the phone rang early, it was Big Ed with bad news. Picking up the receiver and hearing the chief's voice, she braced herself.

"I thought you'd like to know that your brother's out of jail," he said. "All charges were dropped and, in turn, he's dropped his charges against the sergeant."

Ella breathed a sigh of relief. "All Clifford wanted to do was show Manuelito what could happen if he didn't stop his harassment. I can't say I blame him."

"I'll speak to the sergeant today. Do you still want him on your team?"

"I'd like him to stay available, but I intend to use him only as a last resort."

"Noted."

Ella and Justine stopped for gas, then headed directly to the station. An hour later, after signing for another vehicle, a white squad car Big Ed had made available to her, Ella received a call from Wilson. He was being very circumspect on the phone, which wasn't normal for him.

"Can you come over? I want to talk to you in person," he said.

"Are you in your office at the college?"

"Where else? I'll be here until late, too. It's my day to meet with my Science Fair kids."

Ella left the office in her newly assigned vehicle and headed toward the college. Using her cell phone, which had fortunately escaped incineration during last night's fiery debacle, she telephoned Kevin. It took a while to track him down, but she finally found him at home. He'd taken a day off since he didn't have any client meetings and wasn't scheduled for court.

"I need to see you, Kevin. Can we meet today?"

"I can guess what you want to talk about. Grandmother Rena has been here at my house a lot lately, and I understand you've seen her walking down your way a few times."

"We need to talk about that," Ella said.

"I know. Do you want to come here, or shall I meet you somewhere?"

"Will you be alone today?"

"Grandmother has taken her goats and gone back to her hogan. I don't expect her or my family to be visiting for a long time."

She knew from Kevin's tone of voice that he'd finally found out the whole story and hadn't liked what had happened any more than she had. She hoped that would make it easier to talk to him.

"I'll meet you at your house in about two hours. Okay with you?" she asked.

"I'll see you then, Ella."

As she disconnected and closed up the phone, she felt slightly better. Kevin liked running his own life, and he'd find even the thought that someone was interfering with his personal business profoundly irritating.

Ella looked out the window at the river valley to her right, and the arid hills and mesas rising before her on the left. The land looked peaceful, with most of the harvest in and cold weather still weeks away, but there was a restlessness among The People. An intangible force was attacking the fabric of life here, pulling it in so many directions it couldn't survive intact.

She tried to push back the feelings of dread that chilled her spirit. Unless she found answers soon, there would be no harmony and no walking in beauty—not for her or anyone else on the Rez.

By the time she arrived at Wilson's office, her science teacher friend was visibly nervous. He was pacing by the window, and so lost in thought that he never heard her come in.

"Hey, Professor," she greeted, taking a chair.

He spun around quickly. "I didn't know you were there." He went to his desk and sat down, clearing his throat before speaking again. "Do you remember Alice Washburn?"

"Sure. Gloria's daughter."

"Yeah. The little girl with the rabbit that had babies. Well, I saw the one surviving offspring of the rabbit and he's quite remarkable."

"How remarkable can a rabbit be?" she asked, wondering all of a sudden if the trip had been a waste of time.

"Let me describe what I saw and you can judge for yourself. She's taught it tricks, like one would a dog. He can kick a ringing phone off the hook to 'answer' it and, even though it's completely blind, it follows Alice with remarkable accuracy. It can problem solve, too. It's learned to get out of his cage by undoing the locking mechanism." He paused. "I've been around animals all my life, but I've never seen any rabbit do those things."

"So, maybe she's got a budding Einstein."

He smiled. "Funny you should say that. Alice named the rabbit Bunstein."

Ella laughed. "Okay, so there's a very smart little rabbit running around. What is it that's got you so worried?"

"Let me give you the rest of the story which I got from Gloria. Out of one litter, one rabbit was born blind, and the rest of the offspring were so badly deformed they died. In view of all the anecdotal evidence we've been amassing about the fairgrounds, I began to wonder if this might somehow track back there, too, so I asked Alice where she got Bunstein's mom. At first, she kept ducking my questions."

Ella sat up, suddenly a lot more interested.

"Turns out that Alice found Winnie, the pregnant female, hiding in a fairgrounds culvert—near LabKote."

"It can't be LabKote's. They don't use laboratory animals. They sterilize test tubes and beakers and that sort of thing."

"As far as you know."

"Maybe the rabbit was part of the Agricultural Society's exhibition," Ella suggested.

"No, I checked. Some rabbits were there, but no animals, not one, turned up missing. The interesting thing is that there has been a very high incidence of abnormalities among the offspring of small animals who were at or around the fairgrounds the day of the exhibition. If the bunny was wild, then maybe it was at the wrong place at the wrong time."

"Not every animal that was there has been affected. You know that."

"But their owners have been, or so it seems. Face it. No one who was there exhibiting animals has acted right since."

"But it doesn't add up. We haven't found any contaminants. And even if the Fierce Ones had managed to find a substance that hadn't shown up in the tests in order to blame LabKote, they wouldn't have used other traditionalists like Mary Lou and Nancy Bitsillie to spread fear. Those livestock killings do *not* put the traditionalists in a good light, and what the Fierce Ones need most is public support from other traditionalists."

"Are you really sure that the animals were killed by traditionalists? Mary Lou and Nancy have protested, claiming innocence, and maybe they're telling the truth. Did you check the killing methods down to the last detail and verify that they were done according to our rituals?" he said. "I'd expect your brother to know things like that, but you? Heck, Ella, neither one of us

knows stuff like that, not without looking it up or asking someone else."

"Good point. I'll go over everything again."

"Keep me posted, okay? And if you need help, I'm here," he
added.

"Thanks, Wilson. I don't think I say that enough to you.
You've been a good friend."

He nodded, but there was a flash of something in his eyes that
told her it had been the last thing he'd wanted to hear. She mulled
it over as she returned to her vehicle. Was Wilson hoping once
again that they'd be more than friends? She hoped not. That was
a complication she didn't need right now.

Ella drove directly to Kevin's. Although she felt guilty about
letting her personal life interfere with business, she knew she'd
never be able to concentrate on anything until she got the issue of
his "watcher" relatives cleared up.

When she arrived at Kevin's home, she saw him sitting outside on the porch of the small wood-framed house, a can of cola in
his hand.

"Taking a break?" she asked, approaching.

"You bet. I've been painting all morning. You know I built this
place myself. Well, until right now, I hadn't quite gotten around
to worrying about paint in the interior. But the walls were looking
pretty stark."

"What colors did you decide upon?"

"Color. Light yellow. They had several gallons premixed on
sale at the hardware store."

"Glad to know you took so much time selecting just the right
look," Ella teased.

Kevin laughed. "Hey, at least the walls aren't all drywall
white now."

She sat down on the pine porch swing and tried it out. "Hey
nice touch. I like this."

"Good. Come over more often, and you can use it whenever
you like. I find it relaxes me."

Ella said nothing for a while, wondering how to start. "I learned a few things from my mother, Kevin. Disturbing things, you know?"

"I wish I could say I didn't know what you're talking about, but I think I do. At first, I couldn't figure out why Grandmother Rena kept wanting to visit and bring her goats to graze around here. Her home isn't too far from here, and the grazing's no better here than it is over there. She and I have never been particularly close either, so this seemed just a little too strange."

"So, when you pressed her, she told you?"

"I wish it had been that simple. Grandmother didn't say a thing about it to me. I ended up putting it all together after talking to my mother and then my aunt. They're now both part of the new traditionalists."

"The ones who believe in the old ways, but use modern means to spread the word, right?" Ella saw him nod. "I've listened to their group's late night radio show when they discuss plant medicine and rituals."

"Their group is comprised mostly of traditionalists who've grown up with radio and television, press and media, and want to use what's at their disposal to let other people know what they stand for. They hold on to the best of the old ways, but they also work with the new. You might call them cultural pragmatists."

"Yeah, just what we need—a new group with another agenda," Ella said with a wry smile.

"But at least they're easier to talk to and, in this case, it really helped. My aunt is quite a bit younger than my mother, and understood that I had to know what was going on. So, although my mother only gave me a local history lesson, my aunt gave me the details." He met her gaze. "I'm assuming you know about the watchers."

Ella nodded. "Did you have any inkling about that before now?"

"No. I wouldn't have built this house here if I'd known it could serve as a forward observation post for my relatives."

"Why did you, then?"

"As far back as anyone can remember, this land was set aside for my family. No one had built here, so I figured I'd use it."

Ella nodded. "Now what? Do they know I'm pregnant?"

"Yes. I told my mother not long after you told me. That was before I knew the entire story about our ancestors."

"Do they believe it's *your* child?"

Kevin gave her a guarded look. "I see that Rose has figured out the rest of the problem."

"You haven't answered my question."

"My parents remember how close I came to asking you to marry me a few months ago. I think they believe it's my child, too, but it's hard for me to guess what they're thinking. They believe my feelings for you influence me too much, so they've stopped confiding in me."

"If you told them to stop spying on us, do you think they'd do it?"

"Truthfully? No," he said. "But that doesn't mean I won't try. I can still pressure them, and I intend to do that, but I can't promise you any long-lasting results. What I can guarantee is that they'll be far more careful not to be seen. But I'm not sure if that'll be a help or not." He took a deep breath, then let it out again. "I can tell you this—I will *not* allow any member of my clan to threaten you or the baby. Not ever."

"Superstition is hard to combat," Ella said softly. "And that's precisely what's at the root of the problem. To us, the whole thing's nonsense but, to them, it's solid fact."

Kevin didn't answer. "Remember one thing, Ella. It's not just your baby, it's mine, too. We're in this together."

Ella nodded. "By the way, no one at the police department knows about the baby yet, and I'd like to keep it that way for a while longer."

"My family won't talk about it, so you don't have to worry about that. To them, watching you and your brother is part of the way they protect our tribe. It's a lot bigger than gossip. Do you understand?"

"Yes, and it's that fanatical dedication that worries me most."

Kevin took her hand. "I want you to try and remember something. Anyone who comes after you will be coming after me as well. We may not be getting married, but the child binds us."

Ella nodded, accepting the inescapable truth. Kevin was right. This was their problem, not just her own. Yet, despite that, she wasn't quite sure how much to trust Kevin. He was just as much a product of his family as she was of hers. Even during her years on the outside when she'd tried to tell herself that she'd left her family and culture behind, that tie had continued to exist. It was no different for Kevin, whether or not he admitted it.

A short time later, Ella said good-bye to him and headed back to the station. She needed more information on the Fierce Ones, on LabKote, and on the livestock killings. As she considered where to begin, she realized that it didn't matter. No matter which thread she picked up, she was certain it would lead to the center of the problem.

Ella remained at her desk, studying the many notes she'd compiled on the pending cases. As she opened the file on the livestock killings and read it over carefully, she began to see that Wilson may have been right. Although, at first glance the death of Abigail Atcitty's ewe had looked like a traditionalist's work, she just didn't know enough about it to judge. She thought of asking her mother for help, but decided against it. Rose already had too many worries crowding her mind, with the legacy and her upcoming grandchild, and it didn't seem fair to add any more to the burden she carried.

Ella picked up the crime file, then drove to her brother's house, glad that he was out of jail and the Manuelito incident was over. As she approached, the breeze blew the blanket door of his medicine hogan open and she saw him inside.

Ella pulled up and parked, then waited by her car, not willing to disturb him. He'd come out soon enough.

A few moments later, he emerged and waved for her to come in. When Ella explained her problem to him, he didn't seem surprised. "I wondered how long it would take you to realize something was wrong there."

"You *knew*?"

"We only had the words of those who had seen the carcasses to go by, but it was clear there were things that were off the mark. Let me give you an example. I was told that the head of one animal was placed under a juniper, on the north side. A traditionalist should have known to place it to the east. And the meat was allowed to stay on the animal, though there was no telling how long it would be before the animal was discovered. Our people have been taught not to waste the gifts the gods provide." He shrugged. "I thought of telling you, but it was the kind of proof you wouldn't have accepted off hand. Admittedly, these days our people don't always know the right ways, so it was possible it was the work of someone who just didn't know any better, but was trying to follow our way."

"I still wish you'd told me."

"Now do you see that the Fierce Ones are being framed?"

"I've always considered that a possibility. But the problem is, by whom?"

"The Brotherhood from the power plant is no longer a threat," he said, "so there's only one possibility—the Anglos from LabKote."

"But that doesn't make sense. They have no reason to care one way or another about the Fierce Ones or about the different factions within our tribe. The Anglos come, do business, and, eventually leave. All they want from us here is cheap labor and no interference. You know that as well as I do."

"You're forgetting about the dead insects and birds, and the evil at the fairgrounds that has affected almost everyone who was there. It's our belief that their presence has brought this evil to us."

"We've run tests—"

He held up a hand. "You're thinking like the Anglos who are convinced that anything that's real can be measured and tested. But that's not always so."

Ella forced herself not to sigh. That was the way with all meta-physical beliefs. They made perfect sense—to a point. Then, mysticism and superstition muddled everything.

"Do you have someone inside LabKote who can verify that the company is doing something wrong?" she asked, glad to finally have the chance to broach the subject.

"I can't tell you that," Clifford said.

"You want me to help you, Brother, but then you tie my hands. Give me a break here, okay? Your silence helps no one now."

"I can tell you this much. Although there are many Navajos working at that plant, not one of them would have taught strangers about our way, and risk having that knowledge used against us. But there is one person who may have never stopped to think that she was giving away information that shouldn't have been in the hands of an outsider. She isn't a bad person, she just doesn't always think."

"Who?"

"You know her. Martha Gene."

Ella rolled her eyes. "Martha talks just to hear the sound of her voice. She goes on and on and, to make matters worse, seldom gets the story straight."

Clifford nodded. "She's a clerk at LabKote, and works for one of the Anglo supervisors."

"I'll go talk to her."

"Be careful, or she'll repeat every question you ask her."

"Unfortunately, there's no way to stop Martha from doing that. She's incapable of keeping a secret." Ella stood up and headed back to her vehicle. Clifford followed, a few steps behind.

"Be careful, Sister. I heard what happened to your Jeep, and how you barely escaped being burned. We're dealing with one evil that has many arms. You need to keep your eyes and ears open while you're at LabKote. I've been hearing things . . ." he said.

"What things?"

Clifford stared at the ground by his feet, then finally looked up. "Take a closer look at how many trucks come in and go out." He turned and started walking back to the hogan.

"Wait!"

"That's all I have to say."

She kicked the tire. She knew that tone. Wild horses couldn't drag another word out of him now. "It would be easier if we could work together, you know," she yelled after him.

He stood at the door of the medicine hogan and shrugged. "Sometimes things aren't meant to be easy," he said, then disappeared from her view.

As her cell phone rang, she flipped it open, still muttering to herself.

"I've got some disturbing news," Justine said. "The bio report on the dead birds and insects we found at the fairgrounds has come in."

"What's the verdict?"

"Their cell structure has been damaged at a basic level. It's as if they were cooked from the inside out."

"What can cause that?"

"Raging fevers from massive viral infections, microwave and other forms of radiation, and certain chemicals. But we can rule out viruses and chemicals because we tested for them and the results were negative."

"By radiation, you mean like what LabKote uses to sterilize the lab supplies?"

"I was told that strong radiation could have been the agent, but it was highly unlikely that it came from LabKote since the gamma rays used in their process are supposed to be precisely aimed, and of short duration. Also the rays are usually shielded inside a building, and are incapable of getting through the protected walls, though they could easily penetrate unshielded areas."

"The shielding is in place. I saw it myself," Ella said.

"So, where's that leave us?" Justine asked. "There's no other source of radiation here, except for the old uranium mill tailings and background radiation. Yet that would have been widely distributed, not just on the fairgrounds."

"Well, *something* happened at the fairgrounds to cook those poor animals," Ella said. "Keep digging."

Ella called Martha at home, but found out from her husband that the woman was at work. LabKote was trying to finish a big order and everyone was busy putting in a lot of overtime.

Curious about the new flurry of activity, Ella drove to the plant, had the guard notify the supervisors, then waited by the gate until Morgan came out.

He smiled as she saw her. "What brings you back here, Investigator Clah?" Morgan was wearing his side arm and had the knife, but was casually dressed in jeans, a sports shirt, and sneakers. She'd hoped to see him in boots and at least try to casually check those out against the prints she'd seen before.

"I'd like to talk to one of your employees, Martha Gene."

"She's my secretary. Has she done something wrong?"

"No, it's not like that. It's a Navajo matter, and I'd rather keep it confidential. But I need to talk to her in private."

Morgan checked his watch. "She goes to lunch early, but you might still be able to catch her," he said pointing to the field where most of the Navajo employees were now parking their cars. "There she is."

Ella ran to catch her, glad for the chance to question Martha away from LabKote. Inside one of their offices, there was always the possibility that someone might have monitored their conversation. With video cameras in so many locations, she'd wondered about microphones as well.

"Martha, wait up," Ella said, catching up to her in the parking area.

"Hey, Ella! How's your mom doing? I haven't had a chance to visit her lately, but last time I was there, her legs were much stronger."

"She's still making progress," Ella said. "She's a lot stronger than anyone gave her credit for being. Someday she'll throw away that cane."

"I always knew that. I told everyone not to worry," she said, then gave Ella a long, thoughtful look. "But that's not why you came here today. Is something wrong?"

"A lot of trouble has been centered on the fairgrounds, and I'm trying to find out if there's any real basis for concern."

She nodded, understanding. "The traditionalists are saying that there's evil there. I think they're right, but it's just a product of what the *Dineh* themselves have been doing. People got too competitive, you know? We're supposed to work to have enough for our needs, but this craziness about who wins what ribbon . . ." She shook her head in disapproval.

"Did you go over to the fairgrounds during the exhibition?"

She nodded. "Sure, I even took my boss, Mr. Morgan. He wanted to learn about our traditions, and I figured that was a good place to start. I told him how the animals are part of our circle of life, how even today the young women are taught to butcher sheep for food, and about the rules our men keep when they hunt so that the gods will continue to bring game." She paused then looked directly at Ella. "He's trying, you know. He really wants to understand us so that the company can coexist with our ways. They've leased the plant for five years, and he wants the company to help The People, not just make money."

She had her answer now, but who else had Martha Gene told? And if the livestock killings had not been done by traditionalists, had they been staged to divert the police away from something else going on?

"Does LabKote keep lab animals?" Ella asked.

"Animals?" Martha shook her head. "No, just all those fancy machines and stuff."

"Are you sure? I mean have you been through the entire plant?"

"Sure I have," she said, then hesitated. "Well, almost all the plant. I've got clearance for most areas, you know, because my boss is the head of security."

"What about the areas you haven't seen? What's there, did anyone tell you?"

"The only places I'm not allowed to go are the rooms where they try to culture germs on different samples of our products to see if they've really been sterilized. That's the simple explanation, mind you. When they tell it, it's a lot more complicated."

As they stood there, Ella saw a large semi come in and back up to the loading dock. "It sure looks like they're doing a booming business."

"It's more than doubled just the last few days, but all the overtime won't last. We've been told that next week the night shift won't be working. The company has to do routine maintenance on some of the machines, and the production line."

"What kind of maintenance?"

"They clean, calibrate, and run tests on all the equipment. That sort of thing."

Ella watched as two massive boxes were loaded up into the truck. "How big is your production line these days? Those boxes are a lot larger than the shipping containers I saw when I toured the place."

"That's not my department, so I don't know. All I can tell you for sure is that the guys in packing and shipping were complaining because, even though they haven't had to pack up the crates, they still have to load them up using dollies. They're not supposed to use the forklifts."

"Why?"

"I don't know, but I guess the stuff inside is really fragile."

"Do you like LabKote, and the way they do business?" Ella asked.

"Yes, I really do. For an Anglo-run company, they really go out of their way to understand how things work for us here. Mr. Morgan is always asking me questions about people, about things, and our ways."

"What about Dr. Landreth. Do you like him, too?"

"Funny you should ask me that. I was telling my husband the other day that even though he's the boss, at least based on job titles, it always seems to me that Mr. Morgan is the one in control. When people aren't around, Dr. Landreth is always asking Mr. Morgan how to do this and that."

"Scientific stuff?"

"No, the business end, like who he should contact in another company, and that type of thing. Mr. Morgan seems to know everyone who does business with LabKote and he's always telling Dr. Landreth what to ship and who gets priority delivery on orders."

"Do they ever deal with toxic substances or anything like that?"

"Just the germs that sometimes show up if production screws up and stuff isn't really sterile. They've been pulling a lot of stuff from the production line for quality control testing lately, too. But everything that isn't safe gets put into the incinerator. Nothing and no one comes out of those clean rooms without being sanitized, believe me. In that, Mr. Morgan and Dr. Landreth stand together. They have rules and no one is allowed to break those rules. You're automatically fired if you get caught in the wrong section of the plant, or trying to get around the protocols. The clean rooms require electronic keys just to get inside."

"Have you had any emergencies within the past few months other than the Fierce Ones' demonstration? I imagine you know pretty much all that goes on," Ella pressed further, now that she had Martha talking.

"Well, I'm not supposed to talk about it, but Mr. Morgan did get upset about potential contamination during the animal exposition when one of the big doors came open accidentally. The machines shut down, of course, but there was this lady standing there on the other side of the fence, and the guards had to ask her to move on. I heard she was working her horse, and the dust being kicked up was coming inside. I know they had to run the filters all night." Martha shook her head.

"Who was the woman, did you ever hear?" Ella suspected it was Elisa Brownhat. The puzzle was now starting to come together a little more.

"I never heard. Mr. Morgan knows, but don't ask him. He'll know where you heard about it. Okay?" Martha's eyes grew larger. She obviously was afraid she'd gone too far.

"I won't mention it to him," Ella assured Martha, noting the woman was dressed in a comfortable-looking denim skirt and fleece sweatshirt. "Everyone seems to be dressed very casually today. It must be your hectic schedule."

"That's it, exactly. Mr. Morgan said for everyone to dress comfortably. With all the overtime being put in, he's hoping it will keep everyone relaxed and productive." Martha smiled. "I like it."

"Even Morgan himself is taking his advice. Doesn't he usually wear dress shoes instead of sneakers?" Ella ventured.

"Naw. He's a boot man usually. Some of the Rez must be getting into his blood." Martha glanced at her watch. "Oops. I've got to get going. I have less than forty minutes left of my lunch hour."

Ella watched her drive away. As she turned around, a flash of light from behind a window at the LabKote plant caught her eye. She was almost sure that it had come from Morgan's office and, although she'd only caught a glimpse, she suspected he'd used field glasses to keep an eye on them.

Ella walked back to her vehicle, lost in thought. This case was turning out to be a bit like one of those cardboard tube kaleidoscopes she'd played with as a child. Every time she looked at things from a slightly different angle, what was right in front of her would change and become something completely different. She was anxious now to find out what was in those toxicology tests for Mrs. Brownhat. Had the woman been accidentally exposed to radiation, and, if so, would it show up on tests?

Ella arrived back at the station a short time later. She was walking down the hall to her office when she saw Kevin coming out of the chief's office.

He came up to greet her. "It looks like Manuelito will have an official reprimand put in his file, but won't be suspended. Your brother didn't want me to push for that."

"I'm glad the situation's resolved," she said, then waved him inside her office. "I'm also glad you're here. There's something I need to talk to you about concerning one of my cases." She waited as he sat down then continued. "Because you're an attorney for our tribe, I'd like to get your legal opinion. Listen to the evidence I've collected against LabKote and then tell me if you think the tribe would support me if I decided to lean on them."

"Do you think they're doing something illegal?"

"I suspect something bad's going on, but I haven't got any proof. Let me bring you up to speed." She recounted what she'd learned, including the possible exposure to Mrs. Brownhat.

He said nothing for a long time. "Everything you've got is circumstantial," he said at last. "If you start harassing Morgan or Landreth, or their staff, you'll pay a higher price than they will. They've got some powerful friends."

"Or at least they did have. The two at the top of the list have been kidnapped."

"By whom? You have nothing that clearly incriminates anyone. All you've got is based on hearsay—at most. Even positive tests of radiation exposure won't prove Mrs. Brownhat was killed by someone from that plant. If you go after LabKote in any major way, you'll get sued naked."

"So I'll borrow your shirt and pants."

"Then I'll be naked."

"Okay by me."

Kevin laughed. "Okay, so what you really want me to do is stand by in case *you* need an attorney?"

"You bet. I've got a plan in mind, but it'll be risky. I'm gong to see if I can get FB-Eyes, Carolyn Roanhorse, and Wilson Joe to help me out."

"You're picking muscle from the FBI and people with science backgrounds? What are you after?"

"I'm still trying to work out the details of my plan, but the bottom line is we'll be checking the cargo in the trucks leaving LabKote. Carolyn and Wilson will be able to tell me if there's something weird about those shipments. We're worried that LabKote could be covering up for an accident, maybe even a radiation leak during the recent animal show."

"That sounds very serious. Be careful how you do this, or any evidence you get will be completely useless in court."

"I know. Maybe Blalock will be able to come up with a legal way to accomplish what we need, but we have to see what LabKote's shipping in such large quantities and protecting so much."

"You'll be walking a fine line trying to stay on this side of what's legal. Let me know what you find out."

She nodded. "Let me talk to Blalock. The FBI can be very good at finding ways around problems."

TWENTY-TWO

———— ✖ ✖ ✖ ————

A few hours later, Ella stood beside the highway just west of Hogback, inside the Rez borders. Blalock was there with the two men he'd handpicked—one a state policeman in uniform, and the other a drug enforcement agent with a black Labrador retriever trained to sniff out drugs.

The route north through the state from Mexico was an established pathway for drug smugglers, and it was this that had ultimately provided them with the legal muscle they needed. A portable meth lab had also been reported to be in operation in the Four Corners area, and an all-out search was underway.

Blalock and Ella had chosen the location for their roadblock carefully, and it had been approved by the other participating agencies because the road farther up from them branched out and led to Arizona, Colorado, and Utah. The bonus, as far as Ella was concerned, was that LabKote cargo trucks leaving the Rez went right past them and would therefore be subject to a search.

"Are you sure I have to wear this DEA jacket?" Carolyn grumbled. "The sleeves are too long."

"Yes," Blalock said. "Your presence here is official. As a doctor you're more likely to spot lab paraphernalia, even if the perps get creative. All the other personnel on this operation are assigned to other roadblocks east and south, where there's a lot more traffic."

"Not to mention that I need your expertise and Wilson's to check out the stuff coming from LabKote," Ella said, "because we're not really looking for illegal drugs."

Wilson Joe stood near Ella. "If there's something off center here, Ella, we'll find it," Wilson said, his voice soft. "Nothing gets past Carolyn, and I've worked around science equipment enough to know what an operation like LabKote should be shipping and receiving."

Blalock, across from the civilians, glanced at Wilson and Carolyn. "But officially, this is a cooperative effort between agencies. I've worked with these guys before on drug interdiction operations and raids and, believe me, they fully intend to do their job and search for drugs."

He glanced over at the state policeman, who was watching the road with binoculars for approaching trucks. The DEA officer was still in his car with the dog.

Blalock continued. "This is the way it'll go down. I'll work with the DEA agent and state policeman and we'll search outside of the trucks for drugs. Ella, you and the others will check the cargo. We'll run the dog around the outside, then move inside, but the dog is worked quickly, so you'll have to do the same."

They checked two interstate trucks before they finally got the chance they'd been waiting for. Soon they spotted the unmarked cargo truck that their lookout at Shiprock had reported was coming from LabKote. Ella put out a portable barrier and some traffic cones while the state policeman lit a flare, and waved the truck down. The driver stopped and Blalock explained what they were doing.

"Hey, the stuff I carry is presterilized lab and surgical supplies for hospitals and such. If you contaminate it by opening up a package, it'll have to go back," the driver protested.

"We'll just take a look at the cargo, then run our dog through. He can pick up the scent of contraband without opening any packages. We'll be careful," Blalock said.

The driver was directed off the highway, and the barriers were removed from the road.

After the driver opened the back doors to the trailer, the state policeman took him aside to check his permits, license, and shipping paperwork. Wilson and Carolyn quickly climbed into the truck via a small ladder, and Ella followed with an electric lantern. The large wooden packing crates caught their attention immediately. With Ella holding the light, Wilson and Carolyn checked the shipping labels, which were addressed to supply companies out of state.

"These aren't the normal cardboard shipping boxes used for lab supplies and glassware," Carolyn said, her voice low.

"They look more like frameworks to protect equipment," Wilson said. "Can you tell what's in there through the spaces between the wooden slats?" he asked Carolyn.

"The control panel and label are covered by this board, so I can't quite tell what it is," Carolyn said.

"That board's loose. Let me move it aside," Wilson said.

"No, it's not," Carolyn said, testing it.

"Give me a minute." Wilson gave it a vicious tug and pulled the plank loose. "Sure it was. See? It came right off."

Carolyn smiled. "My mistake." She drew near and looked inside. "That's a gamma ray generator."

Wilson pried the lid open partway on another crate. "I have no idea what the heck that is. It looks like a big stainless steel kettle. There's a pressure valve, so I might have said it was an autoclave, if it wasn't so big."

Carolyn took a close look. "It's an autoclave, all right, used to sterilize glassware and petri dishes in large quantities, like for a major biological research lab. Seems overkill for the LabKote operation, though."

The DEA agent appeared with his dog. "You finished?"

"Yeah," Ella said as Wilson pushed the boards on the crates back into position. A moment later, they went back down the ladder giving the agent room to work.

Once the dog and the agent had finished their work, the driver was allowed to lock the doors again, and get underway.

No one said a word until the truck was well down the road. Ella finally pulled Carolyn and Wilson aside. "Well, what did you think of the cargo?" Ella asked.

"I don't know what to tell you," Carolyn said. "What we saw is not entirely out of line with what they claim to be doing. But what puzzles me is why they're getting rid of equipment they supposedly need, instead of shipping out product."

"Let's see what the other LabKote trucks are carrying, then we may have a clearer idea of what we're dealing with," Ella suggested.

They continued the process for another four hours, stopping and checking out three more LabKote trucks before the roadblock was finally taken down. After the other two agents had left, they finally had a chance to talk freely.

"Their business is supposed to be producing sterilized lab supplies, yet there wasn't a single box of lab supplies on any of the trucks," Wilson said. "Just equipment used for the operation."

"And how can they keep production going without the gamma ray machines, for instance?" Carolyn added. "Surely they only have a limited number of those. How can they send back two to their supplier and still stay in business?"

"What if their radiation equipment malfunctioned, maybe leaking and causing an accident, and they're now trying to cover up by sending the equipment back to the vendor?" Ella proposed.

"That's reaching," Blalock said. "If that was the plan, why didn't they do it a long time ago? And why send back other equipment they supposedly need? Are they running out of money, and having to send it back?"

"I don't know, but we can't discount the other evidence. Remember the dead birds and insects we found at the fairgrounds. Their deaths are consistent with overexposure to radiation. And I have reason to believe Elisa Brownhat may have been exposed as well." Ella related her conversation with Martha Gene.

"That might provide a motive for murder. We'll have to see how the toxicology tests come out." Carolyn nodded.

"When you were there at LabKote, did you get a good look at

any of the equipment in the sterile rooms, the ones that were off limits?" Carolyn continued.

"Sure. I saw one of those autoclaves, and another machine that looked like a big stainless steel chamber with lots of valves and electronic panels." Ella tried to recall the details. "It was really strange seeing the setup. It looked like a scene straight from one of those virus hunter movies, complete with the protective suits for the workers."

"Why were they wearing biohazard suits? I don't get it," Carolyn said, mulling it over. "They shouldn't need that level of protection. Ella, if you saw a photo of the machine you just described, would you recognize it?" Carolyn asked.

"Yeah, I think so."

"Let's go back to my office. I'll show you my lab equipment catalogs and see if you can spot it. We'll know more then."

Blalock shook his head. "So, after all this work, what we have is inconclusive? Even if Mrs. Brownhat was irradiated, we still don't have enough evidence to move on anything. We'd still have to link her to LabKote."

"Why don't you come with me to Carolyn's office?" Ella said. "This isn't over yet."

Blalock exhaled softly. "You're never going to let me retire in peace, are you? Watch me get transferred to a post in Prudoe Bay, Alaska."

"Do you feel that you're on to something?" Wilson asked Ella. "All you really have at this point is circumstantial and speculative."

She knew that he was asking her to judge based on her intuition, not just theories. Like many others, Wilson thought it was far more than just police training. "I do," she said at last. "But whether it'll pan out or not, is something else altogether," she said, bringing it into perspective for him.

"I'm worried about you . . . I'm worried about all of us," Wilson said as Ella walked him back to his car. "Don't forget to let me know what happens."

"You can come with us to Carolyn's office if you'd like," Ella said.

He shook his head. "All things considered, I'd rather not," he said with a hesitant smile. "I try to avoid visiting the morgue while still alive."

A short time later, Ella followed Carolyn and Blalock back to the hospital. She was now convinced that there was something going on at LabKote. Maybe it had started with Hansen's death, or the reason behind his murder, and possibly that of Elisa Brownhat. One thing was clear. LabKote was at the center of a lot of the troubles the Rez had seen.

Twenty minutes later, they were seated in Carolyn's office. Blalock, sipping a cup of freshly brewed coffee, was unusually quiet as Ella leafed through the equipment supply catalogs.

"Something's eating at you," Ella said as Carolyn left to type up a report. "What's wrong?"

"I'm worried about what we discovered tonight," Blalock said. "Having LabKote all of a sudden boxing up and sending away equipment smacks of tenants who intend to slip out in the middle of the night."

"You're thinking that they plan to shut down and leave, before anyone can figure out what's been going on and hold them accountable?"

"I don't know," he said with a shrug. "Maybe I'm overreacting, but I always thought it strange that this company set up shop on the Rez, so far away from major airports, rail lines, and the interstates. You would have thought that they'd want to be closer to a major city where they'd have a variety of shipping options."

"Land's more expensive in the city and the tribe did give them a lot of tax breaks."

"Yeah, but I've got to tell you, Clah, if it were me, and I was doing something I didn't want anyone to know about, I'd pick the Rez, too. Even going back in time to the atomic bomb development, this state has always provided a lot of isolation for secret projects."

"If you had to guess, what would you say is going on?" Ella asked.

"I don't know, but I'll tell you this. I'm going to get even more details on Morgan's and Landreth's backgrounds. I'll also see if I can speed up the Marine Corps and get the service file Officer Goodluck requested on Morgan. I'll be gathering background information on LabKote, too," Blalock said, picking up his cell phone and punching out a number.

"Morgan supposedly served in Desert Storm, came back, resigned from the military, then spent some time in Europe doing security work. That's information I got from Morgan himself, and LabKote's personnel file. Maybe you can dig up more. Landreth's background was kind of generic. I'm curious to see what FBI sources can add to that."

"Have you learned anything else about LabKote, other than what's in their brochures?" Blalock asked, still holding the cell phone to his ear.

"Not really. They're too new." Ella suddenly stopped leafing through the pages. "Carolyn? I've got something here."

Blalock rolled his chair back from the table, spoke briefly into the receiver, then disconnected the call.

Carolyn returned to the office just then and glanced down at the equipment Ella was pointing to. "Are you sure that's what you saw?"

"Yeah. I remember seeing those places with the heavy gloves you put your hands into before reaching into the sealed chamber."

Blalock stood and walked over, looking down at the page from over Ella's shoulder.

"Then I've got a news flash for you," Carolyn exclaimed. "LabKote is doing something besides producing germ-free supplies. That's a culture chamber for handling dangerous forms of bacteria. Those built-in gloves are for handling petri dishes and vials without exposing yourself to pathogens. But based on what I've been told about their operation, they shouldn't have any reason to culture any bacteria at all. Whatever bacterial colonies they do end up with would only be a result of faulty sterilization uncovered from sampling as part of their quality control. That's part of their waste and something they probably destroy immediately, or should."

"There's some circumstantial evidence that suggests LabKote may have used laboratory animals at one point." Ella told them about the rabbit Alice Washburn had found and the subsequent events. "That new rabbit is supposed to be a clever little thing."

"The best and the worst. That's another by-product of genetic manipulation or radiation-induced defects. I wonder exactly what they've been experimenting with," Carolyn said.

"Those suits that the men wore in that locked room . . ." Ella shook her head. "There's something really bad going on there."

"You know, if all they're doing is producing germ-free supplies, they wouldn't need biohazard suits and filtration systems. Most of the microorganisms they'd find in unsterile lab supplies are relatively benign. Even bad strains of food bacteria and strep can be controlled using simple sterilization techniques and lab procedures," Carolyn said.

Blalock was leaning forward. "Okay. So what we've got isn't just a radiation leak cover-up. We also have a real good suspicion that they could be handling, and maybe even producing very dangerous bacteria. But to what end? Biological warfare or terrorism?"

"More importantly, how the heck do we get in there to verify any of this? We have no evidence that will get us a search warrant," Ella reminded them. "What would we say we're searching for? Equipment that we *think* may be used for cultivating dangerous bacteria, and all based on my recollection? They'd sue us for harassment, for sure," Ella said.

"And win," Blalock added. "We'll have to approach this from a different angle. Let's see what we can get from behind the scenes. I'm going to request backup and start a twenty-four hour surveillance. We need evidence that will get us a ticket in there." Blalock started writing down notes. "We've had more than one ex-soldier or disillusioned tech-head decide to become a terrorist. We need to look for any foreign or domestic terrorist group connections to these people. I'm also going to request information from Interpol on Morgan. They should have something if he did security work overseas."

As Blalock left, Ella gave Carolyn a worried look. "I've got to tell you, I'm scared to death. I went to the fairgrounds a few times during that animal husbandry event, and I was pregnant at the time. My baby . . ."

"Might have been vulnerable," Carolyn finished for her. "You could get some tests run."

"I was already advised to get a maternal serum alpha fetal something blood test after sixteen weeks. What's that?"

"That's an AFP, a maternal serum alpha-fetoprotein screening test. They check your blood for elevated levels of alpha-fetoprotein. If the test comes back abnormal, it could indicate any of several defects or problems with the fetus. That's when more tests could be run to isolate the concerns." Carolyn said.

"But will anything be conclusive?"

"At that point, probably only major defects, such as spinal cord problems or the absence of brain tissue." Carolyn paused, then added, "But talk to your obstetrician. It's been a long time since I studied anything to do with that field of medicine."

Ella shook her head slowly. "I'll ask, but if the screening test comes out okay, I may pass on the ones that come later. Instead of calming me, I think at this point all they'll do is scare me silly."

Carolyn's eyes narrowed. "You're sounding a little bit like a traditionalist who believes fear can harm."

"Fear *can* be harmful when you allow it to take you over. I really do believe that. Fright causes physical changes and chemical imbalances."

"So, what are you advocating?"

"Something I'd never thought I'd be saying," she said slowly. "I'll go through the normal prenatal tests, but after that I'm going to rely on the old ways, Carolyn. This time, I think that the best chance my baby and I have is if I straddle the line between the old and the new, and take the best of both."

"That's a good plan, but I want you to know that I don't think you really have anything to worry about," Carolyn said gently. "If you'd been exposed to any harmful bacteria, you'd already have shown symptoms. And those gamma ray generators produce a very narrow, directed beam. With the room shielded, you would have had to be in *exactly* the wrong place at the wrong time for it to have affected you at all."

"Then how did the birds and insects get irradiated? Maybe their safety systems failed and they exposed everything outside one of those big doors, including Elisa Brownhat. If Hansen knew about it, that may have been what got him killed. And somebody has been trying to kill me. Is it because they know I'm pregnant with a potentially deformed baby that could lead back to them, or is it because I'm on their case?" She ran a hand through her hair in a gesture of frustration. "It's all the possibilities and the lack of answers that scare me the most."

"If there's anything I can do to help you, just say the word. If what we suspect is true, I'd like to throw those LabKote jerks to the *Dineh* and let our people tear them apart."

"Sometimes primitive justice has definite appeal."

Ella returned to her vehicle, unable to shake the feeling that something terrible was going to happen on the Rez soon unless she could find a way to stop it. She would have liked a court order to tap Morgan's phone, but that was out of the question until they had some solid evidence.

Still considering her options, Ella stopped at the Totah Cafe. George Branch was doing his radio show, so she listened to his tirade. He had now embarked on an all-out attack on tribal politics and was accusing the tribal council of cheating The People.

"The worst part," Branch's voice boomed over the radio, "is that the FBI and the tribal police are running around in circles chasing their own bureaucratic tails. The kidnappings are as phoney as everything about the people who engineered them. While our cops are out looking for kidnappers and missing politicians, our tribal resources are being handed on a platter to non-Navajo businessmen. And, folks, when our land is used up and no good to anyone anymore, that's when we'll finally be left alone. The Anglos will leave, but we'll still be here trying to undo the damage and scratching at the earth to provide enough for our own people. The tribe's best allies right now are the Fierce Ones, despite the efforts of a few to make them look like our enemies. The People are being told so many lies, the truth is getting buried. And we have our politicians to thank for this. Do something about it, listeners. The next time you visit your Chapter House, or go to the ballot box, let your elected officials know that you're as mad as hell, and not going to take it anymore!"

Ella groaned. With Hollywood sound bites like the last one, Branch sounded like *he* was running for office. How much more could the tribe endure?

The waitress, a Navajo girl in her early twenties, came up to her. "What do you think, Officer Clah? Are our politicians forgetting The People?"

"No more than usual. Branch likes to talk about the lies other people tell," Ella said, "but he uses catchphrases and deals in half-truths geared mostly to get him more listeners, not to solve problems. Until we find the answers we need, no one, including Branch, knows exactly where the truth lies. Assumptions are seldom reliable enough for anything except gossip, yet that's exactly what he's using as the premise for all his claims. Always be careful when anyone insists he's got all the answers, because that alone makes him a liar."

Ella threw a dollar on the table. Her appetite was gone, and George Branch was responsible. Without ordering, she said good-bye and walked out.

Ella sat in her office, studying Senator Yellowhair and Ernest Ben's phone records. One thing they had in common was several calls made at about the same time to Morgan's home.

On a hunch, she dialed Sheriff Taylor's number. "You have Hansen's phone records, don't you?" she asked.

"Sure. They're in his file. Whatcha need?"

"I need you to check and see if he called two numbers in particular." She gave him Yellowhair's and Ben's numbers, then waited.

"They're here. He called each of them twice in one month. The last time was the day before he was killed. Have you found a connection?"

"I think so," she said slowly. "Was the first time the day after the animal exposition?" she asked, giving him the date.

"That matches," Taylor said.

"Here's what I think happened. My guess is that Hansen either caused or discovered that there had been a radiation leak of some kind at LabKote. He knew that people and animals were exposed, so he called the two tribal officials he knew, ready to blow the whistle. But Yellowhair and Ben decided to check for themselves and called Morgan. Morgan found out what Hansen had done and either killed him himself or had him killed. Later, maybe suspecting Yellowhair and Ben could still cause problems, or because they asked for payoffs he couldn't provide, Morgan kidnapped them, and made it look like the Fierce Ones were responsible."

"Can you prove any of this?"

"Not yet, but I'm working on it."

"Keep me updated, and let me know if I can help."

"You've got it."

Justine came in as Ella hung up. "I heard the last part of that. So you think Yellowhair and Ben were kidnapped because they knew too much?"

"I'll tell you the picture that's emerging for me. I'm betting that there was an accident the day of the animal event at the fairgrounds and that resulted in a radiation leak. Hansen wanted to blow the whistle but, unfortunately, he called two men who couldn't be trusted. They, in turn, probably demanded hush money from LabKote, and that's when Morgan or Landreth, or maybe both, decided they needed to get rid of them to keep the lid on things a while longer."

"So, you think Ben and Yellowhair are dead?"

Ella considered it. "I'm not sure. If Morgan's behind what's going on, I'd say probably not. He wouldn't pass up the chance to use them as leverage if things got rough."

"How do we get evidence that will either prove or disprove your theory?" Justine asked.

"What we need are LabKote's electric bills, power consumption records, water bills, phone bills, and anything else that would indicate something atypical happened the day of the exposition."

"But how does this tie into the livestock killings, or do you think they were a separate event?"

"I think it's connected. My guess is that they staged those incidents to divert us and help cover up what happened. Remember that all the animals killed were females. That was self-serving on several counts since it would also take care of any questions that might have arisen later if any problems showed up with their offspring," Ella said.

She continued. "Of course, they purposely made it look as if the traditionalists were killing the animals of the progressives so that people would start fighting each other, and the trail would become hopelessly muddied. Mrs. Brownhat had to go, too, because she had been irradiated, and knew about the door being open. All she had to do was mention it to the wrong person, and they were busted. They tried very hard to make it look like an accident, but they failed."

"We still have nothing except circumstantial evidence and not even Judge Chase will give us a court order based on that," Justine said.

Ella cursed under her breath. "Yeah, you're right. That's why I want you to have the electric company check their records and see if there was anything unusual in that power grid, or whatever it's called, around that time. That won't require a court order."

"I'll see to it," Justine said. "For what it's worth, I think your theory's a good one. From that angle, it's easy to link the events to the break-in at the clinic. It seems likely that they were looking for women at a stage in their pregnancy where their fetuses would be vulnerable to radiation. Elisa Brownhat had to go first for a couple of reasons, but she wasn't the only pregnant woman in this area they'd have to murder to remove all risks. Several children born with defects whose mothers were at the animal show could easily have led to an investigation that would have pointed back to LabKote, the only real source of radiation outside a hospital around here. Fortunately, things got too hot for them, and they had to change their plans."

"At the time Elisa was killed, they must have still been planning to stay on the Rez for the duration. I would imagine that they changed their minds after things started getting quickly out of control," Ella said.

"Or maybe they completed what they set out to do faster than they'd anticipated," Justine said.

Ella remembered the terrorist angle and the bacteria culture chamber, and felt a stab of fear. As Justine walked out, she placed one hand over her stomach and closed her eyes. Slowly, an inexplicable peace came over her, and when she opened her eyes again, she knew that her child was going to be all right.

Ella shook her head. Superstitious nonsense. She couldn't possibly know anything with that degree of certainty. Remembering the stories about Bunstein and his stillborn littermates, she shuddered.

Ella stood up and began to pace. It was pointless to give into fear now. She had to trust what her heart was telling her. The connection she felt to the baby was real. Her child *would* be all right. Every feminine instinct she possessed assured her of it.

Holding on to that thought, she returned to her desk and, before she could sit down, her phone rang. Ella grabbed the receiver and identified herself.

"Hello, Officer Clah. This is Barbara Sanchez. I'm the bartender at the Palomino Lounge. You spoke to me about Tom LaPoint, remember?"

"Hello, Barbara. Yes, I know who you are. Did you remember something about the man you knew as Tom LaPoint that might help us?" Ella replied, hoping that was the case. Witnesses seldom called unless they'd thought of something new to add.

"It's not about Tom, or whatever his name was, it's about the man he met that one time, the one with the cowboy hat. I just remembered something about him that may help." Barbara said.

"What is it?" Ella responded.

"The man had a long scar on his arm, like from a bad cut." Barbara recalled. "I remember seeing it when he turned to leave. It was on his left arm, I think."

Ella recalled the scar on Morgan's left arm. "Do you happen to remember if the man wore boots as well?"

"You know, I think he did. I always notice men who have western hats but shoes instead of boots because I think that looks dumb, and I didn't get that impression. I don't remember the style or color, though."

"That's okay, I think what you did recall will be very useful. If you think of anything else, call immediately."

As she hung up and sat down again, Kevin Tolino walked into her office, wearing a serious expression instead of his usual smile.

"I saw your grandmother watching our house again this morning," she said slowly, wishing she had something more pleasant to discuss with him.

"That's one of the reasons I came to talk to you. Don't worry, she won't be doing that anymore."

She said nothing for a long moment, measuring her words carefully before speaking. "So, it's over? Or does that mean I'm just getting a new watcher?"

The expression on his face told her everything. "Let me guess. It's you."

He hesitated, then nodded. "It was the only way I could insure that they'd stay out of your way. And I honestly think that you'll be better off with me, Ella. I won't let anyone pose a threat to the baby. You've got to believe that."

"I do, but I don't need help protecting the baby."

"You're stubborn and independent, but things aren't that simple anymore. There are threats everywhere now, and we'll need each other."

"There's no safety in numbers, Kevin, not in this case. Even if we stay together, we may not be able to counter everything that'll affect this baby," she said slowly.

"I know what you're talking about," he said somberly. "I've been thinking about the possibility you mentioned of a radiation leak LabKote could be covering up, and it really worries me, Ella. I remember you talking about the animal show weeks ago. You were there." His expression grew hard and his eyes burned with anger as he added, "If LabKote is responsible for a radiation leak or for doing anything that could have harmed you, our baby, or The People, I want the ones responsible to pay."

"So do I, and I *will* get them."

"If you need any help, call me."

"There *is* something you can do. You have access to many tribal records. I want you to see if you can find a clear paper trail that links Yellowhair, Ben, and LabKote. If they're in league with LabKote, we need evidence to prove it."

"All right. I'll get on that right away. Anything else?"

"I'm going to want to do an extensive background check on Ben and Yellowhair that'll include accessing their bank accounts."

"You won't have any problem with that. Get Judge Chase to give you a court order. The bank won't fight it because the two are already part of an investigation involving the FBI. Considering the circumstances, you should be able to get the paperwork in record time."

"I also want to see George Branch's banking records, and those of Avery Blueeyes."

"That's trickier. Let me see what I can do for you. Judge Chase and I go back a ways, so he'll cut me some slack. But Branch will scream like a wounded pig, claiming government interference in his privacy."

"I know, but I need to look for discrepancies that might reveal how he's getting his tips, like the one about Judge Chase about to be kidnapped. I nearly got barbecued on that call. Literally."

"I'll get you the court orders, or find a way around them."

As he left, Ella remained seated at her desk, trying to figure out her next move. Everything was in the works, and she had more possible links to Morgan, but until the paperwork gave them the authorization, she couldn't take the next step.

Ella went to Big Ed's office, and updated him on everything that was going on.

"You still have nothing concrete, Shorty, but at least you're on your way to getting it." He nodded slowly. "Once you get the bank records you need, I want Blalock, Justine, and Tolino here.

We'll all work on this, including me. If LabKote really is planning on shutting down and leaving before anyone notices, we've got to move fast. I'm also going to put people around that place so that nothing will go in or out without our knowing."

"I don't think we should. If they have Ben and Yellowhair somewhere on the premises, the last thing we want to do is let them know we're on to them."

"All right. You're in charge of this one. But your head will be the first to roll if this blows up in our faces."

"Understood."

It was close to ten that night when they all sat in the conference room adjacent to Big Ed's office.

"Branch has no financial connections to anyone other than his station and station sponsors," the accountant Blalock had brought in said. "He's not a wealthy man. He's got a good middle-class income, but his financial records are pretty straightforward. He owes money, but not a lot, and he inherited that house."

Tolino then placed several documents on the table. "These are tribal records pertaining to LabKote. It looks like Ben and Yellowhair were critical in helping LabKote cut through the red tape. The checks that should have been done on the machinery and so on were signed, but not dated. They may have never happened. We just don't know. Engineers hired by the tribe were supposed to check out the facility, but LabKote was able to get waivers in order to open on a certain date. There are no records anywhere that the engineers actually made those checks afterwards either."

"There are also some very large deposits made into the accounts of both those politicians the day after LabKote opened," Blalock said, looking at the accountant, who nodded. "The money transfers that came in were from out of state banks, using a corporate name that is hard to trace. Both amounts were deposited on the same day."

"Avery Blueeyes doesn't seem to play a part in any of this. Blueeyes is very nearly broke," Big Ed said. "His accounts are in shambles. I don't have to be an accountant to understand that."

Big Ed regarded them thoughtfully, then continued. "So what we have are bank records suggesting that bribes were paid to two men who were later kidnapped. There are also phone records linking Hansen to Yellowhair and Ben, then those two to Morgan."

"It's still not enough to raid LabKote," Kevin said. "We have nothing against LabKote itself. The only thing our evidence really proves is that, at one point, Yellowhair and Ben both spoke to Morgan. That's not a criminal offense. We can't prove that the deposits were bribes, and we don't have access to either man's tax records."

"What about the lab equipment being shipped out?" Ella asked.

"It could have gone out for repairs, routine maintenance, or been returned at the end of a lease agreement. For all we know, other shipments have come in with new machines."

There was a knock at the door, and Big Ed's secretary poked her head inside. "Something for Agent Blalock, Chief." She held out a packet from a courier service.

Justine, closest to the door, took the packet and passed it over to Blalock, and the secretary left, closing the door.

Everyone watched Blalock as he opened the packet. "It's the Marine Corps file on Walter Morgan. I asked that it be delivered here as soon as it came in." Blalock placed the faxed documents on the table in front of him so he could see them all at once. He picked up a photo and handed it to Ella. "So, this is what Morgan looks like?"

Ella looked at the photo and did a double take. "Damn!"

"What is it, Ella?" Justine strained to see.

"That's not Morgan. Either the marines made a mistake, or our Morgan has stolen this man's identity."

"Are your sure? Here's another photo, glued to his service record." Blalock slid another paper over.

Justine stood and looked over Ella's shoulder. "The birth dates and social security numbers are correct, but I've seen the man at LabKote, and this is not him. A fingerprint check would just confirm it."

Big Ed took a look, cleared his throat, and turned to Blalock. "I'm thinking of the terrorist possibility now, as I think you all are." He looked around the table, and the others nodded. "Can the FBI check to see if Interpol or the CIA might be able to put a name next to *our* Walter Morgan's face?"

"We don't have a photo of him, do we?" Justine asked.

"We can get one. Dwayne, can you ask the local media to give you a print of all the LabKote employees they filmed at the demonstration by the Fierce Ones? I bet Morgan was in some of those shots, and Justine or I can point him out to you," Ella said. "Both Channel Four and Thirteen were there."

"Can do. I'll get on it as soon as we leave."

Justine's cell phone rang, and she left the room for a moment. When she returned, she gave Ella a satisfied smile. "We have even more. Electric company records show that there was a significant spike of short duration in the sector that incorporates LabKote's facility on the day in question. Because their electrical demands are so high, LabKote is virtually by itself on that part of the system."

"That's still circumstantial," Kevin said. "We have no proof anything actually went wrong, and the person at LabKote who could best answer our questions about that is dead. The only solid evidence we have now is that Morgan has stolen someone else's identity."

Ella was about to argue that they could still get damning toxicology reports from Elisa Brownhat's autopsy, backed up with Martha Gene's testimony, when her cell phone rang. Hearing Loretta's voice surprised her and sent a cold chill through her. She knew one thing—her sister-in-law had *never* called her at work without a major reason. Excusing herself quickly, she stepped out of the room.

"I don't know what to do," Loretta said, panic in her voice.

"Calm down and tell me what's wrong," Ella said, using her most reassuring voice, though she was getting more alarmed by the minute. She'd never heard Loretta panic except when her family was in danger.

"My husband spent the day in the medicine hogan working and wanted to be left alone. I did as he asked, but since he hadn't eaten all day, I decided to take some dinner out to him." She cleared her throat, then continued in a shaky voice. "When I went inside, he was gone, and everything was in shambles. The pots with his healing herbs were all shattered, and there was blood on the sheepskin he sits on. There was a terrible fight in there, Sister-in-law, and someone was hurt."

"That doesn't mean it was Clifford. He's very good at taking care of himself."

"I don't know how many men stood against him."

"Less than came in," Ella said. "Now try to stay calm and don't touch anything. I'll be right over."

"But you can't tell anyone what's happened. The ones who took my husband left a note for you. They don't want the police involved. If you disobey, they'll kill him. There's more, but you can read it for yourself when you come."

She heard Loretta's voice harden. Though no one knew the whole story yet, Ella knew she was being blamed for what had happened to her brother. "Read the note to me now," she said firmly.

Loretta cleared her throat, but she wasn't totally successful in keeping her tone steady. "Investigator Clah, if you want to see your brother alive again, disappear for a few days and don't tell the department why. If the police get involved in a search for your brother, he'll be left on your doorstep in pieces."

Fear pried into her, hard and fast. She had no doubt who had taken Clifford. Worst of all, if her hunch was right, he was being held inside LabKote. Inside their well-guarded perimeter, LabKote was nearly impregnable and the law, at least for now, protected the criminals and stood against her.

From this point on she was on her own. If her brother was to stay alive, she'd have to win using her own rules.

TWENTY-THREE

——— ✖ ✖ ✖ ———

Ella went back into the room where the others were meeting. They'd made no progress. Legally, except for what they had on Morgan, their hands were tied until they had enough evidence to get a warrant to search the whole facility. If they went to pick up Morgan now, Landreth would still be free to cover up anything illegal that was going on. She considered telling the others what had happened to her brother, but then decided against it. She knew what she had to do and the fewer people who knew, the less interference she'd get.

"I want you to pressure them, Ella," Big Ed said. "Go over there, question them, harass them a bit. I want to rattle the cage. Let's see what happens."

She smiled. It wasn't exactly what she had in mind, but it was close. "Consider it done."

Ella stood up as their conference ended. As she walked to the door, Kevin accompanied her. "What was that call all about? You looked troubled when you got back."

"It's a family matter, nothing for you to be concerned about."

He gave her a long look. "Are you sure?"

"Kevin, you're going to have to cut me some slack, okay? I've been single for a long time, and it can be nothing short of irritating to have someone watching over my shoulder all the time." She paused, knowing that if she made him suspicious now, he'd never let her out of his sight. "How would you like it if, all of a sudden, I was there every time you turned around? I know you like your privacy as much as I do."

He nodded slowly. "Yeah, I understand what you're saying. I didn't mean to crowd you."

"We'll talk again soon, but right now I need to get back to work."

Ella returned to her office alone. The situation with the kidnappings had cut all her options. There was only one way out. Her brother's life hung in the balance, and it was up to her to take the next step.

She took off her badge, and placed it in her drawer. What she had to do now broke every rule she'd ever followed, but, for the next few hours, she wouldn't be a cop. It was the only way.

Ella drove out of the station and headed to Loretta's. She checked her rearview mirror often, and although she couldn't see anyone tailing her, she had a feeling that whoever had written the note wouldn't be far away.

The minute she arrived at her brother's home, Loretta came out the front door. Julian tried to come out, too, but Loretta forced him back inside the house.

"I'm not staying here," Loretta said, meeting Ella outside. "I'm afraid for Julian. I'm going to my mother's."

"Good idea. You'll be safer with your family now." They would protect her and the boy and it would be one less thing for her to worry about. "I'm going to take a look inside the medicine hogan." Ella started walking off, then stopped in mid stride and looked back at Loretta. "I *will* bring my brother back to you and his son."

Loretta met her gaze and held it. "Yes, but at what cost to all of us? What have you dragged him into?"

She started to answer, then changed her mind. It wouldn't do any good to argue now. "Have you told Mom about this?"

Loretta shook her head. "I knew it would frighten her and I was afraid she'd get sick. What about you? Have you told the other cops you work with what's happened?"

"No one knows—except you and me. Let's keep it that way for now."

As Loretta walked away, Ella sighed. She shouldn't have expected anything different, but it still hurt. At a time when she needed her family's support most, there was no one she could turn to.

Ella entered the hogan, flashlight in hand, and, as she looked around, understood the fear that had gripped Loretta. The interior was in chaos. Her brother's medicine pouch was on the ground, slashed open, and the sheepskin pelt he used as a blanket and cushion was spotted heavily with fresh blood.

Clifford had clearly gone up against a knife-wielding opponent but, without tests, there was no way for her to verify whose blood had been shed. As the last rays of the fading sun found their way inside the hogan, a sliver of light played over something metallic on the ground.

Ella picked it up carefully. It was a lighter. The initials "K. H." were engraved on it. Anger filled her as she realized it was Kyle Hansen's missing lighter, and that her brother could have been implicated in his murder if she hadn't come alone.

She crouched on the ground and studied the now-familiar boot tracks she could make out. The evidence told her that her brother had only fought one man, and knowing her own brother's capabilities, she knew that his opponent must have been highly trained in hand-to-hand. Clifford had always been able to take care of himself.

Landreth wouldn't have been able to take him, not in a million years. But Morgan was another matter altogether. He'd been trained with weapons somewhere, and if not in the military, possibly with a terrorist group. Morgan was linked to murder, attempted murder, and kidnapping—but only by an unproven boot-print.

Somehow, she had to get inside LabKote and search for her

brother, and for evidence that would help her identify the other men responsible for the crimes that had been committed. Morgan was only one person, and he couldn't have done everything on his own. All the answers she needed were at LabKote and that was where she had to go.

Ella went home and changed into her darkest jeans and a black wool sweater. Since her mother was at a Plant Watchers meeting tonight, no explanations would be needed.

Patting Two on the head, Ella started to go out the front door, but then stopped. Two's growls told her she was being watched, but this time it was not by somebody's grandmother. No one was in sight, but the dog's senses matched her own instinct for danger, and Ella knew she'd have to use a little trickery.

Sticking her cell phone in her pocket, Ella slipped out of a window at the back of the house and jogged over to her brother's place. It took her twenty minutes, but she was still in good shape even though she hadn't kept up her daily morning runs.

As soon as she cleared the canyon, Ella saw Clifford's truck parked outside the hogan. Loretta's vehicle was gone, which meant she'd already left with Julian. Thank goodness Clifford had finally taught his wife to drive.

Slipping inside her brother's truck, and reaching for the spare keys she knew he always kept beneath the floor mat, she got underway.

Ella drove to LabKote without a clear plan in mind. There was the electric fence, the guards, and the dog to contend with, but to get in successfully she would have to remain unnoticed. She parked the truck behind one of the fairgrounds buildings and moved to a clear vantage point beside a car in the parking lot.

Even though it was close to eight in the evening, the vehicle traffic seemed to be at an all-time high. In the space of forty minutes, several large, delivery-type vans pulled into the covered dock, picked up cargo, and left.

Ella wrote down the times, truck numbers, and company names each time. Whatever was being shipped out at this odd time had aroused her curiosity.

The open garage-type doors allowed her to see into the building's shipping warehouse which extended outward onto the loading platforms. Observing a large truck approaching from the direction of the highway, Ella made her way carefully toward the gate, staying in the shadows.

Thankful that the moon was not out, she drew even closer. If she stayed on the other side of the truck, maybe she'd be able to slip in. Suddenly the dog, chained to a large stake, began barking furiously. As the guard turned his head, Ella froze and ducked back into the shadows. After what seemed like an eternity, the guard shifted his focus back to the driver. "Blasted dog. He probably saw another cottontail."

Ella stayed still, scarcely breathing. Hearing a soft rustle in the brush, she turned her head and saw a Navajo man come out of the shadows, crouching low. "You timed this really wrong," he whispered. "Come with me, and I can help you get inside."

Even in the darkness, Ella recognized Jimmy Herder. "You're the one who keeps an eye on things for the Fierce Ones, aren't you?"

He nodded. "Something's happening tonight. They've never shipped out anything after four P.M. What made me suspicious was when they gave me the night off with pay. They've always made a great big show out of hiring a Navajo guard, but the fact is they've kept me on a real short leash. Tonight, I plan to do a little digging of my own. If anyone asks, I'll say I came back to get my jacket."

"How are we getting in?"

"There's a new personnel gate that was just installed to allow the guards access to the parking lot from both ends. It's kept locked with an electronic monitoring system. If you try to force it, you alert the guards with an alarm, but I know the security code, and can get us in. After we're inside, though, things are bound to get tougher. If we get caught, I'll get fired, or worse."

"Worse is right. You're more likely to lose your life. Instinct tells me that this is a very dangerous place to be tonight."

Jimmy led her to the small gate, equipped with a large electronic lock, slipped his ID card into the slot, then punched in a number. The gate opened.

"Don't touch the fence on either side, or above the gate. It's still hot," Jimmie said, cautioning her about the high-voltage charge.

They went in, and Jimmie closed the gate behind them.

"That was a lot easier than what I'd expected," Ella whispered. "Do you have any idea how many people are working here tonight?"

"The regular evening crew isn't in. I've seen Morgan, two techs from quality control, the guard at the gate, and another one who conducts random patrols all over the facility. I'm assuming Landreth is here, mostly because where Morgan is, Landreth is, but I haven't seen him. There could be one or two more working in the quality control labs too."

They slipped inside the building through a utility room, using Jimmie's electronic key card to open the locks. He then led her down a hall, showing her how to time her passage to avoid the constant sweep of video cameras that monitored the interior.

"What is it you're after?" Jimmy whispered.

"I believe they've kidnapped my brother, and brought him here. Morgan probably has him locked up somewhere."

"Why didn't you say that before?" he whispered back. "We need to get into the security room. The monitors will show us practically every office and room in the building."

"Practically?"

"I've never counted the monitors and compared that to the number of offices. Some monitors share cameras, too."

Jimmie led the way down a narrow hallway. Although she half expected to run into someone, and then have to try to neutralize them silently, it never happened.

"Everyone's at the warehouse adjoining the loading dock, near as I can tell," Jimmie said.

"Where's the security room?" Ella said looking around.

"Right up there. But let me look inside first."

He sauntered into the room, greeted someone, then came out half a minute later. "We're going to have to work fast. There was a guard there, but I cold-cocked him with his nightstick and stomped on his radio. I'll handcuff him to a table and gag him, but there's no telling how long it'll be before someone notices what happened."

Ella stepped inside the security room, and as Jimmy took care of the guard, she studied the monitors across the tables. Ella could see Morgan as he spoke to two other men in the open warehouse adjoining the loading dock. Then she saw Landreth in a workroom attaching shipping labels to cardboard boxes. Two security guards were outside by the main gate, patrolling with the dog, now leashed.

Ella pushed the buttons on a monitor attached to several cameras, and as the device switched images, she saw two men sitting on the floor of a small storeroom, clearly prisoners. The first face she saw was, without a doubt, that of her brother's, and he had a makeshift bandage on his left arm. As the other man shifted, leaning against the wall, she saw it was Ernest Ben. Senator Yellowhair, however, was not in the room. He was either being held elsewhere, or he was already dead.

"How do I get to that room?" she asked Jimmie.

He was standing right behind her. "I think I know which storeroom that is, but it'll be tricky, maybe impossible to get there. We have to go right through the shipping warehouse that opens up onto the loading dock and, as you can see from the monitors, Morgan's there with half a dozen men."

"Is there another way?"

"No, at least not one that's any less risky. What we have to do is go across silently and hope that there are enough boxes around to use as cover."

"What are they shipping out in such a rush?" Ella asked.

"I don't know for sure. I had heard that LabKote was going to ship out complimentary samples to hospitals and labs across the country. Maybe those are it."

Ella looked around for a phone, and saw one on the wall. "I need to call in the troops."

"Not with that phone. All outgoing and incoming calls are monitored, and go through a relay station in Morgan's office.

Everything is recorded, and, at night, his beeper goes off whenever a call is made. It's unofficial, probably illegal, but it's real. I was called on the carpet for making a personal call one time. That's when I found out about the system."

Ella pulled out her cell phone, but couldn't get through.

"There's too much shielding in these walls," Jimmie explained. "Can't let radiation out, remember?"

She was outgunned and outnumbered. If she made a move now, chances were she'd get both Jimmie and the kidnap victims killed. But all her options were high risk.

"We can't leave the prisoners here without making an attempt to free them," Ella said. "We have to try our best to get past Morgan and the others. If it turns out it's impossible to do that, then we'll see about getting out of here and going for help."

"We'll need actual keys to that room though, and I don't have them. There are no electronic locks around the loading dock area, just the old-fashioned kind."

"Who has what we need?"

"Morgan, Landreth, and some of the guards."

"Like the one in the closet?"

"Doubtful. If he had the keys, he'd be one of those assigned to that area of the building. Very few people here have access to the entire facility."

"Then we'll have to find the right guard and take his keys. After we free the prisoners, we'll leave the same way we came in."

Jimmie led her down the hallways, but as they peeked through the glass in the door leading to the warehouse and loading dock facility, Ella realized that so much had been loaded, the room was virtually empty. Cover of any type was practically nonexistent.

As two men approached, she ducked back into another hallway, Jimmie at her side. Ella listened carefully, scarcely moving. At first, she couldn't make out even one word of what they were saying. The language they were using wasn't Navajo and it sure wasn't English, Spanish, or one of the Pueblo languages. Suddenly she heard a harsh voice interrupt the two who were speaking.

"You are forbidden from speaking in Farsi. Always use English. Is that clear?"

"There isn't anyone around," the man protested.

She heard a scuffle and a loud thump.

"Don't *ever* ask me to repeat an order. Clear? I can break your neck with my bare hands."

"Yeah, sure, Mr. Morgan. English from now on," the man said in a choked voice.

"Now go into the clean room, pick up the shipping boxes, and take them to get their shipping labels. Do it quickly. We're running out of time."

Ella heard the sound of a semi backing up to the loading dock, then approaching footsteps.

Morgan swore loudly. "What do you think you're doing coming back here? You were told to keep an eye on Clah."

"She's at home, sound asleep, Sir. There's no activity there."

"Did you see her in bed asleep? Clearly?"

"Well, no, Sir, but I saw her go in and the lights are out now, and her vehicle is still parked there."

"Underestimating her is a mistake. We can't just break her neck, like with that horsewoman. Clah has escaped us at least three times already. Remember what happened to LaPoint? That woman is extremely dangerous, and not one to ever give up."

"You want me to go back and make sure she's still at home?"

"Yes, and stay with her. If she goes anywhere, I want to know. If we can keep her from interfering for the next few hours, there'll be no way she can stop us. The operation will be a success, despite our change in plans, and that's all that matters now," Morgan said. "Even though we've been forced to cut our mission short, we'll still have the last say."

"What are we going to do about the prisoners? We can't just let them go. They know too much."

"We need to verify the effectiveness of our new strain of anthrax on humans. The prisoners will make excellent test subjects. Soon I'll have them moved to a clean room and exposed to the bacteria. We'll record how long it takes them to die, then dispose of their bodies. At least that way something will be gained from their deaths, unlike Yellowhair's."

"I had to shoot to keep him from escaping." The man was almost whining, more afraid of Morgan than of a murder rap, obviously.

"And it was just a fluke that the bullet was a kill shot? Spare me the crap. Just don't screw up again, or I may stuff your body in the incinerator, too."

As Morgan and the men with him moved away, Jimmie stepped around her and looked into the warehouse. "It's now or never," he said, reaching for the door handle.

Through the window in the door, Ella could see that, for the first thirty feet, there were just enough stacked boxes and crates to give them some cover, but the last forty feet would put them right out in the open.

"I'll go across first," Jimmie said. "If I get caught, I'll try to divert them long enough to give you a chance. Your brother is in the second room to the right."

Ella shook her head. "No, I'll go. This is my responsibility. If they catch me, you'll have to escape and get help on your own."

"That's not a good idea. If you get caught, you'll be shot, and they'll get rid of your body. No one will ever know what happened to you and what we've found out. We'll never stop them. But if I get caught, they'll know I haven't been to the police yet. I'll be locked up with the others to become one of their guinea pigs, and it'll buy you some time." He reached into his pocket and pulled out the electronic key. "Here. Just in case I don't make it."

Silently, he opened the door and they both slipped into the warehouse. Concealed by a water fountain, Ella watched Jimmie sprint forward, her heart at her throat, and the stone badger hot against her skin. He'd almost made it across when Morgan suddenly turned around, spotted him, then yelled. "Stop!"

Jimmie picked up speed somehow. Morgan drew his pistol and shot twice.

Jimmie went down hard, clutching his thigh. Morgan approached confidently but, as he drew near, Jimmie suddenly kicked out with his good leg, sweeping Morgan's legs out from under him, knocking him to the floor.

Ella sprinted across during the diversion. As she reached the other side, she heard another shot, and saw Jimmie wrestling Morgan for control of the pistol while other guards ran over to intervene. Knowing she couldn't help Jimmie by turning back now, Ella hurried down the hallway, then stopped and peered around the corner before going any farther. One man was standing in front of the room where Clifford and Ben were being held. He was looking around, restless, unwilling to abandon his post, but undeniably curious about the disturbance. Certain he was one of the select few with the keys, Ella took a quarter out of her pocket and threw it, hitting the man in the back.

"All right. Who's the joker?" the man yelled, turning around.

Ella reached for her pistol, but remained silent and out of sight.

"You think this is funny?" he growled. "Maybe you'll think it's funny, too, when I haul you over to Morgan."

He strode down the hall in her direction, but she remained around the corner with her back pressed to the wall. He was almost upon her when she jumped out and struck the guard in the side of the head with her pistol.

He went down instantly, but she caught him before he could hit the floor. Moving quickly, she dragged him down the hall and into an unlocked janitor's closet. Using a roll of duct tape she found there, she tied the man's hands behind his back, stuffed rags in his mouth, and then taped his legs together. After searching for keys, and finding a half dozen on a ring clip at his belt, she shoved him into a trash chute built into the closet wall. She stood where she was a moment longer and heard him crash into a Dumpster in the basement. Satisfied, she moved on.

Her luck was holding. Peeking out to make sure it was clear, Ella hurried to where the guard had been standing and, through the small window, saw Clifford near the door.

Ella gave him a quick nod, gestured for him to be quiet, then showed him the keys. She began trying them out one by one.

She'd gone through the first four when she heard loud voices coming toward her.

Ella recognized Landreth's voice. "Once these last few shipments are delivered, the police and the CDC will be too busy trying to stop the public panic to track us down. It might take them days to discover that the anthrax came from our complimentary samples of 'sterilized' labware. Of course, by the time they catch on, medical personnel all over the country will be dying."

Ella looked at Clifford, and could tell from his expression that he'd heard Morgan, too.

"Just opening the packages will start a chain of events that will paralyze this country." Morgan answered. "Thousands will die, and the United States will finally see what its like when war is brought right into their own backyards. They'll bury relatives and friends, and feel what they never could when the war was nothing more than a segment on the evening news."

"The government will be blamed, and those in charge will get what they deserve. Defense department cutbacks cost me my company and destroyed my family. It's payback time for me," Landreth added. "And while this country falls apart, I'll be laying on a beach in southern France."

"Now let's see how our prisoners are doing." Morgan said. "Just keep your distance from Clah's brother. He's dangerous."

The men were getting closer, and Ella felt her blood run cold. This was bigger than a threat to the Rez. She had to find a way to stop these men. She could either try to shoot it out with Morgan and his men right now and save Clifford, or leave before she was seen. If she left, she'd be able to get enough backup to intercept the contaminated shipments and capture the men responsible, but her brother's life and Ben's would remain on the line.

As she met her brother's gaze, tears filled her eyes. She knew what she had to do. "I'm sorry," she mouthed, her heart breaking. "I'll come back, I promise."

He nodded and mouthed the word "go."

Without looking back, Ella slipped away. Sorrow weighed her spirit down but this was bigger than Clifford or her. With death at her heels, she concentrated on the duty she had to see through. Ella eased down the hallway, and made it back to the warehouse and loading dock. Most of the armed men had moved farther into the building, packing up machines and equipment.

A brown step-van truck belonging to a delivery service had apparently just arrived. It was angled sideways to the dock, with the engine running and the driver was talking to one of Morgan's men.

Swallowing back her fear, Ella prepared to make her move. It was all or nothing now. If she failed, death would be the only winner.

TWENTY-FOUR

—— ✖ ✖ ✖ ——

Keeping her pistol hidden, Ella confidently walked the length of the room and reached the edge of the platform without being noticed by the distracted LabKote employee and driver. Jumping off the dock and crouching low, she ran across the loading zone toward the truck, hidden below the level of the dock. A heartbeat later, she climbed into the vehicle, then moved quickly into the rear cargo area. The large pallet of LabKote boxes there told her the vehicle had already been loaded.

Grabbing a small canvas tarp from a shelf, she spread it over herself and waited, huddled behind the driver's seat, pistol ready.

Ella heard the driver climb in, and put the van into gear. Peeking out carefully, she waited, biding her time as the truck rumbled away. Next came the sound of the gates being opened. The truck slowed slightly, then continued past the guards at the fence.

Waiting another ten seconds, she pushed the tarp away just enough so he could see her and the pistol. The driver jumped, but managed to control the wheel. "Whoa. What is this, a hijack?"

"No. I'm a police officer. I don't know if you're working with LabKote on this or are perfectly innocent, but if you do or say

SHOOTING CHANT ✻ 333

anything to give me away, I'll blow your brains all over the wind-shield." She was taking no chances at this point.

"Hey, I'm cool. They don't pay me enough to die for the cargo. Just tell me what you want."

"Keep driving just like you're going on with your business. And stay off the radio." Ella waited until the driver pulled out onto the main highway, then joined him in the adjacent seat. "I'm Officer Clah of the Navajo Police Department. Want to see some ID?" Ella asked, placing her pistol back into the holster. Her instincts now told her the driver could be trusted.

The driver looked over at her, managed a weak smile, then sighed. "No. Actually, I'm just happy to be alive at this point."

"Head for the police station. You know where that is?" Ella saw him nod. "Relax," she added. He was a good-looking His-panic man, but a bit pale at the moment. "You've done just fine so far. If you'll just be patient a little while longer, you'll find out what this is all about."

She reached for her cell phone and dialed Justine. "My brother was kidnapped, but I know where he is. I also have all the evi-dence we need to move against LabKote. It's bigger than we thought. The operation is a front for terrorists, all right. I've taken over a delivery truck that has a shipment of hospital supplies con-taminated with anthrax. I'm bringing it in, but that'll be just the beginning of what we have to do. We'll have to move fast. I don't know how much time we have left."

"Anthrax? What's that?" the driver asked quickly. "Those are supposed to be lab supplies, not germs. Lady, what are you get-ting me into?"

"Actually, I'm the one getting you out of something. Just drive."

By the time she reached the station, Ella had a general plan. The driver was placed in protective custody while Neskahi, Blalock, and the Cloud brothers hurriedly unloaded the cargo, and locked it away in an empty cell. Afterward they met in Big Ed's office and Ella quickly briefed them on the situation at LabKote.

"I don't think they know I was there, at least not yet, and even if they find the guard I took out, he won't be able to swear Jimmie wasn't responsible. He and my brother will cover for me for as long as they can, so Morgan and Landreth and their people probably are still working under the assumption that they have more time. But we have to move quickly. Senator Yellowhair has already been killed, and unless we act right away, the body count is going to go through the roof."

"How do you recommend we proceed?" Blalock asked.

"The truck that got me out can also get us back in. I know they're expecting another pickup so, if our luck holds, when we show up they'll assume everything's in order. The bottom line is that we can't afford to wait for reinforcements. We've got to do something right now."

"You're too well known, Ella," Blalock said. "The second the guard at the gate sees you, he'll sound the alarm. I'll have to drive while you hide in the back."

"I agree," Big Ed said, then looked at Ella. "You said there are possibly up to eight heavily armed men. But there're only seven of us."

"No, eight." Sergeant Manuelito came into the room. "I overheard the driver when he was being questioned. It's what the tribe is paying me for. What do you say, Chief?"

Big Ed glanced at Ella. "This is your operation."

Ella stood and nodded. "We need every experienced officer we have on hand. You're in."

"Good. Now can we go kick some butts?"

While they got ready, Big Ed had the dispatcher radio every available man to prepare to set up roadblocks and cordon off the immediate area around LabKote, as soon as the assault team went in. No one would be leaving LabKote tonight.

Blalock contacted FBI personnel at the Albuquerque office, who in turn began notifying every postmaster and courier service within four hundred miles. No package from LabKote was to be shipped anywhere once it arrived at their facility from Shiprock. Every container was to be isolated instead. The driver's company was assured their man was okay, and told not to make any contact with LabKote.

Blalock was handed a fax just as they gathered in the lobby, and he read it to the group. "This is from Interpol. The man calling himself Walter Morgan is a suspected Middle Eastern terrorist. His family was on that civilian airline accidentally downed by the U.S. Navy several years ago. Morgan must have killed the real Walter Morgan in Saudi Arabia and taken over his identity. LabKote is probably being funded by Saudi dissidents."

Ella nodded, heading for the exit. "It makes sense now. But he's already taken too many lives. It's time to put a stop to him."

Wearing bullet-resistant vests and packing assault rifles or shotguns and pistols, the team quickly climbed aboard the delivery van. Justine, the Clouds, and Big Ed rode in the back where the cargo would have been, out of sight behind empty boxes. Ella was on the floor of the cab on the passengers side, under a tarp, while Manuelito and Neskahi took their place out of view behind the seats.

Blalock wore a baseball cap and the driver's uniform used by the well-known courier firm, but something about him still screamed FBI. Ella knew it, but maybe in the dark he'd pass as a parcel delivery man.

As Blalock drove away from the station, Ella reminded them all of one grim possibility. "If they have the cardboard boxes of lab supplies out on the loading dock, we have to make sure not to hit them with a stray bullet. We could blow anthrax bacteria all over the room and into the air, and if the loading dock doors are wide open like they were, it could spread out into the community."

After that, they rode in silence for most of the ten-minute trip, each officer lost in his or her own thoughts. No one had any illusions. Their lives would be on the line every second of the operation. Ella was wearing two vests now instead of one, but she knew her baby's future as well as her own would depend entirely on her skills and her ability to out think her enemies. Sadness enveloped her as she thought of Clifford, wondering what had gone through his mind when he'd seen her walk away. Would he ever understand and forgive her? If anything happened to him, his death would be on her hands.

As the truck turned onto the lane leading to the plant, she thought of her mother and what would happen to her if either she or Clifford didn't make it. Rose would understand duty, but whether or not she could learn to get over the loss was another matter.

"We're approaching the gate. Now's the time to lock and load, and say your prayers, folks," Blalock muttered.

Blalock stopped by the gate and the guard came over and shined a light in his face. No one moved or made a sound as the beam traveled over the tarp. Ella held still, her pistol out and ready.

"Brother, you've got a pigsty for a cab. Been on the road long?"

"Yeah, too long," Blalock muttered sourly. "Damned graveyard shift. Now I'm behind schedule. You'd better let me get loaded or your packages won't make the airplane out of Albuquerque before tomorrow night."

"Okay, okay. Just follow the driveway around to the other side of the building and stop at the loading dock."

As Blalock drove through, Ella breathed a sigh of relief. "I was worried he might want to step into the truck and look around," she whispered. "Good job, Dwayne."

"Our luck just ran out. Just before we got to the gate, I caught a glimpse of the loading dock. It's lit up like a Christmas tree, and there are at least four guards with shoulder weapons. No way we'll have more than a few seconds before they realize what's going on."

"Then we'll have to flank them," Big Ed said. "Slow down before you go around the corner of the building and Shorty and I will get out. She still has Jimmie's card key, so what we'll do is circle around and enter through the utility room door. You can buy us some time by making a big production about backing in. Take at least two minutes trying to line the van up. Make it look like you're sleepy, drunk, or just a lousy driver. Maybe even kill the engine once. Then back into the dock on the left side so you'll have more cover and keep the truck at an angle so everyone can get out on their blind side."

"I'm going to cut the corner close so the building will shield you and Ella when you get out," Blalock said, slowing down.

Big Ed and Ella jumped out and ran to the side gate, which was out of sight from the dock and the main entrance. Using Jimmie's key card and his number code, Ella and Big Ed slipped through the gate and into the building. It was quiet, and they saw nothing but an empty corridor ahead of them. "I'll go for the hostages while you find a position that'll let you cut off their escape through the building," Ella whispered as they jogged down the hall. "Once I get the hostages out, I'll back you up."

"I'll keep them pinned down, don't worry. With the others attacking from the dock and me coming from behind, they won't have a chance to do much except hide."

They hurried through another corridor, covering each other in turn as they rounded each corner, and smashing surveillance cameras as they advanced. They'd almost reached their objective when the sound of gunfire erupted outside. Big Ed took his position at the door leading into the warehouse.

"If they try to come back through this way, I've got them. Now get ready to move, Shorty." As the gunfire continued from the warehouse, he dropped to one knee, combat style, and braced his arms in firing position. "Go. I'll keep them pinned down while you get your brother and the other hostages."

"I hope Jimmie's still alive."

"So do I. And, Shorty, everyone still alive leaves with us or we all stay. Clear?"

"Agreed." They were in this together. "Here goes." She opened the door and darted across the room, gunfire drowning out her footsteps.

Ella ran across the warehouse as fast as she could, hoping her own people wouldn't shoot her. She'd almost made it to the other side when Big Ed opened fire. There were screams and angry shouts as the suddenly exposed guards went down or sought cover from the unexpected rear assault.

Ella raced down the hall toward the area where she'd last seen her brother, hoping they were still there in that storeroom. Despite the gunfire, which she'd hoped would keep the guard distracted, the man was still at his post when she arrived. He fired a shot the moment she peeked around the corner, but it struck the wall behind her.

Ella dove to the floor and rolled, bringing her shotgun up and returning fire as she came to rest. She aimed for his head, assuming he'd be wearing a vest, and didn't miss.

Averting her gaze from the nearly decapitated corpse, knowing there was no time to lose, Ella scrambled to her feet. She peered into the room through the small glass window in the door, but she saw no one inside. Swallowing back her fear, she found the right key within two tries and threw open the door.

Clifford, Jimmie, and Ernest Ben were behind a large table they'd upended to use for cover after hearing the gunfire. Ella approached, never turning her back to the door.

"We have one man wounded here," Clifford said, speaking of Jimmie, who lay unconscious beside him. "He's lost a lot of blood. I've done my best to stop the flow, but without my herbs . . ." he let the sentence hang.

"Where have you been?" Ernest demanded staring at Ella angrily. "Why did you leave us here? You just ran off!"

"We can discuss this later. For now, let's get out while we can."

"Jimmie can't be moved. I'll stay here with him," Clifford said. "Loan me a weapon so I can ward them off."

"No. *Nobody* stays behind," Ella said, looking out into the hall and hearing a new burst of gunfire from inside the warehouse. "Help my brother carry him," she ordered Ben.

"You're crazy. He'll just slow us down."

"I'll shoot you myself if you don't do as I tell you." She reached for the guard's pistol, which lay beyond the growing pool of blood.

The sight of the dead man seemed to wake Ben up. He stared

at her in surprise, and then went to help Clifford. Her brother's face was expressionless.

"Big Ed is keeping the others from coming back this way, but he'll need help." She handed the guard's pistol to her brother. "I know you won't shoot to kill, but feel free to worry as many of them as you like. Clear?"

Clifford took the weapon. Grabbing Jimmie's arm and pulling it around his shoulders while Ben did the same on the other side, they dragged him down the hall.

Ella remained at point. The shooting seemed to have decreased in intensity, and she hoped it was for good reasons. Other officers in the outer perimeter were supposed to move in if they heard gunfire, and hopefully they'd taken out the guards at the gate and were now backing up Blalock and the others on her team.

They'd just reached the spot where Big Ed was crouched when Ella heard running footsteps behind them, and, as she turned, she saw a familiar figure cross the corridor.

"Morgan's inside!" Ella yelled at Big Ed.

"Leave the others with me and go after him, Shorty."

Ella motioned to Clifford and Ernest Ben, who eased their wounded companion onto the floor beside the wall. Big Ed, crouching on one knee behind the doorjamb, concentrated on looking for targets inside the large warehouse.

Knowing the three were safer with Big Ed than they would be with her, Ella crept back down the corridor, shotgun ready, listening carefully as she moved. A second or two later, she heard cautious footsteps behind her.

Ella spun around and very nearly pulled the trigger of the shotgun. "Are you crazy?" she whispered harshly, staring at Clifford. "Go back."

"No, I'll help you. This man came into my home, threatened to go after my wife and my child, sliced at me with a knife, then brought me here as a prisoner. I owe him. Jimmie also managed to tell us more about what Morgan plans to do. He's a terrorist and has to be stopped. I won't kill him if there's a choice, but he won't escape, not if we work together."

"No, *I'll* see to it. Get back to Jimmie and Ernest Ben. You can help Big Ed protect them."

Clifford held up his hand. "Do you hear it? Morgan went up on the roof."

"I don't hear a thing," she said.

"*Listen!*"

Ella struggled to hear something other than an occasional gunshot from the warehouse. "I'll take your word for it."

"He's probably headed for the metal roof that covers the loading dock. That way he can ambush the officers below," Clifford said.

"Do you know the way up?"

"There's a utility closet with a ladder leading up to the roof. The door was open when they brought us through the building to the room where they locked us up."

Ella followed her brother, but before he could go up the ladder, she moved around him and blocked his way. "I'm going up there but, unless you're going to shoot to kill, brother, don't follow. You'll just be another target for him."

Even though they both knew that he wouldn't fire a kill shot, Clifford followed her up anyway. When they emerged on the roof, Morgan was nowhere to be seen, but the sound of gunfire was much louder from here.

"Look around, but be very careful," she said.

The gunfire suddenly subsided and an eerie silence followed. She'd been in too many gun battles before not to know the calm couldn't be trusted. Almost in response to her unspoken thought, they heard one gunshot, and a hard, dull thump followed almost simultaneously. Clifford ran to the loading dock side of the roof, leaned over and peered down.

"Morgan must have been shot by one of the men below, then went over the edge," Clifford said. "I can't see him. There's an awning, then a truck below that."

"Get back," Ella whispered, running over to where he stood, intending to pull him behind cover. "You're too exposed near the edge."

She was less than three feet away from Clifford when a flicker of movement caught her eye and made her look beyond him. Morgan was on the porch-style roof of the loading dock a few feet lower than they were, huddled against the building. His pistol was swinging around toward Clifford and he had a clear line of fire. There was no way he could miss.

With Clifford in her way, Ella couldn't fire. Instead, she dropped her shotgun and shoved Clifford to the side hard with both hands. Clifford, taken by surprise, stumbled on a projecting vent pipe and fell over the edge of the parapet.

Ella took the bullet meant for her brother squarely in the chest. The impact pushed her back, spun her sideways, and she fell onto her knees, gasping for breath, right next to the roof's edge. The doubled protection of the vests had stopped the round as she'd hoped, but her chest felt as if she'd been hit by a truck. Still on her knees, she struggled to pull out her pistol. The pain was excruciating.

Morgan's attention had shifted back to Clifford, who'd rolled off the awning and landed on the roof of the van parked directly below them. Both he and Manuelito, who was climbing up to help him, were sitting ducks.

She'd only get one shot now. Still trying to catch her breath, she aimed and squeezed the trigger. The bullet hit Morgan in the center of the forehead. He trembled from the shock, then pitched forward, and fell onto the roof. There would be no need to verify he was dead.

Ella glanced back at her brother, and saw Sergeant Manuelito beside him, aiming his pistol directly at her. From their angle, neither could have seen Morgan, and all they were aware of was that someone had fired another shot.

"It's all right. He's dead," she managed, lowering her weapon. Gasping, she finally managed to catch her breath again.

"Who?" Manuelito yelled.

"Morgan."

"I know. I shot him a minute ago when he started to leap onto the trailer roof. But why did you push your brother off the roof?"

"I didn't do it on . . . and you didn't shoot—" She shook her head. "Never mind. We'll sort it out later. We still have work to do."

Grabbing her shotgun with a groan, Ella slid down onto the loading dock roof and moved to a position where she could bring plunging fire onto the terrorists who were still in action. One blast of her shotgun was enough to convince the remaining two men to give up.

SEPTEMBER 17TH

Ten minutes later, the wounded were being tended, and the bodies of the terrorists who'd died were being photographed by the crime team. Fortunately, none of the officers suffered any serious wounds, thanks to their vests and Big Ed's vicious crossfire, which had kept the terrorists pinned down most of the time.

Ella located Landreth, unarmed and alive, hiding in his office behind the remaining anthrax contaminated shipping boxes, and turned him over to state police officers now on the scene.

Big Ed called for a Haz Mat team from the county. "Until I'm certain that this place is safe, no one except those in protective clothing will have further access to this place," he told everyone there.

"With all the deaths here, no one will come near this place again anyway," Ella said, approaching him.

"That's true. Not even a Blessingway will make this place feel safe again. The land here has seen too much."

Ella took in the scene, watching her officers help carry the wounded to awaiting ambulances. "Chief, after this is over, I'm going to take a few days off."

"It'll have to wait. We still need you," he said. "Harry Ute just gave me notice today—make that yesterday—afternoon. He's joining the marshal's service."

"I know, but I'll still need a day or two to settle some personal business. Then, next spring I'll be taking maternity leave."

Ella saw Big Ed's jaw drop. Moving away quickly before he

could gather his thoughts and deluge her with questions, Ella left
to find Clifford.

She finally found him standing in the parking lot, beside the
emergency vehicles, where others were being checked over. "Are
you all right?" she asked. One of the EMTs had loaned him a cane
and he was leaning on it heavily. "Thank goodness for that
awning."

"My leg . . ."

"Let me take you to the hospital."

He shook his head. "You know better."

"If it's a broken bone—"

"I'll handle it my way." He gave her a long, thoughtful look.
"But tell me. Why *did* you shove me like that?" There was no con-
demnation in his eyes, just confusion.

Though Ella kept her gaze on her brother, she could sense that
the other officers around them also awaited her reply.

"Morgan was still up there, hidden, and he was about to shoot
you. I couldn't fire at him because you were in my way. I had two
vests on, and knew they would protect me, so I pushed you aside.
I didn't think you'd stumble and fall over the edge, really." She
opened her jacket and showed him the bullet hole and where the
round had imbedded in the kevlar.

"I understand now," he said. As he glanced around, he saw
most of the others nodding their heads. "They believe you, too,"
he added in a soft voice, moving farther away from the crowd.
"But not everyone will. I know you saved my life, but some will
only remember, that you pushed me off the roof. Remember,
nobody saw Morgan trying to shoot me but you."

"There's nothing I can do about that. People will believe whatever they want, no matter what I do or say," Ella replied. A few of
the old traditionalists would now become convinced that she had
turned to evil, but what hurt most was knowing that some people
would actually believe she was capable of trying to kill her own
brother.

"My fellow captive," he said, referring to Ben, "will also tell
others how you chose to leave us behind when you were only one

locked door away from rescuing us. Everything that happened here today will be seen as evidence that the legacy still holds true. They'll see your child as part of it as well."

"Kevin Tolino is the baby's father, and he's already told his family." Ella wasn't surprised that Clifford had guessed she was pregnant, even though she hadn't told him yet. Her brother was remarkably intuitive.

"That'll answer questions of paternity," Clifford said, "particularly if he doesn't want to hide the fact, but there'll be other problems waiting for you there."

"Because they're our clan's watchers? That's being taken care of. Kevin will handle his family," she said. "I'll provide for my baby and see to it that she has everything she needs."

"And what about acceptance?"

"I've lived through these kinds of problems before. Not everyone will turn against me. Some traditionalists will but, in time, people will see that I'm just a cop, one who works very hard for the good of the tribe."

"You'll have to prove yourself to everyone all over again, just like when you first came back to the Rez."

"Then that's the way it'll have to be, but I'll expect you to help me bring out the truth. People will listen to you."

"I'll do my best, Sister, but, in this case, the truth is a matter of who people choose to believe, and of interpretation."

Ella nodded. "I've always been the type not to worry about things I can't do anything about but, in this case, I don't think I'll be able to do that. The deck is stacked against us, and there are too many frightening possibilities."

Ella sat at home with her mother the following morning. The Haz Mat team had declared there was no anthrax leak at LabKote, but a Blessingway would be done for her and the baby soon. Modern science had no assurances to give her, only more questions.

She still wasn't sure if she'd been exposed to the radiation, and the uncertainties haunted her nightmares. Landreth had admitted to knowing about the accident, but said Hansen had been responsible. No other details were available now, because Hansen's report on the incident had been deliberately erased from the computer files.

"You know the baby will be fine," Rose assured, patting her hand. "Trust your instincts, Daughter."

"I know she's okay, Mother, I just don't know how I know and that's unsettling."

"It's not necessary that we understand the hows and whys. Just accept that you do know."

Ella stood at the window, staring at the stark contrast between the blue sky and the mesa in the distance. It was another cool fall day and, for now, there was peace. She placed a hand on her stomach, wondering how many more weeks it would be before she'd feel her child's first kick. Would that put her concerns to rest?

"But you're still worried about the child," Rose said, not needing to make it into a question.

"If there's anything out of the ordinary about her—whether from the radiation or something else—people won't understand."

"Whatever's different is often condemned as evil, but that doesn't make it so," Rose said. "Your child will be loved by us and by your friends. She'll have enemies, just as we all do, but it will all balance out, and she'll learn to walk in beauty."

EPILOGUE
✖ ✖ ✖

Ella sat on the living room couch, holding her tiny, dark-haired, week-old daughter. She'd been born at home and, in the days before delivery, Clifford had done another Blessingway. Since that ceremony, a feeling of peace had descended over Ella, and it continued unabated even now.

After all, balance had been restored. The anthrax threat had disappeared from news broadcasts months ago, and all known samples of the biological weapon destroyed. The former LabKote facilities had been renovated, and were now being use by an Anglo trucking firm. Most of the truck drivers were Navajo, though few of the *Dineh* were willing to go into the building itself because of its recent history.

The surviving terrorists were in federal lockups now, and Landreth himself was being kept at an undisclosed location. He'd provided testimony and details of the operation in exchange for government protection from those he'd recently sold out.

Ella closed her eyes, held her daughter close, and bathed in the peace for a moment. She opened them again when she heard footsteps.

"She's beautiful," Clifford said, looking at them from the kitchen doorway.

"Yes, she is," Ella said, wondering how it was possible to love anyone or anything as much as she did this little baby. Looking back at her old life, Ella couldn't understand how she could have been happy without her.

Ella looked up at her mother and smiled. "It's time for the ritual. Have you decided on a name for her?" she asked. Although it was customary for the mother of the child to choose the baby's name, the one people would address her with, the secret name had other origins. Bestowed by a close relative, the secret or war name was considered private property and was never used even by members of the family. It was only evoked in a time of crisis, and was said to provide power to its owner.

Rose looked out the window before replying. Kevin was waiting outside on the porch. "Can't we just send him away until we name her?"

"Mom, I've asked him to wait outside so that he doesn't hear the baby's secret name. I've only done that because you insisted, but he has a right to be here for the rest."

Rose's eyes narrowed. "Look beyond him, Daughter, farther up on the hill. It's his grandmother, I'll bet. His own clan doesn't even trust him," Rose whispered.

"Because he's allied with his daughter, and us," Ella answered.

"Maybe."

"Believe what you will, but I won't send him away," Ella said firmly.

Rose sighed, then nodded. "All right, then. I'm ready."

As Clifford looked on, Ella held the baby up straight.

Rose placed her hand on the child. "My granddaughter, your name will be *Deezbaa'*."

Ella smiled. It was the perfect name. "She Goes Off to War," Ella said with a nod. "It's a good choice, Mom. It'll fit her and the life she'll have to build for herself."

"The name *Deezbaa'* will also remind her that life is to be met with courage and strength."

A tiny bit of pollen was placed in the baby's mouth and Clifford sang a *Hozoniji,* a Song of Blessing. It was their special protection, a property of their family alone. After he was finished, Ella looked at her mother, then gestured silently to the door.

Reluctantly, Rose opened the door and invited Kevin inside.

Kevin beamed Ella a wide smile as he carried a beautifully decorated wooden cradleboard into the house. The top ends of the board were pointed, signifying it was for a girl. "I made the cradleboard myself, according to tradition," he said, handing it to Ella. "I carved it from a solid piece of ponderosa pine, bored the holes for the buckskin lacings myself with hand tools, and sanded everything down until it was smooth. I then sprinkled pollen on it and had your brother help me with the proper prayers."

"A Singer isn't needed. Your family didn't help you?" Rose asked.

Ella gave her mother a sharp look, but it was a futile gesture. Rose spoke her mind, and no one had ever been able to stop her.

"I think it was better this way," Kevin said softly.

"They're still out there," Rose said, gesturing outside. "They'll continue to watch us."

"But no one will harm any of you, or my daughter," Kevin said firmly. "You can count on that."

Rose said nothing.

Ella sighed. "Thank you for the cradleboard, Kevin. I need to feed the baby, but stay, and afterwards we'll put her in the cradleboard and say the prayers that need to be said."

Kevin stood. "I'd love to stay, but I can't. I have other business to take care of," he said, looking out at the figure in the distance.

"You're welcome here anytime," Ella said.

"What will her English name be?" Kevin asked, touching the baby's face lightly with his finger.

"I've named her Dawn, for the prayer that was sung at her birth. That Song says that the baby will have a happy voice and will be an Everlasting and Peaceful baby. In that Song is every hope I have for her."

Kevin nodded in approval, then left. As the door opened, Rose saw a crowd of people walking up the road toward their house.

"Many will come to see the baby," Rose said. "Some will do it out of curiosity, others out of love. But we'll never know which is which."

"I know."

"I'm worried about you, Daughter. When you first came back home, you were known as L.A. Woman. No one trusted you. It may be even worse now."

"I'll take it as it comes," Ella said. She was strong enough to face rejections squarely, no matter how they stung, but if anyone came after her child, then they'd see what a bad enemy she could be.

"No one will harm the baby," Clifford said, as if reading her thoughts. "But their fears will become your greatest enemy, and you'll have to look closely before trusting anyone again."

"I'm a cop. That's the way it always is." But even as she said that, she knew that things *would* change. It was the nature of life.